THE
POPE'S ASSASSIN

Luis M. Rocha

Translation by Robin McAllister

JOVE BOOKS, NEW YORK

THE BERKLEY PUBLISHING GROUP
Published by the Penguin Group
Penguin Group (USA) Inc.
375 Hudson Street, New York, New York 10014, USA
Penguin Group (Canada), 90 Eglinton Avenue East, Suite 700, Toronto, Ontario M4P 2Y3, Canada
(a division of Pearson Penguin Canada Inc.)
Penguin Books Ltd., 80 Strand, London WC2R 0RL, England
Penguin Group Ireland, 25 St. Stephen's Green, Dublin 2, Ireland (a division of Penguin Books Ltd.)
Penguin Group (Australia), 250 Camberwell Road, Camberwell, Victoria 3124, Australia
(a division of Pearson Australia Group Pty. Ltd.)
Penguin Books India Pvt. Ltd., 11 Community Centre, Panchsheel Park, New Delhi—110 017, India
Penguin Group (NZ), 67 Apollo Drive, Rosedale, Auckland 0632, New Zealand
(a division of Pearson New Zealand Ltd.)
Penguin Books (South Africa) (Pty.) Ltd., 24 Sturdee Avenue, Rosebank, Johannesburg 2196,
South Africa

Penguin Books Ltd., Registered Offices: 80 Strand, London WC2R 0RL, England

THE POPE'S ASSASSIN

A Jove Book / published by arrangement with the author

PRINTING HISTORY
G. P. Putnam's Sons hardcover edition / March 2011
Jove premium edition / December 2011

Copyright © 2011 by Luis M. Rocha.
Translation from the Portuguese © 2011 by Robin McAllister.
Cover design and imaging by Diana Kolsky.

ISBN: 978-0-515-15017-9

JOVE®
Jove Books are published by The Berkley Publishing Group,
a division of Penguin Group (USA) Inc.,
375 Hudson Street, New York, New York 10014.
JOVE® is a registered trademark of Penguin Group (USA) Inc.
The "J" design is a trademark of Penguin Group (USA) Inc.

PRINTED IN THE UNITED STATES OF AMERICA

10   9   8   7   6   5   4   3   2   1

THIS BOOK IS DEDICATED TO
IOANNES PP. XXIII
ANGELO GIUSEPPE RONCALLI
November 25, 1881–June 3, 1963

And to Ben Isaac as well

PART ONE

Ad Maiorem Dei Gloriam

An agreement was possible.

—John XXIII, *November 20, 1960*

1

—•◆•—

Instruct those you trust to reveal the secret on the first night of each election. The reading of it must be the first official act of every heir of Peter. It is vitally important that they acknowledge the secret. Let them guard it in a hidden place and permit no one else to read it. Any violation of this ritual could signify the end of our beloved and esteemed Church.

—Clement VII, June 17, 1530, Vatican

April 19, 2005

The canonical election of Cardinal Joseph Alois Ratzinger would be remembered, for as long as memory exists, on this day of April, ending the papal vacancy since the fifth of that same month.

As soon as Sodano, the vice deacon of the College of Cardinals, asked him to accept the position that God had selected, at the end of the fourth ballot, he did not hesitate to say "I accept." The five seconds he took to reply "Pope Benedict" to the question "What name do you wish to be called?" also indicated forethought. Don't forget that Ratzinger was the deacon of the college—that is, had he not been the chosen one, he would have asked the same questions to the elected candidate. It's a curious fact that 90 percent of his predecessors preferred a name different from the one their mothers gave them.

The faithful congregated in Saint Peter's Square, hoping that the smoke would be white, not the dark, ashen color it was. Few of those present remembered the first and second conclaves of 1978, in which the same problem arose. Nine million euros to organize a conclave, and they always forgot to clean the chimney of the Sistine Chapel. So, after ten minutes of waiting, with many leaving the square, the bells of the basilica roared with frenzied alarm, spreading smiles instead of fear, through the whole plaza and surroundings.

We have a pope.

Inside the holy chapel the Gamarelli brothers fitted the papal vestments to the body of the new pontiff. There was no surprise this time. The expected candidate had won. It was always easier when the previous pope had expressed his will. John XXIII did so when on his deathbed he named Cardinal Giovanni Montini as his successor. In the case of the Polish Wojtyla, the decision had been made earlier. One should never disobey the last wishes of a dying man, especially someone so close to the Creator. Leaving the decision in the hands of the Holy Spirit subjected the church to surprises like those of Pope Luciani and of Wojtyla himself.

Sodano could not have been happier. His beloved church would remain secure. Ratzinger was a known man in a known place. No one would do a better job.

The Chilean Jorge Medina Estévez was the first to appear at the balcony before the jubilant crowd. A new savior was about to be announced to the city and a world enraptured with the news: the name, the man.

The sixteenth pope with the name Benedict was introduced to history. No one would ever be able to erase him from its pages, even if he reigned only one day.

Ratzinger gave himself totally to this new persona he had created and fulfilled the role with distinction. He was no longer the prefect of the Congregation for the Doctrine of the Faith, no longer a cardinal, but an institution with its own coat of arms and personal security. He made a short speech, composed that afternoon, in which he sensitively recalled the Polish pope, who had been so well loved. He blessed the city and the world—Catholic, naturally—and retired to take possession of all his properties.

From that hour he was responsible for an immeasurable, valuable empire. It would take months to learn of all its possessions, at least those they revealed to him. Of the rest . . . not even the Supreme Pontiff himself could know everything he owned, nor would that be advisable.

When night fell and the world rejoiced at the image of Benedict on the Maderno balcony of Saint Peter's Basilica greeting the crowd, a large committee led by the Shepherd of Shepherds himself began another, more private ritual. The chamberlain Somalo broke the seals on the papal apartments in the apostolic apartments and opened the two massive doors before stepping back reverently to let the chosen of God enter. The chosen one had to enter his future living quarters before anyone else, taking possession of what was his. As soon as Ratzinger stepped inside what would be his final residence, he was followed by a crowd of assistants, religious and lay, who were privileged to serve the new owner.

After such a tiring day, it was late for dining. He answered some phone messages of congratulation from the more important chiefs of state, as diplomacy required, the ones that merited a personal thank-you. For the rest, a written message to the dignitaries of the embassies was enough. No one wanted to forget to congratulate the new pope, but if by chance someone did, there would be a price to pay. Humility and turning the other cheek were left to the religious orders who practiced such benevolence, or to Christ. In politics there is no room for mercy.

He entered his office after a light supper. Grilled meat with green beans, shredded carrots, and a drizzle of Riserva d'Oro olive oil over everything. The last time he'd been there, he had been a mere cardinal, rather more like a prince, but now he was an emperor. Now he felt completely different. He passed his hand over the portentous desk. There he would sign the future decrees of *his* church. He wanted her to be magnificent, matching the vestments he wore, set on steady pillars, shielded in his strong, knowing hands. The reins were his.

He sat down and savored the moment. He remembered

Wojtyla and the decades in which he had observed him sitting down heavily in the same chair and deciding the destiny of the church. Sitting there, it was impossible to forget that he was chosen for the office for life. Sodano and Somalo were watching him. A new pope was taking possession of the church.

At that moment another person, wearing a black cassock, entered and knelt with difficulty to greet Benedict with a kiss on the hand that still wore no ring. Many had already kissed his hand that day, but none so earnestly. The priest was old and breathed heavily.

"I don't remember seeing you before," Ratzinger said, smiling. Nothing upset him today.

"Pardon my interruption, Holy Father. My name is Ambrosiano. I was the confessor of our beloved Pope John Paul after the death of Father Michalski," he explained, panting. "The canon law requires that Your Holiness confess tonight to begin your pontificate free of sin." He apologized, "Not that you have any, Holiness, please don't misunderstand me. Later you can choose your own confessor."

"The Society of Jesus has rigid rules. Didn't Cardinal Dezza also confess Pope Wojtyla?" Ratzinger asked.

"Only in the first few years, Holy Father. But Dezza confessed Pope Montini through his entire pontificate and Pope Luciani. Afterward, Pope Wojtyla named Dezza as superior general of the society until the new election, if you recall."

"Of course, of course. A great servant of the church,"

he said, remembering the past. "And now Father Ambrosiano wants to confess me."

"It's the canon law, Holy Father," the priest repeated.

"And we must always respect the canons. I shall make sure of that," Ratzinger affirmed, brandishing his finger, as if about to deliver a speech.

The priest pulled out a chain he wore around his neck with a key he used to open one of the drawers of the desk. A leather folder with a lock and an envelope with the pontifical coat of arms of his predecessor were inside. He took everything out of the drawer and set it on the desk in front of Benedict.

"Pope John Paul specifically instructed me to have Your Holiness carefully read the contents of this folder today. He left all the information specifically for you in this envelope," Ambrosiano explained, handing over the sealed envelope. "No one else may read it."

Benedict looked at the priest, the cardinals, and the envelope. "I shall respect his will," he said at last.

The two cardinals heard this as a request to retire, and complied without delay. The wish of a pope was an order.

"Read it at your leisure, Holy Father," the Jesuit priest said, going out. "When you're ready, just call."

Benedict closed his eyes and leaned back. Thousands of thoughts flooded his mind. He was going to read a secret shared only among popes. What an extraordinary way to begin his reign. Moments later he broke the seal on the envelope the Pole had left. The paper smelled musty.

Dear Chosen One,

 I congratulate you on your election. History continues its glorious path after two thousand years. You have just accepted the most demanding duty on the planet. Prepare yourself. It will be a hard, ungrateful road, and the worst is that that begins right now.

 Inside this folder you will find information read by few others. Crucial information about our church. You must not . . . you cannot refuse to read it and you must instruct your secretaries to present it to your successor on the night of the next election.

 The ritual began with Clement VII and developed further with Pius IX and John XXIII. It has always been complied with, AND ALWAYS MUST BE. Unfortunately, you'll soon understand why.

 I leave you in the good graces of God. May He illuminate you and give you strength to carry out the enormous duty you will find in the final pages. On your strength the future of our church will depend.

John Paul II P.P.
October 29, 1978

Benedict was filled with curiosity after reading the letter Lolek had written almost twenty-seven years ago. What could be inside this folder?

The envelope held a small gilt key that opened the folder. He took out almost one hundred pages and started reading. Soon he realized by the sting of his tired eyes that he was not prepared. He read some passages again to make sure he had read them correctly, others he raced through as quickly as possible, as if to escape something distressing or inconvenient.

He finished reading after midnight. Exhausted, he locked up the folder and shut it in the desk drawer. Drops of sweat stood out on his forehead. His hands trembled. He laid his head on the desk until he regained some control over his nerves. Finally he calmed down. When he pushed himself up, he felt older, exhausted.

"God have mercy upon us," he said, making the sign of the cross.

At this moment Father Ambrosiano returned to the papal office. Ratzinger looked different. Sorrow was wasting his soul. Silence was punishing him. The Jesuit knew why. This time he didn't kneel to kiss the pope's hand. Ratzinger approached him humbly and fell at his feet. He sobbed with tears that fell in torrents.

"Forgive me, Father. I have sinned," the pope implored, closing his eyes.

Ambrosiano caressed the pope's head with a comforting hand. "I know, my son. I know."

2

———•✦•———

Father Ernesto Aragones knew that his hour would come. It was a question of minutes. Sooner or later he would end up finding him inside. The light given off by the candle flame gave the place a murky yellow look. Shadows swarmed over the walls and the floor like drunken phantoms from other times. But the father was not there to let himself be frightened or enchanted by the spells of the place.

The watchman could not be found anywhere. He was his last hope. Otherwise he wouldn't find anyone to help him. Natural for that hour of the night. The tourists had left long ago to find other attractions, more of the body than of the soul. Sweat spread over his face. He was very nervous, but the moment demanded lucidity. He felt like a crusader in the land of infidels who had to perform one last act of heroism.

Aragones made him out in the apse, next to the stairs that led to the Chapel of Adam, leaning against Golgotha, and escaped as quickly as he could. His eighty years didn't allow him much speed or flexibility. He took off his shoes to silence his steps. He set his shoes very straight on top of the stone of Unction, where supposedly the body of Christ was prepared for burial: not on this one, which dated from 1810, but in this place, at least according to legend. He forced himself to walk under the rotunda and enter the tomb. There was no holier place for Christians, though it was totally unknown to the masses. For Ernesto it was a great privilege, despite his fear. To give himself to God in the place where the body of Jesus Christ had been laid before His resurrection on the third day. How ironic. Ernesto felt fear as he knew he would. Few could go through this moment safely and without fear.

Aragones heard steps in the rotunda outside. It was him. He searched his memory to retrieve an image of the man next to the grilles of the Chapel of Adam. He was tall. He wore a well-cut suit and a blue shirt, but no tie. Unimportant details, but his mind retained them. He couldn't make out the color of the suit precisely, since the place was poorly lit during the day, to say nothing of the night.

My Father, protect Your servant, Ernesto prayed, kneeling on a marble flagstone. He made the sign of the cross unhurriedly, shut his eyes, and prayed. There was nothing more to do.

Shadows still trembled on the walls in an ever more frenetic rhythm, matching the pounding of his heart.

Reaching a certain height, they stretched out gigantically, and despite Ernesto's closed eyes and a moment of apparent calm, his heartbeat accelerated in his chest for what would be the last in his life. He knew it. He remained kneeling on the marble flagstone, which protected the rock that had borne the weight of Christ. But Ernesto wasn't thinking of this. In his final moments, he needed some inner peace.

He felt breath down the back of his neck.

"Good evening, Father," the killer whispered next to Ernesto's left ear, as if he didn't want to disturb the souls wandering through the sacred place. An inhuman coldness, almost lifeless. He got no response, obviously. "I want to ask you a question," the intruder explained. "You may choose to answer or not."

He waited a few moments for this to sink in.

"Where is it?"

It was not the question he expected. Terror filled his veins. *He knows,* he thought without saying a word. *Oh, my God. He knows. How is it possible?*

"Who are you?" He tried to buy himself some time. Sweat dampened his face.

A blow struck on the back of the neck, pushing him forward. He steadied himself on the marble flagstone, a few inches from the floor.

"Don't answer a question with a question. Where are your manners, Father?" the tall man asked, raising his voice.

"Who are you? Who are you looking for?"

Another blow. "Again? You all have a very limited repertoire."

You all? He knew of their existence? Ernesto opened his eyes. He would do everything to protect the secret, but he failed . . . completely.

He felt a cold object press into the back of his neck. Lifeless, without will. The most faithful servant.

"You have ten seconds. Use them well."

Who was he?

Nine. How could he be so well informed?

Eight. Someone had betrayed them?

Seven. The Status Quo had been broken. From this moment on, it would be every man for himself.

Six.

Protect our beloved Roman Catholic Church, which does everything for Your honor and glory.

Five. *I give myself to You, my Father.*

Four. *I serve You at all times.*

Three. A tear slid down his face.

Two. *I die in peace.*

One. He leaned over with both of his sweaty hands on the sacred flagstone and shouted, "Forgive him, Father. He knows not what he—"

The bullet robbed him of the rest of the words. He saw shadows dancing on the walls before collapsing heavily on top of the marble flagstone. Finally he danced with them. He saw and heard nothing more.

3

The less one knows, the more one believes. It has always been that way and will be until the end of time. Today, commonly known natural phenomena that can be easily explained with the efficiency of science, such as thunder and eclipses, were once considered the anger of God, an omen of the world coming to an end. Believers knelt at every altar, appealing to Saint Barbara, Saint Christopher, and others to intercede with the Creator, Our Lord God, Allah, Jehovah; each one choosing an offering to placate the ire of the god, whoever He was. In earlier ages, intercession came through other saints and gods, now lost in the sands of time, forgotten forever. And the world just kept turning, as we know today, with no interest in the beliefs of those who inhabited it.

Nor did these beliefs matter to the man descending

twenty steps, firmly gripping the handrails on each side. Age had not been kind to him. Deep wrinkles were etched in his face, like scars from a whip, reminders of past troubles. The rest of his body bore other reminders: a crippled leg that wouldn't work as he wished it to, eyes that saw poorly, even with the aid of thick glasses—defects of an over-worked, abused body that hadn't been properly cared for.

He took one step at a time toward an underground structure built in the 1950s by five good men. They had constructed a deep shaft with an elevator. However, he considered the entrance, twenty steps up and down, safer. He wasn't thinking about his old age or the impediment of his limbs or the twenty steps he would have to climb up now that he was halfway down. It wasn't a route he took daily; only once a year, on the same date, the eighth of November.

The underground structure was located several hundred feet from a large house, surrounded by leafy trees showing the dead foliage of autumn. The entrance was inside a wooden shed the employees had probably used in times past to store yard tools. It looked abandoned, full of dust and spiderwebs, probably a home for animals that didn't like humans showing up.

At the center of the shed was a bench that hid the entrance to the underground vault. It wasn't as heavy as it looked. It was easier for the old man to move it than to descend those stairs. Once down, the route was short. About a hundred feet to another door, a metal structure a couple of feet wide, with bolts the size of a man's leg.

Sixty years ago, one would have had to insert a key in the proper place to activate the mechanism to open it, but now, with technological advances, an entirely electronic lock had been installed. It opened by an optic sensor, and he looked into it for a few seconds. A blue flash passed in front of the old man's eyes and validated his identity. The eyes matched those registered by the viewfinder:

IDENTITY RECOGNIZED
BEN ISAAC
8 NOV 2010 21H13S04
ACCESS PERMITTED

The mechanism set off an opening operation that, despite its being a logical sequence of releasing locks, sounded to Ben Isaac like disconnected noises coming from within the structure. Only at the end of the process did the two exterior cranks turn, upon which the heavy door opened outward with an exhalation of air, as if it were a living thing. One by one, the fluorescent lights turned on automatically, illuminating the interior of the vault. One hundred square feet of thick stone walls. The interior was two and a half yards high, enough to hold a standing person.

Everywhere the lights emitted a uniform white brilliance, leaving nothing hidden. The place itself was hidden enough dozens of feet above in the abandoned shed among the trees several hundred feet from the large house.

The walls consisted of cold, hard granite, making the closed room cool. The white tiles of the floor reflected the light. There was nothing on the walls. Bare. Three display cases stood alone in the center of the room, topped with three glass panes that prevented oxygen from seeping inside. In the lower left corner of each case, a gauge indicated the temperature of fifty-five degrees. In each of the cases were documents: two parchments and two more recent documents.

Ben Isaac moved to the case on the left that contained a parchment and looked at it. Time had been kinder to that document than to his old body . . . or so Ben Isaac thought, resentfully. What did he know of that document's history? Whose hands it had passed through, and how it had been treated over the years, centuries, millennia, until this day, November 8, the anniversary of its discovery with other scrolls in Qumran in 1947? It had been in his possession in this same place for more than sixty-five years. It dated from the first century A.D., according to the most advanced scientific method of dating that money could buy, and in this regard Ben Isaac couldn't complain. His money could buy anything. It was a small document, compared to the others, its edges worn away and scorched on the upper right side. It must have lain close to a fire on some cold night, or someone may have held it, with criminal intentions, over a flame. Whatever the reason, the burn had not damaged the text that Ben Isaac knew by heart and sometimes recited to himself in the language in which it was written, a dead language for most people, on nights he couldn't sleep. Those nights.

Rome, year 4 of the reign of Claudius, Yeshua ben Joseph,

*immigrant from Galilee, confirms he is the owner of a par-
cel of land outside the walls of the city.*

He couldn't fail to be moved every time he saw that piece
of parchment with those letters written by a Roman scribe
about a man who would change the course of history for
billions of people over the centuries. Jesus himself, son of
Joseph, grandson of Jacob, heir of David the great, Solomon
the wise, the patriarch Abraham, according to ancient legend.

He pressed a small green button below the glass which
beeped before sliding open. Ben Isaac lifted the document
very carefully, as if it were a newborn baby, and brought
it close to his eyes. What emotion! Touching an object
that Jesus himself might have touched two thousand years
before. How privileged he was. He could touch it whenever he wanted. If a pope had succeeded in putting his
hands on this document, any pope, he would have immediately been accused of sacrilege. But Ben Isaac confirmed
it was authentic; he knew it as true.

He returned the parchment to its place and pushed the
button to return the glass to its protective position. He
moved on to the middle case, in which a much older parchment lay, degraded in some parts, so that some of the written characters could not be seen. But it was possible to read
the essential message, which he remembered every day with
a shiver and didn't have the courage to read aloud. He didn't
want to touch this, never wanted to. The parchment was
many years older than the other, but more important. It
wasn't a simple legal authorization, but a gospel known only
to two people: Ben Isaac and a learned man whom he had

approached to interpret the text, under a pact of silence.
Ben Isaac was an expert at this. He let nothing slip.

The last showcase held two documents on letterhead
paper, with the papal coat of arms at the top. Both texts
were in English and easy to read.

November 8, 1960
Vatican City
   I grant Ben Isaac, citizen of Israel, resident of
London, a concession over the parchments found in the
Qumran valley for a period of twenty-five years. While
this agreement is in force, neither party will make the
discoveries public. The Holy See will not attempt in
any way to recover the documents, which it considers its
own by right. At the end of the fixed time my successor
and those of Ben Isaac will have to arrange a new
agreement.

         God be with you.
         John P.P. XXIII
         Ben Isaac (and three illegible signatures)

The other document was similar, with a different coat
of arms and a shorter text.

November 8, 1985
Vatican City
   I grant an extension of the agreement of
November 8, 1960, for the identical term, at the

end of which new arrangements will be made by the heirs.

> *Agreed to and signed by*
> *John Paul P.P. II*
> *Ben Isaac (and five illegible signatures)*

Ben Isaac read and reread the documents. He remembered the negotiations. The cardinals, the prelates, the apostolic nuncios, the simple priests who came and went for two years with recommendations, offers, trivial details, curses, threats . . . the Five Gentlemen. He never met John XXIII or John Paul II, despite their having signed the documents. Perhaps it had been a mistake. Too many special envoys when it would have been simpler to sit down at the same table and talk. A nuncio came and offered him $2 million for the documents before the first agreement. He doubted that John XXIII had offered so much. Certainly, after the contract was signed, he was never troubled again. So many mistakes made over the course of his life. This had nothing to do with religion. He thought about Magda, tears blinding his eyes, and then Myriam filled his thoughts.

With a final glance at the parchments, Ben Isaac sighed. He looked at his watch. It was time. He left the vault and turned back to the stairs. He was too old for the battle, but he couldn't turn his back on it. Life was a battle, nothing more.

Time was up. The agreement had expired.

4

The elderly archaeologist coughed and struggled. He didn't have to wait for the blow, hard and clean, remorseless.

"The next one will knock you out," a voice at his ear whispered, cold, terrifying.

The archaeologist knew he was telling the truth.

He had caught him in the most absurd way imaginable. A telephone call in the middle of the night, unusual, but not crazy. He awoke groggy and bad tempered, but the message woke him up at once. A parchment needed to be translated. It dated from the first century, but the language was unknown. The caller apologized profusely for the late hour, but he would pay whatever was necessary to get such a respected archaeologist to look at the discovery and assess its significance. Nice words his ego seldom heard. The rest was easy. A ticket was waiting at the airport for a morning flight that would carry him to his destination. *Idiot,* he thought. His mother had always told him you never get anything for nothing.

When he arrived, he took a taxi to the address the caller had given him. He encountered chaotic rush-hour traffic that took almost as much time as the flight, but at last arrived at the designated place. It looked like an abandoned refrigerator warehouse. A strange place for such a meeting.

The courteous greeting that he expected was a hard smack in the face that knocked him facedown on the floor. The attacker, a thin man who wore an elegantly tailored suit, placed his knee on his back and shoved his face into the floor with his hand. Immediately, revealing a vigorous physical form, he lowered his head to the archaeologist's ear.

"The rules are simple. I ask and you answer. Any deviation will have consequences. Understood?"

The archaeologist thought the man was going to foam at the mouth like a rabid dog.

"Who are you?" he asked in pain. He could hardly breathe.

Another blow drove his face into the dirty floor again.

"I'm the one who asks the questions, understand?"

"You've got the wrong person. I'm only an archaeologist." It was worth the effort to try to clarify things. Attackers are not infallible, like pontiffs.

"Yaman Zafer. Is that your name?"

"Yes, but . . ."

"See how easy it is? We'll get along perfectly," the man whispered, breathing right over Zafer's ear.

"Listen, I . . ."

Another blow to the neck that left him paralyzed.

"I ask, you answer. Isn't that a perfect relationship?"

Zafer shut up. He didn't have many options. Better to keep quiet and see what the man would do. He could hardly breathe with the knee pressing his stomach to the floor. He was completely subdued.

"If you cooperate, I'll let you breathe," said the attacker. He spoke seriously.

"Okay," he acquiesced. He couldn't make demands there. Why hadn't he asked for more information before he got on the plane? Why had he let himself be persuaded so easily? He was so careless.

The attacker seemed to have heard his thoughts. "It's very easy to say what people want to hear. Let's get to the subject that brought us here," he licked his lips. "Have you heard of a man named Ben Isaac?"

Zafer shivered, despite the pressure on his back.

"I'll consider that a yes," the attacker said. "I want you to tell me everything."

He raised his knee a little, and Zafer took the opportunity to breathe in as much oxygen as possible. Zafer raised his hand to his coat pocket, but the momentary relief was over. He felt the uncomfortable pressure against his lungs again. The attacker knew what he was doing.

"What was the purpose of the project for which you were contracted in 1985?"

"What project?"

Another hard blow to the neck.

"I never did any work for Ben Isaac," Zafer explained. Maybe he would be left in peace.

"If you want to be like that," the attacker warned, "I'll be happy to make a visit to Monica and Matteo. I'm sure they will adore me." He smiled mockingly.

Zafer felt a cold shiver hearing the names of his children. Not them. He couldn't put their lives in danger. He had lost.

The elderly archaeologist coughed and struggled. He didn't have to wait long for the blow—hard, clean, remorseless.

"The next one will kill you," the voice at his ear whispered, cold and terrifying.

The old archaeologist knew he was telling the truth.

"Do I need to rephrase the question?" the attacker insisted coldly.

"No," Zafer said with difficulty. It was hard for him to talk from the lack of air. "I'll talk. I'll tell you everything you want to know."

The knee relieved the pressure, supplying air to Zafer, who gulped it down.

"I'm all ears."

Zafer felt ashamed and humiliated. He thought he wouldn't survive, but he had to protect his children.

Forgive me, Ben.

5

* — * — *

Nothing lasts forever.

Everything is endlessly changing. The river's water, the sea, the wind, the clouds, the body as it ages, the cadaver as it rots, seconds, days, nights . . . nothing is static, not even a chair, this chair inside a grimy, brown room with a forty-watt lightbulb hanging from the ceiling, over the chair itself. The chair's wood is riddled with woodworms; one day it will cease being what it is and turn into something else. The bulb will stop lighting up one day, or one night, but not tonight, and this room inside this abandoned warehouse will be demolished, together with the warehouse, to give way to a luxury condominium, which will later turn into something else.

Everything changes . . . always.

The light from the bulb failed from time to time,

plunging the room into an ominous darkness. At times it flashed like a thunderstorm inside the glass, before glowing again with agreeable intensity, reflected over the chair, leaving the corners flooded in shadowy phantasmagoria.

The room had no windows. A white wooden door was the only way in. Time had worn down the original color of the walls and door with dark stains.

A violent kick threw the door open, adding another dent to countless others. At this precise moment the bulb went out, as if in protest.

"Shit," the attacker swore, turning the light switch on and off impatiently.

After a while the capricious bulb flicked back on.

"I was about to give up," he growled.

He entered the room with a show of power. I want, I can, and I command. A very confident attitude, since he knew of no one who could stop him.

He approached the chair, grabbed the back, and lifted it. Then let the legs of the chair hit the floor in unison. It would support him.

Next to the chair was a small black bag the attacker glanced at. Everything was ready.

He went out and left the door open. The bulb threatened to go out, but when the man returned, it was illuminating the chair as it should. He was dragging someone who appeared lifeless, and sat him in the chair. It was an old man, badly beaten. At first it was difficult to keep him seated, since he didn't have the strength to support himself, and tended to fall forward. The attacker steadied him with a hand on his head. He had time. While the old man recovered consciousness, he would pull himself together.

A blindfold prevented him from seeing the place or his tormentor. Dried blood smeared his lips, a remnant of recent beatings. A bruise marked his neck. This old man had been tortured methodically and brutally.

He coughed a little to open his throat passages, but even that was difficult. He was in pain all over. The attacker interpreted the cough as a return to consciousness, and he was ready. He bent over the sack and opened it.

"Who's there?" the old man asked in a startled voice. "Why are you doing this to me?"

He was so naive. He had attended to the request of a friend who knew someone who needed a translation of a parchment. The next morning he caught a plane, and when he landed, instead of characters written on a parchment, he saw the floor a few inches from his face. A hard blow to the neck dropped him to the ground. He never even saw who attacked him. They blindfolded him and continued to beat him. He couldn't say how many there were, maybe only one, or what the motive was. He offered money, the little he had, but apparently they weren't after money. In the midst of his desperation, he tried to maintain lucidity. His mental faculties were all he had left, but even those he lost momentarily from a harder blow. He regained consciousness sitting in a chair with someone rummaging around in something at his feet.

"I don't have anything that could be of interest. I'm a professor, I live an honest life. Have mercy."

The attacker got up. He had a syringe and a glass container in his hands. He inserted the needle into the plastic top of the container and drew up the colorless liquid. He expelled the air, pressing the handle until a drop appeared at the point of the needle. He let the container fall and it shattered into shards of glass. He stared at the blindfolded old man, who was silent, as if expecting the worst.

"The rules are simple. I ask and you answer. Any exception to this rule will have consequences, understood?" the attacker recited.

6

————•————

"Two books published?" Francesco asked her, rolled up in the sheets of the bed in a suite on the eighth floor of the Grand Hotel Palatino in Rome.

"Sure. They let anyone publish a book these days," she joked, downplaying the importance of the question.

"How did you get such important information about the Vatican?" Francesco asked, looking at the white ceiling. "You must know someone inside with excellent contacts."

Sarah thought about the last two years. They had been too intense. She'd discovered things she would never have imagined about subjects that, until now, hadn't interested her in the least. She could consider herself an expert on Vatican affairs, well versed in John Paul I and II, without ever having lifted a finger to make it all happen. Life could reveal itself in strange ways, certainly. She was at the top of the list of competitive television commentators and print journalists when the subject was the Holy See. Her opinion was so respected that some even nicknamed her the pope's lover behind her back, since much of what she knew could come only from him. It was ironic that the opinion of a woman, highly suspect within the sacred walls, was most respected outside them.

She thought about Rafael, his strength, his sense of duty, his beauty, and what they had gone through together.

It was six months since they had talked. Actually, that wasn't entirely true. She had done all the talking, and Rafael didn't say a word.

They were in London, where Sarah lived. They met in Walker's Wine and Ale Bar. He arrived first and ordered a Bud. Later, when she got there, she ordered an Evian over the noise of the popular bar, but didn't wait for it to be served. She started suddenly on the subject that had brought her to this meeting.

"What do we have between us, you and I?"

Rafael looked at her as if he hadn't understood.

"What do we have together, you and I?" Sarah repeated. "I know you're a priest . . . that you have a relationship with . . ." She felt confused. God, Christ, the church? All at the same time? "Huh . . . but I also know I'm not indifferent to you." Here Sarah looked at him to get some reaction. Rafael remained impassive, listening to her. He could be a bastard when he wanted. Sarah felt increasingly nervous. "I know we got to know each other under unfortunate circumstances." She plowed on. "I know that we went through a lot, our lives in danger, and that probably gave me the opportunity to know you better than anyone. That made me fall in love with you." When she realized what she'd said, the words had already left her mouth. She thought he would have something to say, but she didn't hear anything from him. Should she have declared, clearly and out loud, what she felt? She stared at him even more intently to find some reaction. What she saw was the same Rafael as always: calculating, unemotional . . . impervious.

At a certain point a roar of delirious, shouting voices was heard from inside the bar. The "blues" team had just scored a goal at Stamford Bridge and some of those present had been swept away by the images repeated on the television screens throughout the bar.

At that instant the waitress brought the water, after a long wait. Or at least to Sarah it seemed so, an eternity, hours. Really only a few minutes had passed, but when you've stuck your hand in the fire, a brief time seems much longer.

"It's not an ordinary situation, I know. Nothing is with us," Sarah went on after wetting her lips. "I'm not asking you to divorce God. I'd never do that, but I had to tell you. I know you're perceptive enough to have already noticed." She looked at him again. "Anyway, let's return to my first question. What is it that you and I have for each other? You're not indifferent to me, are you?" It hadn't occurred to her until that moment that she could be hasty. Rafael might simply not feel anything for her. Seeing him take another sip of beer without offering a word made her feel even smaller, like a girl who confesses her love and gets her first rejection. Not verbally in this case, which made it harder. Had Sarah misunderstood everything? Had she deliberately exaggerated the signs? No way. She was intelligent, successful, the editor of international politics at the *Times*, author of two highly regarded books. Had she been deceived by her feelings? Now it was too late. She couldn't do anything. She'd revealed herself. She had to stay firm until the end.

"Aren't you going to say anything, Rafael?"

Only another sip of beer.

"You let me do all the talking and say nothing? Aren't you going to stop me? Put me in my place?"

Rafael badly wanted to talk, and he spoke, but Sarah didn't hear him now. She was leaving after throwing down a ten-pound note to pay for the Evian she'd hardly drunk.

"It's good we had this conversation," Sarah declared. "Now I can go on with my life and put this behind me." She left as fast as possible, infuriated. It was her right to feel exasperated.

If she'd stayed a few moments longer, not gone to the door so quickly, so far from the bar, so far from Rafael, if, if, if . . . probably she would have heard him. A timid, faint "I can't."

The editor of international politics at the *Times*, more sought after than she would have liked, soon found reasons to forget Father Rafael, who returned to Rome. And if, at rare times, she remembered the conversation that had occurred in that bar in Whitehall, while Chelsea was playing some team, it didn't matter to her. The same God Rafael believed in created an opportunity in the form of an Italian Adonis. Apparently she was attracted to Italians. He was a London correspondent for *Corriere della Sera,* made regular appearances on RAI, was thirty-two years old like Sarah, and had a body that would make Eros green with envy. He only had eyes for her from the first second he saw her at a lunch for journalists at the Italian embassy.

It should be said that Sarah avoided this Adonis from the south of Europe at first. But soon the Italian showed a genuine interest and agreeable conversation far beyond his playboy appearance. A native of Ascoli, his name was Francesco. To tell the truth, his sculpted beauty was the reason Sarah agreed to a date. An opportunity for Francesco to show what he was worth and if he was worth it. After this first date came a second. On the third their commitment was sealed with a passionate kiss on the steps of her house in Kensington, and others followed with greater intensity in her bedroom.

In the days that followed, things progressed naturally. More dates, more conversations, more kisses, and more. Francesco seemed captivated by Sarah's directness. There was no role-playing or cover-ups. She was always herself, Sarah, authentic, on the telephone in the office, ordering something in a restaurant, kissing in her room. There was no one but her in his eyes, and he adored this.

"Listen, those books are not bad. I see why you're a celebrity."

"You read them?" Sarah asked with feigned shock. "Who gave you permission?"

"I needed to know if I was going to introduce an anti-Catholic to my mother," Francesco replied, then, seriously, "They put me at ease."

"They're books about men, not about religion," Sarah explained.

"Yes, in fact I think my mom would agree with you on some points. We could drop by Ascoli on your book tour. What do you think?"

"Don't you think that's a little premature?" Sarah argued.

"Not for me. Take the time you need to promote your book. Don't rush. When you're free we can detour to the northeast."

"It's only a conference on La Feltrinelli of the Largo di Torre Argentina," Sarah said as she considered the invitation.

Francesco leaned over her. "You're a very appealing heretic."

"Do you want to carry me to bed, my bad boy?" Sarah smiled with desire.

"Would you let me?" Francesco chose to sound like an innocent boy.

"I would. I do . . ." Sarah said. "I don't know if your mother would let you." She threw herself against him.

"Oh, do you want war?"

A little struggle began with pillows and deep kisses. "You're going to pay for this," Francesco teased.

"Will it be very expensive?" Sarah provoked him.

When the hostilities were over and they lay in bed, out of breath, on their backs, sweating, they smiled.

"I love you," Francesco said.

His words were like a bullet, wiping her smile away. She had no reply. At least not at the moment. Francesco was not just a pretty face, it seemed. He looked at her for a while and changed the subject, paying no attention to the uncomfortable silence.

"You still haven't told me who the bishop or cardinal is who's bringing you these stories," he said, half joking and half serious.

"A woman never tells." She regarded him pensively. She thought about Rafael again.

7

———

Ben Isaac was doing everything to save his marriage. Myriam had lost her patience and given him an ultimatum. The business or her. That was the reason he agreed to go on a cruise when his business was in such a precarious state. His son, also named Ben, would take care of things for a month. Little Ben, twenty-seven years old, had worked administering the business for a long time, but always under the attentive, appraising eye of his father. This time was different. His father was on board a ship with his mother, relaxing in the Mediterranean. Young Ben made a nightly report of what had happened during the day. His mother tolerated this discussion as long as it didn't take more than fifteen minutes. Ben Isaac took advantage of it to counsel his son. He wasn't a good husband, or father, but nobody beat him at his game. He thought his business affairs would be lighter as he got older, but he had deceived himself. His objectives had changed. First he wanted the best for its own sake, then for Myriam, then for his son, and now he simply wanted to leave a magnificent legacy, immune to rough times or bad decisions. "When you die, you leave everything," Myriam warned him. "You can't take it with you."

The cruise could not be happening at a worse time. The negotiations with his Israeli counterparts were at a crucial stage, and little Ben had to conclude the deal. It was a crucial test for the boy.

He'd boarded MS *Voyager of the Seas*, an enormous ship with fifteen decks and more than a thousand passengers. They called it a floating hotel, and they weren't wrong. It had a casino, a spa, a marriage chapel, an ice-skating rink, a cinema, a theater, a shopping center, everything to make the travelers forget they were at sea and not on land.

Ben Isaac could have bought his own ship and crew and sailed where he wanted, but Myriam was inflexible. She wanted to take a cruise like a normal married couple. Arguing with her was not an option. He reserved five cabins on deck 14 and occupied the middle one in order to avoid unpleasant neighbors. Of course, he decided not to tell Myriam this detail. Ben Isaac was like that. He gave in to a certain point, and then arranged things his way. He tried to spare Myriam everything. Business problems, his son's accidents, her brother's detoxification cure, her father's lovers. He permitted nothing to inconvenience her, kept her enclosed in a glass dome. This created other problems, such as a lack of attention, long absences, and a lack of affection. Myriam rebelled and Ben Isaac gave in to her, adapting to the new reality. That was always the secret of his success.

So we find him reading the paper at table 205 in the restaurant on deck 14. Myriam was in the gymnasium swimming, and would join him shortly. Mornings were always the same since they'd boarded the ship. And Ben Isaac, exiled in London since childhood, where he made his fortune, didn't care. If Myriam was happy, so was he. If he got news of the business only at night, then so be it. That was the price he had to pay for innumerable lonely nights. Myriam deserved this sacrifice.

The waiter brought his coffee.

"Good morning, Dr. Isaac. How are you today?" A genuine smile crossed his face.

"Good morning, Sigma. Very well, thank you."

Sigma was from the Philippines and an excellent waiter, in Ben Isaac's opinion.

"Are you only going to have coffee?'

"Yes, just coffee. I'm not hungry before ten."

"Certainly, Dr. Isaac. If you need anything else, don't hesitate to call me. I hope you have a very nice day."

"Thank you, Sigma."

Ben Isaac continued to read the *Financial Times* out of professional interest. No other reading gave him more pleasure. Analyzing the market, reading between the lines, evaluating investment opportunities. One page alone could turn into millions of dollars of income. For this reason he advised little Ben to subscribe and read this paper carefully.

He lifted the coffee cup and drank a little. Black, strong, without sugar. What better way to face the day? Only when he set the cup back down did he notice a small envelope at the edge of the saucer. How strange. Sigma had not mentioned it. He lay the paper down on the table with the intention of returning to his reading and opened the envelope. There was a small piece of cream-colored paper inside.

12am swimming pool Status Quo.

Ben Isaac reread the note three times. He looked around at the tables on every side. Few people had gotten up yet. A family of five in the back, a couple three tables away. No one suspicious, though seeing faces is not seeing hearts, let alone intentions.

He caught sight of Sigma carrying a tray to the table of the family of five, full of croissants, bread, cheese, and ham.

"Sigma, please," Ben Isaac called. The Filipino came over. "Who gave you this envelope?" Ben Isaac asked, trying to hide his anxiousness.

"What envelope, Dr. Isaac? No one gave me any envelope."

"This . . ." But he stopped. This was too much for Sigma to comprehend. "Forget it. I was confused. Thanks."

"Do you need anything else, Dr. Isaac?"

Ben Isaac took a few moments before answering no. Everything was fine.

In spite of the cool air-conditioning, Ben Isaac was

sweating. He raised his napkin to his face to wipe away the film that was forming. This bothered him. He stuck his hand into the pocket of the shorts Myriam made him wear and took out the cell phone. He dialed from memory and pressed the green button to make the call. Soon he heard the beep that indicated the other phone was ringing, or vibrating, or whatever phones did these days.

"Pick up, pick up, pick up," he said almost pleadingly, though his intention was only to think without speaking.

Nothing. There was no answer. Seconds later he listened to the answering machine. You called Ben Isaac Jr. . . .

He put down the phone on the table and looked at his watch. It was eleven o'clock in Tel Aviv. Ben was working. Perhaps in some meeting about important business whose secrecy was the key to success. A tightening in his heart told him no. He got up. He needed to get his thoughts together. *Take it easy, Ben Isaac. He has nothing to do with all this. They're not going to lay a finger on little Ben.* But he couldn't help remembering the message on the cream paper. *Status Quo.* It made him shiver.

The past, always the past, pursuing the steps of the just man. The mistakes, obsessions, excesses of youth gave him no rest or forgetting. Like Myriam, little Ben, and Magda, the past was always with him, and this time it would all catch up to him at midnight in the swimming pool.

8

·•·•·

The professor stared at the students seriously with his arms crossed over his chest. The women considered him fascinating, the men respected him. He looked about forty and was in excellent physical shape. He never smiled or changed his tone of voice. Always confident. He made them think, challenged them, since this was his job as a professor of philosophy at the Pontifical Gregorian University in Rome. He cleared up doubts with new questions and another point of view. He didn't give easy answers. Reflection and reasoning were the best weapons for surviving in the real world. They wouldn't free them from death, but they would prolong their life.

"The church always finds the solution in Holy Scripture. It's all there. No one needs to wander lost, because the Bible is also a book of philosophy," he explained.

What a waste, the female contingent thought. Such an attractive person dedicated to the life of the church, a disciple of Our Lord Jesus Christ, a man of God.

Malicious tongues, anonymous sources, not that credible, said he was close to Pope Ratzinger. It was just a rumor, for no one could say if it was true or not.

"Erotic also, and pornographic," a male voice was heard to say, coming from the door, at once revealing a much older man, with white hair, beard, and mustache. His age showed, along with a gleam of playfulness. The smile of a rebellious child who has done some mischief.

"Jacopo, you never change," the professor said accusingly without altering his tone of voice.

"Were you about to tell a lie, Rafael?" he said, looking at the class provocatively. "The Bible is the first historical, fantastic, science fiction, gospel, thriller, and romance novel since the beginning of time."

"Do you need something, Jacopo?" Rafael asked firmly. "I'm in the middle of a lecture."

"I beg your pardon for sticking my sensible opinion into these minds instead of what you stick in there . . . whatever that is," he joked. "Do you know that after all these centuries and millennia, everything we read in the Bible still has no archaeological confirmation? None. And many of the 'characters'"—he sketched quotation marks in the air as he said the word—"and locations that are cited in this book, so important to so many, are not mentioned anywhere else? Only the Bible mentions them, but since it is the Bible . . ." He stopped talking and assumed a serious tone. "I need to tell you something."

"Can't it wait?"

"Obviously not," and he left the classroom.

Rafael excused himself from the class and promised he'd be only a minute.

"What's happening?" Rafael asked when he left and shut the door. "What is it that can't wait?"

"Yaman Zafer," Jacopo said.

Rafael's eyes lit up. Now Jacopo had all his attention. "Yaman Zafer?"

"Yes," the older man confirmed.

Rafael turned his back and sighed. Jacopo didn't see him close his eyes. He might have cried, but he didn't know how. Life sometimes dries up a person's eyes, making him weep blood inside instead of water outside.

Jacopo was not the type of man who could be called sensitive. Sixty-six years had set a cloak of rationality over his feelings, shielding him from human emotions . . . or at least he liked to think so. Rafael couldn't shield his feelings, but even so he was the coldest bastard Jacopo knew.

"Do you have any more information?" Rafael asked, then turned back to him again, looking at him with sad, serious eyes.

"Someone called him in the middle of the night to talk about a parchment. That's what Irene said. He caught a flight the next morning, and . . ." He left the rest unspoken.

"Where?" the priest wanted to know.

"Paris. An old refrigerator warehouse on Saint-Ouen."

Rafael continued to look at him steadily and then headed for the exit.

"Paris it is."

9

Shimon David was a conscientious old man, or at least he liked to think so. His neighbors didn't use that word, but substituted another, less complimentary one, but he didn't know about that, so he wasn't hurt. For them Shimon was an old busybody, always attentive to the smallest movement on the street and in the neighborhood. If someone wanted to know if a particular person was home or arriving late, Shimon was the person to ask. He would even know whether the delay would be long or short. The limit of his knowledge stretched from one end of the street to the other, and nothing else mattered to him. A widower, he had lived there for more than two decades. All his life he had been a mailman. He could tell a lot about a person from the mail he received. Shimon knew many things about his neighbors, more than they sometimes imagined, because no one wanted to know about him.

The street was in the suburbs of the Holy City. In the distance in the midst of buildings and stores, someone who knew what to look for could make out the gold cupola of the Dome of the Rock within the walls.

From the same window from which he kept track of his neighbors, Shimon could see his beloved city of Jerusalem, the center of the world.

This afternoon Shimon didn't appear at his window. His neighbors came home from work tired and didn't spare a glance to check his absence. They entered their houses as always without looking back, so they didn't notice whether Shimon was at his window or not.

Movements inside the house of Marian, an old woman of ninety who had died two months before without heirs, had caught the zealous Jew's attention. Perhaps someone had bought the house, which was next door to his. Certainly there had not been any changes or repairs. The three men who arrived in a white van entered the house and installed themselves as if they'd always lived there. The situation didn't inspire confidence in Shimon. Information was everything.

He knew Marian's house well. He'd been inside many times when she was alive, crotchety and very gossipy. But he liked to talk to her. She was always someone to talk to. Shimon's first mistake was not knocking on the front door and, instead, trying a sneaky approach. He circled the house by the first-floor patio, one step in front of the other, careful not to make a noise. The first window was for the living room, and he dared not look in. It was shared by too many people to be empty, and Shimon didn't want to risk being discovered. Not because he felt he was doing anything wrong, but to fulfill his duty to his neighbor's belongings that should be passed along in perfect condition to the next owners, whoever they might be. The second window was Marian's room. She'd moved down to the first floor when she realized she would die earlier if she had to climb the stairs every night. She was worn out by the effort. Marian was a very practical woman. But now was not the time to think about her. His mission was to find out who the intruders were. If they were intruders. They could be just three nice young men to add to the list of new neighbors. It would be a change, since the neighbors were starting to disappear as they moved out or died.

Shimon took another step toward the window, which by coincidence was across from his own, separated by a wall. When he got to the window, the curtains were closed. Damn. He couldn't see anything. There was light inside, but the curtain was thick. He went to the corner in back. The sun was setting elsewhere. Already it was dark. His heart beat faster. He was too old for this. He heard a muffled noise. Someone was breathing hard . . . and then a crack. The hard breathing could be his, but the cracking noise wasn't. He turned around to find the source of the noise and found himself again at Marian's window. The curtains hid the interior, but let a pale reflection of light out around the sides. He didn't see shadows. He clearly heard what was going on inside the room. Someone was breathing very hard. Another smack.

"We don't have all night, kid," a harsh male voice said.

"I've already told you. I don't know what you want me to say. You've got the wrong guy," a voice cried. "Let me go, please."

Another crack, very hard, it sounded to Shimon. Chairs scraping and other unintelligible sounds.

"I'm not going to be so gentle next time," the former voice menaced.

"Do what he tells you, kid. We don't have much time," another, more cordial voice advised.

"I'm nobody. You're mistaking me for someone else," the tearful voice repeated.

"Your name is Ben Isaac Jr.?" the friendlier-sounding voice asked. "Son of Ben Isaac?"

The sorrowful voice didn't answer.

A blow sounded. Perhaps to the head. "Didn't you hear? Answer!" the first voice joined in again.

"I am," Ben answered fearfully. "Call my father. He'll pay any amount you ask for." His pain was obvious.

The friendly voice started to laugh. "This is not about money. No one's going to ask for ransom."

"No?" Ben asked. He was completely confused.

"No," the friendly voice confirmed. "But we want something, obviously. And you're going to help us get it, Ben. Do we understand each other?"

Shimon was astonished, leaning against Marian's

window. He had to go home and call the police. Someone had kidnapped Ben Isaac Jr., whoever he was. He is terrified, the son of Ben Isaac Sr., who must have something important for mafia of this caliber. Why were they hiding in Marian's house? Another mystery. One thing at a time. The police first. He walked rapidly toward the street. As rapidly as his age and the strength G-d permitted him. Human life was at risk. When the neighborhood heard about this, there would be an outcry. Shimon passed the window of the living room and . . .

When he came to, he was a prisoner in a chair from Marian's bedroom with a pulsing pain in his neck. Ben was next to him, drooling blood, with his head on his chest. He looked unconscious. Three men were watching Shimon.

"Who are you?" the one with the friendly voice, obviously the leader, asked. He was also the shortest.

"Me?" Shimon gasped in fear. He couldn't think from the pain in the back of his head.

"Yeah, you. Didn't you hear me?" He recognized the voice, the more brutal one.

"I . . . I . . . I'm the neighbor from next door." What else could he say but the truth.

The one with the pleasant voice smiled and approached him, looking him in the eye.

"No, do you know who you are?" he asked sarcastically, while pressing a revolver against Shimon's head, who closed his eyes and pressed his lips together in panic, a cold shiver going over his spine . . . the last. "Collateral damage."

10

The summons arrived at his residence days before, but Hans Schmidt had been expecting it for a long time. The congregation complied scrupulously with every bureaucratic precept without fail, delay, or weakness.

Vienna was having its first cold days. The heat came on, warm clothes were taken out of drawers, and the latest fashions in winter wear were purchased. Hans enjoyed taking his daily walks through the Ringstrasse, indifferent to the freezing rain and cutting cold, filling the air with warm blasts of his breath. He closed his eyes and felt his breathing for a few seconds. He walked with no specific destination, like life itself. It was said that Freud enjoyed similar walking, and the reason was not difficult to understand. Life beat on indifferently. Smiles, cries, someone calling out a name, stores lit up appealingly. Sometimes he stopped by the Café Schwarzenberg to have a cup of hot coffee, and other times to look through the books and newspapers at Thalia.

He found no mention of his case. That wasn't surprising, since the congregation didn't publicize its work. Like many others, he considered himself the victim of hidden attacks by certain historians. Some even demanded that Saint Dominic be removed from the official list of Catholic saints. Wretches. They didn't see the good this man did for the world, a benefit still felt today and in days to come. They demonized a man who saw far beyond the present and stopped at nothing to repel threats to the well-being of the Holy Mother Church. He would be important in the modern world.

Hans was not so obtuse. *Saint Paul, Saint Thomas Aquinas, Saint Augustine would have to be removed from the list along with Saint Dominic,* he thought without saying it aloud.

Like Saint Dominic, Father Hans Schmidt was being judged by similar people in the Vatican. Despite seeing his work suspended for almost a year, he was still a priest. The summons bore his complete name, Hans Matthaus Schmidt, preceded by his title. The congregation usually didn't eliminate the former titles of the accused. Innocent until proved guilty. Although not officially condemned, he felt as if he were in purgatory, not knowing whether to expect hell or heaven. He knew the congregation would decide. In the words of some reassuring historians, in case of doubt, burn him at the stake. And these days there were many ways of burning without fire.

Hans Schmidt was advised by relatives and friends, "Careful what you say or write. It could cost you."

His friends, the few who remained, were starting to avoid him. *Persona non grata* may have been too strong a term, but what did you call someone who was no longer invited by his social circle and relatives?

His mother would have sympathized if she were still alive. His father was unknown. He had grown up without a permanent male presence in the outskirts of the capital, in Essling, during the Second World War. Everything was excusable in that era, even abandoning a pregnant woman. Fortunately, he didn't remember those times very well, but he remembered the Café Landtmann and seeing his real father with his wife and three small children one day when he returned from the seminary. What a dedicated father! He didn't glance at Hans, maybe didn't recognize him. He tenderly wiped away the kisses of his youngest child, ignoring his oldest there, looking at him, the fruit of another life. He didn't remember now how he knew he was his father. His mother would have agreed with what Hans said or wrote, even though she was profoundly Catholic and devoted to the good Pope John, God protect him.

The Ringstrasse seemed different to him today. Full of life as always but with different nuances. Or that was his impression. He passed in front of the Landtmann and let himself look inside, as he did on that far-off day when he saw his father. Maybe he would still be there, decrepit, frozen by the years? He never saw him again after that return from the seminary. He wouldn't be there today. Almost every table was occupied, but nobody fit the description. He was probably sleeping in peace in some cemetery in Vienna. Freud would have enjoyed Hans. Freud would have liked to analyze him there at one of the tables in the Landtmann he frequented. He wouldn't have a coffee today, or leaf through the books in Thalia, either, or the newspapers.

He limited himself to walking, tasting the cold weather that conquered the city. The sun would yield to twilight and set at the time people gathered together at home to relax, eat, smile, and cry. Vienna at the close of day, the same as in every other city in the world, although with a charm of its own. Hans remained a little longer on the Ringstrasse, watching the people, the window displays, the lives passing by, absorbed in themselves and nothing else.

A difficult battle in a lost war awaited him. He had no illusions. Age had brought him wisdom and perspective. He didn't feel lonely in spite of having no one left. He was living well and in peace, giving himself to others without asking anything in return. Perhaps that was why he felt so much. The formal summons sent three months before would not silence him.

*To the attention of the reverend Father Hans
Matthaus Schmidt,*

*The congregation directs the above-inscribed subject
to appear for a standard hearing for the purpose of
clarifying some doubts concerning the volumes authored
by him* The Man Who Never Existed *and* Jesus Is
Life, *which, according to the preliminary opinion of
the Congregation for the Doctrine of the Faith, contain
erroneous and dangerous propositions.*

*Rome, the seat of the Congregation for the Doctrine
of the Faith, June 29, 2010, the day of the martyrs Saint
Peter and Saint Paul.*

> *Signed,*
> *William Cardinal Levada*
> *Prefect*
> *Luis F. Ladaria S.I.*
> *Titular Archbishop of Thibica*
> *Secretary*

Over the last one hundred days, he'd had a lot of time
to read the cold text. And the day chosen to send him the
notice didn't seem innocent, either. The Day of Saint
Peter and Saint Paul, the most important after Christmas,
the birth of Our Savior Lord Jesus Christ, the Lord of
the Universe. It could be either an encrypted message or
his own paranoia.

Hans took an envelope from the pocket of his cassock.
From the quality of the paper it might be mistaken for

the summons, but that was in his briefcase at his residence, ready to go on the trip with him. This one came from the same place, the Holy See, but in place of a formal return address without capital letters, it had a seal with a red background: a miter with triple crown, topped by a gold cross, a white stole that hung down from the crown to come together below with two interlaced keys, one silver and the other gold. The keys that open the kingdom of heaven. Those versed in coats of arms, blazons, and symbols would recognize these in the blink of an eye, since they are the most famous next to those of the Supreme Pontiff. They indicate an envelope from the secretary of state of the Holy See.

Hans pulled out a paper and reread it. He did this often these days. It didn't take long, and as soon as he finished he understood the reason the Ringstrasse seemed different to him. From there in a few hours he would catch a flight to Rome. The next day he would not be here to admire the movement, life, and lights; he wouldn't be buying a hot coffee in the Café Schwarzenberg, the oldest in Vienna, nor would he be browsing through books at Thalia. He wouldn't feel this cold and watch his breath make clouds of vapor in the air.

It was good-bye. An unknown departure, indeterminate, of which he didn't know the outcome. Who knew what would happen. If man planned, God smiled.

He felt good, at peace. Before turning his back on the Ringstrasse, he tore up the paper and envelope and threw them in a garbage can.

"What's it going to cost me to go sooner and help a friend?" he murmured while he walked to his residence. "To give without regard to whom."

If someone had looked over Hans Schmidt's shoulder while he read over the letter, and no one did, he wouldn't have been able to read the hasty scribble, but the signature wouldn't have fooled anyone:

TARCISIO BERTONE, S.D.B.

11

His slow steps showed the heavy weight of years. He considered himself well preserved for his age, but he couldn't fool himself about his own unsteady strength, which he tried hard to hide. His steps had brought him a long way so far, to places he never longed for in his youth, when distances seem shorter than they are.

The small chapel was for his use alone, only for him or whomever he wanted to invite. A statue of Christ at the back on the altar defined the space. Six feet of Carrara granite from which the sculptor, believed to be Michelangelo, removed the excess stone to reveal this immense Christ. His head hung toward His right side with an expression of suffering set there four hundred years ago. Human cruelty. Certainly this was not just any statue by any sculptor. It was Christ in person, in His divine aspect, whom he saw and to whom he prayed whenever he entered the chapel and knelt at His gleaming feet. He did it every morning and night, but today required a special prayer, and he dragged himself along the corridor. He was bending under the effort and worry. This was not an ordinary end of the day. They were never the same, but this one brought an additional weight.

"Your Eminence," Trevor, one of his younger assistants, in a black cassock, called out at the door of the study.

His Eminence raised his hand in an abrupt, rude gesture that called for silence and entered the door of the chapel in front of him. He knelt at the feet of the angelic Christ, made the sign of the cross, and bowed his head more in mercy than in reverence. He whispered an unintelligible litany for a few moments until he realized he was not alone. He didn't need to look up to know who it was.

"Can't I pray in peace?" he protested without looking behind him.

"It's not time to pray, Tarcisio," the other person replied, dressed identically in the scarlet uniform of a prince of the church.

"Maybe not, but certainly it's something we do less and less," Tarcisio argued.

"Do as I say, not as I do," the other replied.

Tarcisio repeated the sign of the cross and got up. He turned around to the one who had disturbed his prayer to at once drop his gaze.

"This is going to have consequences, William," he said.

"We have to minimize them."

"At what price, William?" he said, raising his voice in irritation.

"Whatever price necessary," he replied strongly. "We have to be prepared for everything, whatever it costs."

"I don't know if I have the strength," Tarcisio confessed.

"God gives you the burden and the strength to bear it. You've come far. Look where your strength has brought you. Look what God wants you to do." William's voice was sincerely encouraging. He believed in Tarcisio's ability. He laid his hand tenderly on his shoulder. "And your road is far from the end. He wants much more of you. More still. You know this very well."

Tarcisio coughed uncomfortably. "We don't know what He wants later." He covered his face with his hands. "We don't even know what He wants now." Tarcisio looked perturbed, a sheep lost among the others.

William set both hands on Tarcisio's shoulders and looked at him intensely. "Look at me."

Tarcisio took his time complying with the request, not an order, since Tarcisio was William's superior.

"Look at me," he repeated with the same firm posture. Tarcisio finally looked at him with a beaten, lost expression. "You're concentrating on the problem when you should be thinking of the solution. Things are in play. We can't stop them now. But I need your approval. I myself will try personally to guarantee that everything will work out in our favor." He looked intensely at Tarcisio again. "We've got to do what's right."

Tarcisio freed himself from William and turned his back. He had to think about what he'd said. The moment required lucidity, he recognized this, but it was hard to find it. *Help me, Father. Show me the way. Guide me in the calm sea of Your arms,* he prayed mentally. William was right. Crossed arms and burying one's head in the sand resolved nothing. A firm hand and a very short rein were necessary. He grabbed William's hand.

"Thank you, my good friend. You brought me back."

William smiled. "Not me." He looked at the suffering statue. "Him."

"Your Eminence," Trevor called again fearfully from the door of the chapel. He didn't dare enter.

Tarcisio looked at his assistant without showing his excitement. "What is it, Trevor?"

"Ah . . . you asked to be told when Father Schmidt arrived," he said, awaiting a reaction.

"I'll be right there," Tarcisio only said. "You can go back to work."

The assistant disappeared almost instantly from the entrance to the chapel, as if the devil were watching him from the corner.

William looked embarrassed. "What are you going to say?"

"Nothing. He's here as my friend from the church. I'm not going to intercede, nor do I want to," he deliberated. Now he was the Tarcisio he always was when he assumed control and responsibility. An imposing secretary.

"That seems wise to me." William returned to the

matter at hand. "You're giving me your official approval, then?"

"You can count on it," he said, going to the chapel door. He longed to see Schmidt again. He was playing on both sides at the moment. He wanted to do what was right. Christ would help him.

"We already have people in the field," William informed him as they walked out. "I want to give the final orders and go over to Via Cavour."

"Be careful. Are you sure we can trust them?"

"We don't have another choice."

"Another innocent thrown to the beasts," Tarcisio argued pensively. Traces of conscience.

"Others have done it. Don't worry. We're at war."

"I know."

"It's a holy war, but there are damages we have to sustain. Everything will be resolved quickly."

"May God hear you," Tarcisio replied.

"He'll hear," William said with a smile.

"Were you able to analyze the DVD? Any indication?" he questioned shyly.

"Nothing. Clean. I'm going now."

Tarcisio left for his office in front, not without flexing his right leg and making the sign of the cross out of respect to the figure on the altar. William did the same, and both left to pursue their own affairs. Only Christ remained, nailed to the cross, His head hanging at His right side with an expression of suffering that foresaw the times to come.

12

———◆———

The press conference in the La Feltrinelli bookstore was much calmer than Sarah had imagined. Francesco contributed by asking questions from time to time that called for a light response, without the institutional weight attached to most subjects linked with the Holy See. Even if his questions seemed planted, he did break the ice. Sarah felt grateful, since they had not planned it in advance. She didn't even know Francesco would attend the conference, pen and notebook in hand, leaning up against a wall with a calm, serene expression, attracting the attention of the female contingent and of a few men as well. The Vatican contingent had not shown up, and this, too, helped lighten the atmosphere. The book she was promoting attacked certain people associated with John Paul II and suggested their responsibility for the attempt on the Holy Father's life on May 13, 1981. The most prestigious journalists from *La Repubblica, Corriere,* and *Il Messaggero* were there. They sent professionals who for decades had studied and investigated that case, as well as others tied to the Vatican, and asked pertinent, intelligent questions, which Sarah answered confidently.

In the room of the Grand Hotel Palatino Sarah was sick. Nausea rose up in her throat, dry heaves. She tried to vomit, sitting on the floor of the bathroom with her head on the edge of the toilet. Nothing. Francesco didn't know what to do.

"Do you want me to call a doctor?" he asked worriedly.

"No, it's going away," she answered, starting to gag again. She didn't want to tell him that this was not something that had just started now. She'd felt symptoms since London.

"I'm going to order some hot tea. It'll do you good," he said, picking up the phone in the bathroom.

"Yeah, do that. Thanks," as she dry-heaved once again. Empty. Upset. "Oh, damn," she complained.

Francesco placed the order and hung up the phone. Then he cradled Sarah in his arms.

"Do you want to go to bed?" he asked lovingly.

"Let's see if this goes away." Sarah knew it always calmed down. It lasted a few minutes and afterward it was as if nothing had ever happened.

Francesco gazed at his lover, who was leaning over the toilet bowl like someone who had been drinking all night.

He couldn't help feeling tender toward her, a need to make her feel better. He looked at her seriously.

"Sarah," he said hesitantly, "I know it's not the most propitious time, but maybe it would be better to go to a pharmacy." He waited for her reaction.

"Why?" The sickness was going away.

"You know very well why, my dear," he smiled. "We haven't taken proper precautions the last few times."

Sarah didn't even want to consider this. Pregnancy wasn't in her plans. Not that she had anything against Francesco, far from it, he'd be an excellent father, but . . .

"I'll go to the doctor when we get back," she proposed.

"Are you sure?" Francesco looked at her with concern.

"Yes. After tomorrow we'll resolve it. Help me get up, please."

Francesco pulled her up against himself and embraced her tightly.

"I'll be with you come what may. I'm not going to leave you to go buy cigars," he said with a smile.

Sarah snuggled against his chest and closed her eyes. A tear spilled onto Francesco's shirt. She felt lost, and despite the Italian who swore his love, she felt lonely, with no one to help her . . . Except Francesco, the Italian Adonis from Ascoli who offered his heart to her.

They heard a light knock on the door.

"It must be room service," Francesco said. "Are you okay, honey?" He looked at her face and wiped the tears from her eyes. He kissed her on the forehead.

Sarah looked at herself in the mirror, freed herself from Francesco's embrace, and put her hands on the washbasin, noticing her imperfections, red eyes, livid face.

"I'm all right, Francesco. Would you get the door, please? I'm going to wash my face," she asked, continuing to examine herself in the mirror.

"Of course," Francesco agreed and went to open the door, where someone was knocking again, a little louder.

"I'm coming," he called out in Italian before leaving the bathroom.

Sarah rubbed her eyes with the hope that when she opened them she'd see another woman in front of her. Another color. A new disposition. The will to go forward. That iron will that accompanied her when she left Rafael in the bar six months before, full of anger that softened quickly. He let her pursue her own path in life. He hadn't called her or looked for her since. The protection Rafael provided her dissolved. She missed him and even his prolonged silences. Sarah missed the times when she looked out the window and didn't see him, but she knew he was watching out for her like a guardian angel. All this ended six months before, after that one conversation in Walker's Wine and Ale Bar. Was he in Rome or on a dangerous mission someplace else? She wanted to call him. Find out how he was. If everything was all right in his parish, how his classes at the university were going. Then she'd come back to reality . . . and the ridiculous situation. *Hi, Rafael. I wanted to know if you're okay. And the children in your parish, your students. Oh, and I still love you.*

All this mental diarrhea stopped when she heard Francesco's voice from the other room.

"Oh! I think you better come here, Sarah."

Sarah wiped her face with water and dried it on a towel. She came out and saw Francesco at the door.

"What is it?"

She approached the door and saw a young prelate in a black cassock. He had dark skin with a circumspect expression.

"It's for you," Francesco explained.

"Good evening," Sarah greeted him.

"Good evening, Miss Sarah. I was asked to pick you up."

"You were asked? By whom?" It was very strange.

"I am not authorized to say. I'm sorry," the young priest apologized.

Her journalistic curiosity overcame her fear. She put on her shoes and grabbed her coat.

"I'm coming."

"Do you want me to go with you?" Francesco volunteered.

Sarah looked closely at the young cleric and thought about it for a few moments. "No. This is fine."

They took the elevator down to the reception area. It was already night. She looked around and didn't see anyone. Even at the reception desk, where there was almost always someone behind the counter ready to attend to the most demanding guest. The hotel seemed empty. As if the world had stopped for a few moments and been depleted of people.

Sarah and the cleric didn't exchange a word. She preferred it that way, and it was a blessing to have an escort who also liked silence. Clearly he followed orders scrupulously and didn't want to be questioned about things he shouldn't or couldn't mention. They went outside. It was cold, but not disagreeable. She could tolerate it. She thought about Rafael. Was he the one calling for her? It couldn't be anyone else. This was why she felt so carefree. A car was in front of the hotel at the bottom of the steps. A Mercedes with tinted windows.

The young cleric opened the door of the vehicle, and Sarah looked inside. Her jaw dropped. Inside, comfortably seated and smoking a cigar, was a man in scarlet vestments, a gold cross hanging on his chest, his cardinal's cap on his lap.

"Good evening, Sarah Monteiro," he greeted her. "Let's take a ride, shall we?"

13

—◆—

Conversations between friends are continuous. Even if they are years apart, they always resume them, as if they had just seen each other only the day before. And the day before in some friendships could have been three and a half years earlier. Hans Schmidt and Tarcisio enjoyed this kind of friendship.

An immediate embrace followed their handshake. Then two kisses. Tarcisio let his eyes fill with tears, but none dared to spill down his face. Schmidt was not so overcome, but that didn't mean he had not missed his friend. He was simply less demonstrative. He had always been called "the Austrian iceman."

"How are you, my friend?" Tarcisio examined his friend closely with a smile.

"As God wishes," Schmidt replied, looking at his friend.

"Sit down, sit down." Tarcisio pointed to an old brown leather sofa. "You must be tired. Did you have a good trip?"

"Very pleasant," Schmidt said, accepting Tarcisio's invitation to sit and letting his body rest on the sofa. He crossed his legs. "Without delays or problems."

Tarcisio sat down next to him. They were in his office, which Schmidt had never been inside before. Very spacious, a large oak desk next to one of the wide closed windows that separated them from the Roman night outside.

A tense silence settled in. The small talk was almost exhausted.

"Did you have dinner? Do you want something to eat?" Tarcisio offered.

"I'm fine, Tarcisio, thank you."

Schmidt rarely felt hungry. Often during the time he was assigned to Rome, which seemed like ages past, he forgot to eat. He would faint from weakness. Schmidt was obstinate and dedicated himself completely to the tasks he was given, whether they were his studies or, later, his pastoral functions. For some years he was removed from these duties that gave him so much pleasure, helping Tarcisio with the more administrative and episcopal duties he knew were necessary, but didn't fulfill him. Whether he liked them or not, he performed them proficiently. Tarcisio had enormous appreciation for him as a man, a cleric, and above all a friend.

"Are we going to talk about your problem?" Schmidt

inquired. His approach to problems was simple and direct; he didn't avoid them or turn his back to them. If they existed, they had to be solved at once, so that they did not return to defeat him. God protects the audacious.

Tarcisio looked at the floor to find the right words, but feared words were fleeing him like water through his fingers. He decided to be direct, like his friend. Schmidt would not permit any other way.

"The Status Quo was broken." He got it off his chest, and lifted his gaze to an indefinite point on the wall where there was a large portrait of the Supreme Pontiff, his face with a neutral expression. He waited for Schmidt's reaction.

"Lay it all out" was the only reply, with a German accent to his Italian, normally flawless.

Tarcisio needed his friend's sharp, lucid mind. No solution presented itself unless all the facts were at hand. Tarcisio opted again for the concise, cold recounting of the elements, no matter the cost.

"They killed Aragones and Zafer, and Sigfried has disappeared; so have Ben Isaac and his son." He threw out the names and facts point-blank, as if mentioning them freed him from them or transferred them to Schmidt. He felt selfish for a moment, but it passed.

"When did they die?" Schmidt questioned him without emotion. If he felt anything, he didn't show it.

"During the week. Aragones on Sunday, Zafer on Tuesday, and Sigfried disappeared on Wednesday. We don't know when the Isaacs disappeared."

"Did the entire family disappear?" Schmidt wanted to know.

"Yes, the wife and the son also," Tarcisio concluded.

"Who's going to handle this?"

"Our liaison officer with SISMI and a special agent."

"Who?"

"Father Rafael. Do you remember him?"

"Of course. Very competent. You don't need me," Schmidt remarked. "The situation is in good hands."

Tarcisio did not seem convinced, to the contrary. He was nervous and agitated, tapping his foot on the floor.

"If this explodes in our face . . ."

"The church always survives everything and everyone," Schmidt offered. "I don't see any reason it shouldn't survive now."

"You don't see? They're after documents that prove—"

"That don't prove anything," Schmidt deliberated. "No one knows who wrote them or with what motives. They're only words."

"An order in words wounds and kills," Tarcisio objected.

"Words only have the power we give them," Schmidt disagreed without altering the tone of his voice.

"Is this your defense now?"

"Nothing needs my defense. Much less the church."

Tarcisio got up, irritated, and began to pace back and forth with his hands behind him.

"We're at war, Hans."

"We've been at war for two thousand years. I've always heard this war talked about, and we don't even have an army," Schmidt said ironically.

"Can't you see what will happen if these documents fall into the wrong hands?"

"If I remember well, Pope Roncalli took steps to avoid that scenario. The agreement—"

"The agreement expired," Tarcisio interrupted, raising his hands in the air. "It ran for fifty years. It ended a few days ago."

"I know, Tarcisio. Personally, I don't believe that Ben Isaac would have appropriated the docu—"

"Why not? The contract had expired."

For the first time Schmidt looked at him apprehensively. "Because I knew Isaac when he was renewing the agreement. Ben Isaac could be a victim, but not a villain."

"That was twenty-five years ago. You saw him two or three times. Let's not forget that he is . . . Jewish." He said it as if it were a grave fault.

"He's not a Jew, he's a banker. And we also pray to a Jew, Tarcisio."

"It's not the same thing," the cardinal said, excusing himself.

"I don't see the difference. He never knew any other religion."

"Jesus founded the Catholic Church."

"Tarcisio, please. You are the most influential cardinal in the Roman Catholic Apostolic Church today. Jesus never knew the Catholic Church or any other inheritor of His name. He never founded it or, much less, asked that we construct it."

The subject disturbed Tarcisio. It was a point of friction between the two men. This freethinking of Schmidt's exasperated him and only gave trouble to his friend. He remembered just then that this was the principal reason that his friend found himself in Rome tonight. He sat down again and let the silence spread through the office. Hans remained immobile, his legs crossed, the Austrian iceman, imperturbable.

"Are you prepared for tomorrow?" Tarcisio finally asked.

"I'll see when tomorrow comes."

"I'm not going to be able to help you in front of the congregation, Hans. I'm sorry," he said awkwardly. He was genuinely sorry.

"I'm not asking for your help, Tarcisio, nor would I accept it. Don't be sorry, don't worry about it. The congregation will make their decision. If they think my opinions fit with the church, fine. If not, fine as well. Either way serves me, and none will affect me."

The confidence with which Schmidt offered these words impressed Tarcisio. They came from deep within him; they were sincere, without any presumption or perfidy. Schmidt had changed much in the last years.

"I hope it goes for the best. As Our Lord desires," he wished.

"Our Lord doesn't have anything to do with this," Schmidt concluded.

"Do you also think Ben Isaac has nothing to do with this?" Tarcisio returned to the previous subject.

"I suggest you try to find him, if it's not too late."

"How?"

"Think a little, Tarcisio. They killed Zafer and Aragones. We can very well fear for the fate of Sigfried and the Isaac family."

"But who's behind all this?" Tarcisio asked. "What's their intention?"

"I don't know, but whoever it is doesn't stop at half measures." He stopped talking and thought about it. "Hm. Interesting."

"What?"

"The participants in the Status Quo are all being eliminated," he said with a thoughtful expression.

"And?"

"Two are left."

14

—◆—

History tends to write itself with deep chisel marks that disappear only with the passage of time, dissolving in oblivious rain. Insignificant people will never be remembered on bronze plaques that record their birth, the place they lived, or their achievements. They remain only in the memory of those who lost them, until they, too, disappear under a forgotten gravestone.

No one would remember Yaman Zafer's deeds, not because there weren't any, but because he spent his life trying to conceal them. The last hours of his life proved that his best efforts were not enough.

Rafael leaned over the greasy, disgusting stained floor, examining it in silence, as if hoping that the place would speak for itself. He was sad. He had known Zafer and his sons for more than twenty years. Not that he saw them often. Sometimes years passed, but they felt together at every moment. This had been eliminated.

"I still don't see what you think you'll find here," Jacopo grumbled, standing up, looking at the priest.

"I still don't see what you're doing here," the other replied.

"You know perfectly well why I'm here."

They had arrived in Paris around midnight. The flight had been smooth, covering the miles in the darkness. Jacopo had used the time to talk about his theory about the lack of proof for the stories in the Bible. Rafael listened to him without paying attention.

"Until the end of the nineteenth century, the truth of the Bible was never put into question. The Evangelists were inspired by God. The truth is that, as much as it could, the church didn't allow its faithful to read the sacred book in their language. It was a crime, punished by death." His theatrical gestures didn't impress Rafael. "It was Pope Paul the Fifth, in the seventeenth century, who said, 'Don't you know that much reading of the Bible harms the church?'" he quoted sarcastically. "Now, think about it. What church, especially one called a religion of the book, bases its dogmas on the book but prohibits its believers from reading the sacred book that gives credibility to everything it proclaims?" He paused dramatically. "The nineteenth century initiated a feverish archaeological search for proof of the 'facts'"—he sketched quotation marks in the air when he said this word—"narrated in the Bible. They excavated everywhere there was a site. Palestine, Egypt, Mesopotamia, a host of sites in the Near and Middle East. They wanted to find Solomon's temple, the remains of Noah's ark, anything to confirm the facts of the Bible. Paul-Émile Botta, the French consul in Mosul, began the race; Austen Henry Layard, an English diplomat, was next; then another Englishman, also named Henry, embarked on the search."

Rafael looked at him for the first time. He could do without the history lesson. He'd known this argument for years.

"Do they pay you to teach this?" he asked scornfully.

"After decades of excavations, smiles, delusions, anxieties, what did they find?" He left the question hanging in the air, ignoring Rafael's remark. Jacopo made a circle with his thumb and finger. "Zero," he proclaimed triumphantly. "Nothing."

"Nothing?" Rafael asked.

"Absolutely nothing," Jacopo reiterated. "Nothing to confirm a single fact mentioned in the Old or New Testament. But they came to another conclusion: names of people and places appear in the Bible that the Greeks and Romans had never heard of. They're mentioned only in the Bible, and nowhere else."

"On January 4, 2003, a block of limestone was discovered with inscriptions in ancient Phoenician of a detailed plan for the recovery of the first Jewish temple, Solomon's," Rafael said. "It was found on the Temple Mount, in the old city of Jerusalem."

"The Haram al Sharif, as the Muslims call it," Jacopo added, visibly pleased with himself.

"The fragment dated from the time of the biblical king Jehoash, who reigned more than twenty-five hundred years ago. If you're so well versed in the Bible, then you must remember chapter twelve, verses four, five, and six, specifically, from the Second Book of Kings, where it's related that Jehoash, king of Judah, ordered all the money from the Temple collected to use in its restoration."

"Allegedly," Jacopo offered with a smile. "They never let me see that discovery. Nor was there further information about it."

"In 1961," Rafael continued, "an excavation of an ancient amphitheater, ordered built by Herod the Great in Caesarea in the year 30 B.C., revealed a limestone block, accepted as authentic. A partial inscription was found on it."

Jacopo and Rafael quoted at the same time:

DIS AUGUSTIS TIBERIEUM
PONTIUS PILATUS
PRAEFECTUS IUDAEAE
FECIT DEDICVIT.

Jacopo applauded, smiling. "Pilate's stone. It proves only the existence of Tiberias and Pilate, which was never in doubt, and confirms that Pilate's office was prefect, or governor, and not prosecutor," Jacopo argued. "Do you have more?"

"It's a work in progress. Don't forget we're talking about millennia of history on top of history. But you never know when something new might appear, and you better than anyone know that it's a slow process."

Jacopo lifted his arms and opened his hands. "Let the sophists return. They're forgiven."

A light rain fell on them as they left the terminal, wetting their faces and clinging to their clothes.

"Shitty weather," Jacopo complained.

The police had sent a car to take them to the place where Zafer had been found by an addict who was using the private spot to get high. Instead he found an old man stretched out on the floor on his stomach, lifeless.

The warehouse was in the north of the city, far from the tourist traffic and glow that made Paris the City of Lights. A collection of projectors, powered by a generator that made a monumental noise, lit up the interior and exterior of the building. The cadaver had been picked up during the afternoon. A technician collected all the evidence that could reveal anything about the crime. The rest was pretty clear. Zafer had come of his own free will, received a beating, and an injection of prussic acid ended his suffering.

Some plainclothes police wandered through the area, busy with tasks that would make no sense to outsiders. Others were just talking together, anticipating the end of a long day of work.

"Rafael Santini?" called out a man in a tan suit with a cigarette in his mouth.

Rafael was brought back from the world of possibilities and speculations he'd been absorbed in and got up.

"That's me. Are you Inspector Gavache?"

"Yeah." He extended his hand.

"Jacopo Sebastiani," the other interjected.

"What are you doing here?" Gavache asked, greeting him hostilely.

"We're friends of the victim," Rafael put in before Jacopo answered.

Gavache looked at them with displeasure. He didn't try to hide the fact he was there to keep an eye on them.

"Tell me," he said to Rafael, who was obviously the leader, "who's Yaman Zafer?" He took a drag on his cigarette.

"He's not of interest to the Vatican. We're here personally, as friends of the dead man."

Gavache looked at them again. First one, and then the other, doing justice to his role as an inspector. "Well," he finally said. Cigarette smoke formed a cloud around the three of them. "Friendship is a wonderful thing. Did you know him a long time?"

"Twenty years. He was a respected archaeologist at the University of London. Maybe you know some of his publications," Rafael told him. He had to give him something. Gavache was no fool.

"I don't like reading," the French inspector replied. "Life's already a big enough book to waste time with that. Did he *archaeologize* something for the Vatican?"

"He did some work under the sponsorship of the Holy Father," Rafael confirmed. "Some excavations in Rome and Orvieto." He couldn't tell him everything. "Can we help with anything?" Rafael offered. He felt he was losing him.

"No. If you don't mind my saying so, friends are a distraction in cases like this," he said disdainfully. "Jean-Paul," he called out to someone, who came up from behind. Gaunt and tall with veins sticking out on his neck. If you didn't know him, you would think he was starving.

"Here, Inspector."

"Escort these gentlemen to the city. We don't need them here. *Merci beaucoup.*" He turned his back, lifting his cigarette to his mouth again.

"Follow me, *s'il vous plaît,*" Jean-Paul said.

At that moment Rafael looked at Gavache, who was brandishing some photographs a technician had given him.

"Was this your plan?" Jacopo protested, sticking his hands in his pocket to fight the cold. "A waste of time."

"The devil is in the details," Rafael replied, continuing to watch Gavache.

They headed outside to Jean-Paul's vehicle.

"Do you have the results of the autopsy yet, Inspector?" Rafael asked. He needed information.

"Yes and no. Yes, we have them, and, no, I'm not an inspector. Your friend was badly beaten and injected with cyanide. A quick death."

As they descended some iron stairs, their heavy shoes made them ring with every step.

"Any suspects?"

"No, no one. Everything's clean. Not even a hair fiber.

Everything else is shit, I'd say. Whoever did this chose the place well."

"You're not going to find anything," Rafael said.

"Father Rafael," he heard a voice call out. There was a woman at the door of the warehouse.

Rafael looked.

"Inspector Gavache would like a word with you, if you don't mind."

Rafael went up three steps and entered what was formerly an office.

Gavache was busy discussing something with two of his men. His nasal voice rose above those of the others. He caught sight of the Italian priest.

"Ah, Father. Do you mind if I call you that?" He handed him some photographs. "Do you know him?"

Rafael looked at the three photographs. Each was of the corpse of a male, on the floor, who was not a friend of his. He was darker, dirty also. A wooden chair fallen to the side. He couldn't see the face.

"This is not Zafer," he said with certainty.

"So far we're in agreement."

Gavache gave him another photograph. The corpse was on a gurney in the body bag of a mortuary. Rafael looked at the face and recognized it.

"There was no identification with him. What name are we going to give him?" Gavache inquired expectantly.

Rafael didn't know how the inspector had related the two cases, but he wasn't going to hold back. He needed him to get access to the case or cases.

"Sigfried Hammal. Professor of theology. When did this happen?"

"Today."

"Here in Paris?"

Gavache shook his head. "In Marseille."

He looked at his subordinates. He didn't need to say a word for them to step out and leave them alone. Gavache gave Rafael a prosecutorial stare.

"What's going on here?" he asked suddenly. "An archaeologist, a theologian. Two people tied to the church, dead in the same manner, in the same country."

"I have no idea," Rafael responded without lowering his gaze. To do so would suggest withholding something.

"Some scam. Was he also a friend of the German?"

"I saw him only once."

"For what reason?"

"I don't remember. It was a long time ago."

"How long?"

"Maybe twenty years."

"And the archaeologist was English?"

"Turkish, but he'd lived in London almost since birth."

"Don't you think it's curious you knew both of them?"

"What do you mean by that?"

"Two deaths, one after the other, of two people you knew."

"Are you telling me I'm a suspect?"

"Of course. We all are. Only they"—he pointed to the photos—"are not suspects."

Death frees everyone of guilt and suffering. The true salvation.

"Do you believe in life after death?" the Frenchman asked.

"Excuse me?" What kind of question was that?

"Just curious," Gavache added.

Rafael was speechless. He'd have to respond carefully to avoid being misunderstood.

"I believe there is a world after death where we'll be in communion with God and . . ."

"In heaven?"

"Yes."

"Or hell?"

"For whoever hasn't saved his soul," Rafael explained. Where were these questions leading?

"Do you think the Turk and the Englishman went to heaven or hell?"

Gavache had a gift for leaving him speechless.

"Uh . . . I'd say to heaven." What a strange person.

"Then you think they lived a life worthy of heaven opening its gates to them," Gavache insisted.

"Without doubt."

"So what had they done for someone to so meticulously plan their murders? What did they do . . . or what did they know?" Gavache left the question hanging in the air.

Rafael sensed where the inspector was going. He had no doubt why he held this position. He was sharp.

"There's something else," Gavache continued.

Rafael waited.

"You told me you came for personal reasons, and not in the name of the pope, right?"

"Correct," Rafael confirmed.

"But these crimes have not yet been made public, Father. No journalists know about them. We informed the Holy See for very specific reasons, which makes your presence here very strange, don't you agree?" Gavache didn't wait for a reply. He looked directly at him. "I understand you are a friend of one of the victims, but you have to explain to me why you took the last flight of the day to get here, for personal reasons, to assist in an investigation of a crime that no one knew had occurred. Your friend's body wasn't even cold yet." Having asked the question, he turned his back. A habit of his. "Take your time preparing your answer."

What the fuck was the first thought that crossed his mind, and the second and third. The fourth was a less serious obscenity. *Shit.*

Jacopo came up at this moment, as if nothing were happening. "So? What did the guy want?"

Rafael grabbed him by the collar and lifted him in the air a few inches, lacking a wall to shove him against.

"You bastard," he cursed.

Jacopo grabbed Rafael's hands to get loose, but they were like claws holding on. "What did I do?" he managed to ask.

"Who told you about Zafer's death?" He still couldn't connect the name to the group of dead men. It seemed unreal. "Who?"

"The secretary of state," Jacopo managed to spit out.

Rafael set him down. Things hadn't been right since the beginning. It wasn't what was expected of him. His eyes blazed with fury. He was angry with himself.

"You told me it was Irene."

"Who told me he'd taken a flight to Paris to look at a parchment. I didn't say it was Irene who told me the news." Jacopo finished explaining. "What's going on?" he asked, composing himself.

"Who told you to inform me?" Rafael turned his back to think.

"Trevor, at the request of the secretary," Jacopo explained. "The orders were to go to Paris on the first flight. Isn't that why you came?"

Rafael didn't reply.

"You're completely crazy," Jacopo accused. "I didn't want to come here. I came because they paid me to. I was just fine in Rome screwing my wife."

Rafael remained silent, immobile.

"You came for friendship, didn't you? You thought I would give you news and Irene asked you to come to see what was going on? They hadn't been together for years. Did you think I was here for the pleasure of your company?"

Rafael looked at the photographs of Sigfried's body again. Gavache came up at that precise moment.

"Have we reached a conclusion?" he asked nasally.

"The inspector said he informed the Vatican for very specific reasons. What are they?"

"Welcome, Father Rafael," Gavache greeted him with a half smile. He opened a silver cigarette case and took another from inside. He raised it to his lips and searched for his lighter. He felt his pockets. "Jean-Paul," he shouted.

"Here, Inspector," the assistant replied, stretching out his hand and lighting the cigarette.

Then Gavache handed a cell phone to Rafael.

"For this," he said.

Rafael took the cell phone and looked at it, then at Gavache with a puzzled expression.

"Your friend had great presence of mind, let us say. He was able to turn on the recorder and record a part of what happened. Maybe because the phone has a special button for that. Your friend used it from time to time to record thoughts and ideas. The part that interests us is not easy to understand, but the lab is working on the recording. Anyway, there is something explicit enough here. He took the phone from Rafael's hand and found the recording he wanted.

The sound filled the room. *What is the code* [static noise] *they gave you?* a voice asked. *I know the Vatican ordered the codes given.*

HT, responded a voice Rafael recognized as his friend. *In what order?*

I have no idea. Zafer seemed to be in great pain.

This is over now. You were a great help, Yaman Zafer. May the Lord have mercy on you and Ben Isaac. The pope will pray for your soul, the other voice said.

The rest were disconnected sounds that could be anything, but Rafael knew. Zafer dying. He heard the death rattle that had occurred in this very place. Finally, silence. He heard some steps and a word of farewell. *Ad maiorem Dei gloriam.*

Gavache turned off the phone and looked at Rafael.

"Does this shit tell you anything?"

Rafael looked at him with icy coolness and a dead expression. The devil is in the details. "He's a Jesuit."

15

———◆———

It's said the night is always a good counselor, but under cover of night, crimes are committed, secrets told, and mysteries perpetrated.

They dined at table 205 on deck 14. Myriam wanted them to go see what was playing in the theater—a review called *Broadway Hits,* some of the principal scenes and music from *Cats, West Side Story,* and *Phantom of the Opera*. It wasn't unforgettable, but pleasant, a kind of easily consumable pastiche.

They returned to their room after eleven. Myriam was happy, and that was the objective.

"Are you okay, my love?" she asked him. "You seem very distant today. Do you feel all right?"

"I'm fine, Myr. Don't worry."

"Did you talk to Ben tonight?"

"I did," he lied. "I'm going to call him again at midnight, if you don't mind. Today was an important day for him."

"So late? And even later in Jerusalem?" she objected, wrinkling her brow.

"Yes. He asked me to."

"Okay, but don't stay on the phone an hour. You know I'm cold at night."

"Relax, dear. I'll be quick," his voice rose a little.

He hadn't been able to reach little Ben. The phone was always busy. His assistant wasn't able to locate him anywhere. He wasn't at the property Isaac had in Tel Aviv, or at the office at work. Isaac feared the message he'd received at breakfast was related to his son's disappearance. He had no idea who had sent it, nor who would know the latest about the Status Quo. He'd know in a little while.

He spent the day suspecting everything and everyone: the smiling employees, the other tourists—only Myriam escaped suspicion. He asked himself hundreds of times whether the sender of the message was on the ship, if he were watching him, if, if, if. This in a man who always avoided ifs. After lunch, they'd made port in Livorno, and it could very well have been there the intruder boarded, in time to leave the following day, in Naples, taking advantage of the coming and going from port to port on the western coast of Italy. He was a needle in a haystack of three thousand people.

He kissed Myriam tenderly on the forehead and left for the pool.

"Don't be late," she reminded him as he closed the door gently.

He didn't know what reply to give except an "I'll be quick." The truth was he didn't know what he was going to find. He normally assigned a time frame to everything—a meeting, a telephone call, a lunch, buying a present, flowers for Myriam—but for this appointment, nine minutes before midnight, there was a blank.

He walked through the corridor of deck 14 toward the elevator. Going up a ramp and from there to the pool would not take more than two or three minutes at his slow, nervous pace. His legs trembled as if an abyss were opening before him. He passed some tourists stumbling to regain enough balance to return to rooms whose location they couldn't remember. The employees tidied up the disorder of the day or cleaned up trash thrown on the floor without regard—cigarette butts, plastic cups, bits of food.

Strangely, or maybe not, there was little movement near the pool. Ben Isaac was panting. It wasn't a difficult walk, no steep up-and-downs. No one was around. The water undulated to the motion of the giant ship. The pool water was illuminated by vivid blue underwater lighting, and transformed in appearance to a living organism by its undulation. He didn't see a living thing. Strange. But nothing today was normal. He looked at his watch: 11:57. In his mind, seconds were turning over, or was it his heart pumping into his veins that marked the rhythm? The three minutes seemed six, then twelve, until midnight arrived and . . . nothing happened. True, it was midnight only on his watch, maybe it still wasn't midnight on the other person's watch, whoever he, or she, was.

He looked around and saw no movement. The night was cold and unpleasant. The ship floated slowly toward the south, opening up the waters to the Mediterranean. Two minutes past the hour, according to his watch. He heard the echo of a gunshot. He couldn't pinpoint where it had come from, but wherever it was, it wasn't nearby. Moments after the mysterious shot he saw something slowly descending from the sky. It was about a hundred feet up, descending toward the pool. At first he couldn't figure out what it was. An unidentified flying object. At fifty feet he could give it a name. A parachute. Oblivious to Ben Isaac's attentive observation, the parachute maintained its serene descent. It was about two feet long, and another object, black, was secured to its cords. Seconds later it fell silently into the pool and remained floating.

Ben Isaac kept looking at the parachute that now seemed more like a small sheet in the middle of the pool.

What now? Ben Isaac was cautious. There was no brilliant solution, and he was a pragmatic man. He went to the closest ladder; took off his shoes, socks, and jacket; and slipped into the water. The temperature was pleasant, but swimming was not something he liked to do, especially at that hour of the night. In a few strokes, he reached the parachute. He dragged it over to the ladder and sat on the edge of the pool. It carried a package wrapped in plastic. Frantically, he tore it open. Inside he found a box, and in the box an electronic apparatus. It was a viewfinder the size of a hardcover book. He tried to figure out how to turn it on. It only had an on-off button. With his heart beating like a hammer inside his chest, he pressed it. The viewer turned on. A signal to play appeared in the middle of the screen, apparently touch activated. Ben Isaac took a deep breath and pressed it.

He didn't know how long it took him to get to his room, whether he ran or walked, if he took the elevator or went down stairs, but somehow he found himself in front of the door to his room. He hugged the apparatus to his breast as if it were a sacred object. He was completely wet and left a trail of water. If someone saw him, he saw no one. He entered the room and looked for Myriam, who was sleeping on her stomach like a baby, her face turned toward Ben Isaac. He tripped on a chair and almost fell, just enough to wake his angel.

"Are you okay, dear?"

She didn't see at first with her sleepy glance that he was drenched with water and conflicting feelings. He wasn't the same Ben she knew, but a weak, old, disoriented man. He paced from side to side, soaked, holding on to something. Now, yes, Myriam saw it. She turned on the light, blinking her eyes in the contrast, and confronted Ben.

"What's the matter, Ben? Tell me right now."

Ben Isaac kept his head down, not daring to look at her directly.

"Our son, Myr. Our son," and he began to cry.

16

History never lies. Books that record it can relate what they understand: truths, lies, half-truths equivalent to whole lies, speculation, eulogies, heroic acts that never happened. Glorious acts last because someone was paid to extol them. There's no better example than Rome, the Eternal City, the glory of God on earth, where He chose to dwell, without doubt.

Rome is a whore of a city with a palazzo on every corner.

They entered one of these palazzi, which in this case once belonged to the wealthy family of the Medicis. Two famous cousins had lived there before they moved to other, more sumptuous palaces, Giovanni and Giuliano, who became Leo X and Clement VII, respectively, the most powerful men in the world—by their own estimation, at least. The celebrated Catherine, the niece of Clement, who married Henry II of France, had also resided there. Curiously, none of them gave his or her name or the family's name to the palazzo, which, in an era when influential cardinals or Supreme Pontiffs engraved their names on every place they ordered built or reconstructed for posterity, did not escape notice. So Madama Margherita of Austria baptized a palace that to this day is called the Madam Palace in her honor. The Medicis are long gone—Margaret, too—but the Palazzo Madama today houses the Senate of the Italian Republic.

The Mercedes entered through a side gate and circled the enormous edifice to the back. There it parked. The black priest who had come to Sarah's room was the first to get out of the vehicle. He opened the back door for his superior, the cardinal, and would have opened Sarah's door if she had not already done so.

They'd filled the brief ride with polite small talk, *Are you enjoying your stay? The weather is beautiful for this time of year. The famous, warm Roman autumn.* Unimportant observations that only served to fill an awkward silence. The cardinal, trained to be a good conversationalist, didn't allow a single moment of unease to fill the backseat. Strangely, or not, Sarah was very much at ease. The situation required her to be alert and distrustful, since she was in a car with a cardinal of the Roman Catholic Church, completely at the mercy of his will, whatever that might be, given that his career with the church was not very well known, but she didn't worry about that for one moment.

They invited her to enter the palace through a back hall, a large, ample area with a stairway rising to the higher floors. There was no doubt the Romans of the Renaissance knew how to build palaces. This proved it, if proof were necessary. They went up two flights.

"I didn't know this palazzo belonged to the Holy See," Sarah said to break the silence. She was panting, the result of not having worked out for a while.

"It doesn't," the cardinal replied in a friendly way. "Actually it's the Italian Senate's. We'll see in a minute."

"Then why are we here?"

They reached the second floor, which opened into an immense atrium with enormous closed double-paneled wooden doors at the other end.

"What better place for a private conversation?" the cardinal disclosed.

The priest opened the doors.

"Please." The cardinal motioned Sarah to go in before him.

Sarah accepted with a decisive step inside.

"This used to be the library of the palazzo."

The room had high walls, like everything else in the palace. Sarah tried to imagine it filled with bookcases from top to bottom. Now the walls were hung with paintings by artists who were unfamiliar to her, on various themes: religion, paganism, erotica, all chosen by someone who kept his reasons to himself. Two busts were placed against two facing walls. They were two men, Medicis, Popes Leo and Clement. The painting of a woman dominated the back wall. It wasn't difficult to guess who she was . . . Madama Margherita of Austria.

There were in fact traces of modernity; a temporary exhibition spread across the room with paintings, parchments, and photographs.

Sarah gave herself time to get used to the atmosphere and then looked at the cardinal.

"Why is it that the prefect of the Congregation for the Doctrine of the Faith wants to talk to me?"

"You recognized me? I'm flattered," the prince of the church joked.

They walked side by side. The cardinal looked at the priest assisting him, who, with an obedient motion of his head, left the room without turning his back, and closed the doors.

Sarah looked at the prefect of the Congregation for the Doctrine of the Faith inquisitively. She was still waiting for his reply.

"Did your book signing go well?" the prefect asked, changing the subject with a congenial smile.

"You tell me, Your Eminence," Sarah said provocatively.

"Call me William."

If he'd been dressed like an ordinary man, in a suit, shirt, perhaps matching tie, she might have complied with the request, but not in these circumstances. Not with a man in a black cassock with a scarlet slash dominating his chest, a gaudy gold cross hanging from his neck, and a cardinal's cap.

"I don't think it's standard practice for men so prominent in the church to seek out women in their hotels, drive off with them in their cars, and bring them to a palazzo. We'll have to talk about that eventually, Cardinal William," she said, settling on a half title.

The cardinal looked at Sarah and smiled. Then he stepped forward to a display that showed a poster of Jesus Christ, a common image, recognized by everyone regardless of his or her faith. At the bottom was the title of the exposition in large letters. Sarah found them curious: THE FACES OF CHRIST.

And in subtitle: Artistic Representations of Christ Through the Centuries.

An engraving dating from the first century A.D. was next to the poster. An image of the Nazarene in a somewhat crude sketch that was faithful to the idea of Christ at that time.

Curious, Sarah thought to herself.

"Interesting, isn't it?" William asked.

"Very," Sarah agreed, still looking at the artistic representations.

"We have an image so associated with Him that we don't realize that it came from the mind of an artist, and later from others, and so forth through the centuries,"

William explained. "Look at this one," he said, pointing to a painting in the third display that showed a powerful man with a sparse beard and his hand on the head of a kneeling man.

"Is that Him?" Sarah asked, curiously. "It doesn't look like it."

"But it is. An artist's vision."

Sarah had not expected an evening like this, wandering through a room in a palace side by side with one of the most influential cardinals in the college.

"Why'd you bring me here?" she asked, a variation on the question she'd asked before, like an artist creating something different from the same motif.

William pointed at the various images in the exposition. "For Him."

Sarah looked puzzled at the different representations. Maybe William had not explained himself clearly. "For whom?"

"For Yeshua ben Joseph." He proclaimed. "Jesus, the son of Joseph."

She still didn't understand. What was she there for? She waited for William to continue.

"Sarah has a special talent. Rare in journalists, let's say. Discretion." He praised her.

Sarah decided to stay silent. She didn't know how to respond to the observation.

"It's not just journalism that lacks discretion. A lot of other professions could use it. Seriousness, too."

"Is the church discreet and serious?" Sarah asked.

"There are times when it's not, I confess. Times we don't like to remember, but today I'm proud to belong to an institution that excels in both qualities."

Sarah didn't doubt that William believed what he was saying, but she did doubt the complete honesty of his assertion.

"According to the Holy Father, Sarah also excels in those qualities."

Would the pope speak about her qualities? This remark left her perplexed internally; externally, she remained impassive. She'd learned not to show her feelings with Rafa. . . . *Oh, forget him.*

"The Holy Father?" Sarah smiled. "Surely he has more to worry about than my qualities."

"Everything, Sarah. The Holy Father is a man who worries about all the sheep in his flock."

"Please, Cardinal William. I'm sorry, but I'm not a sheep in the pope's flock."

"You have two books that prove it. That show you want to know the problems, that you want them to be solved, that you worry about them," the prefect argued.

"Two books that, probably, the congregation over which you preside would censure if the Index Librorum Prohibitorum still existed," Sarah replied. She never thought she'd be speaking on equal terms with a cardinal.

"The Holy Inquisition continues to exist, my dear.

And it's important that it does. But with respect to your reply, let me tell you that the Roman Catholic Church never for a moment opposed your books. There has not been one unfavorable review or angry sermon. Nothing."

Sarah wasn't convinced in the least. "Sometimes silence is the best remedy. The church is a master at letting time erase what it doesn't want remembered."

"Let me remind you that you are alive because of this church you reproach and this pope you criticize."

Sarah respected the remark. It was true. Twice. It suited the church to intervene in her favor, but, yes, it had done so.

"Has the time come to collect?" Sarah asked, frowning. Was that it?

William didn't answer. He continued to walk along, looking at the faces of Christ. Some were very similar, others added something more: an athletic bearing, a physical detail, different hair, now blond, now brown, shorter, longer, thin, good-natured, smiling, suffering, contemplative, miraculous, enigmatic, angry, frightened. There were innumerable representations of the same person, each different and yet all the same, if that were possible.

"The church needs you, Sarah," William concluded. "We're in a war and under secret attack. It's not a payback but an urgent request."

Sarah was even more confused. What service could she provide for a church that made a cardinal look for her personally at her hotel?

"In 1947 a Bedouin named Muhammed ehd-Dhib

happened to find some parchments inside some jars while he was looking for a lost sheep," William began.

"Qumran. The Dead Sea Scrolls. I know the story," Sarah informed him.

"Well, that story's completely false."

This was news indeed.

"The person behind the expedition was an Israeli named Ben Isaac. Ever heard of him?"

Sarah searched her memory, but found nothing. "I don't think so."

"He's lived in the same city as you have for more decades than you've been alive," he said with a sad smile. It wasn't a story he liked to tell. "He fabricated the story of the Bedouin to be able to investigate more thoroughly what his team had discovered. He was ingenious. In the ultimate analysis it was providential. The hunt for the scrolls began. Complete and partial parchments were sold on the black market for millions of dollars. Total fraud in the majority of the cases."

William continued the detailed account. The church had its own agents in all the markets of the Near and Middle East looking for any documents relevant to the Holy See or the history of the West. Sarah imagined Rafael as one of these infiltrators, with turban and dagger, or saber, in a white tunic negotiating in the hot sands of Damascus, Amman, and Jerusalem. Of course he wasn't old enough for this.

From time to time there was talk, whispers only to interested parties, about some fragment that appeared in some place in the possession of some person or another. Offers came in from all sides, always in a tent, never in the heat of the sun, and the church managed to acquire some of these fragments of history in exchange for large sums of money. They were translated and authenticated. The Dead Sea Scrolls do in fact exist. For some time they were not seen or heard of by anyone, but then two or three appeared at the same time. Ben Isaac released a few he deemed sufficiently provocative but harmless.

"And how was it they discovered his scheme?"

"It was God.

"They might never have been discovered. Ben Isaac was an intelligent man with an acute, discreet mind. But one of the archaeologists who was part of the Israeli's team quarreled with his supervisor and resolved to abandon the project. Despite a pledge of secrecy, he sent an anonymous accusation to the secretary of state. It was the pontificate of the good Pope John that tried to verify the information. It was confirmed."

William was silent for a few moments to let all this sink in for Sarah, who listened attentively.

"But the story of the Bedouin prevails today," Sarah objected.

"In the beginning we decided not to reveal the false story, until we saw what was going to happen. It turned out to be advantageous for both sides."

"For both sides?"

"For the church and for Ben Isaac."

"He gave you what he discovered?" Sarah was astonished.

"Part of it. Fundamentally, we had the same objectives."

"Which were?"

"To preserve history," William offered.

Sarah didn't exactly agree. She considered the church an institution that preserved only the history that served its own interests, not all of history.

"So what was Ben Isaac's plan?"

"He wanted to keep the discoveries secret at all cost. Not just from the church, but from everyone."

"He didn't want glory, like every other adventurer?"

"No, he was born into wealth. He studied in London, fell in love, and married. He was a hard worker. Then he took on the mission of finding evidence of the Bible. Others before him had tried, without success. The place where the scrolls were discovered was a route of passage for the Jews. Jesus himself might have passed that way. He knew what had to be done and equipped himself with very expert historians and archaeologists. Money was not a problem, so everything came together in a positive final result."

"Yes, but I thought they found the gospels of Philip and Magdalene, which the church considers apocryphal and not credible, along with other irrelevant things. That's what I read or heard, anyway."

"You're well informed. That was only what they made

public." He hesitated before deciding to go on. "The rest is protected by an agreement."

Interesting, Sarah thought. *The church and its secrets.*

"An agreement between . . ." she insisted.

"Between the Holy See and Ben Isaac. It's called the 'Status Quo.'"

Sarah smiled, remembering a rock band with the same name.

"It means the current state of something. It was signed by John the Twenty-third and Ben Isaac, and later, by John Paul the Second and Ben Isaac and their team of historians, archaeologists, and theologians, obviously. It was important to maintain absolute secrecy."

"He must have been very young when he signed the first agreement."

"A little more than thirty years old."

"That's something," Sarah said with admiration.

"Indeed," William concurred.

"I still don't see what I'm here to do!" Sarah exclaimed. Her curiosity continued to grow.

"We'll get there, Sarah. Be a little more patient."

At that moment one of the doors opened to admit William's resolute assistant, who whispered something in his ear.

"We'll go at once," William murmured.

The priest left and the cardinal was available again. It was time for the question a good journalist would ask if this were an interview. "And what documents are included under this agreement?"

William didn't answer at once. He approached Sarah, stopped looking at the faces of Christ, and focused on her. He hadn't stared as intensely all night as in this moment. He felt uncomfortable, even blushed.

"Two documents from the first century," he informed her at last.

"Important?" Sarah asked uncomfortably.

"Very. One of them is the Gospel of Jesus."

17

When a commandment comes from God, it cannot be questioned. It is known that He always writes without error. His will is law, always, even if it is not written. It will come to pass from that day forward. And if to protect Him certain commandments must be violated, commandments that He himself inscribed and gave to Moses to communicate to us; well, then, let His will be done on earth as it is in heaven.

One of the Ten Commandments he violated constantly, *Thou shalt not kill*, but He slept like a baby every night since He knew the majesty of His work in the astonishing Creation.

The mail was delivered every week without the name of the sender or the recipient listed, since it could be for only him, for only he and she lived there.

She always woke up before he did and never went to bed unless she was told to or unless he was not at home, which, fortunately, happened frequently. She rarely spoke unless he asked her a question, though she did speak to herself when she was alone. Every day, like taking medicine, before bed and first thing in the morning, she had a random passage from the Bible to read, or at least that's what she thought.

Tonight he returned without prior warning, and she was still not asleep at nine. She was reading a novel that he didn't know about. Her lip split from the hard slap he gave her and splattered blood on the pillow.

"The sun has already set," he said in a calm voice and with an expression that made it seem the remark should be considered an act of leniency.

"Forgive me," she murmured, her eyes tearing with pain. She got up and ran for her room.

"Stop," he ordered, and approached her menacingly. He grabbed the book roughly. "I'm confiscating this. Go to your room."

Everything had its time, rules, and discipline. A fault, whatever it was, required a punishment, and the slap in the face that split her lip was not itself the punishment but a warning.

These outbursts could be avoided if she followed the rules. She knew them backward and forward. She had no excuse to disobey what had been determined.

He looked at the book and read the title, *The Man Who Never Existed,* by one Hans Schmidt. A heresy in two hundred pages that pretended to point out the road to salvation. He couldn't understand it. God showed them the way. Why did she have to look for other ways? He was too merciful. Some people needed to learn the hard way how to stay on His track.

He threw the book in the fireplace, which was burning with a hot flame, and opened his briefcase. He took out the last envelope he had received. Inside there was a letterhead with round strokes in large letters. On the top line he read *AD MAIOREM DEI GLORIAM*. On the next line was *Deus vocat*, followed by the name of the chosen ones. Normally there was one name, rarely two. This time he read two: Yaman Zafer and Sigfried Hammal.

He threw the letter and envelope into the fireplace.

He got up and went to see her. She was kneeling by the bed to pray. The power of prayer. He didn't interrupt her, since nothing is more sacred than the direct contact with God through prayer. To ask forgiveness, grace, an idea, a suggestion, this was the privileged, sacred channel that should never be interrupted. He waited with his arms crossed, staring at her. As soon as she made the sign of the cross, signaling the end of the communication, she got up and lay down in bed. He went to a chest at the foot of the bed and opened a drawer. His back was turned to her, so he didn't see her eyes fill with tears, which she quickly wiped away. Her shaking lessened, then stopped, for better or worse. He looked at her and came over. He carried a syringe containing a yellow liquid.

"Give me your arm," he ordered.

She wouldn't. He pulled her to the edge of the bed and inserted the needle. He slowly emptied the syringe and waited. He looked at his watch. Two minutes later she'd be sleeping like a baby. Breathing quietly. A sleep without dreams. A holy repose. He undressed, folding and hanging each piece of clothing on a chair. He got on the bed, on top of her, raised her nightgown, opened her sleeping legs, and entered her. He went in and out in a frenzy, and she never opened her eyes or uttered a sign. A few minutes later he finished, with a few drops of sweat on his face. She remained asleep, unchanged, with the same quiet breathing.

He left her asleep and went to look at the mail. A box in the door with a lock only he had the key to. There was an envelope in it, as he suspected. A cold smile, if it could be called that, spread over his lips. He opened the box and took it out. The same letterhead across the top and then the name of those chosen by God to join Him. He had no time to waste. This time there were three names.

18

"Tell me the story straight," Gavache asked as he leaned his head against the front passenger seat.

Jean-Paul was driving the inspector and the two Italians into the city.

"Saint Ignatius of Loyola was the first to use that saying in the Society of Jesus, which he founded. *Ad maiorem Dei gloriam*. For the greater glory of God," Rafael explained.

"Saint," Jacopo mocked.

"Are you telling me the Jesuits go around killing people?"

"No, I'm telling you that *a* Jesuit killed *two* people—"

"Three," Jacopo interrupted to correct him.

Gavache's eyes almost jumped out. An exasperated Rafael stared at Jacopo with disdain.

"Three? The count has now gone up to three? Did you hear that, Jean-Paul?" He looked at Rafael like an inquisitor.

"Yes, Inspector. Someone's hiding information." Jean-Paul joined the party.

"That's exactly what I think, Jean-Paul. Somebody's making fun of us. What can you expect from those who preach morality? They only preach morality when they're being immoral, right? But who's fooling us, Jean-Paul?" he looked around and stared at the passengers behind him.

Jean-Paul didn't answer Gavache's rhetorical question since he knew the inspector could be dramatic when necessary.

"I'm sorry, Inspector. I didn't remember that detail," Rafael began uncomfortably. He hated to apologize. Difficult for someone who normally did as he pleased . . . in the name of God. Jacopo had to learn to keep his mouth shut, but this could wait. "The third homicide, which chronologically was actually the first, was a Catholic priest in the Church of the Holy Sepulcher in Jerusalem."

"When?" demanded Gavache brusquely.

"Three days ago."

"Name?"

"Ernesto Aragones. He was the administrator of the Catholic wing," Rafael clarified. He was still on shaky ground.

"Why do you say the Catholic wing?"

"Because the Church of the Holy Sepulcher is administered by six distinct churches."

"Did you hear that, Jean-Paul?"

"A real mess, Inspector." Jean-Paul kept his eyes on the road.

A light rain continued to fall, glazing over the windshield irritatingly. The wipers dirtied the windshield more than cleaning it off, forcing Jean-Paul to double his focus.

"How can six churches fit into one?" He turned around, facing the road. Spending so much time twisted around to the back was giving him a crick in the neck.

"Do you know the importance of this church?"

Gavache didn't answer, as if he were thinking about it, but Rafael realized that he was just irritating him.

"It's the most important."

"Exactly. It marks the place where Jesus was crucified and buried."

"Supposedly," Jacopo added, as if that one word made all the difference.

"I see your friend is not very Catholic," Gavache offered, amused but not smiling.

"Not at all Catholic," Jacopo added. "Not a drop."

"So why'd you come?"

Jacopo didn't know what to say. He'd rehearsed answers for every possible question, but he didn't know how to answer that.

"Jacopo is an eminent historian at the University of Rome, La Sapienza," Rafael said. "He came because he was a friend of Yaman Zafer."

"And of Sigfried Hammal?"

"I think we met at a conference in '85, but it wasn't

important enough to remember," Jacopo offered in a timid voice.

"And this Ernesto Aragones," Gavache insisted.

"I've never heard of him."

Gavache was silent a few moments. The only sound was the car moving on the street.

"Where were we?" he asked after some time.

"How is it six churches can fit in one?" Jean-Paul remembered, as if it were nothing.

"Exactly. How?" Gavache repeated.

Rafael explained. "As we said, this church is the most important of all the ancient churches, for historical reasons." He stared hard at Jacopo. "A treaty worked out with the Ottomans in the 1850s divided the custody of the church and adjacent residences between Roman Catholics, Greek Orthodox, Armenians, Copts, Syrians, and Ethiopians. They named a neutral watchman."

"Watchman?" Gavache asked.

"The person who locks and unlocks the church," Rafael explained. "They named a Muslim watchman."

"What a happy world in which all the religions live together in peace," Gavache said sarcastically.

Rafael ignored the remark. "This treaty is called the Status Quo."

Gavache absorbed the historical information and wet his lips.

"Now the million-dollar question." He permitted himself a few seconds of suspense and turned toward the back. He massaged his neck to ease the pain. He wanted to see their faces when they replied. "Did Ernesto Aragones, Yaman Zafer, and Sigfried Ḥammal know one another?"

The two passengers in the back looked at each other.

"I have no idea," Rafael answered.

"I don't know what to tell you," was Jacopo's response.

"Hmm . . . do you think they'd give the same answers if they were in separate rooms, Jean-Paul?"

"I have no idea, Inspector. I don't know what to tell you," the subordinate replied.

Gavache was a falcon. He hovered over his prey several times before sinking in his talons.

"Are the crimes related? How did the other one die?"

"A bullet in the back of the neck."

Gavache sighed. "Is this a Jesuit practice?" Sarcasm at a new level. "A priest, an archaeologist, a theologian," he said, speaking more to himself than to the others. "We know the archaeologist and theologian are related. The priest's death differs in the modus operandi. Here I am with a priest and historian who keep the best information to themselves and sweet-talk me. Do you think we can trust them, Jean-Paul?"

"I don't know what to say, Inspector. Are you greedy?"

"I'm greedy, Jean-Paul. Of course I'm greedy. I'd rather have a bag of candy in my hand than have them handed to me one at a time, or have to beg them to give me more."

"There's your answer, Inspector."

Their dialogue irritated Rafael and made Jacopo apprehensive.

"Inspector Gavache, I've given you everything I have," Rafael offered, attempting an excuse. "I didn't mention the crime in Jerusalem because I didn't think it was related. As you yourself said, the modus operandi is different. It could have been the same murderer or not. I didn't try to trick you. I hope you understand that. It's been a terrible week for us."

"And I have two related deaths on French territory, in less than twenty-four hours, in the capital and the south. Do you think that's easy?" Gavache countered.

"That's not what I was trying to say," Rafael said, in his own defense. It wasn't easy to argue with Gavache. Actually, it was impossible. He'd never win this kind of argument. He decided to leave things the way they were.

Silence settled in again. Jean-Paul drove through the heart of downtown Paris. Perhaps because it was still before the morning rush hour, there was not much traffic, and it was easy to drive. Several minutes passed in a deafening silence that could have been counted out by a heavy ticktock. *Ticktock. Ticktock. Ticktock.*

Rafael recognized the street, Boulevard du Temple. Boulevard des Filles du Calvaire followed, farther along rue de Saint-Antoine.

"Why did you ask for help from the Vatican?" Rafael asked.

Gavache didn't answer at once. He looked ahead like Jean-Paul, turning over in his mind everything that had been said, the good and bad.

"The Vatican was mentioned on your friend's recording,"

he finally said. "But something else intrigued me even more."

Rafael leaned against the seat in front. He was very attentive. "What?"

"The murderer said the pope would pray for him. It could have been an innocent remark, but to me it means that your Jesuit did what he did on his orders."

"Are you crazy?" Rafael exclaimed. "That doesn't make sense."

"I'm only a layman. If you have a better explanation, I'm all ears," Gavache said ironically.

"Does it make sense that the Holy Father would hire a murderer and later agree to help in the investigation of a crime he himself ordered?"

"You know as well as I do that criminals sometimes testify in crimes they themselves perpetrated. It wouldn't be the first time."

"What we have here is a Jesuit out of control . . . with his own personal agenda," Rafael compromised.

"To whom do the Jesuits answer?" Gavache asked.

"To the superior general of the society," Rafael explained.

"And to whom does the superior general answer?"

Rafael took longer to answer than he liked.

"To the pope," Jacopo put in.

No one said anything further except Jean-Paul, with a brusque "We've arrived" as he braked hard.

Gavache got out of the car and looked around. The others joined him.

"Another church, Jean-Paul."

"Another church, Inspector," Jean-Paul repeated.

"I hope you're right," Gavache remarked to Rafael.

"I do, too."

And they climbed up the stairs toward the entrance.

19

—◆—

The helicopter shook as it headed into the side wind. The pilot was accustomed to these conditions, and chose a route farther to the north to avoid fighting the wind. The call had come from the *Voyager of the Seas,* a cruise ship sailing along the coast between Livorno and Corsica.

It happened sometimes, someone more critically ill than the ship's clinic could handle or disagreements that had to be resolved by the police. In this case it was a couple who urgently needed to get to Fiumicino. They were alarmed, but spoke a language the pilot didn't understand. It sounded Arabic, but he couldn't say. Hebrew is difficult for anyone. They hadn't explained the urgency, nor did they have to. Must be some millionaire who needed to close a business deal, spoiling the vacation of his wife—or his lover, since she looked younger than he.

Ben Isaac secured himself as well as he could. Myriam clung to the seat and looked at the instrument panel countless times. No father should have to see something like this. His son, little Ben, tied up, bloody, with tape over his mouth and a blindfold covering his eyes. He was holding up a white sign with Hebrew letters written in black:

THE STATUS QUO IS OVER.
AWAIT INSTRUCTIONS.

But she didn't care about the sign or what it said. Only that the boy she had given birth to was suffering, helpless, with no one, without protection, without his mother. She had tears of worry on her face, and kept looking at his image.

"What is it they want, Ben?"

"I don't know, Myr," Ben Isaac answered, keeping his voice under control.

"Money? Pay them, Ben. Pay whatever they want."

Below they began to see lights from the coastal towns. They were nearing the peninsula.

Ben Isaac looked out the window just as a light rain began to strike the glass. In his worst nightmares he had never imagined such a scenario. Had they kidnapped little Ben to blackmail him? He knew exactly what they wanted, but who were they? How did they find the information?

Only a leak could have started all this, and there were not many who could have informed when those involved were so few. He had failed in the most important duty of his existence—protecting his family. Just as he had failed Magda in another life, long ago, in his forgotten past.

The pilot radioed his position to the control tower and followed instructions for landing. A few minutes later they put down on the assigned runway. A van waited to take the passengers to a plane Ben Isaac had leased while still on board the ship.

As soon as they settled into the van, his cell phone rang. It showed his son's number. Ben looked anxiously and turned the screen to his wife, who suddenly snatched the phone from his hands and answered.

"Ben? Ben?" she cried desperately with tears running down her face. She listened a few moments and closed her eyes. Moments later she held out the phone to Ben. "It's for you."

Her husband took the phone and lifted it, reluctantly, to his ear. "Ben Isaac," he answered. He said nothing more. He just listened. Probably as he was ordered to do. Myriam looked at him in suspense. No reaction, no interjection. Nothing. Total silence. The one-sided conversation lasted a few seconds. Ben Isaac hung up, and Myriam, instead of bombarding him with questions, made only one observation. "Don't hide anything from me, Ben."

The van stopped next to a Learjet 60 XR that was ready to board them. An attendant waited next to the steps to help Myriam and Ben climb into the plane.

"Welcome," she greeted them with a brightly enameled smile.

The interior of the jet was a luxury they had become accustomed to, but even if they weren't used to it, they wouldn't have noticed. They were stopped in their tracks by the sight of a cardinal, accompanied by a young woman, seated comfortably in the cabin.

"You're a difficult man to find, Ben Isaac," the cardinal observed.

"I was never hiding."

"Sit down." William gestured toward the seats. "Make yourselves at home."

20

<hr/>

The priest's name was Gunter, and he made them wait awhile. It was just as well that an acolyte received them inside the immense Church of Saint-Paul–Saint-Louis, sheltering them from the rain, which was getting heavy.

Gavache lit another cigarette over the useless objections of the acolyte. Those who enforce the law are always above it.

Jacopo displayed a scornful smile, which everyone else considered idiotic, but no one said so.

A Delacroix looked over them in silence, *Christ in the Garden of Olives*. A statue, the *Virgin of Sorrows,* by a prominent French sculptor, could also be admired. Rafael felt as if he were inside a puzzle with missing pieces. He was used to being a step ahead, not a step behind. It was not a comfortable position.

Jacopo wandered through the side chapels, appreciating the works of sacred art. This was his world. The light was dim and lent an air of mystery, deepened by the rain they could hear falling outside.

"Interesting," Jacopo stammered, his eyes on an altar full of relics.

"What's interesting?" Gavache interrupted with a cigarette between his lips.

"This church. It's based entirely on the Church of the Gesù in Rome. Even the facade outside. The Jesuits are indeed exemplary."

"It's a Jesuit church, anyway," Gavache offered, looking at Rafael. "Do you think they'll give up one of their own?"

"We'll see," Rafael replied, sitting down in a pew next to Jean-Paul. "That isn't the idea."

"What makes the Jesuits so special?" Gavache asked Jacopo.

"They're extremely intelligent. They know how to think about the church. You could say they're specialists in marketing religion."

Rafael smiled. What an absurd idea.

"They always turn to preaching. Unlike the Benedictines, for example, who live in communities and follow daily rituals together, the Jesuits think more about society than community. To convert people after preaching, spread the word of God through the world. Loyola was a very good strategist," Jacopo said, warming to his subject.

"You talk a lot about this Loyola," Gavache noted.

"Naturally. Saint Ignatius of Loyola was the founder of the Society of Jesus. This church, like many others, is due to the work that he initiated. It's the largest Catholic religious order in the world. And everything began here in Paris."

"That's enough of a history lesson for now," Rafael said, saturated. He knew what Jacopo was going to say backward and forward.

"Sorry, Rafael, but the subject interests me," Gavache interjected, then looked at Jacopo. "Please, continue."

That a French inspector was interested in what he had to teach about the Jesuits made Jacopo feel very important.

"Okay, you can always recognize a Jesuit church from its symbol. We're talking about the sixteenth century, and they already had a notion of a sign." He pointed to the altar and to the acronym above the image of Christ. "IHS. You'll find those letters on the facade, too."

"IHS?"

"Yes, it signifies Jesus in Greek, composed of the letters *iota, eta, sigma. Iota* and *eta* are the same in Greek and Latin. *Sigma* was transliterated as *S*, and in some cases *C*, because they have the same sound. They also interpret the acronym in Latin as *Iesus Hominum Salvator,* which means Jesus Savior of Men. If until the Council of Trent the Benedictines were the ones to follow in the matter of ritual, afterward the Jesuits revolutionized everything. Do you see that pulpit?" He pointed to a kind of marble veranda on top of a carved cap on a column supporting them.

"I'm looking at it."

"The Jesuits were adept at preaching, as opposed to turning their backs on the people. Don't forget, we're talking about the sixteenth and seventeenth centuries. Mass was celebrated in Latin, but the Jesuit fathers made a point of preaching facing the faithful, very close to them, in a way they understood." Jacopo was silent for a few moments. Many priests had preached their sermons from those pulpits. "And for me one of the most inspired inventions of the church: the confession," Jacopo added.

"The confession? How so?" Gavache looked perplexed.

"It was the Jesuits who invented confession as we know it today. I know we grew up thinking that these things existed forever, but it's not true. Everything has a beginning."

Gavache had to think about that.

"Marriage . . . ," Jacopo proceeded.

"Don't tell me that was one of their inventions also?" Gavache cut him off.

"No, marriage was before them, but the ritual as we know it today comes from the twelfth century. I mention it to illustrate how things aren't as we think they are. Someone thought them up, someone created them . . . men, not God."

Jacopo let the idea sink in. It was a theory that made people, especially laypeople, think.

"You're a sensationalist, Jacopo," Rafael accused.

"Am I lying?"

"You put things in a very simple way. As if they'd tried to think up ways to exploit the faithful," Rafael argued. Gunter was really taking a long time.

"And didn't they? What was confession?"

"You tell me."

"What better way to create the omnipresence of God," Jacopo said, his face flushed. The subject was dear to his heart.

"Please, Jacopo. That's absurd."

"I don't think it's absurd," Gavache put in.

"You see?" Jacopo agreed. "Any person with any sense agrees. Confession was a pleasant procedure for getting to know the lives of everyone around you. Even today a Jesuit priest hears confession from the pope every Friday. I tip my hat. It was ingenious."

"The confession is protected by secrecy on the part of the confessor," Rafael replied, tired of the conversation.

"What does that matter? As soon as you tell me your secret, even in confession, I have power over you because I know something no one else does. Besides, a superior can oblige a confessor to divulge the confession, as you know very well. There's a reason they call the superior general of the society the black pope."

"The black pope?" Gavache inquired.

"Yes, because the Jesuit suit is black," Jacopo explained.

"There are some who claim that the black pope has more power than the pope himself."

"Interesting." Gavache was visibly intrigued.

"It's the society's mission to serve the Supreme Pontiff wherever he desires, without question, fulfilling his will, always, but it's said that whoever opposes the society finds himself in a war that can end very badly, even for the pope himself. There are rumors that some popes died at the hands of the society."

"That is outrageous," said a thundering voice behind them. It was Gunter, who crossed the nave from the altar with firm steps. "The Jesuits answer only to the pope and carry out what His Holiness wants, when he wants, without question. We preach the word of the Lord all over the world—love, understanding, tolerance—and we help society progress down a good path. We never put a life at risk," he added. "I'm sorry I made you wait. My name is Gunter." He introduced himself to Gavache with a handshake. When he came to Rafael, he embraced him. Two friends separated by distance. He did not greet Jacopo.

Gunter appeared to be in his forties and in great shape, emanating energy through every pore.

"To what do I owe this visit at such an inopportune hour for the servants of God?" Gunter asked.

"I'm sorry for the late call, Father Gunter, but servants have been assassinated and others need your help," Gavache said in his nasal tone, not caring if he seemed sarcastic. Gavache was Gavache. Who could blame him?

"I'm not sure I understand."

"We need your help, Gunter. Show him the recording, Inspector," Rafael said. It would be easier if Gunter was informed about what has happened as quickly as possible. Tell him everything, or almost everything, and show him the recording. Gunter remained pensive. A phrase went though his mind. *Ad maiorem Dei gloriam.* Saint Ignatius uttered these same words in the sixteenth century, in the same city of Montmartre, where he founded the Society of Jesus with Peter Faber, Francis Xavier, Alfonso Salmeron, Diego Laynez, Nicholas Bobadilla, and Simão Rodrigues, on August 15, 1534. It was one of the rules that governed the Society. *For the greater glory of God.* For Loyola this was the most important thing. Gunter listened and watched everything in silence and then went on thinking.

"Did you know the archaeologist or theologian?" Gavache proceeded. He needed to start putting the pieces of the puzzle together.

"I don't believe so."

"Jean-Paul, show the photos of the victims to the father," the inspector ordered.

Jean-Paul did so promptly, handing over the photos he was carrying. Gunter carefully examined the faces but not one was familiar.

"I don't recognize anyone. Sorry, Inspector."

"Do you think it could be the work of a Jesuit father?" Gavache continued.

"It doesn't seem believable to me that priests, Jesuits or not, would go around killing people. We preach love, the way of God, the good. Having said that, anything is possible."

"Let us suppose that these guys"—Gavache pointed at the photos of Yaman Zafer and Sigfried Hammal—"were enemies of the church. The reason doesn't matter. Imagine they knew a secret that could bring down the church. Would you be the people to get to resolve the problem?"

Gunter chuckled, "For the love of God, Inspector. The church doesn't do these things, much less the Jesuits."

"Bullshit," Jacopo stammered.

Gunter didn't respond.

"We're not going to get anything here, Jean-Paul," Gavache muttered, turning his back on the conversation.

"Well, no, Inspector."

"Paris has nothing, Marseille nothing. We have nothing." Gavache was thinking out loud. "Where are we going to start over, Jean-Paul?"

"At the beginning, Inspector. Always at the beginning."

Rafael took advantage of the moment to get close to Gunter so that no one would hear them. "Do you have something for me? You can fool the inspector, but I know it was a Jesuit priest. I want to know who it was and who gave the order."

"Are you crazy?" Gunter whispered. "Bringing a cop with you. Where's your common sense?"

"My common sense ended when Zafer died at the hands of a Jesuit priest," Rafael replied coldly.

"I can't help you, Rafael."

"This Loyola," Gavache mentioned with a quizzical expression.

"Who?" Gunter and Rafael answered simultaneously.

"The Loyola the historian was talking about."

"Saint Ignatius," Jacopo explained.

"What about him?"

"What was he all about?"

Rafael and Gunter looked at each other.

"I don't understand what you're asking." Gunter was confused.

"What was he doing? Why did he found the Society of Jesus? What was the purpose? Do you have to take some special course to join the society? Is it enough to know someone? No one does anything for free, right, Jean-Paul?"

"Nobody, Inspector."

"What was his deal?" Gavache insisted.

Gunter didn't know how to answer. It was a very strange question.

"Saint Ignatius was a Spaniard and—" Jacopo was ready to give another history lesson.

"Please, Mr. Jacopo," Gavache interrupted, lighting a cigarette and exhaling smoke into the holy air of the church. "We have a Jesuit here. I'd prefer some inside information, if you don't mind."

According to Father Gunter, Ignatius Loyola was born in 1491 in the town of Loyola, near San Sebastián, in Basque country. He became a soldier and was seriously wounded in the Battle of Pamplona, which occurred during the Italian War, when Francis the First of France and

Charles the Fifth of Spain were fighting over the Holy Roman Empire. This was in 1521. Loyola spent months recovering and began to read books about Jesus, saints, the road to God. These readings influenced him greatly.

"Books have always been a bad influence," Gavache added, sending a cloud of smoke into the air.

When Loyola recovered his health, he secretly left his father's house and dedicated his life to God. First in the Monastery of Montserrat, where he confessed over the course of three days. Then he abandoned his elegant clothes and decided to live a life of poverty in the monastery of Manresa. He wasn't a monk; he only occupied one of the cells as a guest. He supported himself by begging and not eating meat or drinking wine, and visited the hospital, and brought food to those who suffered. He underwent tests of his soul, visions, and spiritual experiences. In 1523 he decided to ask permission from the pope to go to the Holy Land to convert the infidels. He obtained a pontifical passport and, once in Venice, headed for Jerusalem. He planned to live there, but the Franciscans would not permit it, so he returned to Europe, to Barcelona.

"When was that?" Gavache asked.

"In 1524."

"How could someone so resolute, who asks for a passport from the pope and wants to live in the Holy Land, be convinced to return so quickly?"

"What do you mean by that?"

"What I said. Deciding to live his life someplace and

only staying a few months, simply because somebody didn't want him there . . ." He let the question hang over them. "Not a good story."

"That's your opinion."

"Why didn't the Franciscans want him there?"

"We don't know."

"Well, then."

"He entered the University of Alcalá de Henares on the outskirts of Madrid, founded by Cardinal Cisneros in the sixteenth century and known today as the Complutense of Madrid. He studied Latin, but his preaching and begging brought him to the attention of the Holy Inquisition."

Gavache smiled at the mention of the *Holy* Inquisition.

"He was a prisoner for a month and a half, but they found nothing bad in his writings or what he preached. They freed him, but he was forbidden to preach and had to dress better. He appealed to the archbishop of Toledo, who upheld the prohibition but let him enroll in the University of Salamanca. Again, he was arrested by the Inquisition. He decided to leave for Paris, where he entered the university in 1528. He studied theology and literature, becoming a teacher in 1533. In 1534 he founded the society with six followers. The intention was to go to Jerusalem, but first he needed the permission of the pope. Paul the Third approved his voyage and consented to ordain them priests. The war that broke out between the Papal States, Venice, and the Turks delayed the journey to the Holy Land, so Ignatius remained in Rome.

Paul the Third, who needed missionaries for the Americas and the Orient, verbally approved the new order on September 3, 1539, and a year later confirmed it with the papal *Regimini militantis Ecclesiae*, which contained the statutes of the Society of Jesus. Thus, it was officially born."

"And what happened to the saint?"

"He was named first superior general of the Society of Jesus. His work continued. He founded the Roman College, on donations alone, with the purpose of offering free education. Paul the Sixth made his life a little difficult, and he found himself in economic difficulties, but Gregory the Thirteenth, twenty-five years after the death of Loyola, maintained and supported the project, and that's why today we call the ancient Roman College the Pontifical Gregorian University. Ignatius died in Rome on July 31, 1556. He left one thousand Jesuits in one hundred and ten places with thirty-five colleges. He was canonized in 1622 by Gregory the Fifteenth."

Gunter was like a student nervously reciting a report and afraid to make a mistake. Gavache was silent, looking at the floor.

"That's the official history. What about the secret one?" Gavache finally said.

"Excuse me?"

"The secret one. The history you don't tell anyone, but pass along secretly."

"I assure you this is the history of Saint Ignatius. There are no secrets, and we're talking about a saint from the sixteenth century. He did not commit the crimes against Zafer and Hammal," Gunter joked, though he sounded serious.

Gavache didn't challenge the remark. Actually he ignored it completely. "We've got too many nationalities now."

Gunter shrugged. What did the Frenchman mean by that?

"Someone killed the Turk, a German, and maybe a Spaniard. The Vatican sent me two Italians who brought me to a German in French territory to see if the murderer belongs to a society of another Spaniard who lived in the sixteenth century. What a lot of shit—"

"If you'll permit me, Inspector," Gunter interrupted, "I don't think we have anything to do with this."

Gavache blew a puff into the air. "A lot of pieces are missing in this puzzle. And I need to find out if Zafer and Hammal knew each other. Worked together. If they ever saw each other's faces." He looked at Rafael. "I need you in this department."

Rafael agreed. There was something about Gavache that made him want to help. Perhaps his iron will to find the killer of his friend.

At that moment a cell phone rang. It was Gavache's, and he took it out to answer. He listened and said a few phrases in French in his nasal, firm voice. When he disconnected, he looked at them with wide eyes.

"The lab managed to decipher part of the recording. There's a name." He looked at all of them at the same

time, as if wanting to capture their reactions simultaneously. "Does *Ben Isaac* mean anything to you?"

Gunter prostrated himself on the floor of the church.
Rafael showed no reaction. Jacopo looked at Gavache
openmouthed.

"God help us," Jacopo said, sitting down in the near-
est pew.

"It's never too late to start believing," Gavache offered
ironically.

21

—◆◈◆—

Francesco couldn't imagine making the trip to Ascoli without Sarah. To make the scene more troubling, he didn't know what had happened to her. They were supposed to be going the next day to meet his mother. It was important.

"Not even a phone call to let me know you're okay?" he sighed to himself, annoyed. Had something happened to her?

He pressed his cell phone to his ear with his shoulder while holding the hotel phone in his other hand. Someone must know something.

"Sarah, let me know if you get this message. I'm getting really worried."

He shouldn't have let her leave without finding out where she was going. He'd looked out the window and seen her get into an imposing Mercedes. They went up Via Cavour and were lost to sight. From there they could have gone anywhere. She wasn't coerced. She got in willingly. Still, he'd tried to read the license plate, but he was too high up to make it out.

This had happened five hours earlier. Five hours was a long time. Enough to cross the entire continent. He hung up his cell and took the earpiece from his ear. He laid his hand on the other phone to give his shoulder a rest and continued to wait.

Think, Francesco, think. But he didn't know what to do, except what he was doing.

The operator left him on hold too long, but he wasn't going to give her the satisfaction of hanging up. He couldn't stop. Finally someone answered on the other end of the line. No news. They couldn't help him. Fury mixed with apprehension overcame Francesco.

"Listen up. I know she was called by someone in the Vatican," he lied. "I saw the priest who came to get her. You have an hour," he emphasized, raising a finger, "one hour to give me news. If not, her face is going to be on all the lead stories of the international news media, and I'm going to accuse you of kidnapping a British citizen. Do you understand? I'll turn the eyes of the world on you. One hour." Francesco was fed up.

The operator maintained the same serene, routine voice and said she'd communicate the message to the proper party, wished him good night, and hung up.

Tears filled his eyes, but didn't fall. He covered his face

in his hands and took a deep breath. He was exhausted. He looked at his wristwatch. It was two thirty in the morning. He got up and went to the window, drew the curtain back, and looked down. There was no sign of the Mercedes or Sarah. The pavement was wet, parked cars covered with drops, but it was not raining. On the other side of the street he saw the steps leading to the engineering school and the Church of Saint Peter in Chains, where the chains that had bound Saint Peter on his fateful journey to Rome could be found, as well as a monumental statue of Moses by Michelangelo. The steps passed below the palace of the Borgias—Rodrigo, Cesare, and the beautiful Lucrezia—who in other times wandered through these streets, masters of Rome, but Francesco didn't think about this. He ignored the history of the building on the other side of the street.

Where are you, Sarah? he asked himself.

He felt like waking up the whole place with a huge outcry, but Sarah might just saunter into the room at any time without a mark, calm, with her usual composure, calling him an idiot for entertaining these fantasies. He remembered her nausea and dry heaves, and felt tightness in his chest.

Outside there was little movement. A car or two passing in the direction of the Piazza dell'Esquilino, a car coming down Via dei Fori Imperiali. Rome slept the eternal sleep of night, disordered layers of time flowing together. The streets, plazas, alleys, avenues, and all the roads came together in Rome, this millennial city, and no street ended in a dead end. There was no better city to disappear in than this, where everything was connected, like arteries in the human body.

The phone ringing on the bed startled Francesco so much that he jumped. He immediately grabbed it and looked at the screen. An unknown number. Tonight was not going to be easy. He took a deep breath and answered the call.

22

<hr>

Of all the professions exercised on the surface of the globe, none was as peculiar as Ursino's.

For forty years he had carried out his illustrious office from Monday to Friday, sometimes Saturday, but never on our Lord's day of rest, since if He rested on the seventh day, who was Ursino to do differently?

He was grateful to Pope Montini, recorded in the rolls of history as Paul VI, for having designated him for such a prestigious and picturesque role.

He had the privilege of working in the apostolic palace on the ground floor in a room called the Relic Room. It contained thousands of bones of accepted saints celebrated by the Holy Mother Church and sent them to new churches built every year throughout the world. These relics, diligently sent in small quantities by Ursino, were what gave sanctity to the new place, which without a bone, without the mystery of something used or touched by the saint, would be nothing more than a space without divine aid, a temple in which the name of the Lord could not be invoked—at least not by the Roman Catholic Church, since it would be invoked in vain.

Whenever possible, Ursino took care to send a relic of the saint that the new church celebrated. A piece of Saint Andres's tibia if the church was dedicated to him and if one existed in the thousands of drawers that filled the giant cases with such relics. Of course, that most sacred archive contained only one of Saint Andres's fingers, part of a skull, and pieces of the cross on which he was martyred, all sent to Patras, where he was patron, decades ago.

He was diligent, yes, but the Milanese Ursino had a fault. He wasn't very sociable, perhaps from spending so much time alone caring for the relics, the requests, and the new sacred bones that arrived less frequently now that there were fewer saints. The protocol had become so difficult that today it was extremely hard to pass from the level of sinner to the society of saints.

Although he would deny it if asked, the requests for relics were fewer now, too. Forty years ago he had more than one request a day: a piece of Saint Jerome's radial, a splinter from Saint Margaret's wheel, or Saint Nicolas's metatarsal—back when he was a saint, not long, since he ceased being one under Paul VI. Now Ursino passed weeks in which all he did was organize the immaculate archive of relics so that he knew exactly where something was stored in the immense cases that guarded such sacred content.

In earlier days, the schedule was tight for the amount of work he had. Lots of discipline, rules, and organization were necessary to fulfill all the requests and sanctify thousands of Catholic churches around the world. Now he had the luxury of looking through the shelves and inventing things to occupy his time.

A portrait of Pope Benedict dominated the wall near his dark oak desk. Working in front of the wall, he often looked at it. He was an austere figure, unhappy, without joy, or charisma, but a good man. He had dealt with him a few times over the course of the last twenty years and knew that the Holy Father was a very educated, intelligent man who wanted only to improve the church.

"Is it too late for an old grump?" Ursino heard a friendly voice behind him.

The Milanese didn't turn around and continued to sort some of the vertebrae of Saint Ephigenia, a contemporary of Jesus, into some small linen bags.

"I can ask the same. Has the Austrian iceman come to see me?"

"I had a meeting that lasted all night, and now I'm going to rest," Hans Schmidt explained.

Ursino got up, approached Schmidt, and embraced him. "It's been a long time, old friend." He held up a linen bag. "I'm waiting for a telephone call."

"Late, it seems."

Ursino pulled out a chair and invited Schmidt to sit. "Are you still running around with crazy ideas in your head?"

"What do you call a crazy idea?" Schmidt asked.

"I read your writings. A little avant-garde for me. The idea of the observer over the thinker made me nervous."

Ursino sat in his chair and sighed.

"They're ideas," Hans replied without further elaboration.

Ursino sniffed and stuck a finger in his nose to remove what was there. Forgivable manners for someone who worked alone for decades, and surely not a sin in the eyes of our Lord God. "The idea that my thoughts were not my own went over my head. I couldn't understand it."

Hans smiled. "Have you ever done something that was contrary to the will of your inner voice?"

Ursino thought a few moments in doubt and rubbed his chubby belly. "Yeah."

"Your inner voice is the thinker. That which didn't hear the voice is the observer, or . . . you."

"Are you telling me I'm two people? One is already too much for me," Ursino joked impolitely with a grin.

"No, Ursino. We're only the observer," Schmidt explained, "but we think we're the thinker, and we're prisoners of our thoughts when ultimately our thought is simply a reasoning to help us from a practical point of view."

"Do you control the thinker?"

"Totally."

They didn't speak for a few moments. Ursino mulled over what his friend had said and bit his nails.

"Let's not talk about this anymore or I'll be invited to keep your society tomorrow morning at the hearing." He meant it as a joke, but didn't manage to smile. When the last word left his mouth, Ursino felt his observation was in bad taste. "Are you prepared?"

"For what?" Hans asked.

"For the hearing tomorrow."

"Tomorrow is only tomorrow. Now I'm simply here with you." He looked Ursino in the eye, very attentively, very calmly.

Ursino sniffed again and sighed. "On your way, and don't contaminate me with those ideas."

"Nice seeing you," Schmidt said, getting up.

The phone rang abruptly at that moment, and Ursino answered it. "Hello, Ursino."

Whatever had been said on the other end of the line transformed Ursino in a way that left him confused and indisposed. When he hung up, he raised his hand to his chest. He felt his heart would burst.

Hans looked apprehensively at him and tried to help. "What's the matter, my friend?"

Ursino felt like fainting. It was difficult to breathe; shivers ran up his spine.

"What's the matter, Ursino?" Schmidt's voice was more insistent.

"They know about the bones," Ursino stammered.

"What bones?"

Ursino stopped suddenly, as if he had been miraculously cured. He no longer panted or felt palpitations. He started pacing back and forth, thinking.

"Call the secretary of state, please," the curator of relics asked him.

Schmidt quickly picked up the phone and dialed the extension he knew by heart. Trevor took time answering before he was informed of the urgency to call Tarcisio. The assistant assured them he'd get Tarcisio immediately.

"They're waking Tarcisio. Are you going to tell me what happened? Who are they? What bones are you talking about?"

Ursino continued thinking, thinking, thinking, until he paused and looked very seriously at Hans Schmidt. "The bones of Christ."

23

————◆————

The nausea turning her stomach made her vomit empty gasps of nothing. Try as she might to expel the sickness she felt in her stomach, Sarah succeeded only in dry heaves. She bent over the not very private toilet of the Learjet. She had started to feel bad as soon as they took off from Fiumicino. Leaving the ground provoked a sickening dizziness that made her press against the back of the seat. She tried to find the most horizontal position possible, which was still too vertical, and she knew the nausea was coming. Even before the plane had reached its cruising altitude, Sarah had unbuckled the seat belt and run for the toilet.

It must have taken half an hour to compose herself again. As suddenly as the nausea had come on, it disappeared.

She returned to the cabin, red-faced, overheated, and aching all over. The table in front of her seat held a tray with a teapot, cup and saucer, and a roll.

"Sit down, dear," the comforting voice of Myriam said. "I asked them to make you both some chamomile tea. Drink it. It'll make you feel better," she added with a knowing smile.

That "both" upset Sarah, since she'd tried to hide it. The word hit her in the face and spread to the rest of her body. Could it be? Was she carrying someone with her in her womb? Was she pregnant?

The feeling of happiness that all future mothers supposedly feel was not there. The feeling Sarah experienced was panic, with no joy. Was she normal? She remembered Francesco just then and how anxious he must be without news of her. At once she imagined him at her side, she with an enormous belly almost at the end of her third trimester, soon to embark on an unknown parental sea. She wanted to force a smile, to feel a minuscule portion of happiness, anything positive, but couldn't. Worse, she didn't want it to be true. She enjoyed Francesco, admired him, but she didn't want to have a child with him. Rafael's image invaded her thoughts. She enjoyed Francesco, respected him . . . wanted to enjoy . . . to admire. She should want to have a child with him. Francesco was a marvelous man. He'd be a great father and loving husband . . . but Rafael's image would not leave her mental screen.

"Don't tell me you didn't know?" Myriam interrupted, not knowing she was interrupting anything.

Sarah shook her head.

Myriam put her hand on top of hers. "You don't have anything to worry about, dear. It's a divine condition." Her voice changed, and it was Sarah's turn to offer her a friendly shoulder.

"Don't be afraid, Myriam. Everything is going to be okay," she wished. "We're going to get there on time and resolve everything."

Myriam dissolved in tears as Sarah hugged her. The sorrow was contagious, but someone had to be strong.

"It's not fair, Sarah. No parent should lose a son." Myriam wept hard.

"That's not going to happen," Sarah comforted her. "We're going to look for him. Everything will turn out right." What more could she say?

"Don't speak about my son as if he were dead, Myr," Ben Isaac admonished her from his own seat, not looking at the women. "Little Ben is alive. They're not going to do anything to him."

Sarah asked the attendant for a cup of water with sugar. The plane continued northeast, but for Ben it seemed motionless. He spoke with the pilot to move things along, but they were at the maximum altitude and speed the jet could tolerate. *The more you hurry, the slower you go,* Ben Isaac thought, his heart heavy with sorrow. But he would not be weak in front of a woman he didn't know.

The cardinal who had surprised them didn't continue the trip with them.

"You're a difficult man to find, Ben Isaac," William observed.

"I'm not hiding," Ben Isaac said.

"Let me introduce you to Sarah Monteiro."

"I'm sorry I don't have time for a longer conversation," Ben Isaac said, excusing himself politely. He wanted to leave as quickly as possible.

"We know about your son," William suddenly cut them off. "We received a DVD. I'm very sorry."

Myriam lowered her head and controlled herself. It seemed like a death announcement. Her chest burned with a torrent of tears she forced herself not to show in front of the cardinal and this Sarah, who remained silent.

"You received a DVD? Then you know I'm in a hurry," Ben Isaac proclaimed. He was losing his patience and had no time for the rules of etiquette or good manners.

"Certainly. I'm leaving," William excused himself. "Sarah is current on everything and is going to go with you."

The situation was strange, but Ben Isaac didn't protest. Here was a cardinal prefect of the Congregation for the Doctrine of the Faith telling him he was current on everything, knew about his son's kidnapping, and imposing a woman on him. They were in the same boat or, in this case, the same plane. She had disappeared into the toilet for half an hour. After freshening herself up, the time had come to lay all the cards on the table.

"What's your role in all this?" Ben Isaac wanted to know.

"If you want me to tell you frankly, I don't really know," Sarah answered timidly.

"Did you see the DVD?"

"On the way to the airport."

"What did they tell you?"

"They talked about the Status Quo."

Ben looked at her with different eyes. They'd told her everything. Why was she so special?

The attendant arrived with the sweetened water and gave it to Myriam.

"Tell me about yourself," he asked, softening his all-knowing attitude.

Sarah didn't like to describe herself, but she understood. "I'm a journalist, the editor of international politics for the *Times*. I live in London. My father is Portuguese, my mother English."

"I think I've read something written by you."

"It's probable. I published two books on the Vatican, specifically on the two popes before this one."

"The church trusts you?"

"Let's say it trusts me distrustfully," Sarah said sincerely. She wasn't going to hide anything from Ben Isaac. "You know perfectly well how these things are. Today's enemies are tomorrow's friends. You never know how the world will turn, only that it will."

"What do you have that they want?"

The Jew knew what questions to ask.

"It's complicated," Sarah argued.

"I don't consider myself too stupid," argued the other

with a half smile, the first she had seen. He emanated grief, a life of work and caution.

"Have you ever heard of JC?"

Ben searched his memory. "Jesus Christ?"

Sarah smiled. She wanted to tell him he was right. JC sometimes seemed supernatural, not in terms of love or mercy, but being omnipresent. He knew everything at all times.

"It could be, but no," she answered. "JC was a mercenary, responsible for the murder of John Paul the First."

"Don't tell me he was actually assassinated?" Ben Isaac was truly shocked.

"I remember that day well," Myriam put in. "I cried all day long. It was never satisfactorily explained. There were always doubts."

The day of September 29, 1978, of unhappy memory, dawned with the death of Albino Luciani, the "Smiling Pope," thirty-three days after he'd been elected by the College of Cardinals. Officially, the death was attributed to a massive heart attack. But many strange things came to light, though the official version was never disproved or changed.

"He was murdered," Sarah confirmed. "JC is a very powerful man."

"I never heard a thing about this," Ben Isaac said, trying to remember any situation involving such a man.

"Few people know about it. I found out about it without wanting to, by chance."

"Life is chance."

"Well, yes," Sarah agreed. "Anyway, the Vatican needs him, and I'm the only contact."

"Why do they need him?" Ben Isaac didn't understand.

"I don't know. But it looks like he's important in helping to resolve everything that is happening lately."

"I can't see what JC has to do with the kidnapping of my son."

"He doesn't. He has something to do with the death of three of the Five Gentlemen."

Ben Isaac turned red. Sarah and Myriam looked at him anxiously, fearing he was having some kind of attack.

"What's the matter, Ben?" Myriam asked him in alarm. What a night. "Tell me, honey."

They tore his jacket off and unbuttoned his shirt. He seemed to be having difficulty breathing. He coughed weakly. Myriam tried to get him to sip the rest of her sweetened water. A few moments later Ben calmed down, regained control, and breathed more easily.

Myriam placed herself in front of him and looked him directly in the eyes.

"Ben Isaac, tell us everything you're holding back. Don't hide anything from me or from Sarah." She stared even harder. "It's an order."

Ben Isaac wet his lips and lowered his eyes. He felt destroyed.

"Do you know their names?" he asked Sarah.

"Who?"

"The ones who died."

Sarah took out her notebook. "Um . . . Yaman Zafer, Sigfried Hammal, and Ernesto Aragones."

Each name was like an arrow in Ben Isaac's chest. A tear ran down his face. He was in pain.

"The Five Gentlemen are . . . They were experts who validated the discoveries of 1947 in the Qumran valley. At first there were only three. Later we recruited two more. We demanded a vow of silence, which was never broken," Ben Isaac explained. "This silence was essential for guarding the discoveries and for . . ." He hesitated.

"For what, Ben?" Myriam insisted seriously.

"To maintain the Status Quo," he confessed.

"And what does that mean?" Myriam sounded irritated.

"The Status Quo. Things as they are."

"Why did these documents always remain in your possession?" Sarah asked.

Ben Isaac didn't answer at once. He wanted to find the right words. He didn't want to be imprecise. He looked at Myriam fearfully. "Because it was my team that found them. Whoever finds them is the owner."

"I know you gave some to the church and other institutions. You sold others." Sarah was not convinced.

"Because they had less importance." Ben Isaac's words came out irritated. There was something else there.

"It seems strange the church didn't insist, since one of them is the Gospel of Jesus." Sarah wanted to show him that she knew what they were talking about.

"The Gospel . . . the what?" Myriam couldn't believe it. "It can't be."

Ben looked like a mischievous boy whose pranks had been discovered. Head lowered, fearful expression, absorbed.

"Was it written by Jesus Himself?" Myriam wanted to know.

Ben agreed silently.

"And the other document?" Sarah reminded him.

Ben hesitated.

"There's more?" Myriam was at the same time intimidated and intrigued.

Once more, Ben nodded silently. He took his time answering. When he did, his voice sounded hoarse. "The other places Yeshua ben Joseph in Rome in the era of Claudius."

Sarah and Myriam didn't know why this would be so strange, but neither was an expert in history.

"And what's the problem? Who's Yeshua ben Joseph?" Myriam asked.

"Jesus, the son of Joseph," the Israeli explained.

"Okay, Jesus was in Rome. What's the problem?" Myriam still didn't see.

"Jesus was in Rome in the fourth year of Claudius." Ben Isaac's voice was firmer.

The women still didn't see what was wrong with that. What was so bad about Jesus being in Rome at that time?

Ben Isaac sighed. They still didn't understand. "The fourth year of Claudius's reign is the year 45 A.D."

The two women looked at each other. This certainly was a surprising revelation. Jesus in Rome in the year 45. That was incredible.

"What about the Crucifixion, then?" Sarah asked, her heart beating fast. She wasn't sure she wanted to know the answer.

Ben looked at her this time. "It never happened," he said, as if throwing a bomb.

Sarah never realized she'd made the sign of the cross when Ben Isaac said that. "What?"

He looked at the journalist piously, as if he wanted to ask forgiveness.

Sarah wasn't able to say anything else. It was incredible.

"That is very serious," Myriam said finally. "Extremely serious."

"I know. I didn't want anyone to know in any way. We guarded this secret for fifty years and wanted to continue doing so," Ben Isaac said ashamed.

"And this is why they kidnapped my Ben?"

Ben nodded.

"Who are these people?" she asked angrily.

"I don't know, Myr. I have no idea." He looked at Sarah, who still seemed half stupefied. "Do you know how to contact this JC?"

Sarah had never contacted him. From the beginning it was a one-sided relationship. He contacted her. She suspected that her position at the paper was through his influence, but she also thought it could have been Rafael. In those moments of success, which during the time she'd worked there had been considerable, she liked to think it was purely her merit. And, ultimately, it was. From time to time she received a file in her mailbox about something that deserved attention. Normally these were overrated scandals, not all about the Vatican, for which the journalistic community called her the pope's lover. She knew JC watched over her, she preferred to think only to a certain extent, and was always alert. She was sure this would call his attention. More than sure.

"I do." Was this a half lie or completely false? In any case, she was sure she'd succeed in doing so.

"What was it the kidnappers said?" Myriam asked, remembering the phone call Ben Isaac received at the Fiumicino airport.

The plane began its descent. The flight attendant approached them.

"We're landing at Gatwick, Doctor. I'd appreciate it if you'd fasten your seat belts."

Ben Isaac grabbed the belt quickly, while Myriam continued to stare at him, awaiting a reply.

"They said to wait at home."

24

—◆—

"Cough it all up from now on," Gavache ordered. "We'll begin with the recently converted historian. Who is Ben Isaac?"

"He's a legend, a myth," Jacopo answered, amazed.

The rain outside was falling harder. A flood that inundated the City of Lights, freeing it from evil, amen.

"He seems alive enough," Gavache contradicted him. "I'll have his record shortly. Continue, Mr. Jacopo."

"According to what is known, in very restricted circles, he was behind the discovery of the Dead Sea Scrolls. Those the Holy See declares apocryphal gospels."

"What are they?"

"Non-canonical gospels, not approved as belonging to the sacred Scriptures, in other words, writings not considered inspired by God."

"Why? Are the others considered inspired?"

"According to the church, yes," Jacopo confirmed.

"And how do they know what was inspired or not?" Gavache questioned. What a hell of an idea.

"They don't know. It was a question of politics."

"Absurd," Gunter protested. "Of course they knew."

Gavache turned to Gunter menacingly. "Quit protecting your own interests, Mr. Priest. It doesn't suit you well." He indicated for Jacopo to continue his explanation.

"The theologians of the church had to decide what to include in the sacred book and what to leave out. There are five Bibles—the Judaic, Hebrew, Catholic, Protestant, and Orthodox. The most important are the Judaic and Catholic, the latter because it has the largest number of faithful; the former, for historical reasons. As you ought to know, the Jews and Catholics share some books of the Bible. Those they call the Old Testament, but the Jews don't recognize them as old because they don't accept the new, since for them Jesus is not the Messiah. Both are called religions of the Book. Muslims are, too, because they base their faith on another book, the Koran, of course.

"The Judaic Bible is composed of twenty-four books. It was what Jesus read and quoted regularly. The Catholic Bible has seventy-three, seven of which are considered apocryphal by the Jews. Don't forget, the New Testament is not included in the Judaic Bible, nothing of the Acts of the Apostles, the Gospels, Letters, or the Apocalypse. And, obviously, the New Testament comes long after Jesus Christ. He never read it."

"So you're telling me the Holy Scriptures have very little holiness."

"That's your opinion," Jacopo defended himself. "To each his own. But I agree with you. Besides, it's said the Septuagint and, later, the Vulgate left a lot out."

"The Septuagint?"

"Yes. The Bible was translated from Hebrew into Greek for the Jews living outside of Palestine who no longer spoke those languages. Greek became the second language of Palestine. Even Jesus spoke it, according to the evangelists. The Septuagint was translated by seventy erudite Jews from Alexandria, from which they call it the Bible of the Seventy, or Septuagint. It's curious that the four evangelists of the New Testament quote biblical texts from this Greek translation rather than the original. Saint Jerome translated the Greek into Latin and called it the Vulgate. Every day in all the Catholic liturgical celebrations, one passage from the Old Testament and another from the New are read."

Gavache listened attentively to the history lesson. Any detail might be important, but he was under no illusion that these people were here to help find the murderer, but rather to help their church, including Jacopo.

"And what does this have to do with Ben Isaac?"

Jacopo took up the thread of the discourse again, now that he'd launched into historical considerations of the Bible. "Well, according to what's said in these restricted circles, Ben Isaac discovered some important documents that relate to what's said about the Bible."

"This is what we call a motive," Gavache declared.

"Excuse me?"

Jacopo didn't follow. Gunter didn't seem to understand, either.

"That's a reason to kill," Gavache explained. "What did Zafer have to do with Ben Isaac? The murderer who asked about him, certainly, was aware that they knew each other."

No one said anything for a few moments. Only the rain filled the silence with constant pings.

"Suggestions? Speculations?" Gavache demanded.

No one answered.

"Mr. Jacopo. Any idea?" Gavache insisted.

"Maybe . . ." Jacopo began timidly. "Maybe the Turk was one of the Five Gentlemen. Hammal, too," he suggested.

"Absurd," Gunter interjected. "A historian's fiction. This never existed."

Gavache was interested in knowing more about these Five Gentlemen. The story was getting more complicated and more elements were appearing all the time; more questions and few answers. Was he going to have to investigate the background of Christ's family and His disciples? He smiled at the idea.

"The Five Gentlemen were the people who made up Ben Isaac's team. They were sworn to silence about the discoveries, according to what's said."

"According to what's said means a lot of things. . . ." Gavache added. "More all the time."

Gunter got up. "I can see this is going to be a long

night. Would you like some coffee, tea, or some refreshment?" the Jesuit father offered.

Gavache asked for coffee, Jean-Paul also. Jacopo and Rafael accepted some tea.

"Maurice," Gunter called out. The acolyte who'd brought them to the nave appeared at once and took the order. "Take it to the sacristy. Then tell us as soon as it is ready."

"Certainly," Maurice answered subserviently, and left to prepare the hot drinks.

"The Five Gentlemen. What do you think of this, Jean-Paul?" Gavache asked. His expression revealed he was about to tie together everything Jacopo had said.

"A mess, Inspector."

"A mess," his superior concurred. He looked at Gunter. "I see you contradicted everything the prestigious historian said, but you recognized the name Ben Isaac when I mentioned it." It was a statement, not a question.

Gunter swallowed dryly. Nothing escaped the inspector.

"Who is Ben Isaac, Father Gunter?" Gavache insisted with an unfriendly look.

Gunter adopted an arrogant attitude and got up from the chair where he was resting. "I'm not on French territory. I don't have to answer your questions."

"Did you hear that, Jean-Paul?"

"He's shameless, Inspector."

Rafael approached the German Jesuit. "Cooperate, Gunter. Tell him whatever you know. You can help catch the murderer."

Gunter refused to back down. Rights had to be exercised. Gavache went up to him and stopped so close he could smell him.

"Silence is your right, Father. It's true we're not on French territory."

"This church belongs to the Society of Jesus, to the Roman Apostolic Catholic Church, to the pope," Gunter argued coldly. He couldn't tell what he knew. . . . Never.

Gavache drew even closer, if that were possible. "Listen to me well, Father"—his tone was menacing—"you can hide behind the Concord to keep a criminal free. Your conscience is your conscience. But eventually you're going to have to step outside this church to go shopping, administer last rites, get into some whore's bed . . . whatever it is. I guarantee you that when you do, I'm going to be waiting for you, and you won't have the church or any saint to help you. Not even your friend Loyola." Gavache's breath struck Gunter's face with the revolting stench of cigarettes. But even more repugnant than the odor were the words. "But if you make trouble for me I'll have a warrant made out for Mr. Gunter, not Father Gunter, and give you a load of shit before I ask the first question. And just so you know, sometimes I forget to ask the first question for a month or two while you wait in the slammer for my signature to be sent back to Germany because, no matter how much the little priests love you here, the French, believe me, are not going to let you return here." He was silent for a while to let his point sink in. He turned his back. "Think hard."

Rafael tried to advise his friend. He knew the situation wasn't easy. The secular nature of the state complicated things. No one respected the confidentiality of the church. The state superseded everything, the church, faith, and salvation. The state was the religion of the new times. So the church always had to act indirectly, not always truthfully, manipulating public and private opinion, creating diversions to distract those watching from its true interests. Rafael knew all this. He was an agent in the service of these very diversions and manipulations. He preferred to wait and conceal, reveal little, always be in control, one step ahead of the others. . . . But this wasn't an ordinary case.

"Say what you can, Gunter. Who's Ben Isaac?" he pressured him. "What are the documents?" He lowered his voice. "You don't need to be specific or get into details. Speak in generalities."

Gunter maintained a thoughtful expression, and his foolish arrogance softened the lines of his face. He'd follow the advice of his Italian friend. A soft reply placates fury, as the wise Solomon said.

"Inspector Gavache," the Jesuit called.

The inspector was smoking another cigarette while looking at the Delacroix. He didn't shift his attention, and it wasn't clear whether or not he admired the work.

"Have you decided to follow the path of goodness and love proclaimed by the first superior general of the Society?" he said ironically. He wanted to show that every detail was important to him.

"I'm going to tell you everything I know about Ben Isaac," Gunter declared, ignoring Gavache's sarcasm. His initial arrogance probably deserved it.

Gavache sat down near Gunter and invited him to do the same. The German did so carelessly. He was nervous. The inspector read his reaction as that of someone about to tell something he shouldn't.

"Ben Isaac's story is real. . . ."

At first, the reason for the interruption went unnoticed. Only when Gunter got a glassy look and started drooling blood before falling heavily on the floor of the Church of Saint-Paul–Saint-Louis did those present realize that someone had shot the Jesuit. There was a bullet hole in the back of his cassock. The rest happened much faster. Jacopo, Rafael, and Gavache were still looking incredulously at Gunter when they heard Jean-Paul, gun in hand, shout, "Drop it, guy."

Trembling, the acolyte Maurice tried to steady a gun with a silencer in his hand.

"Drop the gun, kid. You're not going to shoot anyone else," Jean-Paul repeated.

Gavache joined him, aiming his gun at Maurice, who was beside himself, tears running down his face, panting.

Rafael bent over Gunter, who was suffocating.

"Gunter," he cried out as if it would help. "Call an ambulance," he shouted.

The Jesuit bled fast and groaned. Jean-Paul took one hand from his gun and grabbed the cell phone to make the call.

"I . . . I'm . . . I'm sorry," Maurice stammered.

"Calm down, kid," Gavache said while moving closer with short steps. He spoke in a whisper. "Everything can be resolved. Drop the gun. Let's talk."

Maurice looked at him with eyes filled with rage. He still pointed the gun at everyone and no one. "There's nothing to talk about. Shut up. He couldn't. He couldn't." Fury mixed with disgust was upsetting the young man.

"Calm down. You don't want to make the situation worse."

Jean-Paul ended the call and put the phone back in his jacket pocket. "The ambulance is on the way."

Rafael stayed with Gunter, who was fading fast. "Rafael," he murmured.

"Don't talk, Gunter. Don't try. The ambulance is coming."

With a last effort Gunter raised his hand to Rafael's head and pulled him down lower. "Plaza . . . plaza," he whispered.

Rafael listened to his words fading away. With each second Gunter's life was draining away.

"Saint Ignatius." He sighed before giving himself up to God. The pain was over. He was at peace. Rafael closed his dead friend's eyes and blessed him. He folded his hands and prayed for God to receive his soul. "Peace be with you."

Gavache continued to try to calm the acolyte, who trembled more and more. "Don't do anything foolish."

Rafael got up and fixed the acolyte with a hard stare. "You killed a good man."

Those words stirred him up even more. "I had to. It had to be. He couldn't tell. He couldn't tell."

The siren grew louder as the ambulance got closer to the church. It would be transporting a dead man, not a wounded one.

"Drop the gun," Gavache ordered. "I'm not going to warn you again," and he cocked the Glock. Jean-Paul did the same.

Maurice raised his hand to his head and shut his eyes. He made the sign of the cross and kissed the crucifix hanging on his chest.

"Ad maiorem Dei gloriam," the acolyte muttered before placing the mouth of the barrel under his chin.

"Don't do it," Gavache shouted.

The bullet made more noise exiting from his head than it did from the gun. Maurice fell helplessly, without life.

For a few moments nothing but the siren was heard. Not rain, or breathing, or heartbeats. Nothing. It wasn't the usual scene inside a church. Corpses were common, but during funeral rituals, not from some priests killing others on holy ground.

The doors opened and the paramedics entered.

Rafael and Jacopo watched silently. Gavache came over and looked at them coldly.

"What the hell is going on?"

25

———•═◦═•———

The secretary dragged his left leg as he walked as fast as he could. The light was dim at that hour of night, and he'd asked that no lights be lit at all. There was no need to raise trouble among the staff of the apostolic palace. The intrigues of the day were enough. Trevor followed at his side in silence, submissive, respectful. Tarcisio knew it was more fear than respect.

His leg pained him, but that was nothing compared with the reason Trevor had awakened him. That indeed was eating at him.

"Did you alert William?" he asked with effort.

"Yes, Your Excellency."

It was important that Cardinal William know about this. There still weren't a lot of facts, but Ursino had been blunt. They were in open war with an unknown enemy who had an advantage over them. They possessed confidential information that indicated that someone in the bosom of his church was the source. Christ had to separate the wheat from the chaff more than two thousand years ago. Saint Peter and he also had to do it, as did all those who succeeded them. The struggle never ended. It was a permanent war; the battles only changed generals from time to time.

With a commanding air befitting a general, a brilliant strategist, Tarcisio entered the Relic Room, where he found Ursino and Hans Schmidt.

Ursino asked for his blessing, knelt, and kissed Tarcisio's ruby ring. "Pardon me for disturbing your sleep, Your Eminence."

Tarcisio helped him up quickly. "Tell me everything, Ursino. Who are they?"

Ursino explained. The voice that had spoken to him on the phone was male. He called during the afternoon office hours and said he would call back later, after midnight, and it would be in his interest to be there. He used a friendly tone, conciliatory. Ursino wondered why he had to wait for a telephone call so late in the night. He was used to going to bed right after sunset. The speaker said it was about Yaman Zafer and important.

"Zafer?" Tarcisio interrupted. "Are you sure?"

"I am, Your Eminence. These ears God gave me work perfectly. He said Zafer."

"Did he sound like a young man or older?" Schmidt asked.

"Middle-aged, but I can't really say. You know how it is. Voices are confusing."

"Of course. Continue," Tarcisio asked, raising his finger to his lips. He was all attention. He wanted to know everything.

"I confess curiosity got the best of me," Ursino continued, trying to be as precise as possible. The past mixes up thoughts and desires, dreams, all in the same stream of consciousness, and it is necessary to separate what happened from what was wished for, what was real from fiction.

After midnight he returned to the Relic Room and waited for the call. Father Schmidt appeared unexpectedly to keep him company. Just then the call came. Same voice, another tone. Arrogant, sarcastic, cruel, vengeful. He said Zafer was dead and very soon the world would know about Christ's bones.

"Holy God," Tarcisio exclaimed, raising his hand to his sweaty face. "Christ's bones."

"It could be a bluff," Schmidt warned with a calm voice that settled the atmosphere as much as possible.

"I don't think so," Ursino said. "He mentioned Ben Isaac."

Tarcisio stretched out in Ursino's chair, exhausted. He'd heard that name too many times already in the last several hours. It was never a good sign to hear Ben Isaac's name.

"The agreement expired," the secretary said at last. "Any connection between the Holy Faith and Ben Isaac is over." Again he had mentioned the name.

"The question is whether Ben Isaac will have any conditions for protecting the documents, now that the contract has ended," William commented as he entered the room. "And they've kidnapped his son."

"I should leave." Schmidt started to go.

"Please, Father Schmidt, if it's for my sake, stay," William said, walking over to the desk next to the portrait of Benedict XVI.

"I don't think its proper for us to meet before the hearing of the congregation," said Schmidt, excusing himself.

"Nonsense," William blurted out. "We're not going to talk about that, are we? This has to do with the church and defending her, and we're all together on that. Please stay."

Thinking quickly, Schmidt agreed to stay. His case had nothing to do with this situation, which at the moment demanded more attention.

"I am very worried about this, too," Tarcisio declared. "On the one hand he guarded the documents competently for more than fifty years. But a son is a son. That changes everything."

"Zafer, Hammal, Aragones." Schmidt counted them off. "Ben Isaac Jr. Apparently they know more, and we know less. We don't even know who they are."

William paced from one side to another, thinking. "I don't think we should trust Ben Isaac. Not for his honesty and competence, but because of the delicacy of the situation. I think we should get possession of the documents as quickly as possible."

Tarcisio shook his head no. "It's not going to be easy. Pope Roncalli was forced to enter into the agreement with him because he couldn't get his hands on the documents. I don't think he's going to give them up for free."

"Let's pay," William cut in.

"Do you think we haven't offered money? Ben Isaac is a multimillionaire. Any offer is small change for him, and he'll laugh in our face. He would pay us instead to keep them. The second agreement was so difficult that Pope Wojtyla limited himself to extending the term without discussing other deal points at all."

"Why does he want to hold on to the documents so much? He can't use them. He gains nothing with them. As far as we know he's never mentioned their existence to anyone. On the contrary, he's kept them under enormous secrecy, which, fortunately, is in our own interests. No one can come within two hundred yards of the papyrus without swearing an airtight oath of complete silence. I don't understand his fixation on them," William declared.

No one did. Maybe only Ben Isaac could explain, if there was an explanation. Sometimes there are no reasons for human obsessions. They just are.

No one said anything in the minutes that followed. Enemies should be kept in sight, under vigilance. The worst enemy was the one you didn't know, whose movements could not be predicted because you didn't know who he was.

Tarcisio got up painfully. The night was already late. The following day would be a series of important meetings with foreign dignitaries, and he couldn't appear as if he needed rest. Certainly, makeup could turn a frog into a prince, but that was only a facade. The secretary of state's meetings required intelligence and preparation, not a pretty face.

"Well, tomorrow we have a full day, right, Trevor?"

"Yes, Your Excellency. In the morning the ambassadors of Pakistan and Brazil."

"The afternoon with Adolph, right?

"Correct, Your Eminence."

"Damn, this is going to delay everything," William grumbled.

Tarcisio turned to William. "Any news from our agents?"

"We have one with Ben Isaac at this precise moment. Rafael still hasn't reported anything."

"I think it's best to recover the documents. They'll be better with us," Tarcisio deliberated.

"I already gave orders to recover them," William said, "but what if Ben Isaac won't give them to us?"

Tarcisio thought about it a few seconds, then started out of the Relic Room, where the bones of the saints reposed. "We'll use whatever means are necessary."

26

The morning darkness was cold. It wasn't raining, though the pavement was wet. He continued on foot, going down Via Cavour toward the Via dei Fori Imperiali. He turned right and followed the long street toward the Piazza Venezia, turning his back on the Colosseum. Francesco shivered, but couldn't tell whether it was from the chill. Cold sweat made him anticipate the moment of truth a few hundred feet ahead. The man had said Sarah needed him. Everything was all right, there was no problem, not to worry, but he needed to meet her in the Piazza di Gesù, which was after the Piazza Venezia on the left side. Just a few steps down Via del Plebiscito. Spread out on both sides of Via dei Fori Imperiali were the vestiges of what was once the Roman Empire. History didn't lie and was there to be seen. At the end on the left was the Vittoriano, commonly known as the Altar of the Fatherland, an eccentric work by Giuseppe Sacconi in homage of Victor Emmanuel II, the father of the country, the first king of a unified Italy. The building was jokingly called the *torta nuziale,* or "wedding cake," by the Roman citizens.

Francesco ignored all this, thinking only about Sarah, not what was waiting for him in the Piazza di Gesù. The man spoke with a Tuscan accent, which in itself meant nothing. Sarah was a mystery. How she was able to make such influential contacts in the inner circles of the church and politics, he had no idea. Only she could say, and she never did. She was very reserved, and Francesco's hot blood, even if it boiled, always respected her will and her space. He'd be excluded entirely if Sarah felt he was invading her privacy.

He crossed the Piazza Venezia to the left side and walked beside the Palazzo Venezia, which had once served as the Venetian embassy. He rounded the corner and walked down Via del Plebiscito.

At the end, the small Piazza di Gesù, dominated by the Church of the Gesù.

Two beggars slept next to the church door, rolled up in dirty clothes that covered them to their heads. With the exception of these two souls, forgotten by God, he saw no one else. From time to time a car or motorcycle passed. A bus emptied out its few passengers, on their way to work.

Where could Sarah be? Or the man who had called him? Was she in danger? He put the thought out of his mind. Absurd. Sarah left with a priest. What danger could come of that? It was true there were many examples of despicable acts committed by the church, but they wouldn't have the courage to hurt a journalist, or two, if they considered him.

He tried not to think about it for a while. His mind always looked for patterns, labeled situations: good, bad, cold, hot, comfortable, uncomfortable, restful, uneasy. He was nervous now because he let his mind elaborate on innumerable theories about what would happen next. Not one true because the future is always unknown . . . always.

His phone pinged, indicating a text message. He took it out and looked at the screen: *Continue toward Largo di Torre Argentina.*

The sender was unknown. Had they called him to come to this location and were now changing it? What did it mean? He'd asked to talk to Sarah when they called, but the man said she was busy, but wanted to see him. Later they called him on his cell, which meant they had his number. Sarah could have given it to them, or, of course, whoever was responsible for this could have his own methods for finding out his number. His curiosity was greater than his fear, so he turned toward the Largo di Torre Argentina, which was close by. According to legend, it was in these Roman ruins of the Theater of Pompey, protected by a wall, that long ago some conspirators, including Decimus Junius Brutus Albinus, stabbed Julius Caesar twenty-three times. No place was more opportune for a meeting.

The yellowish light from the streetlamps created a mysterious atmosphere. A group of drunken partiers passed him, singing louder than was appropriate for the hour. Finally he reached his destination after covering several yards on Corso Vittorio Emanuele II. Some people were wandering out from a bar after the alcohol they'd enjoyed had awakened their spirit of adventure.

"Do you have a match?" a completely drunk man startled Francesco.

"I'm sorry. I don't smoke."

The guy mumbled some unintelligible curse and continued limping in the direction of Via dei Cestari, where he disappeared.

Small groups came and went, but didn't stop. This was a passageway, not a place to linger.

"Do you have a light?" the drunk again asked. He had suddenly reappeared.

"I just told you I don't smoke," Francesco repeated with irritation.

"You're a son of a bitch," the man insulted him, turning back toward Via dei Cestari. "You're not the man for her, you bastard," he murmured before disappearing.

What did he say? Did he say what I thought he said? Without thinking, Francesco followed the drunk, who continued down the street, limping with his left leg. He didn't notice Francesco, who gained ground on him with each step. Had the idiot been talking about Sarah, or just muttering nonsense? He wasn't exactly credible, having downed countless drinks. At a certain moment he lost his balance and almost fell. He laughed hard at himself.

That guy couldn't know anything about Sarah. At least that's what Francesco thought. He followed along out of nervousness and anxiety. It would be better to turn back. This was the place specified in the message he'd received. He gave a half turn and sighed. *Ah, where are you, Sarah?* he asked himself, but unfortunately there was no reply.

"Do you have a light?" Behind him, Francesco heard the voice of the drunk, who should have left him behind by now.

Francesco walked faster and didn't reply.

"Do you have a match, you fool?"

Francesco ignored him. It was the alcohol talking. He didn't have to listen to someone in that state. It was a mistake to have followed him.

"You're not the man for her," he said again.

Francesco stopped and looked at the man. "What did you say?"

Francesco lost control and grabbed the drunk, but when he recovered, it was he who was pressed against the wall by the other, who drove a powerful hand into his throat. He tried to free himself, but couldn't.

"Now you're not so brave, are you?" The words were no longer slurred, but firm and dry, his movements precise. He was more sober than Francesco.

"What . . . what do you want with me?" Francesco

asked fearfully, his voice constricted by the hand on his throat.

"Me, nothing," answered the man close to his face, with a Tuscan accent.

Francesco could smell his breath.

"But Sarah does," he added.

"What?" Francesco was confused. What was he saying? "Sarah?"

The man loosened his grip. "Is Sarah important to you?"

"What?"

"Can't you say anything else?" the man joked. "Is Sarah important to you?"

"Yes," Francesco replied with difficulty.

"Would you die for her?"

"Yes."

The man released him completely. He took off a dirty jacket and dropped it on the ground, revealing an impeccably tailored Armani suit. He straightened his jacket, shook off the dust, and assumed a cool but annoyed expression.

"Good. Let's see if she'll do the same for you."

PART TWO

Perinde Ac Cadaver

(Just like a corpse. Loyola demanded
a vow of complete obedience to
the pope, *perinde ac cadaver.*)

———

*Let this warning be added to that of our brother Leo X
so that they know these new developments nearly set
us back. I plead with my successors not to liberalize
the regulations. If possible make them more restrictive.
The traitors have to be silenced.*

—Pius IX, *August 13, 1863*

27

David Barry liked to get up early. Even before the first hint of sunrise he could be seen on his morning jog in Hyde Park. A full hour around the serpentine path at a fast pace, rain, shine, or drizzle. A thick fog limited his field of vision but not his desire to keep his usual pace. He trusted his reflexes to get him around any obstacle—a slower runner or a morning walker. Even on nice days it was unusual to see a lot of people. The park started to fill up when David finished his daily run.

His morning routine continued with a hot shower and shave. He put on blue tweed slacks, a blue shirt, and a blazer without a tie. He had a light breakfast, just coffee and toast. He didn't have children to take to school or a wife to kiss before leaving, since they were 3,663 miles away on the other side of the Atlantic in Washington, D.C., and still sound asleep.

His office was ten minutes away by car, depending on the traffic. Learning to drive on the wrong side of the street was not as tricky as he had first thought. After three days it was as if he'd done it his whole life. He'd even started to think the English were right in the first place. He entered his building at ten minutes before eight. The doorman said good morning, and he returned the greeting, waited for the elevator, got in, and pressed a random button, then swiped his ID card through a digital reader that accessed a floor that did not appear on any button. Seconds later the doors opened on a floor filled with activity.

The CIA headquarters for Europe.

"Good morning, David," a man in corduroys and a T-shirt greeted him.

"Morning, Staughton. Quiet night?"

"Weird," Staughton commented, before disappearing into a room full of monitors.

Aren't they all? David thought as he went to his office.

The frenzied activity at that time of morning was incredible. People were shouting into telephones, at each other, into microphones and monitors. People walked with others, or alone, from every side of the office to another, holding a stack of papers, files, trays with Starbucks cups, empty trays, sandwiches, and cameras. Fuck, fuck off, fucking work, go fuck yourself, fucking Iraqis, fucking Afghans, fucking Russians, fucking Israelis, fucking

Muslims, fucking Osama, fuck them all. We'll make America safe.

Every day was the same. It wasn't a job for just anyone, only for the best of the best, men like David Barry, who at forty years old had the qualifications to replace Geoffrey Barnes, the former station chief who had died in service, may God rest his soul.

The director barely had time to enter his office and hang up his coat.

"David," a harried woman called.

"Good morning to you, too, Samantha," he greeted her pleasantly.

"Good morning, David. Sorry." Samantha's hair was mussed up, but David chose to ignore it. "We have a problem."

"We always do," he said dismissively, then immediately showed her a smile. "Talk to me."

"Last night two priests died in a church in Paris," she told him.

David sat down and gestured for Samantha to join him.

"Two priests in Paris," he said, as if making a mental note.

"But there's more."

There always is.

"According to our sources, this happened while they were being questioned by inspectors from the Sûreté Nationale."

David frowned. "The French police? What were they questioning them for?"

"Two other murders that had occurred earlier."

"That's complicated," David yawned. "Let's take one thing at a time. Who killed the priests?"

"We don't know yet."

"We don't know a lot, do we?" he said, a little disgustedly. "We can't waste resources on unimportant things, Sam." He sighed and smiled to lighten his condescending tone. He liked his people happy. "Anything else?"

Samantha was reluctant to say the rest, and David was an expert at reading people's expressions.

"Out with it."

"Jack . . . Jack Payne was with them," she finally said.

David's eyes got wider. "Rafael?"

Samantha nodded and lowered her eyes.

"Was he one of the victims?"

"We still don't . . ."

"Know," he finished her sentence, irritated. He got up. "Call Aris, please."

Samantha got up and left the office to do it.

Jack Payne, aka Rafael Santini, was a legend in the recent history of the CIA. A real son of a bitch who had been exposed as a double agent in the service of the Vatican. A priest of sorts. David Barry had been close to him, a friend, and felt betrayed when he discovered the truth in 2006. He felt hurt, and he wasn't alone. He still hadn't gotten over it.

Two minutes later, a huge, heavyset man in a well-fitting suit came in. "David," he greeted him.

The two shook hands in support and loyalty.

"Tell me everything you know," the director asked. "Something new with Rafael?" The name still stuck in his throat.

"My team is on the ground, but those French bastards aren't going to be open with us." He took out a cigarette and lit it. "But we know that the Sûreté was there at the time and the questioning involved two other murders in Paris and Marseille."

"What's in the news?"

"This is interesting, too. Nothing, because they know nothing."

"The French are fuckers," David considered scornfully. "No press, then?"

"Not yet," Aris said, taking another draw on his cigarette before putting it out in the ashtray on David's desk.

"Do we know who the other victims were?"

"I should have that information within the hour," Aris replied.

"Do we know whether Rafael was among the victims in the church?" He felt no sympathy for a Judas.

Aris shook his head no. "But there's a simple way to find out."

Barry waited for his suggestion.

"Call him up," Aris said with disdain.

"Who?"

"You."

Barry sat back down in his chair. What a hell of an idea. It was the logical thing to do. Aris was intelligent and pragmatic. He was good at analyzing situations, seeing the options, and coming up with solutions.

"This could scare off the game," Barry objected.

"On the other hand we'll find out if he was one of the victims and if he's trying to hide something. Either way, we win."

Barry thought a few moments. What would Rafael be doing in Paris with the Police Nationale? Was he being questioned by them? Had he died? When he came to himself again, he took out his personal cell phone and checked his contacts under the letter R. No number for Rafael. Strange. He knew he had his number and hadn't deleted it. A CIA agent never deleted anything, since he never knew when he'd need it someday. Finally he remembered. He pressed J, and after several Jacks, Jack Payne appeared. He was listed under the name by which Barry had first known him. The bastard.

After a few seconds of hesitation, he pressed the green key and brought the phone to his ear. It started to ring. One ring, two, three. *Pick up, pick up,* he said to himself. Four rings, five, six, and . . . someone answered.

"Rafael?" he asked with a firm voice. He congratulated himself for having waited. It was he. "Hello. It's David."

Rafael said something David listened to carefully. "Yeah, we haven't talked in a long time." More words neither Aris nor Samantha heard, since David hadn't activated the speaker. "I'm in Rome," he lied, "and I thought of you. Are you free for coffee?"

A few seconds later Barry disconnected the call with a *Perfect—I'll see you there.* He looked at Aris and Samantha.

"He's alive," Barry stated the obvious. "And he's lying, too."

"What did he tell you?" Aris wanted to know. Curiosity was an occupational hazard.

"He was about to hear confessions at six, but we could have dinner at eight," he said as he left the office.

The others followed him.

"Sam, I want you to check flights leaving Paris for Rome around five and see if Rafael is on any of them."

"He's on one," Samantha guessed and left them.

"Are we certain Rafael was in Paris this morning?" Barry asked.

"Absolutely. He's on the manifest for Alitalia. The French confirmed this. He used his own passport."

They went into a room crowded with monitors and agents carrying out surveillance on them. The various images were from satellite or closed-circuit video, covering different points all over the world. Barry saw Staughton, who was manipulating a joystick while also looking at a screen.

"Staughton," Barry called.

"Hi, David. To what do I owe the pleasure?"

"Are you busy with something important?"

The monitor showed a woman talking on a cell phone on a busy street. She was carrying two shopping bags from Burberry. She was being filmed from above by a satellite four hundred miles high. Staughton zoomed out, and the monitor displayed the island of Britain.

"Nothing that can't wait," he answered.

"I need to find the location of this number." Barry showed him the screen of his cell phone.

Staughton pressed a key that focused on the number. He rapidly dialed some keys and entered the number. He continued to send orders with impressive speed.

"Are you kidding me?" Staughton asked as he read the information that appeared on another monitor, along with a photo of Rafael, aka Jack Payne.

"Do you know him?" Aris asked.

"Everyone knows Rafael. He gave me a lot of trouble." He also didn't want to say a few ugly bruises. "When Barnes died he was there, too. He's a tough son of a bitch."

Barry knew the case. Rafael had nothing to do with the death of Geoffrey Barnes, Barry's predecessor.

"I need you to tell me where he is now."

Moments later a red blinking signal appeared over a map on one of the screens.

"He's moving," Staughton informed him, continuing to strike the computer keys.

"Where?"

"In France. North of Paris, and taking off at high speed."

The screen showed the red signal shifting toward the north on the map. Every time it blinked it shifted farther north.

"Where is he? In a car?" Aris asked.

"No. He's moving too fast."

"In a plane?" Barry suggested.

"We can't pick up cell phone signals in a plane. Wait a minute," Staughton said, concentrating on his operations. A few moments later he left the keyboard and pressed the joystick: the image that hovered over the British Isles defined itself more and shifted to the south to focus on a long, narrow object moving very fast.

"What's that?" asked Aris, who couldn't see well.

"The Eurostar," Staughton and Barry answered in unison.

28

The cherubim gave the room a kind of solemnity. There was one for every aesthetic taste, all probably commissioned to one artist, but produced by different pupils. There were the dandies, full of flowery details, with a shiny luster; the mischievous, who didn't even try to hide their bad dispositions or, on closer analysis, their irritation; the indifferent, uncertain where they were looking, as if they could have been anywhere; others, with an austere expression, who confronted whoever looked at them; and then there was the one Hans Schmidt found most amusing, considering where it was placed. A small cherub, hovering over the prefect's chair, was winking his eye, laying a finger over his lips to demand silence or, as Schmidt preferred to think, to warn him not to say anything incriminating. He made a mental note to find out who the artist of that piece was.

Hans Schmidt was calm, despite a sleepless night, thanks to the events that had tormented Tarcisio, which is to say that had tormented the church, but would not be alluded to in this hearing. The business here was something else, delicate also but more personal, between the Apostolic Roman Catholic Church and Father Hans Schmidt—nothing so alarming that it could place the Roman Catholic world in crisis and bring down the Vatican like a house of cards. No. Here, the only person who could be ruined, if they desired, would be the Austrian iceman, though he appeared imperturbable.

Schmidt rose when the prefect of the congregation, in the person of Cardinal William, entered the hearing room accompanied by his court of jurors, though that term was never used. Secretary Ladaria followed him with five more counselors, the preferred title as Schmidt well knew. They all carried files and piles of papers. The Austrian knew very well that those learned, circumspect men had read his writings line by line and analyzed his books word by word so that nothing would escape. The congregation dedicated itself completely to its investigations.

As soon as the prefect sat down, the others followed his example, including Schmidt, who cast a complicit glance at the angel hovering over William's chair.

"Let us begin this hearing called by the prefect of the congregation in the name of the Holy Father Benedict

XVI for the Reverend Father Hans Matthaus Schmidt regarding two of his publications, *Jesus Is Life* and *The Man Who Never Existed*," Secretary Ladaria, also a cardinal, proclaimed in a solemn but weak voice.

"It is important to know that this is not a trial. No accusation has been made at this time," Cardinal William clarified. "The congregation has doubts about some of your writings and only wants to dispel these doubts. Understood?"

"Perfectly, Most Reverend Prefect."

"I ask you kindly to respond to our doubts as best as you can. After the hearing, the congregation will decide if the ideas you advocate are damaging to the church or not."

The rules and procedures understood, the prefect gave the floor to Monsignor Scicluna, a man whose wizened face looked a century old. Obviously he would have to be twenty years or more younger, since the positions consecrated to His Holiness required retirement at seventy-five without loss of honor and privileges. Even the servants of God are attacked by old age and senility. All are equal in the eyes of the Lord.

"Reverend Father Hans Matthaus Schmidt," Monsignor Scicluna began faintly. "Having read your works attentively, I confess I am struck primarily by the titles, which are certainly peculiar. The first is *Jesus Is Life*, which I must say I agree with, though I'll ask you to explain certain ideas in it. The second is *The Man Who Never*

Existed. In both books we are dealing with the same person." He sipped some water to moisten his dry throat. "My first question to you is how can Jesus be life if, in your own words, He never existed?"

Schmidt had anticipated that this would be the first question. He hadn't wasted time thinking of hypothetical questions. If the roles were reversed, he would logically ask this same question.

He straightened his back, not so much that he would show nervousness or disquiet, but because he wanted to be comfortable. He took his time opening a bottle of water sitting on the desk in front of him and poured some in a glass. He wet his lips, put the glass down, and smiled.

"Good Morning, Reverend Prefect, Mr. Secretary, and you other counselors. I understand your doubt perfectly, my dear Monsignor Scicluna. On the one hand Jesus is life, and on the other, He never existed. What an outlandish idea . . . at first glance." His voice reverberated through the room. Everyone listened intently, and the cherub had closed his eyes, as if he didn't want to listen. "The message I want to convey is that one can live in two ways. There is no one right way with Jesus or another wrong way without Him, or, if you wish, with whatever other divinity." Schmidt noticed some red faces and a deepening irritation in Scicluna's. He wasn't there to be friendly. He wanted to start out forcefully. "What I intend by *Jesus Is Life* is to provide teachings about how to live day by day in Jesus by abstracting the essence of His words, and in *The Man Who Never Existed* the same message without Jesus, because it is possible to live with Jesus or without Him, in God or without Him. However God is understood."

"What are you saying?" Monsignor Scicluna protested, rising and bracing his hands on the table.

"I have come to the conclusion that all forms of religion are true. The Jewish Bible is true, as is the Catholic, and all the others. The Torah is true, along with the Talmud and the Koran. We are neuro-divine." A clamor arose among the counselors, the prefect, and the secretary.

"All forms of faith are true. Even believing in nothing is true," Schmidt concluded in the same reasonable manner.

"That is heresy," Monsignor Scicluna accused, the veins in his neck protruding in fury.

"That which in this room is a heresy," Schmidt returned, "would also be so in any synagogue or mosque, but that doesn't really matter . . . to me."

William covered his face in his hands. Schmidt was a fool. He knew very well what he could and could not say in that room. He'd chosen something else . . . something more difficult.

"Are you saying that the Word or the Mystery is of secondary or little importance?" the monsignor demanded.

Schmidt shook his head no. "No, nothing like that. I'm saying that the Word or Mystery have the importance that the believer wants to give them." He let the idea sink in. "Great importance," he paused dramatically, "or nothing."

"The gentleman is putting himself into a very delicate position," Monsignor Scicluna warned in a cold, dry voice.

Schmidt got up and confronted the others with an attitude that some would consider disrespectful. "Everyone in this room knows I am right. Isn't that so?"

29

It's not a good sign when a ritual changes, especially if it's repeated, like a sacred act, without variation in content or feeling. The purpose of rituals is to evoke, venerate, and honor relevant events, whether historical, political, religious, or—no less important—personal.

The year 2010 would be registered in Ben Isaac's storage safe, five hundred feet from the main house, below the toolshed, as the year when it was opened twice, a unique occurrence in more than five decades.

He positioned his eyes in front of the visual reader so that the computer could recognize him as the owner. Another change to the ritual was that this time Ben Isaac would not descend the twenty steps alone, but with two other people. The fluorescent lights came on as they advanced and went out behind them, creating a sensation of endless darkness in front of them and unknown secrets behind them.

"I cannot believe that you've always had this here and I didn't know, Ben Isaac," Myriam complained, alert to every sound, her eyes wide open.

"I couldn't tell you, Myr. The less you knew, the better," the Israeli argued. It was never a good sign when Myriam called him by both his first and last name.

"I'm your wife, a part of you. You can't keep secrets to yourself."

Myriam was visibly angry and disillusioned with him. Ben knew she was right, but this was how he was; he kept things to himself. It was an immense effort to bring them there.

The mechanism opened the heavy door with a sigh and, for a few moments, they just looked inside without moving. Myriam took the first step decisively. Sarah followed her, and Ben was the last to enter the room.

Sarah had not imagined such a bare space. Three display cases, nothing more, and cold, unadorned walls. She thought she would find shelves full of other singular things, of lesser significance certainly, but full of sacred relics with many stories to tell. She never thought that the large room would contain only three cases. She joined Myriam, who was examining the parchments displayed under glass. She couldn't understand a single word written there. Elaborate letters written in an ornate style, unintelligible to her.

"Can you understand anything, Myriam?" she dared

to ask, as if she were creating an explosion in the awkward silence.

Myriam looked at the small document in the first case and shook her head no.

"No." Myriam looked at Ben Isaac. "Is it Latin?"

Her husband affirmed it.

"I didn't study Latin, but it looked like it," Myriam offered, her eyes fixed on the parchment. "Yeshua ben Joseph. And it talks about Jesus in Rome," she said, more to herself than to the others.

She moved to the second case and frowned. Sarah looked at her but couldn't tell whether or not Myriam understood what was written there. For Sarah it was impossible. She couldn't begin to unravel whatever was written there. It was not in the Roman alphabet, like the other one, but in a series of strange letters.

"What is this? Ancient Hebrew?" Myriam wanted to know. Her voice seemed worried.

"Aramaic," Ben Isaac answered. He had remained behind, observing his wife.

"Of course Aramaic." Myriam looked at the parchment in a different light. "I still don't understand anything all this time."

"Aramaic is similar to ancient Hebrew," Ben Isaac explained.

"Is this the gospel?" Myriam asked in a halting voice.

Ben did not respond. Silence meant yes.

"Walk over here next to me," Myriam said, more like an order than a request.

Ben approached her step by step, slowly, timidly, as if walking on shaky ground, until he was next to Myriam, who continued looking carefully at the gospel. For a few seconds no one said anything.

"Read it to me," Myriam finally ordered.

"Myriam," Ben sighed, as if it were a painful experience.

Myriam gave him a hard, pained look. "Read it."

Ben hesitated. It troubled him to reveal something only he and a few others knew about. Myriam needed to know what the text said. If that piece of lamb or calfskin was worth more than a human life, than that of their son, their Ben, who had left her heart weeping in such a deep sorrow.

"Uhh . . ." Ben began.

Whether it was divine intervention or the coincidence of fate, a providential ringing of a cell phone interrupted Ben's reading. It was his own.

"Excuse me, dear," Ben said, moving away a little.

Sarah hugged Myriam. "Be calm. Everything is going to work out."

Ben Isaac took out his phone. Some instruction from the kidnappers. Poor little Ben. He remembered the image of his son tied to a chair, tortured, bloody. He shivered. He looked at the screen and opened the message. He couldn't wait to read it. His heart began to beat faster suddenly. *How can this be possible? Who are these people?*

He read the message again in the hope that he had read it wrong, but no. The text was the same.

If you want to see your son alive again, get rid of the journalist.

30

———•••———

Circumstances.

All of life is an accumulation of unknown and imponderable factors, uncontrollable and totally unforeseen, that can be summarized in that simple and powerful word: circumstances.

Rarely do we think about them or even give them any value, but the fact of turning to the left instead of the right, planning a trip to a certain place and not another, deciding to take one course instead of another, all this, and much more, will completely change the circumstances of everything and everybody.

Rafael was not so given to thinking about circumstances. He evaluated them, whenever necessary, but lost no time thinking about the reason to be in a certain place at a certain time under certain conditions. Whenever he entered a place, he immediately studied all the possible exits. An occupational hazard that could not be called a defect, derived from years of dedication and involvement in dangerous missions in the name of God.

So it wasn't natural for Rafael to still be troubled about Gunter, who might still be alive if Rafael hadn't come to ask him for help in clarifying certain evidence of the crime that had sent Yaman Zafer to his Creator. Unlucky circumstances.

If he hadn't gone to the Church of Saint-Paul–Saint-Louis, Gunter would still be alive, along with Maurice. If he hadn't heard those words that Saint Ignatius had pronounced more than 450 years ago. *Ad maiorem Dei gloriam*. If, if, if . . . Or if he were not in the habit of speculating about what could have been. Rafael was a man of action and reaction, not reflection. He had to turn the page on Gunter once and for all. Maybe that would only happen when he resolved the situation. He had to clear up that confusion.

"Gavache has a big problem on his hands," Jacopo said, interrupting the priest's thoughts.

The train was traveling at more than two hundred miles an hour toward the station of St. Pancras International, right in the heart of London. They were now passing through Her Majesty's land, a few minutes from their destination.

"Gavache? What about us?" Rafael answered.

Jacopo let himself mull over the priest's reply for a few moments while he looked down at the screen of his laptop.

"How tragic," Jacopo lamented. "Why would the acolyte have done that?"

"I don't know," Rafael answered. "No one kills or is killed for nothing. Something very serious was going to happen."

"The boy seemed desperate," Jacopo commented, remembering the scene, which was still vivid in his memory. "Are we going to help Gavache?"

"Only insofar as he lets us help solve the murders," Rafael deliberated. "It's all very confused."

"Yeah, it is. And this change of location to London is extremely strange." He typed an address into his computer. "William could have been more explicit."

"Sometimes it's better not to know much," Rafael replied. "And that's *Cardinal* William to you."

Jacopo didn't acknowledge the remark. He was absorbed in a search for information about the mysterious Ben Isaac.

The car was full of passengers. Executives finalizing presentations for some important meeting, Muslims talking on their cell phones as if they owned the world, tourists, married couples, criminals who resembled executives, lonely travelers, beautiful women, handsome men, some reading erudite books of French philosophy with dazzling or monotonous titles, others reading the best seller of the moment about sacred lies, assassins of popes, and Vatican secrets, crimes to solve, and bits of ancient legend.

"We have a problem with the Jesuits," Rafael finally said.

"You're just figuring that out now?" Jacopo's sarcasm was obvious.

"I'm not talking about unfounded suspicions," Rafael argued. "We saw last night there's some secret they're guarding with their lives."

Jacopo comprehended what Rafael meant. "Do you think it's a secret known by every member?"

"I don't know," Rafael replied, but Maurice had been the one to pull the trigger, which meant that the lower orders knew something. "I don't know," he repeated.

"Tarcisio is going to meet with the black pope today. Maybe he should bring this up," Jacopo suggested.

"There's only one pope," Rafael objected, showing some irritation. "There is no black pope. He never existed."

Jacopo had referred to the popular designation for the superior general of the Society of Jesus. The head of the Jesuits, in other words. "Black" referred to the color the members of the society wore and also to a certain dark power of the order. It was said that the black pope has more power than the pope himself, and whoever occupied the Apostolic Palace of the Vatican had to swear allegiance to the Curia Generalizia on Via Penitenzieri, a few feet away from the palace, if the pope wanted to have a peaceful reign. But these were legends and myths that lacked legitimacy.

"Call him the superior general if you want, but what's certain at the moment is he seems to know more than the pope."

Rafael didn't want to admit that Jacopo was right.

Something dark was happening in the society. Gunter, Maurice, Zafer, Sigfried, and Aragone were proof of that. Ben Isaac was the answer to the whole puzzle, at least Rafael hoped so.

He thought about William's final words when he had called Rafael with new instructions. *Your friend Sarah is now with them*. He hadn't expected that development. The journalist always seemed to be in his face. Without wanting to, certainly, but always on his trail. Maybe this meant something.

He had taken the opportunity to inform the cardinal of the tragedy that had occurred in the Church of Saint-Paul–Saint-Louis. The prelate said nothing. He absorbed the information and didn't want to know any more details. *Follow the instructions I gave you. Without mistakes. And don't let anyone kill anyone else or commit suicide this time* were his final words, without even a good-bye.

Later, already on the road, David had called. He was in Rome and wanted to meet him for dinner. Accustomed to analyzing situations in fractions of a second, he'd agree to meet him that evening. He had to do everything to make this happen. At least he had to land in Rome at the end of the day. He didn't understand David's call. He was a friend from another life, a life that was over. He thought about not accepting the invitation, but the American could be useful in the game that was unfolding.

His thoughts were interrupted by a female voice coming over the public-address system.

"Passengers, in a few moments we'll arrive at St. Pancras

International Station. Please check to make sure you have
your personal belongings with you. We hope you have enjoyed
the trip, and it will be a pleasure to welcome you aboard
Eurostar next time."

"Finally," Jacopo complained. He shut his laptop and
put it in the case.

Rafael's cell phone rang just as the train slowed to
come to the platform. He answered and listened for a few
seconds. He ended the call without saying a word.

"Everything okay?" Jacopo asked, visibly tired.

Rafael nodded his head yes. Before the train came to
a stop, a line was already forming by the door. Passengers
crowded to leave—their business more important than
anyone else's. Rafael remained seated, along with Jacopo,
more out of deference to the priest than his own wishes.

As everyone started to leave for the platform, Rafael
looked at Jacopo with a serious expression.

"As soon as we step outside the train, we're going to
do things my way."

Jacopo swallowed dryly and agreed.

31

———◦◦◦———

"Total concentration. Don't take your eyes off of them," David Barry said, looking at a large monitor that showed several images of the interior of St. Pancras International Station and some even inside the train.

There was no better city than London for this kind of surveillance. The thousands of cameras spread over the city offered a vast view of everything and everyone in practically all public places, and with the proliferation of video cameras and cell phones, there was no place that couldn't be watched. And, of course, there was the cherry on top: the high-definition spy satellites that surveyed the earth, four hundred miles in space, and could capture the glow of a cigarette with greater detail than a conventional camera a few feet away.

Barry resembled the commander of the *Enterprise* in

full battle with the Klingons. He was in the center of the room, alert to every movement, ready to give orders as things developed.

"I want to see and hear, folks."

"The train stopped. It's showtime," Staughton alerted them, moving the joystick that controlled the high-definition cameras of the satellite.

"Anything from Sugar Grove?" Barry asked.

"We've intercepted two communications from the French police," Aris reported. "We've got the names of the victims now. There are four. Three in Paris and one in Marseille." He handed some papers to Barry, who looked at the names.

"Okay, I want to know who these people are. All their strengths and weaknesses, who they associated with, the life they led, secrets, lies, heroic actions, even the size of their shoes."

"I'm on it," Samantha replied, taking the papers from Barry's hand.

"Sooner than later," Barry said, half-joking and half-serious.

The images showed people leaving the Eurostar from several angles, in a hurry, absorbed in their own lives, oblivious to the invasion of privacy in the name of the law.

"They're on the platform," Staughton informed them.

"Okay. Pay attention. We can't lose them. Who has the camera in the station?"

"Davis," replied a technician with the same name.

"Keep a sharp eye out, Davis."

"They're not going anywhere without taking me along," he said confidently.

In the image Rafael appeared, followed by another man, walking toward the exit.

"Who's that with him?" Barry asked. "I want to know who he is, folks. His name, Social Security number, and who he voted for," he ordered in a firm voice.

"The agents in the main terminal are in position," Aris reported.

Barry looked at him seriously. "What agents?"

"We have a team on the ground."

Barry pointed at the monitor. "We have cameras. They're our agents in the field. Get rid of the people on the ground before Rafael notices them," he demanded irritably.

"But . . ." Aris was going to object.

"But nothing. It's an order. You don't know Rafael. He'll notice them in a second," he turned from Aris and spoke slowly. "Take the team away immediately."

"Stand by, Travis," Aris spoke into a headphone, visibly unhappy.

Travis said something over the static.

"Abort the operation. Repeat. Abort the operation."

"Roger. Operation aborted," Travis said.

Several cameras continued to follow a serious-looking Rafael. A handful of technicians controlled various areas to let nothing escape. The two men were in a customs line to show their identification in order to step onto British soil.

"Who has the cameras for the exterior of the station?" Barry asked, always a step ahead of what was happening.

"Davis," the same technician replied again.

"Where can they go out?"

"The station has five exits. One by metro, two for St. Pancras Road, and two for Midland Road. In the street they can take a bus, taxi, or rental car. Or walk," Staughton informed them.

"Or take another train to another destination," Aris pointed out.

Barry shook his head no. "Whatever they've come to do will be in London," he said, raising his voice. "Pay attention to all the exits. We're dealing with a professional who can make fools of us."

A couple of technicians looked at Barry, amazed. Was that true? Then they turned to concentrate on the monitors. They could not afford to lose the target.

"The suspect is in the main terminal," Staughton said. "He's going toward the north exit to Midland Road. There's a taxi stand there."

Barry didn't miss a detail. Rafael. How long ago did he last see him? Maybe more gray hair, but, all things considered, he was in good shape, as always. Cold eyes, calculating, scanning the surroundings. He would calculate all possible exits, but only he, and he alone, knew his plan. No matter what the movies said, the CIA still could not read minds.

"Confirm the Midland Road exit," Staughton reported. "The taxi stand is next to First Capital Connect."

"Control the exit, Davis," Barry ordered.

They watched Rafael leave with the still-unidentified person and wait in line for a taxi. The priest took out his phone. Someone was calling him.

"I want to hear that call, folks," Barry demanded. "I need to hear it," he pressured.

"Direct from Sugar Grove . . ." Staughton said.

Rafael's voice could be heard all over the room. He was speaking Italian. *We just arrived. We'll continue directly to the location agreed upon. We're waiting for a taxi.*

God protect you, the other person said, and hung up.

An image appeared of Rafael putting his cell phone in his pocket.

"Who was he talking to?" Barry asked agitatedly.

"Just a minute," a voice said.

"We don't have a minute," Barry grumbled.

"Someone at the Vatican," Staughton answered.

"Shit," Barry cursed. "Shit, shit, shit."

"Why?" Aris asked.

"We're not going to be able to find out who called," the director said.

"When calls are sent to or from the Vatican, that's about all we're able to know," Staughton added.

"Why?" Aris insisted.

"Because it's the country with most telephones per capita," a technician explained.

"There are more telephones than people," Barry continued.

Aris smiled.

"I'm not joking," Barry said, with his eyes fixed on the enormous monitor. Rafael and his companion were next in line, only the taxi hadn't pulled up.

"Okay, here comes a cab," Staughton said.

The image showed one of the famous London taxis pulling into the entrance for passengers.

"Pay attention to the address," Barry warned. "Keep your ears open."

Great Russell Street, Rafael was heard to say.

"Great Russell Street. What's on Great Russell Street? Quick, folks," Barry took control of the operation.

"Ah . . ." Staughton entered the information into the computer. "I thought so. The British Museum."

"The British Museum. Why didn't he just say 'British Museum'? Do we have access to the cameras there?"

"Main entrance, Great Court, and some rooms on the ground floor. Not all have cameras," said Davis, the person controlling the ground cameras.

"Okay. I want a map of the place. Put some agents there just in case," the director said.

"Okay," Aris communicated the order over the radio.

"Does the taxi have cameras?"

"No," Davis responded quickly. "I've already verified that, sir."

"Call me David, Davis."

The image showed the companion getting in the taxi, followed by Rafael, who looked around and up toward the sky before getting in.

"What's he doing?" Barry asked curiously.

"He's looking for somebody. Are there buildings around?" Aris observed.

"He's looking up, Aris," Staughton put in. "Maybe he's going to pray?"

Finally Rafael got in, and the taxi moved on to its destination.

Barry sighed and raised his hand to his chin. "Pay attention to the taxi, Davis." He turned to Staughton. "Go back to the image and focus it more."

Staughton pressed some keys and in seconds recovered the image of Rafael looking at the sky. With further definition it seemed as if his eyes were looking directly at the satellite camera.

"Bastard," Barry swore.

"But where's he looking, and what's he looking at?" Aris asked, concentrating on the image.

Barry smiled slightly. "At us."

32

———❖———

Sarah shivered. Cold sweat dampened her face, and fear overpowered her. She shut her eyes, but not even that stopped the sensation of imminent danger. The cold barrel of the gun pressed the back of her head, and fear gave way to panic. She could feel the end.

"Don't do it. Please," she managed to stammer out.

"You know too much, and at the moment you're an obstacle for us," a male voice said. "Your grave has been dug for a long time."

How could this be the end? So slow and so fast at the same time, unforeseeable, unknown. The place was dark. She couldn't see anything inside or out. Eyes shut, making a huge effort to keep from opening them, she felt only herself and the barrel of the gun.

"Good-bye, Sarah," a voice said.

Sarah's body tensed, but her panic vanished. She resigned herself.

"Francesco" was the last thing she said before her face exploded in a sea of blood and flesh.

"Time to wake up," he heard a male voice say, followed by two slaps to the face.

Francesco woke up from the nightmare, frightened. He was lying in a double bed. The man who had woken him up was the same one who'd approached him on Via dei Cestari. He was wearing a well-tailored Armani suit, and limped with his left leg. Francesco couldn't say whether it was the same suit or not, but then he hadn't had much time to observe. The man tossed a towel and some clothes in his direction.

"The bathroom is out there," he pointed. "Take a shower and get dressed. You have five minutes."

"Where are we?" Francesco asked, half lying and half sitting.

The man turned his back and left the room.

Francesco tried to remember the strange events of the night before: Sarah's departure with the priest, the waiting, the phone call instructing him to go to Piazza di Gesù and then along Largo di Torre Argentina, where the drunk had approached him. He couldn't remember what had happened after that. He must have been drugged. He couldn't believe he'd have slept so easily without knowing where Sarah was. Where was she? Still in Rome? He was clearly in a luxurious hotel room, but it wasn't the Palatino. He got up and went to the window.

He opened the curtain and looked out over buildings stretching toward the horizon. It was morning. Below, the traffic was building up to a frenzy. He didn't recognize any building in particular. He was not in Rome.

He looked for his watch, but it had disappeared. *Damn.* He looked for his cell phone but couldn't find it, either. All of his belongings had disappeared. The clothes the other one had tossed to him were new. He sat down on the edge of the bed and rubbed the back of his neck. He felt tired and disoriented. Someone had to have answers. Only he didn't know if he was ready to know them.

He got up and took a quick shower before the crippled man returned to the room. He used the shampoo and gel from the hotel—a five-star, no doubt. He couldn't understand the words on the bottles. No matter how much he washed, he continued to feel dirty, a filth that stuck to him even when he dried off. He was still devastated. He wanted to know about Sarah. His heart beat fast with anxiety and exasperation. He lacked the one feeling that gave a person well-being: control. Without it, he was totally lost, more than just geographically.

The man in the Armani suit returned to the room while Francesco was tying his shoelaces. He looked at the journalist disdainfully and opened the door.

"Let's go." It was an order, not a request.

Francesco went out hesitantly, unsure which way to turn.

"Straight ahead," the other said.

"Are you going to tell me where we are?" Francesco asked.

"This is not the time to ask me questions," the other warned. "Left."

Francesco went left. There was a long corridor with innumerable doors, but they didn't enter any of them. He came to a hall with elevators.

"Push the button," said the man in the Armani suit.

Francesco obeyed. An elderly couple came out of a room and waited with them. The woman greeted them in English.

"Hello."

"Hello," they both replied.

Francesco was apprehensive.

"Don't take the next elevator," the unknown man whispered.

A bell announced the arrival of the elevator. The two men let the elderly couple take it and waited for the next one. Francesco went in first. The man in the Armani suit pressed a button that Francesco couldn't see. The doors closed and the elevator began to rise.

It was only a few moments, but to Francesco it seemed an eternity. He felt more anxious and alarmed as they ascended. The thought struck him that the unknown man would tie him up on the top floor, and he imagined falling down the stories, desperate, helpless, until he struck the floor below. On the other hand, it was hardly credible that whoever was behind this would plot such a complicated scheme for so simple an ending. They could have killed him more easily anytime.

Stop thinking about it, he ordered himself. *Whatever will be, will be.*

The doors opened onto another corridor full of rooms. Francesco went out first, completely ignoring the luxurious decor.

"Left," said the other one following him. "Keep straight ahead."

Francesco complied with careful steps, neither too fast nor too slow, expecting the worst.

"Here," the other said, moving ahead to a door and lightly knocking twice.

From inside came a "Come in."

The man in the Armani suit, always with an unfriendly expression, opened the door and let Francesco enter. Then he shut it, leaving him alone with whoever was inside the room.

Francesco found himself in an enormous suite. He couldn't see who had told him to come in.

"Buon giorno," he heard a man say. "Come closer."

The voice came from a room on the right. Francesco found a very old man, seated in a chair, looking out a large window. He was dressed in white. He spoke perfect Italian without an accent.

"Closer, Francesco," the old man insisted.

Francesco approached cautiously, never taking his eyes off the man. Who was he?

"Who are you, sir?" he finally worked up enough courage to ask.

"Who I am is not important," the old man replied.

He got up painfully with the help of a cane with the gold head of a lion on the top, and approached the window. Francesco stood by him and looked out at the city spread before them. This time Francesco recognized it. He'd never visited it. He recognized the gold dome from news broadcasts. In front of them lay the holy city of Jerusalem.

"Where's Sarah?" was a more important question.

"In the service of God."

What a ridiculous answer. What did he mean by that?

"You in the service of God, too?" he asked somewhat recklessly.

"I?" he smiled. "I have no master. Call me JC."

"JC? What do you mean by that?"

"JC," the old man repeated.

Francesco pointed toward the city.

"What are we doing here?" He couldn't hide his irritation.

JC didn't answer right away. He looked at the city for a few moments and then sighed deeply before he finally spoke, as coldly as an iceberg. "Jerusalem. It was here everything began. . . . It'll be here that everything ends."

33

—◆—

The Bible.

The most prodigious book ever written. The majority of its words were inspired by God, and those that were not were written by His own hand.

He always carried it with him in a paperback edition worn out from so much reading. He gave special attention to the synoptic gospels, especially John, as well as the Acts, but what really satisfied his soul was the Apocalypse. He chose specifically for today *Jesus said to him: I am the way, the truth, and the life. No one comes to the Father but through Me,* from the Gospel of John. He read it and re-read it until he didn't need to read it again, it was so deeply fixed in his memory. He looked at another paper with the names of those whom God was calling to Himself and he had the pleasure of dispatching. Three names, three people who would come before the God of judgment. God would deal with them as He knew best.

He had no great admiration for the Old Testament, though he'd read it several times with the greatest respect. Certain passages struck a deep chord with him, especially the story of Abraham, who in certain respects resembled him, since he obeyed the will of God without question. He had no doubt that he would kill his father, mother, and children, if he had any, if it were asked of him. The Exodus from Egypt was one of his favorites, and he found great wisdom in the Book of Proverbs, written by the great Solomon, the son of the no lesser David. The Book of Job, the prophecies of Jeremiah and Ezekiel, Jonah in the belly of the whale, Noah, Absalom, Jacob, Joseph, and many others, the history of the Chosen People, who deserved all the suffering they endured. Caiaphas was guilty of sending the Son of God to His death. He considered himself an avenger, or rather, an avenging angel, a savior, freeing His world from evil. Thanks to Him, he did it extremely well.

He frequently used a personal ritual with Him. He shut the holy book and thought about some extremely important event in his life, then immediately opened it at random and placed his finger on a verse. God would tell him what to do through those prophetic words, sanctioning what would occur; He never failed, since He was omnipotent.

He did the same when he looked at the first name on the list of three below the words *Deus vocat*. He shut the

Bible and opened it at random. Put his finger on a verse and read it. He smiled. *I know well what you can do, and none of your desires will be denied*, from the Book of Job.

God had made His judgment.

He hit the brakes as he reached his destination. He looked at his watch and unbuckled the seat belt. Right on schedule.

34

A re you sure it'll work?" Jacopo asked.

"No," Rafael answered.

Jacopo sighed. The cold London morning penetrated to his bones. They hadn't stopped since yesterday. He needed to rest. He'd tried to sleep on the train, but with no success. He wasn't used to seeing people killed in front of him. Gunter and Maurice were the first, and it wasn't pleasant. He admired Rafael's presence of mind. He had helped Gavache with the investigation, answered every question succinctly, as if he had not been present at a tragedy and lost a friend. Probably he'd lost so many in such different ways that one more didn't matter. Life can make us immune to anything. He shivered at the image of a shot exploding in his own brain. He didn't want to be Rafael's next friend to die . . . one more.

"I can't believe I'll ever get to Rome," Jacopo confessed.

"Tonight you're going to be sleeping with Norma," Rafael asserted.

"I hope so," Jacopo replied, thinking of his wife, whom he normally didn't have the patience to put up with. Her shrill voice asking him for money to go shopping wasn't so unpleasant anymore.

"Did you remember everything?" Rafael wanted to check.

"I'm a historian. Of course I remembered everything," he joked to lighten the mood.

"A historian tends to remember things his own way."

"Do you think we'll be successful?" A serious question.

Rafael didn't answer.

"Fighting with Ben Isaac and Jesus Christ," the historian said, "is not going to be easy."

"If it were easy, we wouldn't be here," Rafael replied.

Jacopo had to acknowledge this. The Holy Father would not have sent him just anywhere. The truth was that the Holy Father didn't know he'd sent him anywhere. Jacopo was too insignificant for the pope even to know his name. The secretary was the one who gave the orders, the mediator between the earth and the god who rested in the Apostolic Palace. Despite not being a believer, Jacopo was the one Tarcisio relied on most to carry out the duties asked of him, evaluating works of art and ancient documents. This work was the reason for his loss of faith. Thousands of parchments, papers, bones, pottery jars, and coins passed through his hands. If a document said one thing, another soon appeared to contradict the first. There was an erroneous understanding of the people who had lived in antiquity. Most imagined them as savages, not very hygienic, who lived short lives, killed one another, and were always at war. This could not be further from the truth. The ancients were as intelligent as modern people. Everything the world was today, for better or for worse, was due to them.

"Great Russell Street," the taxi driver informed them.

"Okay," Rafael said, immediately looking at Jacopo.

"I'm ready."

"That's good. Don't forget that not everything is what it seems."

"Look who's talking," Jacopo said eagerly. "I hope Robin will collaborate. Don't let them kill him."

"That doesn't depend on me," Rafael asserted. "You take care of your part, and let him decide how to do his."

"Is that how it works?"

"That's how you survive."

35

Not everything is what it seems. Who would guess that a simple London taxi, one of thousands cruising the British capital every day, would be the target of intense surveillance by the CIA?

David Barry remained at his command post, monitoring every detail transmitted on the screens and simultaneously anticipating and providing for every eventuality.

"Great Russell Street," Staughton alerted them.

"Is the team on the ground?" Barry asked.

"Affirmative," Aris assured him. "Prepared and waiting."

"Remember, we're only going to observe. Any change in the plan must come from me and me alone. I don't want any extemporizing, understood?"

Aris, Staughton, Davis, and the other technicians answered with an okay, so there would be no doubt.

Samantha burst into the control center at precisely that moment. Barry looked at her.

"What do you have for me?"

Samantha made a brief report on each of the victims and their professional and personal background. Barry listened carefully while keeping his eyes on the monitors.

"Jesuits?" Barry commented when Samantha was through reporting. "What's the common denominator?"

"All worked for the Vatican, but at different times," Sam informed him.

"Is that all?" Barry didn't want anything to escape him.

"Apparently so. I'm still checking on what they did for the Holy See. They could have even been working on the same project at different times," she replied.

"Well done," he said, raising his voice. "Do we have the museum cameras?"

"They're with me," Davis said.

"Staughton, man the satellite. We're going to depend on it for the first few yards."

"It's secure. No one will get away," the technician assured him.

"Stand by, folks," Barry alerted them.

The taxi entered Gower Street and then turned to the left at Great Russell Street, where the museum appeared on the right. The taxi pulled over. For a few moments nothing happened, but then two passengers got out into the cold.

"They're with you, Staughton."

The technician, so used to these situations, handled

the joystick calmly. The image focused to show the two men crossing the street and entering the gates of the museum, which at that hour already had thousands of visitors. It was a great archive of human history, with thousands of objects from every continent, the most remote locations, and the most ancient civilizations.

The Ionic columns stood imposingly at its entrance, marking a separation between two worlds, the frenetic, modern one and the dead past.

"Alert the agents on the ground," Barry ordered.

Aris communicated with his men.

"Don't be careless. I don't want them to detect us," the director said.

"They're going into the building," Staughton said. "Now it's up to you, Davis."

The cameras of the Great Court, an enormous dome with windows, became the eyes of the control center. Various angles of the Great Court appeared on the central monitor.

"There they are," Davis said.

"Where can they be going?" Barry asked.

Staughton superimposed a map of the museum on his monitor, defined the specified location, and designated the possible exits.

"There are several possibilities," Staughton said. "They could go into the Reading Room, the circular library in the middle of the Great Court that only has one entrance and one exit. To the right they could go to the King's Library, left to the ancient Egypt room, or straight ahead to the Wellcome Trust Gallery. Each location connects with other rooms."

"We have the Great Court well covered with cameras, so it's better to place the agents at the exits. We don't want to lose them," Barry ordered. "What are they doing there?" he was asking himself more than the others. "What's your plan, Rafael?"

"It's a good place for a meeting," Aris suggested. "You have to admit it."

Barry said nothing but silently agreed.

The images continued to show the two men, the dark one and the white-haired man.

"Define the image more, Davis," the director asked.

"It's at maximum."

The maximum wasn't much, and, additionally, the cameras lacked the resolution of the satellite image. They were not made for surveillance but only to save money and dissuade theft.

"They're going toward the cafeteria," a voice over the radio alerted them. "They're passing me."

"Okay, Travis," Aris said. "Keep your distance."

There were two cafés next to each other at the extreme north end of the Great Court. They served hot and cold drinks, sandwiches for every taste. Jews, Arabs, and believers of other faiths, including those of the church, could find something to eat there. No one was left out. The two targets chose the cafeteria on the right that had a line of about five people.

Barry was impatient. Too much suspense and too little information. He needed more than he had.

"Are they going to eat?" he wondered.

"Looks like it," Staughton confirmed.

Barry looked at the technician as if he'd just had an inspiration. "Can you see through the glass of the Great Court?"

Staughton sat down in his chair and began playing with the controls. "If it's not reflecting too much sun."

The image that showed the outside of the building focused over it until it met the glass. The reflection on the east part was too much and obscured the image, just a white brilliance, but when it passed the Reading Room, it cleared and captured movement below.

"Good," Barry said. "Go to them next and focus the image."

Staughton executed the order quickly, and in seconds the image displayed the two men. Jacopo in the front of the Court Café line, Rafael behind.

Something was wrong about the picture. Barry smelled something funny and shook his head.

"What's going on?" Aris asked about the gesture.

"Something's not right," Barry said.

Aris looked at the image, just like all the others. He felt he was missing some detail the director had noticed. What? All those cameras and agents, and the director saw more than they did.

"What's the matter, David?" Aris insisted.

Jacopo and Rafael stood in line. There were two people in front of them waiting to be helped.

"Son of a bitch," Barry swore.

The others continued in their ignorance. Barry grabbed his cell phone and dialed a number, then engaged the speaker so the whole room could hear. A beep indicated the call was beginning. The agents still didn't understand.

"What's wrong with this picture?" Barry asked.

No one answered. They looked blankly at the director and the image.

"Does anyone know?" Barry demanded.

Aris was the first to see it. "The phone isn't ringing there."

"Order your men to go in, Aris. Detain them, *without making a scene*," Barry emphasized.

Aris gave the order over the radio. From the various internal cameras in the museum, agents could be seen converging on the cafeteria on the right.

"Without making a scene," Barry repeated.

"What's going on, David?" Staughton insisted.

Barry raised his hand to ask for silence. His eyes never left the central monitor.

The two men saw the six agents coming from different sides with their eyes fixed on them. They wasted no time leaving the line and starting to run away.

"There they go, making a scene," Barry criticized, and then turned to Staughton. "The taxi. Can you get it?"

Staughton looked at him without understanding.

Jacopo and Rafael were caught quickly and brought outside the building.

"Check their identity," Barry ordered. "Quickly."

The images showed one of the agents searching the men. "We have here a Jacopo Sebastiani, Italian, and a . . . Steve Foster, English . . . taxi driver."

Staughton finally understood Barry's question. "It's going to take time to find him," he said apologetically.

"That son of a bitch," Barry swore again.

"Uh!" Travis interrupted over the radio. "Rafael would like to give the director some information."

"What is it?" Aris asked.

"Eight o'clock, the Osteria de Memmo I Santori, number twenty-two, Via dei Soldati. Don't be late."

Barry was furious, but he tried not to show it to the team. Rafael had made fools of them.

Not everything is what it seems.

36

That story sounds like a cheap thriller written by a hack writer."

"It's the pure truth, Jonas," Ursino said.

The scene could only be the Relic Room, which Ursino oversaw religiously every working day.

Jonas was seated comfortably in a chair, legs crossed, in a dark suit with a matching shirt and shoes of the same color, listening to his friend recount the events of the night before. There were no secrets between them, and their friendship transcended the difference in their age, despite Jonas's being half as old as Ursino.

"So they killed a priest in Jerusalem and kidnapped Ben Isaac's son?" Jonas summarized with his hands behind his head, in a relaxed pose.

Ursino gave Jonas's upper leg a little kick in reproach.

"And that's just the half of it, kid. There was also a Turk and a German in France." He raised a finger to his lips. "Don't repeat this to anyone."

It was Jonas's turn to look offended. "When did I ever repeat anything said in here? And you talk a lot."

Ursino had to agree. Jonas visited him from time to time. They had met in the year of Jubilee at a fund-raising dinner and had hit it off. Another friend, Hans Schmidt, had introduced them. They talked all night and many nights afterward. Jonas was a missionary, always traveling, but on his regular visits to the Holy See he never neglected a visit to see his friend in the Relic Room. Then he returned to the jungles, to mosquitoes, hunger, illiteracy, wars, intolerance, encephalitis, and illness. For seven months he hadn't heard from Jonas. When Ursino feared the worst and was about to ask the secretary, for the love of God, to bring him some news, good or bad, Jonas gave signs of life, ill, but with the same spirit of mission he was familiar with. Fever had kept him in bed in a hut in Angola for months, and only God managed to save him, since there was no medicine capable of doing so. Ursino enjoyed Jonas more than he did any other person, probably because he had nobody else to enjoy, except the Holy Father, the secretary, and God, but with them he couldn't have a good laugh or tell stories, and months could pass without seeing them. That might have been why Ursino tended to talk too much with Jonas, and Jonas had given proof of his trustworthiness.

"But whoever's behind the murders is very well

informed," Ursino continued, carefully carrying over a kneecap of Saint Thomas Aquinas to be sent to a church being built in Campinas, Brazil.

"Why?" Jonas asked, stealthily fiddling with some fragments in a linen cloth on top of the desk.

Ursino put down the kneecap less carefully than he liked, and slapped the other's hand. "Leave Saint Theresa's wrist bones in peace."

"That's her scaphoid?"

"What's left of it," Ursino explained while he folded the fragments up in the linen to protect them from Jonas's curiosity.

"Why?" the missionary repeated his question.

"Because they know about Christ's bones."

"What?" Jonas was so astonished he got up. "How could they know about that?"

"Don't ask me. Fewer than ten people know, I thought. Three are dead. The others are me, the secretary, the pope, Adolph . . ." He was counting in his head. "And that's all."

"And me," Jonas added.

"You don't count. Three of the Five Gentlemen are dead. Two are left," the missionary speculated.

"How do you know about the Five Gentlemen?" Ursino asked, truly surprised.

"You yourself told me about them last year, you addled old man."

"They're not going to get the other two," Ursino ventured to say.

"Why not?"

"They're well protected inside the walls of the Vatican."

They let the silence spread over the cases full of human history, a true hymn to their existence. Ursino sat down on a small chair to rest his bones. Jonas beat his foot nervously on the floor in a rhythm only he knew.

"Can I smoke?" Jonas asked.

"Outside," Ursino said, pointing. "That habit is going to kill you."

"The doctor's given up on me," Jonas said calmly.

"Is that right?"

"Yes. I've got a life expectancy of only seventy or eighty years," he joked.

"You rascal," Ursino said. "How long are you going to be here this time?" He changed the subject.

"Only tonight."

So little time, Ursino lamented silently. He liked having a friend around. Normally Ursino came in without speaking and left silently. Days passed without speaking a word. After a long time, he ended up almost grunting like a caveman. Sometimes he shouted just to give his larynx some exercise. A telephone call left him smiling the rest of the day. Yesterday and this morning were exceptions that proved the rule.

"Where are you going next?" Ursino wanted to know.

"Do you know a priest named Rafael Santini?" Jonas asked, ignoring his friend's question.

Ursino was surprised by the question. "I do. Why?"

"I need to find him. Do you know where he lives?"

"Do you?" Ursino asked apprehensively.

"I don't. That's why I asked."

"You can't," Ursino answered abruptly. Partly he felt jealous that Jonas wanted to meet him, but that wasn't why he'd been brusque. "Who told you about him?"

"He's here on the list," Jonas said, tossing a paper down on the desk.

Ursino picked it up and read it. He found Rafael's name after his own.

"Why is my name on this list?" He didn't understand. "And what does this mean at the top?" He referred to the title dominating the upper part in big letters. It said *Deus vocat*.

"God calls," the other said.

"Yes, I know. It's Latin."

Jonas approached him and lit a cigarette.

"Don't forget what I told you about smoking in here," Ursino cried, getting up also.

Jonas stuck the piece of fibula from some unknown saint into his friend's eye. The holy relic also served as a weapon. Ursino gave a brief cry and sank heavily to his knees, while Jonas drove the bone deeper.

"Jonas," Ursino whispered with a sad grimace.

"Dead men don't talk," the other said, suddenly yanking out the bone and stepping aside to avoid the blood that gushed from where there had once been an eye. Ursino, or his corpse, remained kneeling for a time before tumbling over, his legs sprawled under him.

"*Ad maiorem Dei gloriam*," Jonas murmured. "Your Jonas died today with you."

The man looked at the body as if for the first time.

I know well what you can do, and none of your desires will be denied.

He blessed himself before picking up the piece of paper and leaving the holy Relic Room, where the silent witnesses of history reposed.

37

<hr>

It was strange how decorative figures—static, immutable—could change their expression depending on the scene they were witnessing. The same rebellious, mischievous cherub, who held his finger over his lips to ask the Reverend Father Hans Schmidt to restrain himself, now seemed wide-eyed in the silent call for judgment.

"Your theory is that the mind is our enemy," Cardinal Ricard, another counselor, said with a sarcastic smile.

"Let's say the mind possesses us," Schmidt added serenely.

"Do you mind explaining? Lay it out, please."

"Certainly. Our mind, a voice we have inside our head telling us to do one thing or another, that judges and reacts to situations, was made for a specific purpose. To aid us in a practical way. Just as our immune system recognizes the characteristics of an aggressor to overcome constant attacks, the purpose of our mind is the same. We never stick our hand in the fire because we know it burns. How do we know that? We store that information. Unfortunately, we corrupt the whole purpose of the creation of the mind by letting it possess us."

Everyone looked at Schmidt with evident interest. A few shook their heads in a gesture of disapproval, but listened to him attentively.

"Aren't we the ones doing the thinking?" the same cardinal countered.

"No, Your Eminence. We are the ones who know, who have the idea of thinking, which is very different. If we can listen to our thoughts, then we are the ones who listen."

"Does that mean that someone thinks for us?" another counselor spoke.

"No. It means we give too much importance to thinking. Thought exists for practical purposes, not for speculation. Thought exists for me to say that it's cold outside, and so I have to dress warmly, not for saying, *Oh, damn, it's cold outside. The hell with the weather.*"

"But through thought I know who I am, who I was—I have a notion of my history," the first cardinal argued.

"A false notion of self. A false notion of your own history. The self is the root of the problem."

"What are you saying? Why false?"

"Because everything is mixed up here," Hans said, pointing at his head. "The real, the unreal, the imaginary, the past, desires, dreams."

"Can we not distinguish between reality and dream?"

Schmidt stopped for a moment and smiled. "I'll give you an example. Do you remember the last trip you took?" he said to the cardinal.

"Very well," His Eminence replied.

"Can you tell us where it was?"

"Certainly. Croatia. I was in Zagreb a few days."

"Think of a place in Zagreb where you were."

"I'm doing so."

"Where was it?"

"The cathedral."

"Now imagine me next to you. Can you see us having coffee on the esplanade of Ban Jelačić Square?"

The cardinal said nothing, and a sarcastic smile faded from his lips.

"We're not able to distinguish what actually happened from what we wish had happened or from a suggestion that might have happened," Schmidt explained with passion. "The past serves for nothing. It's not for remembering or for mentally reviving. It was what it was, and there is nothing you can do to change it. Certainly, it's not worth crying over. It's not worth judging ourselves and others." He paused briefly. "Salvation is always in the present. We can only make a difference in our life now. Not yesterday, not tomorrow, only now."

The room looked at him in silence. The prefect, the secretary, the cardinal counselors shifted their papers and moved uncomfortably in their chairs, impatient, constrained, some dry coughing, others with too much phlegm.

"I ask myself," the secretary began, "if you realize the outrages you've told this congregation. You've polluted this holy place with a mountain of heresies."

·There was a concurring mutter and shaking of heads around the table.

"Salvation is always in our Lord Jesus Christ," the secretary added, gaining the approval of the prefect.

"I agree with Your Eminence," Schmidt affirmed.

"But not completely," added Cardinal Ricard.

"The extent of my agreement isn't important. As I said previously, believing or not believing is equally correct."

The cardinal got up indignantly. "There is only one belief," he shouted. "In our Lord Jesus Christ. It was He who said the kingdom of God is always at hand." He stuck his finger in the air, as if that sanctioned what he said.

Schmidt chuckled.

"When Jesus said that, He was not talking about time."

"What was He talking about, then?" Secretary Ladaria asked.

Schmidt looked at his listeners with a genuine smile. He was very amused. "About distance."

"Distance? Explain that, please." William spoke now. He'd been silent so far.

"Jesus meant that the kingdom of God, salvation, was near, that is, it was ready, within reach of anyone. But he wasn't talking about a place or time. . . ." He let his words sink in before proceeding. "He was referring to a state or condition."

"A state," the secretary repeated, as if awakening from a trance. "And what state was that?"

"The state of illumination."

The entire congregation waited for an explanation.

"Jesus almost always lived in this state," Schmidt continued. "It's what happens when you live free from permanent control of the mind. The mind judges, classifies, files everything that surrounds it. It's hot, cold, bad, good . . . this one's an idiot, that one's a thief, and everything is conspiring against us. . . . Everything that passes before our eyes suffers instant classification. It happens often we meet a person, and in five minutes we've formed a fixed opinion. We like him or not, according to *our* mental classification. Nothing is more erroneous."

Indignation was growing among the counselors. The prefect was the only one who showed no reaction.

"Jesus didn't judge and classify things. He was in a permanent state of enlightenment. Always in contact with the vital energy of the universe. He didn't make value judgments or predictions, didn't worry about problems that might or might not occur, and never tried to imagine how to correct things, because things never happen as we imagine. Jesus didn't live in the past or in the future, only in the one state in which one can live: the present. *Consider the lilies of the field. They neither toil nor spin,* He said. There is no other way to live. You can't do it thinking about what is going to happen in five minutes or ten or an hour, a day or a year. We can only make a difference now in the present. Jesus made all the difference living in this way."

No one said anything for some time. They didn't know what to say. The counselors tried to assimilate the outrageous words that the reverend Austrian father had uttered with such fervent passion. The entire session was a horrendous profanation of the holy, a sacrilege. In a way that Schmidt might have considered disrespectful, if he were a man given to classification, the counselors began whispering among themselves. William stayed out of the conversation in the beginning, but was compelled to intervene when whispering turned into a murmur and, later, into a heated altercation.

"Gentlemen," the voice of Schmidt, whom everyone had forgotten about, broke in. "Reverend Prefect, Mr. Secretary, and Your Eminences, I understand that you don't agree with me. I want to tell you that my first duty and priority is to the church, which I serve and obey, in humility and abnegation." With those final words he lowered his head in a gesture of submission until he showed his bare neck to indicate he was at their mercy.

The prefect of the Congregation for the Doctrine of the Faith rose from his chair, assumed an arrogant pose that matched his function, and looked at Reverend Father Hans Matthaus Schmidt sternly.

"Good . . . this session was without doubt . . . intense." He hesitated to characterize the proceedings. "The prefect and the other counselors will deliberate and—"

The doors suddenly opening interrupted the prefect's discourse. Four Swiss Guards, in dress uniform, entered and took position on either side of the door. Four more of their countrymen immediately followed.

"What's going on?" the prefect wanted to know.

One of the guards, clearly the most senior, advanced to the center of the room.

"This room is sealed until further notice."

"How ridiculous," the secretary spoke up. "You owe us respect, Daniel."

"I'm sorry, Your Eminences, but there has been a breach of security. At this time I have maximum responsibility for the Vatican. I beg your understanding."

"A security breach? What happened?" the prefect asked.

Daniel hesitated. He didn't know if he had to answer.

"Don't keep it secret, Daniel. What happened?" William insisted.

"A murder within the walls of the Vatican," the commander of the Pontifical Swiss Guard explained.

"My dear God," the prefect let slip and sat down exhausted.

"But who?" the secretary inquired.

"I'm not authorized to say. I am sorry to inform you that no one may enter or leave until further notice." He turned his back and looked at the Austrian priest. "Father Hans Schmidt?"

Schmidt confirmed with a nod, and then the other three guards surrounded him.

"I must kindly ask you to accompany us."

Schmidt got up, blushing slightly.

"Where are you taking him?" the secretary asked.

"To the papal apartments. Orders of the Holy Father."

38

From the street, the church could not be seen. It was hidden under a dark, filthy viaduct. Above, the constant noise of trains made the foundations vibrate in that same place where it had stood long before there had been trains and viaducts. The church wasn't always set in that kind of subterranean underworld, but within a community, and its tiled roof had shimmered in the weak British sunshine. People came to the small Catholic church for morning services, especially on Sundays. These days it was just a grimy, forgotten building under a viaduct, which sheltered Rafael from the light rain that had begun to dampen London.

He had abandoned the taxi a half mile from the British Museum, walked another few yards to Tottenham Court Road, and called another taxi, which left him a few hundred feet from the church. He quickly covered the distance to the Church of St. Andrew and found the door, bare of paint from the passage of time, open. He entered without making any noise. No one was there. A candle burned next to the altar. The church couldn't hold more than fifty people, but rarely had that many over the years. Perhaps a handful of faithful still attended, more out of fear of God and respect for the priest than for any other reason. The walls, once white, looked darkened by cars and trains. The light was faint. Next to the candle were one or two low-voltage bulbs.

Rafael kneeled at the altar, blessed himself, and prayed briefly.

"Hello," he heard a voice say.

Rafael got up and looked at a man with completely white hair. "Hi, Donald," he greeted him.

"What the fuck," the other cursed.

Rafael smiled. "You were always gracious."

"What are you doing here, you prick?" Donald was clearly not enjoying the visit.

"Seeing a friend."

"You must have the wrong place. No one is your friend here."

Rafael didn't give the slightest sign of being offended. Donald greeted all his friends like this.

"Have you got yourself into a mess, Santini?"

"Have you ever seen me not in one?" Rafael responded.

Donald said nothing for a few moments. He looked at Rafael disdainfully, then looked around the minuscule space and turned his back. "Follow me . . . or get out. Whatever you want."

The sacristy was to the left of the altar as one approached.

When Rafael entered, Donald had already poured the golden liquid of a bottle of whiskey into two glasses. He opened a wooden box from which he took some tobacco and filled the bowl of his pipe. He struck a match and held it above the tobacco, sucked vigorously to get it lit, and in less than a minute was relaxing in a chair to enjoy the drink and tobacco. Rafael sat down also, without Donald's invitation, and grabbed the second glass of malt scotch. He wasn't in the habit of drinking in the morning, but he needed this one. It had been a long night. There were some who drank for lesser reasons than this.

"How are things in Rome?" Donald asked, finally breaking the silence.

Rafael sipped a little of his drink before replying. "Same as always."

Donald frowned. "Still fucked up, huh." The Englishman got up and went over to a closet. "How many do you need?"

"One."

"Only one?"

"Only one."

"And they? How many are there?" Donald's voice was friendlier as he continued looking through the closet for something, with his back toward Rafael.

"You never know, Donald."

"Of course not. That's shitty."

Donald approached with a package and a box and put them down by Rafael. "Take your choice."

Rafael unwrapped the tissue around a Glock 19 9mm. He tried it out, chambered a load from the magazine he attached, and aimed. Then he opened the box that contained a Beretta 92FS of the same caliber. He didn't even test it. He put it in his jacket pocket along with two magazines of 9mm bullets. Donald looked at him curiously.

"Made in Italy," Rafael explained, getting out of the chair. "Has any Jesuit asked for your help?"

"The Jesuits don't need me. They have their own methods. Besides, they have Nicolas."

"Who is Nicolas?"

Donald got up and accompanied Rafael out of the sacristy. "Nicolas is the man who carries out their jobs. The Jesuit front line. He's the one who solves their problems."

"Where can I find him?" Rafael was visibly interested in this information.

"I have no idea. I don't even know where he's from. Some Jesuit will know. He's one of them. Talk to Robin."

The two men went to the door.

Donald offered his hand. "I'm not going to wish you good luck because you're a tough son of a bitch."

Rafael smiled. "Keep your head down for a few days," he advised. "Things are going to get hot."

39

—◆—

"Spill it, Sam," Barry ordered. He was not in the mood for bullshit. "I don't want to hear *We don't know*."

The meeting was in the same room where they held briefings on ongoing operations or those being planned. Aris sat on Barry's right, Sam on the left, Staughton, Davis, and Travis followed. No one sat at the opposite end.

"The Italian and the taxi driver?" Barry wanted to know.

"They're being interrogated as we speak," Aris informed him.

"Let's begin, then," the director ordered.

Sam got up and pulled her skirt down. She seemed nervous, tense, a little feverish, judging from her red cheeks.

"Everything began about fifty years ago with an agreement between Pope John the Twenty-third and Ben Isaac."

"Ben Isaac." Barry thought it over. He tried to flesh out the name with more information, give him a face. "The Israeli banker?"

"The same," Sam confirmed. "In 1947 he was one of the discoverers of the famous apocryphal gospels."

"The *what*?" Aris asked.

Sam shrugged her shoulders in irritation. "The Dead Sea Scrolls from Qumran."

Aris raised his thumb to show he understood.

"It seems there were some very important documents in these discoveries," Sam continued. Her nervousness disappeared as she got used to the male eyes focused on her. "Some of them were never made public, since they were covered by an agreement between the Israeli and the Vatican. That agreement was called the Status Quo."

"Interesting," Barry said. "Okay, let's throw some light on the reason Rafael was in Paris."

"And in London," Sam added.

Barry looked at her, puzzled.

"Ben Isaac has lived in London for more than fifty years," Sam explained confidently. "But there's more . . . much more."

"Put Ben Isaac under surveillance as soon as possible."

"Already done," Sam replied.

"Don't keep us waiting, then, Sam," Barry said with a smile. "Go on, please."

Sam continued. Ben Isaac and the agreement with John

XXIII, John Paul II, the Three Gentlemen, the Five Gentlemen, Magda, Myriam, Ben Isaac Jr. . . . Jesus Christ.

All the participants were silent. No one knew what to say. They considered the information silently.

"Wow," Barry finally said. "That's a lot."

"Why did those four people die?" Aris threw in.

There was so much to know. Doubts, questions, misunderstandings, all the reasons for anger, wars and tortures. Jesus Christ? It wasn't every day that a case like this came up. Nothing like this had ever appeared in the history of the CIA, a short history compared to that of the church.

"There weren't four. There were six," said a voice that had just entered the room.

"Thompson. Welcome," Barry greeted him. "Have a seat."

Thompson pulled out the chair across from Barry and sat down.

"Six dead? What are you telling me?" Barry asked.

Thompson threw a bunch of papers on the table. Transcripts, texts, and photos covered the surface.

"Ernesto Aragones, Spanish priest, assassinated with a shot to the back of the head on Sunday in the Church of the Holy Sepulcher in Jerusalem."

The others began to look at the papers.

"This morning they killed a priest inside the Vatican."

"A what?" Barry was scandalized. "What the hell is going on? Who was he?"

"The curator of the Relics Room. Don't ask me what it means."

"What's the connection between all these people?" Aris asked again.

"Yaman Zafer, Sigfried Hammal, Aragones, and the priest today, Ursino, were part of what was called the Five Gentlemen," Thompson replied.

"And the others?"

"The others were Jesuits. According to what I was able to squeeze out of the Italian. The acolyte killed the priest to silence him, then committed suicide."

Barry shook his head. "Who are we fighting with, folks?"

"They don't know themselves, from what I could find out," Thompson suggested.

"Okay," Barry said thoughtfully. "Now we have something to work with. This Ben Isaac. Could he be Rafael's target?"

"He could be," Aris commented.

"We need to find out what that agreement covers, and what Jesus has to do with all this." Barry thought rapidly, trying to sketch out a preliminary strategy.

"I can try to pry out a little more, but I don't think the Italian knew much to begin with," Thompson suggested, always practical.

"Sam, did you book a flight to Rome?"

"Of course. It leaves at five in the afternoon from Gatwick and arrives in time for supper."

Barry was pleased. As director of the Agency for the European theater, he had a fleet of vehicles at his disposal. A Learjet 85, two Bell helicopters, several cars. He usually chose to fly commercial when his schedule permitted. His rule was not to waste taxpayer dollars, long before any president recommended the cost cutting.

"Something is bothering me," Barry added.

Everyone looked at him, waiting for him to finish.

"You mentioned Five Gentlemen, right?" he asked Sam.

"Yes."

"Four have died. There's a pattern. Someone is out to kill these Gentlemen."

He let the implication sink in.

"There's one left," Aris said. "Could it be Ben Isaac?"

"We'll have to set up a security perimeter in that case," Barry ordered.

"No, Ben Isaac is very well protected. He doesn't need our protection. They have a good security system, some former and current Mossad agents," Sam explained. "He's not the fifth Gentleman."

"Who is, then? And why do they call them 'Gentlemen'?" Barry asked.

"Because they had a gentlemen's agreement of silence among them," Thompson explained.

"The question is this," Barry advised, getting up. "They've assassinated four of the five, so someone is in danger. Find out who the fifth Gentleman is."

"Uh . . . we know," Sam said timidly.

"Then spit it out, Sam. That person's life is in danger."

"The fifth Gentleman is Joseph Ratzinger . . . the pope himself."

40

Ben Isaac had a maxim he'd used for a long time in life, especially in business: everything has a price. An object, a jewel, a house, a business, a man—everything could be bought and sold. All you needed was capital, and Ben Isaac had more than enough money. But tonight the Israeli banker would learn a lesson that would strike down that maxim. There are people no amount of money can buy, even if all the coffers in the world are emptied. Ben Isaac had dealt with such a person only once before in his life, and it had not gone well. He felt lost, disoriented, and could think of nothing but his son, tied to a chair, mistreated, bloody, and beaten. Just the idea made him shiver, heartsick, and panic flooded his veins. He remembered Magda, his daughter, dead in the womb, and how he had not been there when she died. Some deal or some excavation, something more important, had required his attention at the time.

Myriam, alone in London so often, watching the rain fall or freeze, or the weak sun rising, without her husband. A day or two, a week. A phone call from Tel Aviv, another from Amman, an unexpected negotiation in Turin, a meeting in Bern, a meeting with the excavation team, who knows when and where, another with the team in a university in the States, to deepen his knowledge of something excavated, no big deal, he'd be back as soon as possible, a kiss.

Myriam never lacked money, not a penny to buy anything she wanted. Ben made sure of that. Myriam sometimes thought that for him money was a more sacred bond than the one by which God united them. On bad days she wished Ben weren't so successful, that he'd fail, and on the worst days, that he'd go bankrupt.

Their daughter, Magda, died on November 8, 1960. His hands were trembling when he called the house from hundreds of miles away to say he'd be home that night. He finally had an agreement in his pocket that Myriam never suspected or would suspect.

Myriam didn't answer that phone call or the others that followed insistently. Ben would find her in a hospital bed at St. Bart's, sound asleep from the strong sedatives prescribed by the staff doctors. She remained that way for several days and nights, without regaining consciousness, breathing quietly, her face as white as a corpse. The doctor on call explained nothing to Ben Isaac, deferring to his superiors. It was not his place to say what was happening to the patient; her own doctor had left this instruction.

The young, prestigious banker, used to doing and undoing, ordering and contradicting both his subordinates and heads of state who clamored for the money he had and they didn't, waited by the bed for her personal physician to deign to appear.

"Myriam tried to commit suicide," was the doctor's greeting. "I can't stay. I'm getting married," he explained.

Ben Isaac was unable to say anything. He couldn't even make a gesture. He stared silently at the doctor, subdued, disgusted, with a three days' growth of beard.

"She didn't eat for days and filled her stomach with barbiturates. She repented and called an ambulance. While she was waiting for the paramedics, she was probably anxious and inattentive, and she tripped on the stairs and fell. When she arrived here, she was crying out . . . for Magda."

Tears ran down the face of young Ben Isaac, the multimillionaire whose wife was so unhappy to want to kill herself and the daughter she carried in her womb.

"I'm very sorry, but we weren't able to save Magda."

Ben Isaac covered his face in his hands and trembled with a smothered wail. Sorrow exploded in his chest and punished him with blows of agony and disgust.

"When are you going to stop sedating her?" he managed to ask.

"Myriam isn't under sedation now," the doctor informed him.

"But she's still sleeping!"

The doctor sighed and leaned toward Ben Isaac. "Myriam will wake up when she understands . . . when she feels ready. Help her. She's going to need it."

The doctor murmured "Good luck" before leaving the couple in the cold hospital room, on his way to church to a ceremony that would seal a sacred compact, not necessarily infallible, even if marriage were not a human invention.

It took seven days for Myriam to wake up, and when she did, it was as if he were not there at all. She didn't say a word, didn't respond to his encouragement or questions, excuses or promises, or love. Ben Isaac would not hear her voice for the next nine years. The absences that he'd curtailed resumed, but it didn't bother Myriam, who was involved with her garden, her friends, her book club, exhibits, tea parties, the theater, the culture that London offered, faithfully, without fail. She didn't share any of this with Ben. It was as if she were living two lives and were two women, Ben's wife when he was home and Ben's wife when he was absent.

One Saturday lunch Myriam said to Ben Isaac, "I'd like to get to know Israel, Ben." It was as if they'd been talking about it just yesterday, seconds ago, forever, without the hiatus of almost a decade in which Ben had not heard a syllable, an interjection, a complaint, or even a sob.

Ben Isaac took her to Israel, Cyprus, Italy, Brazil, and Argentina, and they talked all day about the things normal couples who have a lot of money, and normal couples who don't, talk about. They smiled, laughed, made love again, kissed, felt their bodies breathing, felt the other's sweat—everything a couple feels or ought to feel, except Magda. They never once talked about her. She was a sealed subject, forbidden, taboo.

Ben Isaac lived with silent bitterness, tied up with the strong cords of guilt, resigned to getting through the day, losing himself in his work, filling the hours, attending to Myriam. He didn't return to excavations. Magda served as warning, a punishment from the Almighty, a closed door he could not open again.

All this went through his mind as he read the message he'd received on the cell phone. *If you want to see your son alive again, get rid of the journalist.* Sarah and Myriam continued to look over the ancient documents, neglecting the papal agreements that held no interest for them, despite the fact that they were the only documents whose language they could understand. The rest exercised a hypnotic fascination on them. Ben Isaac had felt it several times. The characters—ornate, stylized, but without pretensions or arrogance, unlike the papal blazons, which in those days didn't yet exist.

He couldn't lose little Ben. He couldn't lose another child. Where was divine justice? Would he always be punished for sticking his nose into something he shouldn't have? No. He had paid an enormous price. Magda, Myriam, and nine years of sepulchral silence.

How could they possibly know about the journalist? The leak had not come from his side. He was absolutely certain. He remembered when Cardinal William had introduced him to Sarah. The leak came from the Vatican at the highest level, and that was serious. He had to get Myriam to safety and put an end to the situation.

"Myriam," Ben called. "A moment, please."

Myriam returned to her husband, who showed her the phone screen. She read the message and raised her hand to her mouth in shock. Sarah noticed.

"No, Ben. We can't," stammered Myriam shakily, her legs weak. "It's not true."

"We have to do it, Myr. Ben's life is at stake." Ben put both his hands on Myriam's shoulders. "We have to do it."

Both of them looked apprehensively at Sarah. She realized something had happened that had to do with her.

"What's going on?" she asked timidly.

Ever since she'd entered the underground storage vault, her heart had been beating nervously. She knew what she had to do. William had been completely explicit in the Palazzo Madama. A sacrifice that would make all the difference for millions of the faithful.

Myriam collapsed on the floor, sobbing. "No, Ben."

"I'm sorry, Sarah," Ben said, approaching her slowly. "I have no alternative."

Sarah backed up until she bumped against a showcase. It was now or never. Ben's threatening attitude helped her make up her mind. Ben clicked a number on the phone and said something in Hebrew. He was calling security.

Sarah put her hand in her jacket pocket and took out

the small, six-shot revolver that William had given her. She aimed at Ben.

"Not one more step."

Ben looked at her, surprised. How was it possib— Cardinal William. Who would have suspected the cardinal?

Myriam raised her head, analyzing the situation.

"Give me the documents," Sarah ordered, her voice stronger than she felt.

"Put away the gun, Sarah. You won't get out of here alive. Besides, you're not a killer," Ben warned. "You don't have what it takes to kill."

"Myriam, get up and come over here." Another order.

Myriam got up with difficulty and approached Sarah suspiciously. As soon as she was within reach, Sarah grabbed hold of her, turned her around, and pushed the barrel of the gun into her right temple. Myriam closed her eyes.

"Still don't think I have what it takes?" Sarah asked. She hated herself at this moment. "Now, give me the documents so Myriam and I can take a walk."

"Do you really want to do this?" Ben asked very calmly.

Sarah trembled with the gun at Myriam's head. She tried not to press too hard, to avoid hurting her. Myriam was actually calmer than she was.

"Don't do something you'll regret," Ben pleaded in a low voice.

"Give me the documents," Sarah insisted.

"That's not going to happen, Sarah. Understand this very well. It's the life of my son at risk."

Sarah was losing her options. She'd never pull the trigger. Her bluff was about to be called.

"Lower the gun, Sarah. My men are almost here. They're pros and—"

"Good evening," a male voice said in perfect English.

"Hadrian," Ben called without looking for him. "Do me the favor of disarming the lady, who's beginning to annoy me."

"I'm sorry, but Hadrian couldn't come," the voice returned.

Ben Isaac looked at the man perplexedly. What was going on here? Who was he? One of the kidnappers? "Who are you?"

"You can call me Garvis. I'm an inspector for the Metropolitan Police, and I'm here to help."

"To . . . help with what?" Ben asked.

Sarah and Myriam were just as perplexed. Sarah kept the gun resting lightly at Myriam's head.

Two men came into the vault. No one recognized them.

"Lower the gun, ma'am. I'm sick of killings," he said in heavily accented English.

"Who are you? How dare you invade my property?" Ben Isaac was indignant and nervous.

"Who am I?" The man was scandalized. "Who am I?" Then he looked at the second man. "Who am I, Jean-Paul?"

"Inspector Gavache of the Police Nationale," Jean-Paul proclaimed like a herald.

"And you can call this a surprise visit," Gavache added, taking a drag on his cigarette.

41

Everything that exists is perfect and sacred because it was created by God in His great glory for the use of those who believe in Him, amen.

He believed this blindly, so he needed nothing more than he already had. He met her at the same time for lunch, grilled dorado with sautéed vegetables and an original touch of two tiger shrimps, also grilled.

She asked him about the verse of the day, which she almost chanted with respect and explained its meaning as he had done when he left the verses each week on her bedside table. *It was the LORD who made this, and it is marvelous in our eyes.* Everyone should be required to read the Bible, but that reading should never be done in private or independently. It should be done with the aid of a priest or theologian to understand what is not clear and to avoid bringing mistaken ideas to the Holy Scriptures. The unguided reading of the Word of the Lord was an evil that the church had always combated, not as severely as it should, in his opinion, and spread erroneous opinions about what God had really proclaimed. God wanted everyone to read the holy text without misunderstanding or difficulty.

He savored the dorado, vegetables, and shrimp frugally, along with a glass of white Frascati '98, with a slightly sweet aftertaste that went down well. She drank water, since the blood of Christ was exclusively for men and denied to women, whose obligation was to subordinate themselves to a man and do what he ordered, or so taught the great Saint Paul, the father of the church, on a par with Peter.

After lunch she took the dishes from the table to the kitchen to wash them, as was her duty. He wasn't long in joining her and putting his arms around her as she ran the dishes through soapy water. He whispered in her ear, ordering her to go to the bedroom. She put down the plates, turned off the faucet, and went.

The syringe expelled the sedative drug into her veins, and two minutes later she lost consciousness. He positioned himself over her inanimate body and enjoyed his carnal pleasure. It didn't take long, two or three minutes, to empty himself in a quick climax that left him feeling disgusted with himself and her. He bathed, scrubbed himself well to wash the stains from his body, the weakness of the flesh. He felt nausea. When he was finished, she was still sleeping. It was time to go back to work.

A third of the order had been completed. Two names remained. Rafael Santini and the other. He wasn't interested in who they were or what they did. If God had called them, it was because their hour had come, and no one could escape his hour. The message said that Rafael's hour had come, so he would try him first. He always worked one name at a time.

He decided to take the cell phone. He opened it, took out the battery and programming card, and inserted another. He put in the battery and started the phone. As soon as it was on, he entered a code: MONITASECRETA.

The call was placed automatically without his doing anything. Seconds later the screen showed a phrase: *Call completed.* He wrote, *Deus vocat.*

In a moment a word appeared: *Nomini.*

He entered, *Rafael Santini.*

The reply did not take long: *Tonight. Via dei Soldati. Wait for instructions.*

He disconnected. He opened the Bible at random and put his finger on a verse. He read it and smiled.

42

The cold penetrated his bones mercilessly, making his joints ache. He zipped up his jacket, raised his collar to protect his neck, and kept walking. The pain in his arm when the temperature dropped reminded him of an old fight with someone he'd forgotten, but his arm still remembered. There'd been so many fights that he'd lost count.

He turned the corner onto Mount Street and proceeded toward his destination. There were a lot of people out at that hour, eleven in the morning, and a lot of traffic, too. The glamour that Mayfair displayed at all hours didn't impress him at all. He didn't look in any store windows. Nothing distracted him. He was a man with a purpose, and that purpose was right in front of him, the Church of the Immaculate Conception.

After Father Donald's small church below the viaduct, this church was much larger, more monumental. He looked at the Gothic facade but didn't stop long.

He went inside the holy temple. Jesuit churches were normally dark, but not this one. A simple nave, supported by stone columns and a clerestory with sixteen windows. Rich side chapels on the left and right, carved and decorated, the relics of numerous saints, full of mystery. Rafael was uninterested in the sacred objects and architecture. He analyzed the exits, checked who was present: a woman kneeling in the front, a man with a Bible pressed to his heart, a line of people in back, and a Japanese couple taking photos of the brass altar created by Pugin. Rafael walked to the center of the nave, cautiously, alert to every movement and noise. A falcon hunting prey, silent, lethal.

He noticed the confessionals at the back, one on each side. The one on the left was empty. An orange light indicated confession time on the right. It was a wooden structure, totally closed, protecting the vicar and the sinner from the temptation of the world. He approached the confessional. Someone was there asking for mercy for his sins, whispering his weaknesses while the priest listened. Rafael overheard *therefore* and *because,* enough for him to know that the man was speaking English. His own sins were enough for him. He didn't need to hear those of others. Since no one was waiting, Rafael would be next. He looked around the immense space again. The same penitents agonizing in prayers for wisdom, grace, pardon. The Japanese had moved on.

The sinner must have received purgation and left the place of penitence, free, light, clean, and immaculate to confront reality anew and commit the same sins and other, new ones.

Rafael let the man leave and went in. He kneeled on the prie-dieu next to the wooden screen that hid the confessor from the sinner.

"Good morning, Father," he greeted him.

"Good morning, my son. What brings you here?" the priest asked in a melodious, complacent voice.

"Forgive me, for I have sinned," Rafael said disquietedly.

"Tell me the nature of your sin, my son. What is troubling you?" the curate said in a bored way. He was more than accustomed to people's pain. A word from him would quiet all. That was the power of confession.

"I have a gun pointed at a priest's head," the sinner said coolly.

"What did you say?" He couldn't have heard what he thought.

"I have a gun pointed at a priest's head," Rafael repeated. "If he doesn't answer my questions, I'll have to kill him."

43

Hans Schmidt entered the papal apartments escorted by Daniel and two more plainclothes Swiss Guards, who stayed in the background. Two others in uniform were standing at attention by the doors giving access to the papal privacy. They saluted the officer passing by them, and he returned the gesture to his men.

"Have they caught the murderer?" Schmidt asked, out of breath with the fast pace imposed on him.

"We can't reveal details of the investigation," the commander of Pontifical Security told him.

"I understand."

They made the rest of the walk in silence, except for the sound of shoes and boots striking the floor. Schmidt had not been there for several years. The first time was in the 1980s in the time of Pope John Paul II, or Lolek, as he asked to be called in perfect German. That first time was always an unforgettable experience. Meeting the Supreme Pontiff, for a priest, was something transcendent, practically like meeting God in person. Lolek was the personification of Him. With the passage of time and more visits, Schmidt grew accustomed to the sumptuous place, the niches with statues of Pius IX, Benedict XIV, Pius XII, and Leo XIII, in a papal pose, all with the tiara on their heads, the symbol of eternal and secular power. Schmidt recognized the door that led to the pope's study a few feet away, with two sentinels with lances, immobile as the walls, ready to give their life for the Supreme Pontiff at any moment.

Two empty niches waited for history to fill them with new personages, from the past or the present, by some patron closer to the arts than politics.

The sentinels saluted their superior and opened the doors. Schmidt examined the study. It was different from what he remembered. More austere, less happy. In Lolek's time it was completely disorganized. Papers stacked everywhere, even on the seats of chairs. This study seemed arranged and decorated to appear in the next issue of a design magazine. Even the sun seemed shy about illuminating it with its rays. It was from that window that Ratzinger addressed the world every Sunday, but the Supreme Pontiff was not in the office, only Tarcisio, who looked through a crack in the white curtains at the square below, teeming with tourists and faithful completely ignorant of the blood spilled inside the walls of the holy state.

"Your Eminence," Daniel called, since Tarcisio had not noticed their presence.

The secretary turned as if he were returning to earth. "Ah, you've arrived." He extended both hands to Schmidt like a cry for help. "My good friend."

Schmidt took Tarcisio's hands in his own. "Difficult times, but they will pass, Tarcisio, that is certain."

Tarcisio looked at the Swiss Guard. "Leave us, Colonel."

Daniel and his men retired without turning their backs.

"Pope Benedict?" Schmidt wanted to know.

"He's in a secure location. The two of us cannot be in the same place. Security protocol. We are under threat, Hans." He was silent a few seconds. "Since Albino Luciani, no one has died this way on this soil," he shared with Schmidt.

"Who was the victim?"

Tarcisio hesitated before speaking the name of the person, who was a man of the church yesterday, and at that moment was no more than a story; it was as if saying it would transform the name into a truth Tarcisio didn't want to confront. "Ursino," he finally said, closing his eyes to contain his suffering.

Schmidt helped him to the papal chair, where Tarcisio sat down, drained.

"The murderer?"

Tarcisio shook his head no. "Still nothing."

"Just tonight I spoke with him," Schmidt remembered.

"How do you deal with such a tragic death?" Tarcisio asked. He was a man falling in a well of doubts.

"Like all the others, my friend," Schmidt reassured him in a firm voice. "Death is a part of life. Celebrate his good moments and don't consider the process a loss but rather a privilege. You were part of Ursino's life. You illuminated the way, each for the other."

"But we'll never do it again," Tarcisio protested.

"But you did once. Don't feel sorrow for what cannot be. The future doesn't belong to us. What's important is that it happened when it happened and it was good. Life is always changing. Nothing is forever. You're old enough to know that."

"That's easy to say," the secretary argued.

Schmidt continued to console him. "I understand, Tarcisio, but remember that mourning is a selfish act. To weep for someone who dies is an offense to the life that he lived and we lived with him."

The two men concluded what was a strange conversation, at least as far as Tarcisio was concerned. He was confused and didn't want to explore that philosophy. The church would always prevail in its ancient ways; that's how it was.

"Why did you call for me?" the Austrian iceman finally asked.

"Because . . . because I don't know whom to trust," Tarcisio confessed. "Someone murdered a priest inside our walls. An important priest, as you know. I'm walking blindly. I need light."

"You must be cold, Tarcisio."

The secretary looked at him, overcome. The situation called for urgent measures. It was a century since the church had been attacked by such an implacable enemy and, worse, an invisible enemy. Who could be behind such a diabolical scheme? What devil wanted to finish off the church? With a face, a description, one could plan a counterattack, take a position on the chessboard. It was better than nothing.

"We're living in difficult, ungovernable times."

"We have to steady our minds and analyze things coolly," Schmidt explained. "Let's start with what we know."

"We know they killed four of the Five Gentlemen."

"We should have put Ursino under security as soon as we knew about what had happened to the others," Tarcisio lamented.

"No, no, no. Nothing you think now will change what happened. Ursino is out. They've killed four Gentlemen. The fifth is left, and then there's Ben Isaac. Do you think we should put them under security?"

"The fifth is always safe. Ben Isaac takes care of his own."

"Okay, what else do we know?"

Tarcisio put his face in his hands. He was exhausted.

"We don't know anything else," Tarcisio said.

At that moment the doors opened, admitting Cardinal William.

"We know that the assassin is a Jesuit," he informed them with a smile.

"A what?" Tarcisio and Schmidt asked at once.

"I've just obtained confirmation. The murderer is a Jesuit. But there's more . . . the society should be current with the situation.

Schmidt's placidity changed to perplexity. "The Society of Jesus?"

"None other," William confirmed.

"But why?" Tarcisio wanted to know.

"It doesn't seem possible to me," Schmidt argued.

"It's being verified at this very moment," William told them. "You're going to be meeting with the superior general of the society this afternoon, right?"

Tarcisio shivered, remembering the scheduled meeting. "Yes."

"You have to press him. Don't meet behind closed doors."

Schmidt smiled. "Please, Your Eminence. Do you think the superior general might attempt something against the secretary of state of the Vatican?"

William didn't reply.

"Are we to consider the Jesuits our enemy?" Schmidt asked.

Tarcisio and William shared a conspiratorial look for a few moments.

"It's possible," William finally said.

Schmidt remained skeptical.

"What now?" Tarcisio asked.

"Now . . . we wait for a woman to play her part," William said, looking at the square below. *And a man*.

"The church in the hands of a woman. Ironic," Tarcisio observed.

"Not for the first time," William remembered.

44

The dining room of Ben Isaac's mansion resembled a command post. Computers, communication equipment, copiers, a commotion of technicians and agents from the Metropolitan Police, who entered and left in a whirl of activity that only they understood. Ben Isaac and Myriam were seated on a leather sofa, feeling upset. What would happen to little Ben? The kidnapper seemed to know everything. This meant the end of their son, everything they had tried to avoid from the beginning.

"They told you to wait for instructions at home," Gavache recalled. "And you didn't try to contact law enforcement?" he asked angrily, with a reproving shake of his head.

"It's my son's life at stake," Ben Isaac argued. "He could already be dead because of this whole circus."

"Don't say that, Ben," Myriam cried out. "Let the officers do their work." She didn't add that it was because they'd always done things his way that they found themselves in the present situation, but she thought it. Blame wouldn't solve anything.

Garvis hurriedly joined the group. He was in charge of the whole operation. "Dr. Ben, everything is ready. Would you come with me, so I can explain the procedure when they call?" He was there to help, and he knew what the father and mother were going through, more than he wished.

"If they call," Ben grumbled as he got up.

"They'll call, Doctor." Gavache reassured him. "You have something they want very much. They've already proved how far they'll go to get it. They're not going to give up."

Ben Isaac went with Garvis to the heart of the machines and connections that, God willing, would track down the kidnappers' hiding place. Gavache was sitting in an armchair smoking, much to Ben Isaac's disapproval. Myriam watched him, intimidated.

"Do you believe what you're saying?" Myriam asked. She needed to know if Gavache was just talking.

"Another one of my faults. I always say what I think," Gavache assured her again, blowing a puff of smoke into the air, "and I have to smoke to think."

"I understand," Myriam said, more at ease with Gavache.

"Where's that amusing young lady, Jean-Paul?" Gavache wanted to know.

"She went into the bathroom ten minutes ago," Jean-Paul informed him, appearing behind his boss.

"Do you think she needs help?"

"No, Inspector," Myriam interjected. "She's not feeling well. She's been nauseous lately."

"Did you hear that, Jean-Paul?" Gavache asked.

"I heard, Inspector."

"One more to keep us busy."

"But we need to work, Inspector," Jean-Paul contradicted him.

"We already have enough for this lifetime and the next."

Myriam found the exchange between them curious.

"Tell Garvis to treat the young lady well. No interrogation and threats. There are enough psychos in this world without our creating another. Let me talk to her myself, with all respect for his command of the operation."

"Okay, Inspector," Jean-Paul answered, leaving to carry out the order.

"You have a good heart," Myriam said, praising him for the sensitivity he had shown.

"No, I don't, ma'am. Almost all my arteries are clogged. Someday they'll do me in," he joked, without showing any humor at all. "Not much to go."

Sarah came out of the bathroom and joined them. She was flushed, tired, and sat down by Myriam.

"Welcome," Gavache greeted her.

"Sorry for the delay," Sarah said weakly. She was shaky.

"We didn't notice. Do you feel all right?" Gavache wanted to know.

"Better," Sarah said, recovering her courage a little.

"We could call a doctor for you," Myriam suggested.

"No," she immediately replied. "Thanks, Myriam. I promise you it'll be the first thing I do when all this is over."

Garvis and Ben Isaac returned from receiving the technician's instructions. Ben Isaac was still angry. He was impatient for the call to come, but at the same time feared it. As a father he needed the call; as an old man, he just wanted to go to sleep and wake up from the nightmare the next day and discover nothing about it was real.

Ben Isaac sat down by his wife, and Garvis took an armchair.

"What now?" Myriam asked.

"Now we wait," Garvis said.

Everyone felt self-conscious except Gavache, who continued to savor the aroma of his tobacco. The others exchanged glances, hoping something would happen.

"Instead of looking at each other like idiots, why don't we tell each other something about ourselves," Gavache suggested.

"What about your history?" Ben asked.

"Mine is boring. From home to work, and from work to home. It's tedious. But yours, Dr. Ben, I'd like to hear. Ultimately, this circus is because of you."

Ben blushed with all the eyes turned on him. As a banker, he was used to being the center of attention, but usually he had everything in control—that is, he had the money—and that wasn't the case here. The money that for so many years had been infallible in corrupting the human soul was useless now. He had lost control of the situation, if he'd ever had it. One of his mother's sayings came to mind as a sign of wisdom: *Man proposes, but God disposes.* In fact, when it was least expected, life easily exposed the fragility of human control, and everything collapsed like a house of cards, as if everything had never existed.

Everyone waited for him to say something, except the technicians and other agents who kept busy maintaining the state-of-the art instruments at top operational capacity, or at least enough that they would not break down when it was time to use them. They weren't interested in Ben Isaac at all, just the opposite.

"You can start with Loyola," Gavache offered, to the surprise of everyone present, including Ben Isaac.

"Loyola?" Ben Isaac inquired.

"Isn't he the indirect cause of all this?"

"No." Ben Isaac smiled, cynically, as if those present were not prepared for a greater truth only he knew. "Loyola only intervened in a story that was two thousand years old. Everything began with Jesus of Nazareth."

Garvis shifted uncomfortably in his chair.

"Hell," Gavache exclaimed. "Maybe we should have something to drink with this. Do you have any coffee?"

"Of course," Ben agreed. "Myriam, could you do us a favor and ask in the kitchen for coffee, tea, milk, something to eat?"

Myriam got up. Sarah started to follow her, but Myriam didn't let her. "Relax, dear. I'll go."

"Let's begin with Jesus of Nazareth, then," Gavache insisted. "We're all anxious to hear about Him."

Ben thought about all his options, but realized he didn't have any. He would tell the truth and hope God was merciful.

"The historical Jesus has nothing to do with the one the Christian world worships. The truth about Jesus has suffered from an enormous conspiracy. Jesus was born—"

The ringing of his phone interrupted this story. The instructions were on the way.

45

JC was an intriguing man. Perhaps if Francesco had met him under different circumstances, his opinion would be different . . . or perhaps not.

From the top of the King David Hotel, Francesco was looking down over all the Old City of Jerusalem, which in the early afternoon swarmed with life. It was cold outside, about thirty degrees. The hotel marked the boundary between the old city and the modern, outside the walls.

Though he didn't feel like a captive, Francesco didn't feel as if he could just open the door and go outside, either. He was in a foreign country with no idea how he got there, no documents, no identification, and no money. He couldn't stop thinking about Sarah. He hadn't talked to her for more than fifteen hours. Was she all right? Where was she? He pictured her. She had such a pretty smile. She could seem bitter and withdrawn, but she was always lovely.

At midday they served lunch in the suite. The *salatim* consisted of *tabuleh*, a *kibbe*, and a salad of peppers and eggplant. The main course was grilled lamb chops with vegetables. Everything tasted good, but Francesco had no appetite.

"Eat. You don't know when you'll have your next meal," JC recommended, drinking some tonic water and lifting a forkful of meat to his mouth.

Francesco didn't want to admit that his stomach was turning over, and that because of his nerves he'd probably vomit anything he ate. The image of Sarah throwing up intervened. Was she better? He forced himself not to think about it. He'd cope with only what he could, and at the moment, that was JC and what he wanted from him. The old man obviously knew that Francesco was nervous and couldn't eat, only drink, because his mouth was so dry that he was constantly moistening it and, as a result, was constantly going to the bathroom.

"Calm down, my friend," JC encouraged him. "History doesn't reward the weak."

"Have you ever felt fear?" Francesco worked up the courage to ask.

"I always killed everything that put fear in me," JC said, putting another piece of meat in his mouth, as if he were just talking about the weather. "There's no reason to be afraid. Your role in this affair is just as an extra with a few lines to speak," he said, smiling.

A crucial question struck Francesco. After several successful years of his career, he knew how to recognize a crucial question. He'd done it many times in press conferences, interviews, at some governmental official's door, elbowing his colleagues on all sides to get the best position, the best angle. But those crucial questions never had anything to do with him. It was always about a case, a personality, an official inquiry into a life not his own. This question was different. The most important he'd ever asked.

"What's going to happen to me when my participation in this *affair* comes to an end?"

JC didn't even look at him when he replied. He continued eating eagerly, as if he had not done so for a long time. "We'll put you on a plane for home. This never happened."

"How can I trust you?" He was afraid to push his luck, but he needed some guarantee.

"You can't. A person's words are worth very little. Things are always changing. What works today doesn't work tomorrow. It's human nature," JC said with his mouth full.

Francesco was increasingly unhappy. Some things were better not to know.

"That said, you're the boyfriend of someone important in all this. Your head is always at risk . . . if you don't act right," JC warned.

The man in the Armani suit entered the room, bringing with him a note of dread. Everything made Francesco shiver. It was surreal. The old man practically threatened him with death if he didn't treat Sarah right.

"How are things?" JC asked his lame assistant.

"Dispersed."

The old man stopped eating and looked at him. "Then the time has come to bring everything together." He wiped his mouth on a napkin.

JC held out his arm to ask his assistant to help him up. The cripple raised him to his feet and gave him his cane.

"Shall we go?" JC said to everyone and no one.

"Go where?" Francesco asked, getting up awkwardly.

JC walked to the door of the suite, aided by the cripple on one side and the cane on the other, leaving Francesco behind. "Let's take a walk. It's time for you to play your part."

46

What were you doing in London?"

"What were *you* doing in London?"

"I'm the one asking the questions here."

"You know perfectly well that you don't have any valid reason to detain me here. Sooner or later you'll receive an angry call from the Vatican asking to release me, and you'll have no other choice."

Jacopo was right, and David Barry knew it. Two countries were abusing the confidence of a third that had no idea what was happening inside its own borders.

The two men were alone in the interrogation room. Jacopo was sweating, it was so hot in the room. He'd taken off his jacket and unbuttoned his shirt halfway. He hadn't been tortured, at least not in the true meaning of the word. No one had laid a finger on him or threatened him physically, except for the heat in the room.

David Barry sat in a chair opposite from him and rested his arms on the table. The white light shone uniformly through the small room, reflected everywhere, even on the door.

"Jacopo Sebastiani, tell me what I want to know, or when the pope calls, I'm going to say that I have no idea what or who he's talking about, have nothing to do with your disappearance, and when you next appear, your decomposed body will be floating in the Thames."

Jacopo swallowed dryly at the idea of finding himself in the dirty, cold river, and shivered despite the heat.

"I don't understand your interest in this affair. There are no Americans involved," Jacopo argued, aware that this wouldn't move things along.

"Everything that concerns our allies concerns us."

"How nice. You're just busybodies, if you ask me."

"Are you going to be like this all day?" Barry was losing patience.

"No, you have to be in Rome by eight tonight," Jacopo joked.

Barry banged his fist on the desk. "If you want to joke, I know how to joke, too. Playing with me is playing with fire."

"Wasn't that what he said?"

"Who?"

"Rafael."

"What is he doing in London?"

"Not even he knows."

"I'm losing patience, Mr. Jacopo." Barry decided to quiet his voice to calm the mood. He had more to gain if Jacopo cooperated. "Rafael may be in danger. We can help him if you tell me the purpose of his trip."

"Rafael knows the hazards of his occupation. Today we're alive, tomorrow only God knows. Don't worry about him."

"What's your function in the Vatican?"

"I'm a historian specializing in comparative religion."

"What's that?"

"Analyzing the similarities and differences between religions."

"Is a course necessary to know that?" It was Barry's turn to be sarcastic. "Why did you come with Rafael to Paris?"

"Who said it was I?"

"Didn't you?"

"I'm here. He's not."

An annoyed sigh escaped Barry. They were going in circles, getting nowhere.

There was a knock, then Aris's head appeared through the half-opened door. "Do you have a minute, David?"

Barry gave Jacopo a dirty look and got up. "I'm coming."

The door closed, leaving Jacopo alone with dozens of images of himself reflected in the mirrored walls. Sweat ran down his face and stained his shirt under his arms. He was weary. He longed for Rome, to return to the comforts of home, even for Norma's strident voice calling him to dinner. Anything was better than this. "Can't you turn off the heat?" he grumbled to himself or whoever might be spying on him.

Then he remembered that someone was probably watching him through one of the mirrors, and smiled. *Go fuck yourselves.* Everything was going as foreseen. *To hell with them all.* The plan was almost concluded.

Barry returned to the room, out of breath. He leaned on the desk and leaned his head into Jacopo's face.

"What's going on here?"

"The heat's on too high," Jacopo enjoyed replying.

"You son of a bitch. You're going to talk, one way or another, you bastard," Barry insulted him. "I'm going to ask you for the last time what you were doing in London. What is Rafael's plan?"

Jacopo smiled cynically. "It's incredible. All this technology, and it doesn't help you at all," he confronted the American. "Ask him tonight. He won't keep it secret."

"I don't like being behind the curve."

"I know what your problem is," Jacopo asserted. "There's a big circus going on in Ben Isaac's house, and you don't have any eyes or ears there. You have no idea what's going on," he said. Despite being fed up with being there, that fact amused him.

"Are you telling me that that's all your doing?"

"Of course. Wherever you go, we've been there already and know more than you."

"Rafael's there, then?"

"What a fixation, man! You still don't see that Rafael is just a pawn in the game? He follows orders, nothing more."

"And the circus is part of those orders?"

Jacopo sighed. "Rafael has no idea what's happening in Ben Isaac's house. All this is much bigger than him."

47

One can, and should be, suspicious of assumptions. Just because a sinner says he has a gun pointed at the head of the confessor doesn't mean it should be believed. Empirical proof is necessary, and the wooden screen between them does not allow for that. But the confessor opened the screen and saw the barrel of a gun pointed at his head, followed by a hand and body, and identified the man holding it.

"Rafael?"

"Robin."

"What are you doing here? Drop that shit." He tried not to change his voice too much. Confessionals are not soundproof.

Rafael didn't answer the question. He kept the Beretta

pointed, holding it only in one hand, with the safety still on.

"What's going on?" Robin asked.

"You tell me. Put your hands where I can see them." He wasn't joking.

Robin looked confused, but Rafael didn't believe it for a second. He needed answers and was there to get them.

"Please, Rafael. We're men of God. Put that down, for the love of God," Robin argued, visibly uncomfortable.

"Men of God don't murder innocent people. Tell me who the Jesuit is who's going around killing people who helped us in the past, and why." Rafael's voice expressed some anger.

"What do I have to do with that?"

"You should know what's going on in your society. Where can I find Nicolas?"

Robin did not reply. Rafael removed the safety. Robin remained pensive for a few moments. He considered the options, then opened the door of the confessional and got up.

"I forgive you. In the name of the Father, the Son, and the Holy Spirit." He made the sign of the cross as he said each word. "Follow me, and put that away. Show some respect for my church," he whispered, and left.

Rafael waited a few seconds, holstered the gun in the front of his jacket, and left the confessional, lighter, free of sins. He followed Robin to the sacristy. He looked around for acolytes, priests, auxiliary people; he didn't want to be surprised. It was ironic not to feel safe in the house of the Lord. If you couldn't find safety there, it existed nowhere in the world.

They left the church from a side door, which opened onto a cream-colored corridor. They passed a door with a plaque that read *Sacristy* and two more, *Secretary* and the other unidentified. At the end Robin opened a final door. The plaque bore his own name, Father Robin Roth. He waited for Rafael and let him go in first, as good manners dictate, then he closed and locked it.

"Would you like a drink?"

"I'm fine, thanks."

"Sit down," he invited, pointing at two stuffed chairs in the office. A desk at the back displayed a computer screen, which was on; two bookcases with shelves from floor to ceiling filled one of the walls. A simple cross hung on the other wall, without Christ, but only an engraving on the horizontal arm with the three letters that were the soul of the Society, IHS.

Rafael kept his hand on the gun, inside the pocket of his jacket, as if he were cold.

"No one's going to hurt you in here," Robin assured him.

"Start talking, Robin. I don't have all day."

Robin sat down and sighed. It wasn't a subject he wanted to take on. "Were you with Gunter?"

"Until the end."

"That must have been shitty."

Rafael agreed. A silent look said it all. Sure, it was shitty, one more image to forget, a friend to erase from memory, a past, a life. Fuck it. He'd deal with it later, one day when everything was confounded in a mass of dreams, thoughts, things that were and others that were not, a fog that time always had the ability to create to attenuate sorrow and happiness, the good and the bad.

"Have you ever heard of the *Secret Monition*?" Robin asked, crossing his legs for more comfort.

"Of course. Its authority was attributed to Claudio Acquaviva, one of the first superior generals of the Society of Jesus in the seventeenth century. According to my memory, it was all a forgery by some Pole who was expelled from the society."

"Do you know what it was for?" Robin asked in a professorial tone.

"According to malicious tongues, it was instructions and methods for helping the society gain importance and influence in communities they infiltrated and in other institutions of power. Am I right?"

"Correct."

Robin got up from the chair and went to the desk. He took a key out of his pocket and opened a drawer. Rafael took the gun inside his jacket pocket in his hand. Robin took out an ancient book, whose cover was coming apart. It had seen better days. He returned to the chair and handed the book to the Italian.

"What's this?"

"Read it."

Rafael felt the book, turned it over in his hands, looked at the cover, the title page, the back page, tried to identify a certain odor; the exterior gave no clue whatsoever, no engraving, just brown leather, worn by time. He opened it. The first three pages were blank, yellowed, frayed, almost sticking together. On the fourth page he understood everything. Stamped in capital letters, *MONITA SECRETA,* and in smaller letters, a subtitle, *Methods and Advice.* The name of the author was below, a little indistinct, Ignatius Loyola, and the year, 1551.

"Interesting," Rafael murmured. He turned to the next page, where the text began in Spanish.

"The *Monition* is one of Loyola's works?"

"Exactly. He always knew what he wanted for the society, and he left it in writing. What you have in your hand is the reason for our success and longevity," Robin explained.

The *Secret Monition* was a polemical work that many insisted didn't exist or was a fraud. There was always constant doubt about its authorship. It was attributed to Acquaviva, the superior general between 1581 and 1615, always with great uncertainty, but no one dared once to claim that Loyola was the author. This fact was new.

"Why was this necessary?" Rafael wanted to know. "Why such intransigence?"

"Don't speak nonsense," Robin criticized him. "We're not a religious order, and you know it."

"Then what are you?"

Robin didn't answer. He was searching for the right words.

"What are you, Robin?" Rafael insisted.

"We are the front line of the Roman Catholic Church."

"Please, Robin. Spare me the bullshit."

"Since 1523."

"Now you have ten more years?" Rafael mocked. "Didn't the founding in Paris occur in 1534 in Saint-Denis?"

"You don't know the half of it, Rafael. Only two minutes ago you didn't know Saint Ignatius was the author of the *Monition*," Robin admonished.

Rafael had to concede the point. He was there for answers, and Robin was providing them. Rafael let him go on.

"You should know about Saint Ignatius's voyage to Jerusalem in 1523." Robin didn't wait for Rafael to confirm. History said that Saint Ignatius had had visions and various spiritual experiences in Manresa. He decided to go to Jerusalem and devote himself to saving souls. He and some followers had gone to Rome at the time of the event to ask for Pope Adrian the Sixth's authorization. That's the official version. But Loyola was never interested in going to Jerusalem. That was meaningless for him. He had a project, a vision, and if, in order to achieve it, he had to do a favor for someone, he would do it."

"Then who sent him to Jerusalem?"

"The cardinal of Florence, Giulio de' Medici," Robin revealed.

"It was Clement the Seventh who asked him to go to Jerusalem?" Rafael wanted to verify. He couldn't afford any misunderstandings.

"Of course it was."

"What did the pope want him to do there?"

"Note that Giulio de' Medici was still not pope in September. He became pope only in November, and Loyola helped him with that. The correct question is, What did the cardinal of Florence want him to look for there?" Robin clarified, stroking his beard.

Rafael waited for the answer. What the hell would it be? Robin delayed on purpose.

"I'm dying of thirst from so much talking."

"You're not going to stop now, are you?" Rafael grumbled.

Robin laughed lightly. He was enjoying this.

"What was he looking for?"

"Papers," Robin answered, watching the reaction.

"Papers?" Rafael was surprised.

"Parchments," Robin specified.

Rafael had been sent several times for parchments and papyri that the church considered important for one reason or another. Jordan, Syria, Israel, Iraq, Saudi Arabia, as well as western Europe. Sometimes as a mere courier, other times as a thief or buyer, depending on the case or who possessed them. There was a black market in manuscripts, Rafael knew well. It was more than probable that it had existed for centuries or even millennia. Given that Loyola went to Jerusalem to recover parchments for the church five hundred years ago, the idea was not unbelievable.

"Loyola went to Jerusalem and returned shortly afterward," Rafael reflected.

"It was extremely quick," Robin added. "If it were

today, he would have gone and returned the same day. Considering the travel conditions in the sixteenth century, he traveled fast. He spent only twenty days in Jerusalem."

Rafael nodded his head in agreement. "So what were the parchments?"

"Parchments that mentioned parchments that talked about bones," Robin said cryptically.

Parchments that mentioned parchments that talked about bones, Rafael repeated mentally. Nothing strange. Many of the sepulchers most visited by tourists in modern times owed their existence to information about their exact location found in ancient texts. It was customary to record in several places the locations of those who had departed this world.

"You know as well as I do that Jewish funeral rites in Jerusalem in the first century were very different from ours," Robin continued.

"I have some idea, but I'm not well versed in the subject."

"I understand. You're more versed in how they put their dead in caves rather than burying them," Robin said a little scornfully.

Rafael said nothing. He who speaks truth does not deserve punishment.

"In general, the Jews did not bury their own as frequently as we do, or didn't bury them completely. They put them in tombs carved in the rock. There could be one or many chambers, well carved or not, depending on the owner or how much money he had, and they were constructed for entire families, except for the women who married into other families. They washed the corpse with water, always from top to bottom, so that impurities from the feet didn't contaminate other parts of the body. Then they applied oils and perfumes. The corpse was wrapped in a linen shroud, a *sadin*. Sometimes they used expensive, imported, woven cloth, but we know that He was wrapped in a new linen shroud. This whole procedure was carried out by Joseph of Arimathea and Nicodemus, according to the Holy Scriptures. The arms were stretched along the sides of the body, and the feet were tied before wrapping the corpse in the shroud. There was a clear separation between the head and the body. The head was never covered by the *sadin*. What covered the head was called a *sudarion*."

"A burial cloth," Rafael repeated.

"This way, if the *dead* man"—Robin sketched quotation marks with his fingers—"should come back to life, he would not suffocate. There are numerous stories of relatives who found their dear departed sitting up, waiting for them inside the tomb. One of them is about Anaias, who was found waiting for his family sitting in the tomb, and went on to live more than twenty-five more years."

"I've heard of him."

"From this custom in antiquity, the Byzantines began to install small bells in their cemeteries connected by a cord to the coffin. They would be activated if the dead should wake up."

Rafael knew about this custom. There was even possible evidence from very ancient European cemeteries. With advances in medicine these customs disappeared, but in Latin countries, where they interred the dead as quickly as possible, it was not rare to find on the lids of excavated coffins fingernail scratches of those who had awakened too late.

"The Jewish custom was to keep the corpses in niches carved in stone walls in places called *kokhim*. Unless the death occurred from mutilation or execution, relatives always wanted to be certain their loved one was dead, and not in a kind of coma between *sheol*, the world of the dead, and that of the living. People were afraid of being buried alive. So they visited their dead for three days or more, not only to verify the actual death, but because this was part of the ceremony. They prostrated themselves before the corpse in respect and used lotions and potions so that the passage to *sheol* was made correctly. In any case, the subsequent visit to the tomb of Christ was a perfectly normal custom established in the Jewish community. The body remained in the *kokhim* for a year or more. Because of the geological and climatic conditions of Jerusalem, at the end of a year the body would be totally decomposed, and another ritual began. The bones were taken from the *kokhim* and placed in ossuaries—stone chests—normally engraved with the name or names of the dead inside. They were then deposited in another place in the tomb, another chamber or space, depending on how the tomb was constructed. No two tombs were alike. Also there were excavated trenches, the *ossilegium*, where the bones of previous generations reposed. It was not uncommon for the dead man to awaken during the ritual of three days' visitation. There are even some who claim . . ." Robin hesitated. Even for him it was a sacrilege to suggest such a theory.

"That's what happened to Lazarus," Rafael concluded for him.

Robin looked disdainfully at him. "Do you also believe this theory?"

"I neither believe it nor disbelieve it. It makes no difference to me whether Jesus rose from the dead or never died. I'm an arm or leg, not the head or heart of the church," he explained coolly.

"You're the arm or leg because the church today doesn't have a head. The society was always the front line and cornerstone of the Catholic Church."

"*Perinde ac cadaver,* Robin. Your oath," Rafael quoted with a sarcastic smile. He opened the book and leafed through it. "I'll bet it's here somewhere."

"Cut the shit," Robin swore, and got up and grabbed the *Secret Monition* out of Rafael's hands. "Don't give me demagogy."

"To obey the pope like a cadaver. Loyola's fault. It was your idea. If it doesn't serve you now . . ." Rafael continued to provoke him.

"You know perfectly well why it doesn't serve us," Robin pointed out bitterly. "Ratzinger himself made his decision. You can't blame us for that."

"I'm just saying you obey the pope blindly, as was proposed from the beginning, all the time, not just when it's convenient for you."

"Fuck you, Santini," Robin said, furious. "You don't know what you're talking about."

Rafael controlled himself. He didn't want Robin to lose patience completely. There were still things to explain.

"Maybe you're right. You're much better informed about these things than I." He tried to calm their tempers.

"The society always has the higher interest of the church in mind. History proves it," Robin argued, still a little irritated. "We went out on missions to every corner of the earth, converting more faithful than any other religious order, new people for the ranks of the church. We went where no other Christian had ever gone, and are still established there today. We preach the word of the Lord in the language the faithful understand, thinking about them and not the costs. We invented confession, plenary indulgences, and gave the church the power of omnipresence. If the leaders of the church weaken and decide to betray us, should we continue to serve blindly?" He paused to let his words sink in. "*Ad maiorem Dei gloriam* is what the society proclaims, and not *Ad maiorem papam gloriam*."

It was not worth pursuing the argument. Rafael shifted uncomfortably in his chair. He wasn't going to continue a one-sided discussion. It was obvious to him that the society owed respect to the pope, and once they depended on him directly, even more respect. There was a huge divide between the Holy See and the Society of Jesus, the white pope and the black pope. Which one was most powerful? He couldn't say. His duty was to defend Ratzinger, and he would do it until the end.

"You mentioned parchments that referred to other parchments that spoke of bones." Rafael returned to the subject that really interested him.

"There were."

"Put it simply."

Robin sighed. This was the most delicate subject. He'd already told Rafael too much, more than he should have, some of which might blacken the reputation of the society and the good name of Saint Ignatius, but nothing compared with what was coming. Rafael had been the one to ask, and would be the one to suffer the consequences.

"Since Jesus died, though, there have always been questions"—he searched for the right word—"what happened to him."

"He arose on the third day," Rafael objected.

"That's the fairy tale they tell in catechism."

"We don't need any other," Rafael argued. One shouldn't complicate what was simple.

"It was good enough, Santini—in fact, for many years—but things changed with the Inquisition."

"The Inquisition is always to blame," he replied.

"The Inquisition, as you know, created antibodies. The Jews, who had no love for Catholics, earned our hatred, a hatred that endures even today."

Robin continued to relate how the Jews who fled

started actual expeditions to the Holy Land, sometimes disguised as converted Christians or even as Muslims. The remains of parchments began to appear. Nothing special at first, later parchments from Jerusalem, Qumran, Syria, and the Middle East. *Miqwa'ot*, tombs, ossuaries. The church tried to keep on top of these discoveries, paid thieves and tomb robbers to intercept whatever was excavated, but that *Hanukkah* gang—Robin's words—always defended themselves well. In the time of Leo X in 1517, rumors were heard for the first time of the discovery of a parchment that identified the location of the tomb that held Christ, and that text mentioned another parchment that had never been heard of before . . . the Gospel of Jesus.

"The *what*?" Rafael asked, astonished. Had he heard right? He got up and took off his jacket. He needed air. "What parchment is it that mentions that gospel?"

"The Gospel of Mary Magdalene."

"But that didn't appear until the nineteenth century."

"It *reappeared* in the nineteenth century is a better way to put it. Loyola never succeeded in bringing it to Rome."

"It's too much to take in at one time," Rafael complained.

"Do you think?" Robin asked, seated with his legs crossed and Loyola's book on his lap. "That's nothing. The worst is yet to come."

48

—◆—

"M anuscripts? What manuscripts?" Schmidt asked, looking out the window.

A downpour with heavy wind was pounding Rome. Below, in Saint Peter's Square, a few brave souls tried to zip up their raincoats, and others ran under the arcade to seek shelter. Banks of black clouds closed over the Eternal City as if preparing for the universal flood. The tourists and faithful looked like insects scurrying from the water and sheltering under its immense roof. It was afternoon in the Vatican, but it looked more like nighttime.

"The weather's not going to change today," William observed indifferently.

"If it's confidential, I understand," Schmidt said, excusing himself. He didn't want to put Tarcisio in a difficult position. Whatever was going to happen was enough.

William shot a constraining look at the secretary. Obviously he wasn't going to share a papal secret with a simple priest, especially if he might cease to be one soon.

"It's confidential," Tarcisio confirmed uncomfortably. He wanted to reveal everything and let the logical, rational mind of the Austrian iceman analyze the case and come to conclusions, but he couldn't do that in front of William.

Whether by fate or divine intervention, Trevor, the secretary of state's assistant, knocked lightly on the door and came in with a cordless phone in his hand.

"Excuse the interruption, Your Eminence," he said fearfully.

"What is it, Trevor?"

"A call for Cardinal William."

"Who is it?" William asked, approaching Trevor.

"David Barry, Your Eminence."

William took the phone from Trevor, or, more correctly, snatched it from his hand. "If it's all right with you, I'll talk outside, gentlemen."

"Do as you wish, William," Tarcisio said.

William left with Trevor behind him, and the two men continued to watch the heavy rain come down on the square.

"If this keeps up, the Tiber will overflow its banks," Schmidt observed.

"Let's hope it stops. I'm going to pray it does." Tarcisio turned his back on the window and went to sit on the leather sofa. He was too old to confront the Sodom and

Gomorrah that contaminated society. The world was going to hell, and at an amazing speed. To find young people capable of devoting themselves to more than video games and iPods was like looking for a needle in a haystack. Consumerism was the new religion and, with every day that passed, gained followers more easily than any other faith.

A lightning bolt lit up the dark day for a brief instant, followed immediately by a deafening thunderclap.

"God save us!" Tarcisio cried out, terrified. "Sit next to me," he asked Schmidt. "I'm going to tell you the story of the manuscripts."

Schmidt approached his friend and held up his hand. "Tarcisio, I don't want you to tell me things you cannot or ought not tell," he said forcefully. "Friendship should not override duty."

Tarcisio smiled. An admonishment like that could come only from Schmidt, who was always more concerned about the welfare of others than his own. Friends like Schmidt were becoming extinct.

"Sit down, my friend," he sighed with consternation. "The problem is that I don't trust William."

"Why not?" Schmidt asked curiously, sitting down by his Italian friend.

"I'm not sure he can be trusted."

"He's a cardinal in the Apostolic Roman Catholic Church, a prince of the church, like you. He is the prefect of the Congregation for the Doctrine of the Faith. What more do you need?" Schmidt argued.

"I know his credentials, Hans. That's not the problem, nor is his dedication to the church," Tarcisio replied, choosing his words carefully. "I don't know what side he's on or what his goal is."

"Is that your impression?" Schmidt asked, almost condescendingly. "His methods have gotten results. Rafael has gotten information. The girl is with Ben Isaac. Skepticism aside, he's given us a suspect, and what a suspect. The glorious Society of Jesus."

Tarcisio listened attentively. A cold analysis, based only on facts, relegating opinion and feelings to second place. That's how Schmidt was. That's why Tarcisio needed him.

"Maybe it's just an impression," Tarcisio agreed.

"It is. He's on our side," his friend assured him.

"Let's forget that," the secretary decided to change the subject. "The parchments I was telling you about were mentioned for the first time during the time of Leo the Tenth, specifically in 1517."

Egidio Canisio, a prelate whom Leo X named a cardinal, had a prestigious professor of Hebrew with vast connections in Jerusalem. His name was Elias Levita. It was he who told Leo X about a document that mentioned where the bones of Christ reposed.

"That would be a disaster," Schmidt remarked.

"Leo the Tenth knew that. He was an astute businessman before he became a man of the church."

"I know. He was the one who had the bright idea to sell indulgences," Schmidt mocked.

"Don't remind me. He offered a license to sell indulgences in all the Germanic territories to a Dominican, Johann Tetzel. That's why Luther did what he did."

"That's another story," Schmidt said, going back to the subject they were discussing.

"Well, moving along, Leo the Tenth kept everything secret and appointed his nephew to personally investigate the matter."

Giulio, the nephew, understood that to control the situation they had to get the parchments and get rid of the witnesses. He had just the man for the job.

"Who?" Schmidt wanted to know.

"Saint Ignatius," Tarcisio suddenly answered.

The Jesuits, Schmidt thought.

Tarcisio noticed the connection his friend was making. Rafael's suspicion was not as crazy as it sounded.

"Loyola completed his mission," Schmidt said, with a gesture for Tarcisio to go on.

"The Society of Jesus was the reward. Loyola brought the parchments and much more," Tarcisio said thoughtfully.

"The bones of Christ," Schmidt added.

The secretary nodded, as if putting it into words was too painful.

"Where are those documents?" Schmidt asked.

"The Jesuits are their faithful keepers. They confide them to the pope only on the night of his election."

"And the bones?"

"Also in their possession," Tarcisio said, exhausted.

Schmidt got up and went to the window again. Historical facts, holy men, prestige, legends—none of this mattered. Only information, validated with some skepticism. Feelings were inimical to thoughtful decisions. He paced back and forth from one window to another, from the desk to the sofa, comparing the facts Tarcisio gave him with those he'd assimilated the night before.

"All right, if Loyola recovered the parchments and bones and remained the faithful guardian of them, from which the Jesuits derive their power, only one question remains, assuming the Jesuits are involved in this." Schmidt paced back and forth with his chin in his hand.

Tarcisio waited expectantly for the question.

"What piece is missing for them?" Schmidt concluded.

Tarcisio looked as if he didn't understand.

"Leo the Tenth was the first to struggle with the problem. He appointed his nephew, the future Clement the Seventh, to investigate. Clement, for his part, recovered the documents and the bones. Problem solved. What is it that they want? What could be more important than the . . . *bones of Christ*?" he said in a whisper.

"The Gospel of Jesus," Tarcisio informed him.

Schmidt looked at his friend incredulously. "What did you say?"

"Just what you heard. That's what they're after." It was Tarcisio's turn to connect the dots. "As you said, they have everything except that piece of the puzzle. They eliminated everyone they fought with, directly or indirectly, for the relics and became the faithful guardians, as happened with Loyola." That was it. It could only be that. Simple, silent, bloody.

"With one difference," Schmidt interposed. "This time without the pope's consent."

"Jesuit dissidence is not a new thing. It goes back to the beginning of John Paul the Second's papacy. There were also some quarrels with other pontiffs that were resolved. The greatest interference, involving Wojtyla, was over Superior General Pedro Arrupe's resignation. A pope had never named a papal delegate to preside over the General Congregation that was going to elect a new superior general. The Jesuits were resentful and offended. They considered an insurrection against the pope," Tarcisio explained.

"But Paolo Dezza, the delegate Lolek chose, was a Jesuit," Schmidt argued.

"But he wasn't named by the superior general."

"Because Pedro Arrupe was in no condition to do so," Schmidt said, showing some indignation. "A stroke had left him partially paralyzed and unable to speak clearly."

"Go explain that to them. For many Jesuits it was an outrage," the secretary continued.

Schmidt frowned and changed the subject. "I assume it's in Ben Isaac's possession."

Tarcisio nodded. "That gospel is very intriguing."

The gospel was mentioned for the first time in the apocryphal Gospel of Mary Magdalene, the same one that revealed the correct location of Christ's tomb. Who better than Magdalene to know where He was buried? Who better to guard a gospel written by her own companion, Jesus?

"So Loyola didn't recover the Gospel of Jesus?" Schmidt asked.

"He couldn't find it. The Gospel of Magdalene, as you know, was not complete."

Pius IX got involved in the nineteenth century. He read the secret and formed a trusted group to investigate. They found three more parchments that mentioned the Gospel of Jesus and, more seriously, when and where and by whom it was written . . . but not the gospel itself."

Tarcisio wiped the sweat from his face.

Every previous attempt to find the Gospel of Jesus had failed. The only certainty was that it did in fact exist.

"Until Ben Isaac," Tarcisio declared.

"Until Ben Isaac," Schmidt repeated, looking at his friend. "Something's bothering me, though. The society and the church are on the same side. Why all this conflict? Couldn't they negotiate and arrive at an agreement? The Jesuits wanted the Gospel. Why not negotiate with Ben Isaac?"

Tarcisio smiled as he got up, bent over with the effort. "The society and the church haven't been on the same side for a long time." He looked down again on the empty square below, lashed by the wind and incessant rain.

"They must have talked about it?" Schmidt asked.

"Many times," Tarcisio answered painfully. "Today I have to meet with Adolph."

"Let him know you know what's going on. Lean on him," Schmidt suggested.

"It doesn't help, Hans. I'm going to be talking with the CEO of a large corporation. There are many interests at play. The Jesuits know they can't attack us directly." He sighed and wiped his face again. "Nor can we attack them."

William returned to the papal office, flushed, obviously tired.

"The CIA is on to us," he said.

"That's all we needed," Tarcisio grumbled.

"What do they have to do with all this?" Schmidt asked.

"What do they have to do with anything they get involved in?" Tarcisio protested, and looked at William. "Excuse me, William, but your compatriots are always sticking their nose into situations that don't concern them."

William could have said, *Look who's talking,* but he was silent. Tarcisio had a point.

"What do they want?" the secretary inquired.

"They want to know about Rafael, Ben Isaac, and Sarah. They know something, but don't really know what they know. They have Jacopo. I gave them a few crumbs of information in exchange for his release."

"You didn't have to give them anything. He could have

been released if he'd been patient. Are they going to be a problem?"

"I don't think so."

"Any news from Rafael?"

"He's going to have dinner with the director of the CIA at Memmo. Now he's lying low in Mayfair at the Church of the Immaculate Conception."

Tarcisio whispered, "Let's hope he gets away intact."

49

David Barry was better informed after talking with Cardinal William on the phone. Jacopo had revealed almost nothing, but had said that, if he wanted to know more, Barry should contact Jacopo's superior, who by coincidence was a fellow American. David Barry played this same card, talking about Long Beach and the RMS *Queen Mary,* the transatlantic liner that now served as a hotel and museum, permanently anchored at that California city. He also talked about Houston's incomparable museum and theater district, aware that a cardinal, unfortunately, always owes his duty to the pope and not his country of birth. That's how careers are. Everyone sells his work and loyalty to his job.

"Did you call me?" Aris asked from the director's office door.

"Yes. Come in and close the door."

Aris came in and sat down without being asked.

"I talked with the Holy See," Barry informed him.

"Okay, you've got my attention."

"It was the only thing I could drag out of that son-of-a-bitch historian. The name of his superior, Cardinal William, who happens to be from Long Beach," Barry muttered.

"Long Beach? How does someone from Long Beach become a cardinal?" Aris asked curiously.

"The conversation was cordial. They have almost everything under control," Barry continued, ignoring Aris's remark.

"Do you believe that?"

"Of course not. I threw him a few crumbs to let him know we're informed without letting him know we're just outside the door."

"And the door is still shut," Aris added, jokingly. "And locked."

"Well, he half opened it. An Islamic terrorist group kidnapped Ben Isaac's son."

"Who's claiming it?"

"Islamic Jihad."

"Those bastards."

"They go after the very rich, study them, analyze their weaknesses, and then strike. In this case, Ben Isaac's son," Barry explained, joining his hands together on the desk.

Aris thought about the story for several moments and then found flaws. "That doesn't explain what happened in Paris, or Rafael's presence."

"That's what I thought," Barry agreed.

"What did Cardinal William say?"

"That Ben Isaac was a devout Catholic and well thought of by the church. Besides, he has *partnerships* with the Vatican and the Bank of the Holy Spirit."

"A banker with interest in banks. Tell me something new," Aris said sarcastically. "So the guy gives money to the church, and that's why the priests want to save him. This doesn't explain the murders. Or the agreement, the Status Quo."

"The agreement was another weakness for Ben Isaac. An agreement between financiers. They used the excavations as a way for Ben Isaac to transfer money to the church legally as investments. Islamic Jihad eliminated almost everyone involved to demonstrate they weren't kidding, and would kill his son in the blink of an eye."

They thought over William's explanations, looking for a flaw.

"Does that seem believable?" Aris asked finally, lifting his hands behind his neck to stretch.

"Not at all. The English and French have taken charge of the rescue operation. Let's wait and see. Then in Rome we'll know everything. Tell Sam to investigate these *partnerships*," David said, making quotation marks in the air, "between Ben Isaac and the Vatican and the Bank of the Holy Spirit."

"Okay." Aris got up promptly, went to the door, and turned toward Barry. "Does this mean that Rafael doesn't know what he's doing?"

"Apparently." Barry took out his gun, checked the bullets, and returned it to his holster.

"Are you leaving?"

"Let's go," Barry said, grabbing his jacket. "Take care of the calls and come with me to the garage. It's time to deal the cards."

50

The voice echoed from the speakers in perfect English. Everyone listened in tense silence, some scarcely breathing. Garvis kept his hand in the air to restrain gestures or words. Ben Isaac was standing up next to the dining room table full of electronic paraphernalia. A few technicians were seated with headphones, listening in. Others connected the call to special software that displayed the voices in graphic color on the computer screens.

Sarah put her arm around Myriam, who remained seated on the sofa, shivering with every word from the cold voice issuing from the speakers. This was the man who had hurt her son. Calculating and implacable.

"Stay calm, Myriam," Sarah whispered in her ear. "Everything is going to be okay. It's almost over."

Myriam wanted to believe those sweet words, but knew they were only painkillers for her soul.

"Listen carefully because I'm only going to say it once," the male voice said. "Since you ignored our instructions to get rid of the journalist, we're going to give you a *final* opportunity." No one missed the emphasis on the word *final*. "She'll be the one to hand over the parchments. If Sarah Monteiro isn't at the Gare du Nord in two hours with the parchments in her hand, your son will die. We won't call again. *Ciao,* Ben Isaac."

The call ended abruptly. The man had been very clear. There was no room for doubt. All eyes were on Sarah. Since she'd left Francesco in their room at the Grand Hotel Palatino, everything had been out of her hands. The conversation with William in the Palazzo Madama, his instructions, going to meet Ben Isaac, the flight, the morning sickness, everything had unfolded with a will of its own that she didn't recognize at all. It was enough to show her that even the remote appearance of control was pure delusion. She'd known it for a long time, since Florence, since JC, Rafael, Simon Templar, and John Fox. Ben Isaac, Myriam, and their son, the French inspector, the English one, all the paraphernalia to detect the undetectable, the phone call, Francesco, Rafael again, always . . . None of this had impressed her. No one controlled anything except God, if He existed, who controlled everything.

Myriam hugged Sarah tightly. "Bring me my son, Sarah," she pleaded desperately. "Don't let them hurt him. Don't."

Garvis lowered his hand, and frenzy broke out in an ordered chaos that only those involved understood.

"Do we have a location?" Garvis asked.

"Rome," two technicians said.

"Jerusalem," said another.

"London."

"Düsseldorf."

"Oslo."

"Does this mean we don't have a location, Jean-Paul?" Gavache interjected.

"We're lost, Inspector."

"What's going on? The call lasted for more than a minute," Garvis asked uncomfortably.

"One minute and fifty-six seconds," Jean-Paul added, to give some precision to the information.

"We are unable to locate the origin of the call," one of the technicians said. "They obviously know they're being monitored."

"I agree," Gavache said, taking a draw on his cigarette. "Or now they're monitoring us."

Ben Isaac was exhausted and pulled out a chair to sit down. "And now? And now what's going to happen to my son?"

"Now? And now, Jean-Paul?" Gavache asked, looking at Ben Isaac.

"We'll do what they say."

Gavache turned his glance from Ben Isaac to Sarah hugging Myriam. Garvis approached her. "Are you willing to do what the kidnappers demand, Sarah?"

Sarah didn't answer right away. She felt Myriam's arms squeezing her ever more tightly. It was as if not only the life of her son, little Ben, depended on Sarah's reply, but her own as well. There was only one answer.

"You can count on me," she finally said, timidly. She didn't feel like a heroine, just the opposite.

Myriam's embrace tightened even more, if that were possible. "Thank you, Sarah. You're an angel."

"I wasn't just talking, Myriam," she whispered in the ear of the stricken woman to calm her. "Everything is going to be all right."

"Excellent," Gavache applauded.

"We need your help," Garvis advised Gavache. "We don't have much time, and a crucial part of the operation is going to take place in your country."

"*Bien sûr.* Relax, Garvis. I'm going to convey the situation to the minister of the interior and prepare the team," Gavache said calmly. "I need to have them in place at the location in Paris the kidnappers specified."

"I'm going to commandeer a plane immediately," Garvis informed them, taking his cell phone out of his pocket.

"Jean-Paul," Gavache called.

He appeared at his side almost before his boss finished pronouncing his name.

"You're going to accompany Sarah from the first minute to the last. Give her all the protection she needs. Don't forget about her condition. Provide her every comfort possible. Understood?" he asked in French.

"Perfectly, Inspector."

"Guard her with your life if necessary. I'll find you later."

Gavache went over to Ben Isaac, who was holding his face in his hands, as if he were carrying the weight of the world, his world, and put his hand on Ben Isaac's shoulder. "We're going to fulfill our part. Now it's time for you to fulfill yours."

Ben Isaac uncovered his face and looked at the Frenchman arrogantly. "Tell me, Inspector. What do you mean by 'fulfilling your part'?"

"Look around." Gavache raised his hand and pointed around the room. "An international team dedicated to solving *your* problem. No one here knows your son, but they're doing everything possible to rescue him. As if he were their own son. They could lose their life doing it. A woman who could very well just turn her back on all this is risking her life without asking anything in return. We're going to complete our part, Ben Isaac."

The banker remained seated, staring into space. He analyzed all the options, and finally looked disdainfully at Sarah. "Why?"

Sarah didn't understand the question. With her exhaustion and nausea, she was slow to respond.

"Why are you risking yourself for us?" Ben Isaac continued. "You've only known us for a few hours. You tried to kill her."

Sarah lowered her glance. Duty, solidarity, ethics, love of one's neighbor—there was no shortage of reasons. Ben Isaac could choose the one he wanted.

"The kidnappers didn't leave me any option," she chose to answer, with a half smile. She was nervous.

"I don't want to turn over the parchments," Ben Isaac finally confessed.

Garvis, who'd gone off, returned to the group. "The plane is being serviced now. It'll take off from Gatwick in twenty minutes. We've got to hurry."

"We're waiting for Dr. Ben Isaac," Gavache told him. "It looks like he doesn't want to cooperate, is that right, Jean-Paul?"

"Right, Inspector. He doesn't want to pay the ransom."

"We'll have to give them something," Garvis explained. "We'll place a detector in the parchments, so we can keep track of their location at all times."

"You've seen what kind of people we're dealing with, Inspector Garvis. They're always one step ahead," Gavache warned.

Garvis approached Gavache conspiratorially. "We'll have to improvise with whatever bait we can use."

"If an agent were making the delivery, I'd risk his neck, Garvis. But we're dealing with professionals, and it's an inexperienced civilian who's going to be exposing herself to the bullets." He looked at Sarah, who was listening apprehensively. "Speaking figuratively, of course. I don't think it's a good idea for her to carry bait instead of the originals."

"There must be another solution," Ben Isaac offered.

Myriam shrugged off Sarah's arm and turned to her husband. Tears were running down her face. The slap she gave her husband was hard, and echoed through the room. "This is all your fault, Ben Isaac," she said, giving him a sorrowful, cold stare. "Do you want to kill my son? Is that what you want? Do you want to send an innocent person to her death, carrying false papers? This is not the man I married." She turned her back and left the room.

The room was in shock.

Garvis looked at his watch and frowned. "We don't have much time."

"What's it going to be, Dr. Ben Isaac?" Gavache pressured him as he brought a cigarette to his lips.

Ben Isaac took a pen, wrote something on a piece of paper, and handed it to the French inspector with a resigned expression. "The code to open the vault."

Gavache gave it to Jean-Paul, who hurried toward the underground chamber.

"Sarah, we're going to wait for the parchments in the car. We have to hurry. Time's running out."

Two agents escorted Sarah to the car. Garvis put on his jacket and saw Gavache sit down next to Ben Isaac. "Aren't you coming?" Garvis asked.

"Jean-Paul's going to escort the woman. I'll come later."

"As soon as I have Sarah sitting in the plane, it's your problem."

"Don't worry. Everything's under control. Thanks, Garvis." Gavache looked at the defeated Ben Isaac. "Now I want to hear that incredible story that was interrupted by the phone call. Tell me about Jesus Christ."

51

The conversation had reached a pause. Robin excused himself, his full bladder urging him. Rafael felt uncomfortable, and the Jesuit noticed it.

"It's out there to the left," Robin pointed to a door down the corridor. "You'll see it. Relax. No one's going to do anything . . . unless I give the order."

Robin went into the second door on the left and didn't take much time. Two minutes later there was a flush, followed by the priest washing his hands. He came out with his hands dripping and dried them on a towel hanging behind the office door.

"Still afraid of germs?" Rafael joked.

"Laugh away. You have no idea of the pests that surround us. If we're not careful, they'll do us in," Robin said with conviction.

"We have bigger things to worry about now."

"Do you know it was a Jesuit who discovered the microbes invisible to the naked eye that are responsible for the black plague and other diseases?" Robin asked, assuming a professorial tone.

"Athanasius Kircher." Rafael sounded like a student who thought he knew it all. "The master of a hundred arts. He was one of the first people to observe microbes through a microscope in the seventeenth century. German by birth, he was considered the ultimate Renaissance man. He was the author of innumerable treatises, not only on medicine but also on geology, magnetism, and even music. A true Da Vinci, this Jesuit."

Robin looked at him with mock disdain before sitting down. "Now, where were we?"

"You know very well where we left things. Keep going."

Robin crossed his legs and licked his lips. "What do you know about Jesus?"

"He was born in Bethlehem and crucified at thirty-three. . . ."

"Okay, I see you know nothing," Robin scolded him.

"That's what they taught us in catechism and at the seminary," Rafael argued.

"Is that still taught in seminary? No wonder the society is so far ahead. How curious that they teach you to think better than most people and invest years and years in your moral, philosophical, and religious education, yet so often you fail to see the obvious."

"And you do?" Rafael challenged, fed up with Robin's know-it-all attitude.

"What did the Jews in the first century call Him?"

"I have no idea."

"By his first name, followed by the name of his father or place of birth. Yeshua ben Joseph; Jesus, son of Joseph; or Yeshua Ha'Notzri, Jesus of Nazareth. I never heard of anyone calling him Jesus of Bethlehem."

Rafael had never thought of that, but he wasn't going to give Robin the pleasure of knowing it. He played it down. "Okay. He was Jesus of Nazareth and not Jesus of Bethlehem. There goes business for the Church of the Nativity," he joked again.

"If the church was mistaken or, more accurately, gave misleading information about the birth of Christ, don't you think it would do the same with other events in His life?"

As a matter of fact, yes, Rafael thought. He himself was living proof that the church defended herself by hiding, eliminating, and getting around every obstacle. He wasn't the person to ask about the Holy See's good intentions. He, better than anyone, knew they didn't exist.

"Look at me, Robin. I'm the guy ready to blow your brains out. Do you think I believe in the holiness of the church?"

"Why do you, then?" Robin wanted to know.

That was a question Rafael avoided asking himself, but more and more frequently occurred to him. Why did he believe? Because others had believed before him? Because life carried him in that direction? Why? Because, despite all the errors and injustices, the church was still the institution that prevented the world from falling into chaos. He still believed that, and perhaps that was the only reason, the one that made him get out of bed without knowing if he would do so the next day, not knowing if he would sleep that night, if he survived, where he would be, what the next step would be, in what direction it would take him. Every day, hour, minute, and second were unknown to fate. He only thanked God for the time He gave him.

"I believe because I want to," he said.

"Whether you want to or not, you do it for mistaken reasons," Robin warned him.

"And I presume you do so for all the right ones."

"You can believe I'm not going around deceived," Robin admonished, irritated.

"So, set me straight. Why do they say He was born in Bethlehem, when he was actually born in Nazareth? Let's begin there," Rafael asked, losing patience with the argument.

Robin also seemed willing to move on and began an explanation in the professorial tone of one who has always known the truth, and not some deluded version made up for gullible believers.

Jesus Christ was not born in Bethlehem or in Nazareth, but first saw the light of day somewhere in the outskirts of Jerusalem in 5 B.C., according to the Gregorian and Julian calendars. The reason for this strange date had to do with the calculation of the calendars. Agreements and disagreements about counting made it possible, according to theory, for Jesus to have been born five years before Himself, that is, the year 5 B.C. Herod the Great reigned until the year 4 B.C., and since the heir of David had to flee the insanity of that lunatic king, according to Robin, He had to have been born before the death of Herod.

"Forget everything you know or thought you knew about Jesus," Robin said.

Jesus's father was never a carpenter. Joseph had royal blood, descended from Jacob, Solomon, Abraham, and Isaac, and his son was therefore of royal lineage, too.

"According to Matthew," Rafael interrupted. "Luke traces Him back to Adam and God."

"Whoever tells a story . . ." Robin returned to his account. "Why was it necessary that Jesus be born in Bethlehem and not in Jerusalem, or Nazareth, if you prefer to fall into this error?" Robin asked rhetorically. "Because the prophet Micah foretold: *And thou Bethlehem, in the land of Judah, art not the least among the princes of Judah, for out of thee shall come a governor that shall rule my people of Israel.*"

Rafael recognized the words of Matthew.

"There's more. Let's begin with the birth of Jesus, who was conceived"—Robin sketched quotation marks in the air—"by the power of the Holy Spirit. Why? To fulfill what the Lord spoke through His prophet Isaiah: *Behold a virgin will conceive and bring forth a son, and they will*

call him Emanuel, which means God be with us. Either
Matthew had a great propensity to make things up or was
a poor reader with a bad memory because, as you very
well know, Isaiah never said such a thing.

"A young woman with child will bring forth a son,"
Rafael quoted.

Robin nodded in agreement.

"Then Herod secretly called on the magi to set out for
Bethlehem"—more quotation marks in the air—"to discover the hiding place of the child, who, in the meantime,
would flee to Egypt, since God appeared to Joseph in
dreams and ordered him to go there and stay until he
received new direction." Robin got up and assumed a
dramatic pose: "As announced through the mouth of the
prophet Hosea: *Out of Egypt I shall call my son.*"

The deceived Herod then ordered every male child
under the age of two to be killed, fulfilling the prophesy
of Jeremiah: *A voice is heard in Ramah, a lamentation
and loud cry: it is Rachel weeping for her sons and refusing
consolation because they no longer are alive.*

Herod died, and an angel of the Lord appeared again
in Joseph's dreams, ordering him to return to Israel. Since
Arquelaus, the son of Herod the Great, was the tetrarch
of Judea, Joseph decided to settle in Galilee, specifically
in Nazareth, where the tetrarch was Arquelaus's brother,
Herod Antipas, fulfilling another prophesy: *He will be
called the Nazarene.*

Here Robin stopped and sighed. He was tired from so

much talking, and his mouth was dry. He sat down again heavily. "I don't know what prophesy Matthew is alluding to. In the Old Testament there is no mention of a Nazarene or Nazareth. Presumably he confused the name or didn't interpret it correctly. Probably it wasn't Nazareth but Nazarite, like John the Baptist, someone consecrated by God—"

"Where are you going with all this?" Rafael interrupted, fed up with all of it.

"Can't you see your hand in front of your own face?" Robin complained. "You're an idiot."

Rafael didn't bother to reply. He saw nothing.

"Do you think Jesus and his family didn't read the Bible?" Robin asked suddenly.

"They read the Old Testament," Rafael responded, remembering Jacopo's lecture to Gavache the night before in the Church of Saint-Paul–Saint-Louis.

"Exactly—that is, they knew all the steps they had to take to present the heir of David, the Messiah, to the world."

No carpenter in the first century in Israel would have the resources to make a journey to Jerusalem every year to celebrate the Passover. Nor was it necessary, according to Robin's vivid account, to consult apocryphal texts to know that Jesus's family went every year, as was the custom of those who could afford it. Some of these journeys are described in Holy Scripture.

Jesus continued to make them as an adult with his disciples.

"He even died during Passover, if we choose to believe this."

"Don't tell me that's not true," Rafael grumbled uncomfortably.

Robin got up suddenly. It was not something he could say sitting down. He was visibly upset. "We still don't know."

"Then who does know?" Rafael asked impatiently.

Robin looked up at the angry Italian priest, who was acting like a petulant child.

"You don't have any idea what's happening, do you?"

Rafael shook his head no, as if he didn't know and didn't care.

"Remember the manuscripts that mention manuscripts that mention bones?" Robin reminded him.

"Of course."

"We're talking about the bones of Christ."

"What? Repeat that." Rafael was astonished.

"We're talking about the bones of Christ," the Englishman repeated.

It was Rafael's turn to get up. What the hell was he talking about? He could only be joking. Rafael shivered from nervousness. Had Loyola gone to look for those bones in Jerusalem? "Are you kidding, Robin?"

"I wish." He smiled slightly. "For nearly five hundred years the Society of Jesus has been guarding these relics with their lives, under constant threat, inside and outside the church."

Rafael was not feeling well. This went against everything he'd been taught. The Gospel of Mary Magdalene mentioned the place where Jesus was buried. This discredited everything. Everything he had learned, for which he'd fought, was based on a lie? He wasn't in shock, but he had difficulty breathing. Then there was the so-called Gospel of Jesus. What confusion.

"Tell me, my friend, how can you hope to save the church if they don't even tell you the truth?" Robin continued, twisting the knife.

Rafael sat down again, let himself sweat, opened his collar and took a deep breath to regain control.

"Have these bones been tested?" Rafael asked.

"Obviously. Science indicates that the bones belong to someone who lived in 1 A.D. or B.C. They were excavated from a tomb, no longer accessible today, carved into the rock of the Church of the Holy Sepulchre. They were in an undecorated urn with only one inscription, *Yeshua ben Joseph*."

Rafael closed his eyes. He didn't want to hear this. Every word out of Robin's mouth was like a knife stabbing him.

"Of course, Yeshua and Joseph were common names in the first century," Robin continued. "Like Mary, Magdalene, Martha, Peter, James, and Andrew."

"Are you trying to give an excuse to the historians paid by the church to refute the idea?" Rafael accused him.

"But it's true. That recent discovery was featured among all the international media on the Discovery Channel with that documentary directed by James Cameron.

The tomb of Talpiot underscores the idea that they were common names."

What was the probability of having two tombs with the same name in different places in Jerusalem? There was a Jesus, a Joseph, and another that could be Mary, Magdalene, or Mary and Magdalene in the same urn, or it could be neither the one nor the other, but Martha, another common name, which also could mean Mary or be Martha herself. The doubts were too many, and the answers too few. The only difference was a tomb no one had heard about, while the tomb of Talpiot . . .

"Do you mean that the bones that Loyola found in Jerusalem might not be His?" Rafael asked. He preferred doubt, mystery, to an irrefutable certainty.

"In spite of being found in the exact place the Gospel of Mary Magdalene indicated, that's exactly what I'm telling you. At that time secrecy was extremely important. The Jews were experts at hiding things and giving misleading directions. The Church of the Holy Sepulchre may mark the place where he was buried . . . or not," Robin said distastefully. "And don't forget we have the question of Ben Isaac, who guarded the Gospel of Jesus, supposedly written by Him in Rome in A.D. 45."

Rafael snorted. This was too much.

"That's what Ben Isaac guarded for more than a half century. He had an agreement with the church, the Status Quo. They say he paid a lot for the church to let him keep possession of the documents." Robin sighed deeply. He was tired.

When the agreement was renewed in 1985, Peter, the superior general of the society, demanded that Wojtyla not sign an extension, but the Pole wouldn't listen to him. He wanted to get rid of the hot potato as quickly as possible. Robin agreed with the superior general at the time. It was a mistake. Probably in exchange for millions of dollars.

"Now you don't want to run the risk of Pope Ratzinger doing the same," Rafael concluded.

"We can't, Santini!" Robin shouted. "One of the reasons you're hearing this story for the first time is because of us," he said, striking his chest with his hand. "If it were up to me, nothing would be known about it at all."

"Ben Isaac and the church have done a good job of hiding it, too."

"How much longer?" Robin complained. "This proves that the pope doesn't trust us, Rafael."

Rafael sighed. The priests of the Society of Jesus were stubborn, and it wasn't worth arguing about.

"Do you think it's worth killing people over this?"

"Don't you understand the seriousness of what I just told you?" Robin answered.

"You don't even know if the bones are His. With respect to the Gospel of Jesus, anyone could have written it. You know perfectly well that the authorship of the gospels, apocryphal or canonical, has never been established definitively. The writing of the Pentateuch was attributed to Moses, in which he narrates his own death. Damn. Everything is uncertain. No one knows anything."

Robin tapped his foot on the floor nervously.

"However serious it might be, it's not worth four deaths, Robin."

"I am not involved with these strategic decisions." The English Jesuit sounded defensive, as if washing his hands of it.

"I understand, but nothing in all this justifies kidnapping Ben Isaac's son. I really hope he's not going to be victim number five."

Robin looked at him, astonished. "We didn't kidnap Ben Isaac's son."

"Robin, don't fuck with me," Rafael cursed. "You murdered four men and kidnapped Ben Isaac's son. There's no point in denying it, after all you've told me."

"Rafael, I give you my word we had nothing to do with the kidnapping. At least as far as I know, and I usually do."

Robin seemed sincere. Whether he was or not, only he knew, since no one has found a way to discover if someone is lying; even the lie detectors can be fooled.

Rafael got up. He still felt hot, and his heart was racing. He looked at his watch and saw it was twelve thirty. "I think that's enough for today."

"It's always a pleasure to serve an envoy from the Supreme Pontiff, even one pointing a gun at my head," Robin said sarcastically.

"How's this all going to end?" Rafael asked.

"Do you want to know what I've discovered in all my years of experience?" Robin paused to get Rafael's attention. "The end makes everything clear."

Rafael walked to the door. "I hope so."

"It'll be easy for you to predict," Robin offered, going to the desk and picking up the phone. "After everything I told you, you don't expect to leave here with your life, do you?" Someone answered the phone. "We have an escape attempt. Code red," Robin said.

52

It wasn't a pretty sight, and none of the three men would have been there to witness it if they could have helped it. It would not have been humane or pious to let Ursino leave such a sacred place without a moment of prayer and expiation for the services he so diligently performed for His Holiness, four of them, always taking into consideration the greater interest of the Holy Mother Church, submissive to the dogma and teachings of our Lord.

The paramedics had placed the body on a stretcher. A white sheet covered him to the chest and left his face visible. The fibula was still stuck in his eye, shocking the three men of God who observed him in silence. His face was black on the side with the wound, striped with dried blood. His mouth and chin were white as chalk. Ursino looked at peace, the kind of quiet that emanates only from the dead, who know a greater truth, their mission accomplished here on earth, problems resolved or left for others to deal with. . . . What better reason to be at peace, with no debt collector to hassle them, the worries of borrowing a car, marriage disputes, loneliness, loss behind them. Death can be good.

"Your Eminence," the doctor called, shutting a first-aid kit that had been of no use. He had cleaned the wound a little so that the dead priest would be at least slightly more presentable for the secretary of state. He would not remove the fatal bone for legal reasons.

Tarcisio didn't hear him. He was absorbed in his prayer.

"Your Eminence," he called again.

"Yes, Lorenzo?"

"Do you want me to inform the family?" the doctor asked politely.

"No, thank you. Father Ursino had no living relatives," the secretary informed him in a weak, sorrowful voice.

At that moment he noticed the trace of blood that had dripped from Ursino's eye to the floor next to the desk. He tried to avoid vomiting as he imagined the sordid scene that had unfolded there. A sacrilege. William and Schmidt continued to watch over the corpse, whispering prayers to the All-Powerful Father to receive their brother in His merciful arms.

"Clean up that blood as soon as possible, please," Tarcisio ordered, pointing at the dark red stain.

"Certainly," the doctor answered. He looked around for one of the paramedics. "Tomaso, clean up this blood—"

"I don't think that's a good idea, Your Eminence," Daniel, the commander of the Swiss Guard, interrupted. "It's evidence."

Tomaso waited while they decided, bent over the spot, ready to make it disappear. The secretary of state gestured to continue, a decision that did not make Daniel happy, but he swallowed silently and said nothing.

Lorenzo cleared his throat before speaking. The subject bothered him. "What about the body, Your Eminence?"

"He will be buried in the German cemetery."

That seemed strange to both Lorenzo and William. Schmidt laid his hand on his friend's shoulder. He knew how difficult this was for him.

"I'm sorry to ask, but the law requires an autopsy—"

"The law requires nothing, Lorenzo," Tarcisio interrupted with irritation. "You're confusing Italian law with the law of the Vatican. Italian law requires, Vatican law recommends. There will be no autopsy. According to the will of the Holy Father."

"I'll comply with that, Your Eminence." Lorenzo cleared his throat again. Another question remained, and he wasn't happy to ask it. His conscience demanded that he do so. "Cause of death?"

Tarcisio reflected a few moments. His reply would determine how history would hear about this death. It would be the first murder within the high walls of the hill of the Vatican since the nineteenth century, if it were officially deemed murder. There was no other option.

"An accidental cerebral hemorrhage," William proposed. "The cause of death was a stroke."

Lorenzo looked at the secretary for confirmation. Only he was able to give it. A nod of his head sealed Ursino's cause of death, wounded in the right eye by a bone, a fact that would be suppressed in the official records. No murder had occurred within the walls of the Vatican, according to any record.

Lorenzo left the Relics Room, leaving the leaders of the church to contemplate the corpse, Tomaso to clean up the blood, and Daniel with two Swiss Guards to protect the prelates.

"He is at peace," Schmidt affirmed.

"Yes. Surely looking down on us from the Almighty's side," William added.

Tarcisio said nothing. He didn't know any words appropriate for a moment like this. Human life was sacred. The disrespect for it by some, capable of taking it, as if killing a chicken or a cow, lives that God disposed for our nourishment. To take away God's greatest gift was like renouncing Him.

While Tomaso cleaned up, his colleagues approached with the stretcher. "Can we remove the body, Your Eminence?" one of them asked.

Tarcisio made the sign of the cross with his hand pointed at Ursino and wondered whether to cover his face with the sheet. Only then did he authorize them to carry the body off. As soon as the stretcher left the room, the atmosphere became lighter and more breathable. At last . . .

"Now what?" Schmidt asked.

"I'm going to make the funeral arrangements," Tarcisio said. "But first . . . a meeting with Adolph."

"Do you need me?" William asked helpfully.

"Maybe later."

"I'm going to try to get some rest," Schmidt said. "I'm feeling the effects of all this."

"Of course, my good friend. You deserve it. I'll ask Trevor to speak with the Daughters of Charity of Saint Vincent de Paul to prepare a room for you in the Domus Sanctae Marthae," he offered.

"There's no need."

"I insist. I won't accept a refusal," Tarcisio said, closing the subject. "Trevor, go with Father Schmidt and get a room prepared for him. He is our guest," he ordered.

Trevor complied immediately.

"Tonight you'll be notified of a new date to hear the sentence of your hearing," William informed Schmidt solemnly.

"This is not the time for that, William," Tarcisio admonished him, and then looked at Trevor. "Go with Father Schmidt and make sure he has everything he needs."

Trevor and Schmidt left the Relics Room. Daniel ordered one of the guards to go with them.

"Commander," Tarcisio called.

"Your Eminence." Daniel was ready to hear his orders.

"Order this room sealed. Until a new curator is appointed, no one must enter this space."

"I'll do so, Your Eminence."

"Is the investigation concluded?"

"According to your wishes, Your Eminence."

"Let's go, then. We can't keep people waiting," the secretary said, looking one last time at the room that guarded the sacred relics of the church. Someone else would be chosen to continue Ursino's work and take care of this almost immeasurable treasure with the respect and devotion it deserved. Tomaso had finished cleaning and disappeared, like the blood that had stained the floor. Now all that remained was to try to forget. He looked at William. "I'm at your service."

The two men left the room, escorted by Daniel and the other guard. William looked at Tarcisio with an open smile, which the secretary returned.

"I'm really in need of good news," Tarcisio said.

53

The noise was deafening. Vehicles of all kinds circled the runway in an ordered chaos typical of a big city at rush hour. The jet waited for Sarah, ready for departure.

They arrived in a black SUV with tinted windows, driven by one of Garvis's agents; Garvis sat in the backseat with Sarah and Jean-Paul.

Sarah carried only a simple leather folder pressed between her hands. Inside it contained the most important parchments in Christianity, and Sarah was deathly afraid of losing them. Her nervousness made it hard to breathe. The sickness threatened to return. She should never have agreed to do this. Who did she think was judging her? Mother Teresa of Calcutta, who was ever ready to resolve the problems the church got into? Friendly couples like the Isaacs? How she longed for a normal life, without thousand-year-old secrets, or any secrets; without the human cruelty that prevailed everywhere, especially on the highest levels. God was said to have created man in His own image, but she knew this was a lie and, worse, the terrible truth that contradicted that affirmation. It was man's fault. It was he who created God in his own image—cruel, intolerant, spoiled, punishing, greedy, fearful. How could billions of people believe in an all-powerful, omnipresent, moral being with so many faults and such a bad temper?

"Thanks again for cooperating, Sarah," Garvis said in a baritone voice with a West Country accent.

Sarah hadn't noticed his voice before. It was curious how concentrating so hard on one thing could block out everything else. Sarah would not make a good detective. Sometimes the obvious escaped her, even though, as a journalist, a certain nose for things was essential.

"What will the procedure be?" she wanted to know.

"Are you feeling all right?" Jean-Paul asked worriedly.

"Yes. Everything's okay. A little weak, maybe," she excused herself. She didn't want to admit that she was nervous, even if it was obvious.

"You can eat on board. Don't be nervous, Sarah," Garvis instructed.

The limo followed an unidentified vehicle, a kind of low tractor with a fork in front. Several identical ones were busily working the runway. Their function was to move the planes from the gate to the taxiway, ready to follow them to the runway, since planes can only move forward on their own.

They stopped at a kind of crosswalk, though nothing Sarah could see identified it as such. Across the way she noticed a fleet of four private planes. One of them would carry her to her destination, and then . . . who knew? She felt as if she might not survive.

"Aren't you going with us, Inspector Garvis?" she asked, to hide her discomfort.

"No, Sarah. Relax. You're in good hands. Inspector Gavache's team is first-class. Too many people just get in the way."

She had no more questions. In this case they would know the international protocols better than she.

Leaving behind the crosswalk, the limo drove a few hundred feet to a Cessna that awaited them. Garvis was the first to open the door and let Sarah and Jean-Paul out. The noise of the engines was deafening.

"All ready?" he shouted at a worker in a fluorescent jacket and ear protectors.

"Everything's ready, sir," he answered respectfully, loud enough to be heard, and gave a thumbs-up.

Then Garvis shook hands with a man in a suit. "Garvis, Metropolitan Police," he introduced himself. "Are you the one I have to thank for the plane?"

"Not me, but the American people," the other answered, maintaining his grip in a firm, courteous way. "David Barry, FBI," he lied.

"Sarah, once again, thanks for all you're doing," Garvis said to the journalist. "And don't worry. They'll defend you with their lives if necessary."

Sarah got most of what was screamed at her. The noise was immense. A plane started to take off on a runway next to them, lifting off with a roar that filled the surroundings. Sarah acknowledged Garvis with a nod, but Garvis kissed the back of her hand. A gentleman. Then a handshake for Jean-Paul.

"Bon voyage."

"Merci."

Sarah gripped the folder securely and followed Jean-Paul to the steps of the plane.

"Oh, and Sarah?" Garvis shouted seconds before another plane took off nearby.

Sarah looked at him from the door.

"Greet him for me," Garvis asked.

"Who?" Sarah asked.

"You know who," Garvis said, getting in the front door of the limo, smiling slightly, leaving behind the confused noise and vehicles.

Jean-Paul disappeared inside the plane when his phone began to ring. The American was the last to enter.

A pretty flight attendant and steward with everything in its proper place greeted the passengers.

Jean-Paul exchanged some words in French, of which Sarah barely understood half, not enough to connect with the conversation.

"It was Inspector Gavache. He's on his way to the airport, but he has to take a short detour. We'll have to wait a few minutes."

"That's all right. We have time," Barry said.

Sarah didn't care. She wasn't in charge of anything. Her purpose was only to hand over the documents and hope for the best. How idiotic to play the role of Saint Sarah.

Jean-Paul led her to her seat. The backs were very comfortable, but Sarah was already familiar with the perks that money, public or private, can buy.

"Hello," an older man greeted her, who Sarah thought must be a French agent, seated with a half-open newspaper on his lap. "You must be Sarah Monteiro," he said, taking her hand and kissing it. "Nice to meet you." He snatched the folder with the parchments out of her hand without even asking. "Let me take this weight off your hands."

If circumstances had been different, she might have enjoyed this gallantry, but unfortunately they weren't.

"And you are?" Sarah asked suspiciously.

"Jacopo Sebastiani," he said, lowering his head humbly. "At your service."

54

Disorder, disquiet, disillusion, affliction. This was the state in which Gavache had left Ben Isaac in his mansion in one of the richest neighborhoods of London after Ben Isaac had revealed a completely different story of the life of Jesus Christ. Even though Gavache was not a believer, the account had left him troubled. Something of the disquiet and disillusion had followed him from the house and stayed with him in the police car assigned for his use.

Ben Isaac had begun the story without hurry and confusion, except the two interruptions when Gavache received phone calls.

According to the Gospel of Jesus, which Ben Isaac uttered from memory with a tremor in his voice, Yeshua was born a year before the death of Herod the Great, during the Jewish month of Tishri in the year 3755 on the first day of Sukkot in Bethanya, a small village a mile and a half to the east of Jerusalem, at the foot of the Mount of Olives.

"Do you think I have any idea what you're talking about?" Gavache interrupted.

A discouraged Ben Isaac frowned. "September 14, 5 B.C. A Saturday. The first day of the Feast of Tabernacles."

What the fuck. Gavache didn't need precise dates. He forced himself to keep his mouth shut and not show his skepticism.

Jesus was prepared from an early age to assume an important role. He was a descendant of Abraham, David, and Solomon, who had ordered the building of the Temple. He was expected to restore the glorious time before the exile, the glory of Israel. But the Jerusalem that Jesus knew was not the Jerusalem of the Old Testament. That city had fallen under the yoke of Babylonia, which razed the city and destroyed the Jewish Temple. The Ark of the Covenant had been lost forever in the sixth century B.C. The Jerusalem of Jesus's time was reconstructed from scratch by the Jewish rulers of the Hasmonean dynasty in the second century B.C., and the Temple was reconstructed by Herod the Great a year before Jesus's birth.

Herod wanted Him dead, not because he was a lunatic, but because Jesus was a noble Jew who had been proscribed with all His family. Herod had to eliminate any possible challenge to his throne.

"For the Jews the word *Messiah* didn't mean the chosen one or the one sent by God. *Messiah* simply referred to the heir from the house of David. Joseph was also an heir, and Jacob before him," Ben Isaac continued.

"But why Jesus? Did He know he was an heir to the throne?" Gavache didn't understand.

It wasn't difficult to find the answer in the Bible. The accounts place the family of Jesus in Bethlehem, later in Egypt, Nazareth, Jerusalem, Caesarea, Cafarnaum, Jericho, Betabara, Enom, Betsaida, throughout the Jordon valley and along the Sea of Galilee, among many other places. Jesus's family, a royal family, was in permanent flight. In one place His father was a carpenter, in another a stonemason, an artisan—always manual crafts, which those sent by Herod never paid attention to. Joseph never stayed in one place too long. Of course, this information was not explicitly mentioned in Holy Scripture, since the authors of the gospels wanted to emphasize the importance of the virgin birth, of conception without sin. From the beginning the intention was to emphasize Jesus as the Son of Man, the Messiah, a man greater than all other men, who could perform miracles as if He were the Son of God Himself. Everything else was history.

"In the middle of the night, without warning, Father awakened us. It was time to leave again," Ben Isaac quoted.

"Is that in the Bible?" Gavache asked.

Ben Isaac shook his head no. It wasn't necessary to cite the source of the quotation. For Gavache it was a completely different picture of Jesus from what he knew.

The life of Jesus bounced back and forth until his adult

years. He became a renowned and respected rabbi because of His humility and wisdom until . . . John the Baptist. Gavache frowned and redoubled his attention at this point in the account.

John the Baptist was Jewish, the son of the priest Zacarias and Elizabeth. He was born on the outskirts of Jerusalem in Ein Kerem, six months before Jesus, and began his Nazarite education at the age of fourteen in Ein Gedi.

"Nazarite education?" Gavache asked.

"Yes, the consecration of someone to God. It involved some physical sacrifices, never cutting one's hair, never drinking wine, never touching a corpse, never eating meat. One had to maintain a purified state against all temptations," Ben Isaac explained, with the patience of Job. "Jesus was also a Nazarite."

"Jesus the Nazarite, as opposed to Jesus from Nazareth, the Nazarene," Gavache deduced, absorbed in the story. "A Messiah consecrated to God?"

"See how it all connects," Ben Isaac tossed out.

Jesus was fascinated by John the Baptist for his abnegation, but even more for his personality. He saw a wandering preacher who advocated baptism instead of fanatical extremism. Like all the Jews of his time, John had a preoccupation with purification by water. Even today archaeologists are constantly discovering the basins for ritual baths, the Jewish *miqwa'ot*. Practically every Jewish house had one, and any traveling Jew that entered one had to be purified. They had to dip themselves in a pool, which was filled with spring water, but, before going in, they had to wash their hands and feet, especially the lower limbs, which were the source of impurity. After dipping, their feet and head were rubbed with purifying oil. The woman who anointed Jesus in the house of Simon the Leper in Bethany two days before the Crucifixion, according to the canonical gospels, was just performing a Jewish ritual with ancient roots.

"Okay, they took a lot of baths. What does that have to do with anything?" Gavache asked.

"The baths were Jewish rituals. John the Baptist performed the same ritual in the Jordan River, but for gentiles," Ben Isaac explained.

"And baptized Jesus," Gavache added.

"But this didn't have the enormous outcry that the apostles and His followers claimed it did. The majority didn't understand what had happened. Not even John understood."

Jesus was a flexible, open, intelligent man; a rabbi, a master, a healer of souls, a preacher who greatly admired John's methods. John the Baptist was an enormous influence. In reality, John marked a break with the past. After him, Jesus intensified his rituals and preaching, presenting variations that were not pleasing to conservative believers. Jesus created a new branch of Judaism, a kind of sect. When John was beheaded by Herod Antipas, Jesus was his natural successor.

"John never performed a miracle," Ben Isaac said, and then sighed deeply, as if in sorrow. "Neither did Jesus.

The Jesus who gave sight to the blind and cured cripples exists only in the Bible."

"How boring. And where does Bethlehem and Nazareth fit into all this?" Gavache asked, disillusioned.

"The authors of the New Testament had to emphasize that Jesus was the Savior, the Anointed One, the Son of God, Emanuel, and that there was no doubt about this. The prophets of the Old Testament had pointed the way and described the steps to follow. He would be born in Bethlehem, flee to Egypt, return, and be called the Nazarene. But, as you noted, they confused 'Nazarene' with 'Nazarite.'" Ben Isaac smiled slightly. "The only time that He stepped foot in Nazareth, as an adult, he was poorly received. People wanted to kill him. Do you think that would have been possible if he had belonged to one of the good families of the region?"

"What a confusing story." Gavache was speaking in general, not referring specifically to Ben Isaac's account, which made sense. "Why did Pontius Pilate wash his hands of all this and order the Jews to decide?"

"That's more nonsense," Ben Isaac replied. "Do you know who the dominant force in the so-called civilized world was from 27 B.C. through the next four hundred years?"

"I assume you're referring to the Romans."

"You assume correctly. Do you know what happened during this time?"

Gavache shrugged. He was an expert on life, not history.

"Roman expansion, which lasted for several centuries, and in the case of the Eastern Roman Empire, more than a millennium." Ben Isaac counted off on his fingers. "The birth and death of Jesus and of Paul of Tarsus, the author of the Epistles. During this time, the canonical and apocryphal gospels were written, and a new religion was born, Christianity."

"In other words?"

"In other words, everything happened under Roman influence. There are no originals of the sacred texts, only transcriptions of unknown authorship and motivation. Christianity is a patchwork quilt, based on historical misrepresentations. Why do you think the Vatican is always so attentive to archaeological discoveries? Always so quick to refute or control any new fact unearthed? Because they're living with a time bomb. They know that everything they have established is based on a lie. The New Testament is a purely political document, created to control the people. I think it also aimed to control the Jews, only it didn't succeed."

"And why do you think it didn't succeed?" Gavache asked.

"Because they knew the truth." Ben Isaac got up now and paced the room. The subject annoyed him. "Pontius Pilate wasn't the good, courteous man the Bible portrays, nor was he intelligent. He was a bloody man with wicked instincts, a perverse schemer. He never washed his hands or let the Jews decide Jesus's fate. Washing the hands was a Jewish ritual of purification, not Roman, the *netilat yadaim.* Barabbas, whom the Jews chose to free in Jesus's place, according to the New Testament, was a Zealot, from a violent, fanatical sect of Judaism, different from the Nazarites, though they shared some methods. Barabbas had killed Roman soldiers, a serious crime; today he would be considered a terrorist. The Zealots led innumerable rebellions, always put down by the Romans, and in their final hour committed suicide en masse—men, women, and children. Pilate would never have freed a killer of Romans. It's not only improbable but impossible."

"That doesn't necessarily mean he didn't wash his hands of it," Gavache insisted.

"How does the Bible say that Jesus died?" Ben Isaac asked.

"Crucified."

"Exactly," Ben Isaac answered, as if expressing an obvious truth that Gavache didn't get. "If you had doubts, the Crucifixion was proof that Pilate never washed his hands. He was the one who condemned Him, and not others."

Gavache was confused, and Ben Isaac realized it.

"Crucifixion was always a Roman sentence, not Jewish," he explained. "If he'd been condemned by the Sanhedrin, the Jewish council, the punishment would have been death by stoning."

"A devil of a choice," Gavache said ironically.

"But He wasn't sentenced to the Jewish punishment, was He?" Ben Isaac ignored Gavache's comment. "Jewish participation in the death of Christ was greatly exaggerated."

"You mean they had nothing to do with His death," Gavache said.

"Not only did they have nothing to do with it, they tried to help Him."

When the Roman soldiers and the Temple Police arrested Jesus in the Garden of Gethsemane on the Mount of Olives, they didn't bring him before Pilate. The first stop occurred during the night at the house of Caiaphas, the high priest of the Sanhedrin, in front of the Praetorium, the governor's palace. It wasn't at the Temple or the place where the Sanhedrin met, which indicates an informal meeting, not an audience. Also, the Sanhedrin never met at night. One of its members was Joseph of Arimathaea, who aided Jesus along the route of the cross and offered his tomb to receive His body.

"It was the beginning of Passover, the celebration of the freeing of the Israelites from Egypt, and the Sanhedrin never condemned anyone to death during this period. It was prohibited," Ben Isaac continued. "There are many indications in the Bible that suggest that the Jews never at any time mistreated Jesus."

The prophet said that the Messiah would enter Jerusalem on the back of a donkey, and the crowd would hail him as the Son of David. Jesus did that in the final days of His life, but the event was not as grand as Holy Scripture describes. The Romans reinforced all the gates of the city during Passover. If the event had had all the significance the Bible gives it, Jesus would never have entered the city without being arrested. It was a capital crime for a nobleman to proclaim himself king of the Jews. Another story has Jesus expelling the money changers and sellers of doves from the Temple. It was obviously an insignificant event, exaggerated by the apostles and the writers of the gospels. Any major altercation within the Temple would have called the attention of the Temple Police, and there's no reference to this having taken place. Jesus couldn't have created a great scandal without being expelled from the Temple and the city itself by the authorities.

"Or killed?" Gavache suggested.

Ben Isaac shook his head. "The maximum would have been jail awaiting sentencing. As I told you, during Passover, there were no executions."

"But that's not what happened. They did execute Him," Gavache contradicted him.

Ben Isaac didn't reply; he stopped suddenly, as if he were revealing too much. Too late. Gavache noticed.

"It's possible they didn't have Him executed," Ben Isaac finally said, leaning back in the chair, defeated. "It's possible that the evangelists and Paul changed certain events and exaggerated others, blaming the Jews and speculating about what they didn't know. Only Saint John the Evangelist and Saint Matthew knew Jesus. No one else witnessed anything that occurred. All the other accounts are based on hearsay. There is also the problem that the evangelists relate conversations that occurred in private without any witnesses. How could they have known what was said?"

Gavache sat down in a chair next to Ben Isaac. "None of this means that Jesus wasn't crucified."

Ben Isaac sighed. "Do you know what documents the lady just carried out of here?" he asked sorrowfully.

Gavache didn't know.

"An inscription placing Christ in Rome in A.D. 45 and a gospel written by Him around the same year," he said.

Gavache listened without expressing an opinion. He was used to stories being a string of lies. In his profession he had caught many charitable souls, defenders of morality, some prominent in society and politics, with their hands in the cookie jar, caught doing the very thing they criticized and even prosecuted publicly. Everyone lied for one reason or another, or for no reason at all, because it was easy to complicate life, maybe a human need. The church had no reason to be any different, and wasn't.

"Do you believe what was written in the gospel?" Gavache asked.

"I don't know. It has the same errors as the others—contradictions, incoherencies, coincidences. It's a testimony in the first person up to the final days before the Crucifixion, with some interesting information—mysterious, even—and other news. It gives Him a real human dimension that's different from the other gospels. He seems to have been in search of a state of permanent illumination. Perhaps it was His consecration to God from the cradle that nurtured this. He said, *I am not the son of God, but the way to Him.* The gospel places Him in Jerusalem at the time of the Crucifixion . . . and then ends abruptly."

"At least he didn't narrate his own death, like Moses," Gavache joked.

Ben Isaac didn't react.

"Tell me, Dr. Isaac, like you're explaining to an eight-year-old kid, what all this means."

Ben Isaac took a deep breath. He was worn out. "It means He could have been simply a man whom the accidents of history ended up deifying."

"I understand," Gavache said thoughtfully. "What do you think?"

"Excuse me?"

"Do you think He's the Son of God or just the product of legend?"

Ben Isaac didn't hide his shock at Gavache's question. How dare he ask a question so personal, so profound, that Ben Isaac had asked himself for years without an answer.

"Did I upset you, Ben Isaac?" Gavache asked without a trace of pity. He waited for a reply. "Come on. You should know better than anyone. You've guarded the secret for more than fifty years."

"What does it matter to you what I believe?" Ben Isaac snapped back angrily. "Is that going to bring my son back to me?"

"That's in the hands of God and the Son of God," Gavache replied scornfully.

Tears ran down Ben Isaac's face. "What do you want me to say?" he said, sobbing. "That I believe He was a man like me and everyone else? That every day I pray He wasn't the Son of God? That I need that document to be true because that means that my daughter died because that's the way life is and not because He took her from me? Is that what you want to hear? That I could lose another child, and that to keep my sanity I need to believe that it has nothing to do with divine intervention?"

Gavache looked at a point beyond Ben Isaac toward the back by the stairs. Ben Isaac looked toward the same spot and saw Myriam. He swallowed dryly, unable to react or take a step in her direction. She clenched her fists, turned her back on him, and went upstairs angrily.

Myr was the only thing he managed to say, silently, to himself.

Finally he got up and rushed to the stairs. The cell phone on top of the table began to ring, making him stop. It was his. Was it the kidnappers again? He answered reluctantly. He didn't want any more news. He thought about little Ben and closed his eyes, wet with tears.

Gavache answered the phone without asking. He spoke some words in French and then in English, and immediately handed the phone to Ben Isaac. "It's for you. Your son."

"What?" Had he heard right?

"Your son. He was freed and wants to talk to you."

Ben Isaac was incredulous. He heard Myriam running down the stairs.

"Ben? Is it little Ben?" she asked.

Gavache nodded with the phone still extended toward Ben Isaac.

"But the woman hasn't even had time to land in Paris yet," Ben Isaac reasoned, grabbing the phone.

Inspector Gavache hurried toward the door to leave. "So long, Ben Isaac," he said as a farewell.

Myriam took the phone out of her husband's hand and began to talk. It was her son. Tears of relief streamed from her eyes. The nightmare was over, even if she would be at peace only when she saw him in flesh and blood, safe and sound.

"What's going on, Inspector?" Ben Isaac was unable to make sense of anything. "Where are Sarah and the documents?"

Gavache looked back and took another drag on his cigarette before answering. "Your son is safe. That's all that matters."

"Sir, sir," Gavache's driver called out when the car reached the corner and stopped by the curb.

"*Oui?*" said the other, leaving behind what had happened in Ben Isaac's house.

"We're here, sir," he told him.

Gavache looked outside across the street. "Here?"

"Correct, sir."

Gavache opened the door and stepped outside. "What's your name?" he asked the driver.

"Paul, sir."

"Paul, if things get violent, call for reinforcements."

"How will I know, sir?"

"You'll know, Paul. Trust me." Gavache left.

55

—◆—

"That threat only shows you don't know me," Rafael said with a gun in his hand. He locked the door of Robin's study and wedged the back of a chair under the knob to hold it.

Robin smiled mockingly. "What are you going to do? Hold me hostage?"

Rafael remembered Maurice and the coldheartedness with which he had murdered Gunter, the despair with which he had later taken his own life. "No, Robin. You're like an Islamic terrorist," he accused, "capable of killing and dying for a cause, even if you don't know what it is."

"Isn't that what you do, too?" Robin argued irritably.

"No, Robin, don't compare me with your insanity. I don't kill innocent, defenseless people."

"Fuck you, Santini."

"That's how all our conversations seem to end."

The door handle began to turn. Someone was trying to open it from the other side.

"He's here," Robin shouted. "Kill him. He knows too much."

Rafael struck him with the back of the gun, making Robin lift his hands to the wound in pain. When he looked at the palms of his hands, he saw blood. His lip had been split. He looked up with an expression of help-less fury.

"Now shut up," Rafael threatened.

Somebody continued to try to force the handle before suddenly stopping. Rafael knew what the next step would be and anticipated it by firing a shot halfway up the door. A heavy weight was heard falling to the floor on the other side of the shut door.

"Son of a bitch," Robin swore.

"Aren't we all?" the Italian replied, more to himself than to Robin. He stepped forward. "It was a pleasure, Robin. Until we meet again, God willing."

Robin was swearing at him, but Rafael didn't hear a single word. His priority was to get out of there alive. He needed to stay alert. He shot through the door twice more just in case, and waited a couple of seconds. He heard nothing. He opened the door carefully. A young man in a black cassock was lying on the floor, eyes staring life-lessly. A Glock pistol lay a few inches away. Rafael bent down and placed his fingers on his neck to see if there was a pulse. Nothing. He closed the corpse's eyes and sighed. Another life lost for no reason. He took the Glock and shoved it under his belt in the back.

He got up, keeping his gun pointed, and locked the door behind him, leaving Robin captive, and proceeded step by step in silence. The other doors were closed. He tried to open them, but they were locked, except for the door to the bathroom, which was empty; one less problem.

He looked through the door to the high altar. Only the table in the center could shield him from a threat. He ran and rolled over as quickly as possible until he was behind the table, and stayed there a few moments. From there he moved to a corner, from which he could see the nave.

An acolyte behind the confessional, another by a column in the back. He didn't see anyone else, but with so many hiding places it wasn't going to be easy. He risked looking to see if some believer had come to pray at the wrong time in the wrong place. A woman was in the second pew, kneeling, head lowered over her hands, praying for mercy, a girl by her side, seated on the pew playing a video game. The kid probably prayed every night before bed that her mother would spend some money and buy her a new PlayStation. A few rows back was a homeless man in ragged clothes.

"Santini," he heard a voice call from somewhere in the nave.

"Robin," Rafael replied. "What a talent for escaping from locked offices."

The faithful looked around. How disrespectful. Shouting like that in a place of silence and devotion.

"Shhh . . ." said the woman in front.

"Come out, Santini. I want to see you," Robin ordered, moving to the center of the nave.

"No, I'm okay. I know when I'm not welcome," Rafael replied mockingly. "You guys don't wish me well."

"Shhh . . ." the woman repeated. It was too much. Not just a lack of respect for a sacred place but for common civility as well.

"Don't be afraid," Robin protested, approaching the first row of pews, next to the altar in the transept. He made an apologetic gesture to the woman, along with a forced smile. Then he took the Glock out of his cassock and held it against the head of the mother, who could not believe it. "Do you want this pretty girl to become an orphan?"

The little one raised her eyes from the game and noticed what was happening. Instantly her tears began to flow. This wasn't a game for points.

Rafael got up from behind the altar table, hands in the air, and kicked his Beretta away. The acolyte behind the confessional aimed a gun at him with an angry look.

"I knew you'd end up surrendering," Robin said.

"You're an excellent negotiator," Rafael said in mock praise.

"You think you can come to *my* church and do what you want?" Robin continued. "You're so naive. Throw down the other gun, please."

Rafael took the Glock out from the back of his slacks, put it on the floor, and gave it a kick away from him. "Let her go now."

The mother and little girl were terrified. A priest aiming a gun at her head. Two armed acolytes. What a horrible scene. The beggar in the back had disappeared. Life, even without shelter, is priceless.

"Shut up," Robin ordered, visibly angry. "I'm going to deal with you, you son of a bitch." He looked at the woman and turned the gun away from her head. "Get out of here fast. Forget what you saw here, or I won't forget you."

It took less than five seconds for the woman and child to cross the nave and leave the church, completely traumatized.

"You're real brave, Robin," Rafael sneered.

"Put a bullet in this guy's head," Robin shouted at the acolyte aiming at Rafael.

The young man cocked the gun without hesitating, but before he could squeeze the trigger, he was hurled against the confessional, breaking one of the doors and falling inside. A bullet in the head had taken his life.

Instinctively, Robin fired at the column from which the shot came. Nobody had counted on that.

"Only a bastard like you could drag me to this den of fags," someone was heard to grumble. The ragged beggar strode pungently into the center of the nave.

"I'm glad to see you, Donald," Rafael greeted him sincerely.

"Fuck you, Santini. You're as much of a fag as they are," Donald insulted him in his usual affectionate way. Then he dropped the gun and sat down on the floor in pain. Robin's random shot had hit him in the stomach.

Rafael smiled sadly. Donald was always bad tempered, but always there at the right time. Long ago, he'd been an agent like Rafael. His aim was still perfect.

"What do you want, you smelly bum?" Robin said.

"Don't talk, asshole."

The other young acolyte looked at Robin in confusion, as if asking for instructions.

"Kill him," Robin said without a trace of feeling.

"I'd think twice before you do that, cocksuckers," Donald warned. He pointed at the dead acolyte. "Your friend is now sucking cocks in hell."

"You're going to die slowly, Donald," Robin said disdainfully. He aimed his own gun at Donald's head.

"Cut the shit, Robin." Rafael came forward, leaving the altar and approaching him. "No one else but me has to die." He struck his chest. "This is my fault. Do what you need to do, you bastard. Aim at me and get it over with." He came on with firm, quick steps. "Shoot me and let him go. He doesn't know what I do."

Robin watched Rafael come nearer. "Stop, Santini. That's enough."

Rafael obeyed. "Do what you have to do. Shoot. Get it over with."

Robin observed the scene as if he were hovering over it.

Rafael continued to stare hard at Robin. "Shoot."

Robin smiled disdainfully. "As you wish."

A sharp, echoing shot followed. "Amen."

Rafael's head should have exploded, but instead it was Robin who spit mouthfuls of blood before falling on the cold floor of the sacred temple that had seen so many sins over the last few minutes.

"It seems like today's the day for priests to die in church," Gavache spoke out, gun in hand, his shot taken. Amen.

"Police. Drop the gun," he ordered the acolyte, who immediately threw it down, as if it were red-hot. "Get on the floor. Hands behind your back."

Gavache looked at the corpse of the acolyte in the confessional and shook his head. "This world is going to hell.

"Is everything okay, Inspector?" Paul came into the church to see what was going on, gun ready, and kneeled over the other acolyte to handcuff him.

"Look at this, Paul. Does it look like everything is okay?"

"This is my last hour," Donald said to Rafael, trying to grab the pew to get up. "Give my regards to William and tell him to fuck himself. All he ever does is put me in tight spots. He never gives me a break."

Rafael ran to help him. "Don't try to get up, Don." He looked at Gavache. "Can you call an ambulance?"

Gavache bent over Robin to take his pulse. "Call an ambulance for this one, too," he told Paul.

"How did you know I was here?" Rafael asked Gavache.

"Reinforcements are on the way," Paul informed them.

"Okay, let them clean up this shit." Gavache straightened up and walked toward the door. "Come along, Rafael."

Rafael looked around the church one last time. His

head was filled with confusion. Much needed to be explained. He bent down over Donald.

"Thanks, Don."

"This shit didn't come out so well," Donald excused himself.

"It could have been worse."

Gavache interrupted them. "Boys, leave your conversation for later." He looked at Rafael. "Let's go. It's time."

"An ambulance is on the way. I'll see you later," Rafael said to Donald.

"Fuck you. Who said I want to see you? Get out of my sight."

Rafael smiled and followed in Gavache's footsteps. "Where are we going?"

"We have a plane waiting for us."

"Why do I feel like I don't know what's going on?"

"Because you don't."

56

No office in the world could compare in size and sumptuousness to Tarcisio's, with the exception of the pontifical apartments. Not even the Oval Office was in the same league.

Tarcisio occupied a chair that resembled a throne behind his solid antique desk.

Adolph sat down on the other side in a smaller, less luxurious, but equally comfortable chair. The difference in size was not accidental. It served to show whoever sat in it the superiority in rank and power of the person on the other side of the desk. The secretary of state was the most powerful man in the world, except for the pope. He was responsible for an empire of incalculable value, influential throughout the civilized world and in parts less civilized according to the standards set by the civilized. All his power was exercised without weapons or an army, and this was extraordinary in a world in which order was imposed by military might. Tarcisio never tired of telling how Pope Pacelli, during World War II, ordered his Swiss Guard to go unarmed, so that no accidental shot would create an international crisis with the Germans. History testifies that Hitler in all his power, capable of the most execrable massacres, master of the world, or at least pretending to be, with all his military might, never permitted a single German soldier to cross the defenseless Vatican border into Saint Peter's Square. It wouldn't have taken half an hour to capture the Supreme Pontiff and to occupy the Vatican state, but as Pius XII said, *My army is not of this world*. Hitler never had the courage to test this assertion.

Adolph smiled cynically. He adjusted his glasses and waited for Tarcisio to begin their meeting as usual. Outside, rain continued to fall in a constant torrent, the sky blackened with heavy clouds, and the wind keened in the windows. Adolph and his cynical smile.

"I wonder if you have anything to say to me before we begin," Tarcisio began in a serious tone, his duty in the best interests of the church.

Adolph felt superior to Tarcisio, as if the secretary of state did not deserve the distinctions he received. "Not that I know of."

Tarcisio took off his glasses and began to clean the

lenses with a velvet cloth. "Cut the bullshit. We know everything."

"About what, Your Eminence?" Adolph said, showing no surprise.

"Ernesto Aragones, Yaman Zafer, Sigfried Hammal, Ursino. Who's next? Joseph Ratzinger?" The secretary showed his anger.

"Should I know those names, Your Eminence?" Adolph asked with the same smile on his lips.

"If you want to continue lying, that's up to you, Adolph. I'll only say the following, we know everything."

Tarcisio finished cleaning his glasses and put them back on.

Neither one said anything for a few moments. Seconds, minutes, a tense silence.

"We were always the right arm of the church," the superior general finally said bitterly. "Our methods were never questioned."

"Well, when you interfere in matters of the church and kill innocent people and dedicated servants within our own walls, we have to begin to question, don't you think?" Tarcisio argued.

"Not when we're dealing with traitors." He raised his voice and dropped his cool attitude, revealing the true Adolph under the cynicism.

"I'm ordering you to stop what you're doing immediately," Tarcisio demanded. He received a harsh laugh in reply.

"We're the guardians of the church," Adolph asserted, half laughing. "Don't give us orders."

Tarcisio got up suddenly, leaning on the desk. "Don't defy me, Adolph. Guardians of what? Of some bones that could belong to anyone and some documents that, with all due respect, could have been forged by Loyola?"

"I disagree," Adolph warned. "Everything was analyzed scientifically. Everything is proved."

"It that right? Then you have until tomorrow to show me those results."

"I told you not to give me orders," Adolph repeated.

"Do you want to know what I think?" Tarcisio didn't wait for his reply. "I think everything was a fraud. I don't believe that Loyola brought back the bones of Christ."

"But you believe in the Gospel of Jesus," Adolph argued.

"Because it in fact exists and was proved genuine. Scientifically dated, and I can show you the results. Whether it is the Gospel of Jesus or not, we'll never know. As far as I'm concerned, He died on the cross, and everything else is fiction."

"In any case, there's nothing you can do. This operation can't be stopped. Tonight the gospel will be in our power," Adolph informed him again, cynically.

"You're deceived."

"You might be in the larger chair, but that doesn't give you superior insight. Tonight the documents will be in the possession of the Society of Jesus, and then I shall communicate our demands to you," Adolph said sarcastically.

"Why later and not now?" the secretary asked.

"Haven't you understood me?" Adolph was angry.

"On the contrary. I understand you. But we're going to do things differently."

He pressed the button of the telephone on top of his desk, and in less time than it takes to say *God*, the doors of the office opened to admit Cardinal William, talking on a phone with two Swiss Guards at the ready.

"What does this mean?" Adolph asked in astonishment.

"Yes, yes," William responded to the person on the other end of the line. "Just a minute. I'm going to transfer you."

The prefect pressed a button on the phone and handed it to Tarcisio.

"Is it on speakerphone?" the secretary asked.

William nodded yes.

"Good afternoon," Tarcisio said.

"Good afternoon, Your Eminence," Jacopo's voice replied.

"Do you have any news for me?"

"Everything went as planned. The church is in possession of Ben Isaac's documents."

"Would you mind repeating that? I have someone here who didn't quite hear," Tarcisio said, looking an incredulous Adolph in the eye.

"The church is in possession of Ben Isaac's documents," Jacopo repeated.

"Thank you. We'll talk later." He hung up without

taking his eyes off the superior general of the Society of Jesus.

He wanted to laugh in Adolph's face, but the moment demanded seriousness. For the first time in a long time, Tarcisio felt good. "You're too late, Adolph. Later I'll communicate my demands. Now get out of my presence."

57

The temperature rose that afternoon, and the day was sunny and pleasant. Jerusalem was a city that permanently swarmed with building cultural, artistic, and intellectual activity, the capital of eclecticism, with a people who adapted rapidly to the modern world and what it had to offer.

The Holy City knew how to prepare for the future. Every year it received millions of tourists eager to visit the places where Jesus walked. It was the most important city for two religions of the book, and the second most important for the followers of an equally important book. It was those books that gave meaning to all this history. Without them, the world would be different.

The car was parked in the middle of a residential street. Francesco and JC were sharing the backseat. There was no sign of the cripple in the Armani suit. Francesco was afraid of JC. There was something about him, an invisible power, extrasensory almost—as ridiculous as it was to think—that radiated omnipotence more than any other person Francesco had known.

"Now what?" he asked suspiciously.

JC took something out of his jacket pocket—an airline ticket, a passport, some shekels—and handed them to Francesco.

"Your participation has come to an end," JC declared firmly. "I don't have to tell you that none of this ever happened."

Francesco was puzzled. What kind of random plan was this?

"Is that it? Call someone to instruct them to give some documents to Sarah to take to the Gare du Nord? Couldn't you have done that?" He wanted to understand, no matter what happened. "Why did you kidnap me in Rome and bring me here?"

JC looked at Francesco with a sardonic smile and raised two fingers. "Two reasons. The first, so Sarah would know everything was going as planned. Hearing your voice meant everything was under control. And there's a second reason." But he said nothing.

Francesco waited for clarification, but he had to ask for it. "What is it?"

JC looked out at the street, calm in the midst of Jerusalem frenzy. "What are your intentions toward Sarah?"

"What?" What kind of question was that?

JC didn't repeat himself. Francesco had heard him.

"Are you her father?" Francesco asked, irritated by the invasion of privacy. Although he did not personally know Raul Brandao Monteiro, retired from the Portuguese army, he knew who Sarah's father was.

JC didn't react, but only waited for an answer.

"Sarah is an astonishing woman; discreet, professional, very responsible, and until recently I thought we might have a future together. But now, the truth is, I don't know," Francesco confessed. It was not worth the trouble to make up a reason for the old man; besides, Francesco was afraid JC would have sensed the lie.

JC thought about Francesco's words briefly. He was a practical man.

"I'd like to give you a glimpse of what Sarah's life is like. It's not always luncheons at embassies and ministries, nights at the paper, a movie at the Odeon in Leicester Square or the Empire, a play at the Adelphi, lunches at Indigo or home to fuck all night."

Francesco felt totally naked after that list of very specific, very real, intimate nights that he thought belonged to his private life.

"Part of her life has no schedule or plan," JC continued. "Don't expect that she'll fulfill all your expectations, because she won't. Or that she'll come home after work every night, because there'll be days she won't. Or answer all your phone calls; some she'll hang up on."

"Why are you telling me this?" Francesco wanted to know, his heart full of foreboding.

"So you'll know how your future with her will be. I know about her morning sickness."

This old man knows everything, Francesco thought.

"If you're thinking of continuing your relationship with her, you need to know these things. Marrying Sarah implies bringing me along. That's why we're having this conversation."

"You're trying to dissuade me from having a relationship with her."

"Of course not." JC smiled and coughed. "I'm showing you the whole picture. I know it's not common to do so in relationships. Only much later do you see the dark side of the one you marry. Consider this conversation a bonus. You can make a concrete decision about your future. Risk it or not, knowing all this implies."

It was too much to digest at one time, and this wasn't the place to do it.

He saw the cripple leave one of the houses on the other side of the street and come over to the car. He had a young man with him.

"We're going to take you to the airport. Don't forget: you saw and know nothing. Only that will guarantee I forget about you," JC warned.

The cripple put the boy in the backseat with those already sitting there. He had dark bruises on his face and traces of dry blood in his nose and mouth. The rest were covered up by clothes.

"Who are you?" he asked fearfully.

"Your father sent us. Don't worry. Everything is fine," JC reassured him.

"Where's my father?" he asked, looking around uneasily.

JC took his cell phone and dialed a number. A little later someone answered and spoke in French.

"How did everything go?" JC asked.

"Just fine. The woman has the documents and is on the plane," someone responded.

"Perfect. Can you get little Ben's father on the line? His son wants to talk to him. Good work, Gavache." He handed the phone to the young man. "Talk to your parents. They're very worried."

While little Ben calmed parental anxieties, JC lowered the window of the door. The cripple bent down to listen.

"Our work is almost concluded," JC whispered.

"What about Jerome and Simon?" the cripple asked, without looking at JC.

"Thank them for taking care of the kid, and tell them to put in a good word for me when they meet their Creator."

The cripple took a gun out of his holster, checked the chamber, and put it away again. "It'll be done. I'll be back in five minutes."

Little Ben said good-bye to his father and gave the phone back to JC. "Thank you so much. That was terrible. I can't thank you enough," he said breathlessly.

The old man smiled with satisfaction.

"You're going home now."

"What is your name, sir?"

"You can call me JC."

58

The Domus Sanctae Marthae was a five-story building ordered built by John Paul II in the 1990s to give some comfort to those visiting the Holy See on business or for devotion. Cardinals, bishops, or priests, some emissary from another country—it was for anyone who came under the good graces of the Holy Mother Church. It was best known for lodging the College of Cardinals in 2005. It was built on the site of the former Saint Martha Hospice, which Leo XIII constructed during a cholera epidemic, and served as a refuge for Jews and others with troubled relations with the Italian government during World War II.

It was certainly not a five-star hotel, but it provided all the necessary comfort for anyone whose only requirement was a good night's sleep.

Hans Schmidt rested a little, not as much as his body would have liked, since he was no longer at an age when he could stay up all night and part of the following day without rest and food. He remembered he hadn't had a decent meal since arriving the previous night. He'd had coffee, some water, eaten half a sandwich, but nothing nutritious.

He opened his eyes. The room was dark, but the afternoon was only half over. He turned on the light over the bed and looked at his watch. It was four fifteen. He'd slept only an hour. He'd give himself fifteen minutes more of rest before going to see Tarcisio and finding out the final developments in his case.

He turned off the light and shut his eyes again. He shut off his mind, refusing to think about anything. During the hour of rest one shouldn't think. Besides, any thought that had no practical effect was an excuse not to do what should be done when reality required it. People revived too many scenes from the past that they later embellished in the way they wished things had happened or anticipated events that had not yet come. Most people lived in expectations and illusions. Hans didn't. He knew perfectly well that expectations grew to the extent they were imagined, and developed according to one's own wishes. Illusion, or delusion, was also a hope, just different, since one hoped that something one didn't really possess would bear marvelous fruit. Both attitudes were mistakes.

So when his cell phone began to ring in the room, interrupting his expected rest, it left him irritated, but he answered the phone with a smile.

"Good afternoon." Even if it was dark as night.

Whatever the call was about, whoever was calling didn't give Schmidt a chance to reply to anything that was said, not even an interjection or expression of surprise. The flush on his face indicated that the subject was uncomfortable to him in some way. Expectations and illusions could be controlled in theory, but not in real life.

"Okay, I'll find a way," he said. Just as he was hanging up the phone, someone knocked timidly on his door. "Who is it?" he called out loudly.

"Trevor," he heard from the other side.

Schmidt got up from the bed, still in his clothes, and went to open the door.

"Good afternoon, Reverend Father."

"Good afternoon, Trevor. Come in, please. I was just getting up to go see the secretary," he explained.

The secretary's assistant came in with a certain shyness appropriate to his position.

Schmidt sat down on the edge of the bed to put on his shoes.

"His Eminence asked that you come to see him. He has news," Trevor informed him.

"Oh, yes? What news?" he asked, tightening the laces on his shoes.

"The parchments are in the possession of the church," Trevor said, uncertain if he should reveal anything, but prompted by the obvious affection between Schmidt and Tarcisio.

"Yes, I was informed."

Trevor looked at him in amazement. "May I ask by whom?"

"By Cardinal William. He called to say the congregation was meeting to decide my future," Schmidt replied.

"I see," Trevor replied, a little confused by the explanation. Cardinal William had been with the secretary when he was asked to go look for the Austrian priest. There was no meeting of the congregation.

One of the two was lying, either William to Schmidt or . . .

There was no more time to devise plausible or credible explanations. A belt tightened around his neck with suffocating intensity. He couldn't breathe. He tried to resist, but Schmidt twisted harder from behind, applying more pressure. The fight for life under these unequal circumstances couldn't last long, not two minutes, and Trevor's life left him.

Schmidt removed the belt from around the corpse's neck, and slipped it through the loops of his pants.

Finally he took the phone and dialed three numbers, sat down on the edge of the bed, and looked at Trevor's body with a serious expression. When the call was answered, he assumed a stricken tone.

"Tarcisio, please, come here, for the love of God. Come quickly. The murderer. The murderer is still in the Vatican."

59

When a routine is broken, altering the natural predisposition of events that, normally, are governed by a well-outlined chronology, it is God's way of showing believers and heretics that everything obeys His will. At least that's what he believed as he returned down the Via degli Astalli for the second time, looking for suspicious eyes. No one was following him.

He'd received the message on his cell phone at his personal number and not on the other card, the black one, where he communicated when he needed information, locations he couldn't find on his own, or some request that required special authorization. This time, against all rules, they demanded his presence, overriding all the standards of security, a sign of urgency. Although the message included a security sign that only his mentor used in the name of God, he couldn't be too careful.

He looked at his watch and decided to take a third turn around the neighborhood to remove all doubt. Ten minutes later he came out on the Piazza di Gesù. He glanced at the passersby, few at that hour, perhaps because it had rained hard earlier in the afternoon. A smattering of tourists were admiring the facade of the Church of the Gesù, designed by Giacomo della Porta, and taking pictures; others walked by in a hurry, paying no attention to what was around them. The traffic was heavy, since the plaza was a central location of the Eternal City with access to the heart of Rome and a transfer point for many other locations.

At first glance all the doors were closed, but he knew that was not so. Not for him.

He walked to the door on the far left, opened a glass-paned door and another wooden one painted green. The creaking hinges announced his presence.

The interior was grandiose. Ten side chapels dedicated to various religious subjects from the Passion to the Sacred Heart, and to the mortal remains of Saint Ignatius, the helmsman for eternity for the society.

At the back, next to the high altar, a man in black was kneeling, hands joined, head bowed. With his back turned he couldn't see who it was.

"Come nearer," the man in black said.

He came forward slowly, checking each niche and exit where he might hide in case of an attack. His senses were fully alert.

"Come, my son. Don't be afraid," the other said. "*Ad maiorem Dei gloriam*. We don't attack our own. *Perinde ac cadaver. Deus vocat.* You have been a faithful servant," he said irritably.

He walked more quickly. He remembered the verse that came to him in the street and smiled. *Have no fear, for the Lord, your God, will fight for you*. He was welcome. He knew it. He felt it.

When he came to the transept, he stopped at a respectful distance from the man who was praying to the Almighty.

"Come closer," the other ordered. "Kneel beside me."

He obeyed hesitantly. Terrified would more accurately characterize his feelings, but he knelt down, blessed himself, joined his hands, and shut his eyes.

He didn't even try to look at the other man out of the corner of his eye. All he could see was the stem of his glasses.

"The enemy deceived us," said the man in black.

What? He hadn't expected this revelation. He had to say something or look like an idiot.

"How did that happen, sir?"

"I lack men like you, my son. Dedicated, competent, believers. We are living in difficult times."

"You can count on me, sir. My purpose is to serve God and God only." This escaped him before he could control his tongue.

"You're my best servant, my son," the other repeated sorrowfully. "Two names are left on your list."

He confirmed that with a nod, though he knew it wasn't a question.

"You're going to have an opportunity to fulfill the will of God tonight. I'm going to give you all the necessary information."

"I'll do it with dedication, sir," he asserted.

"I know, Nicolas. I know," the other said, calling him by his name in a clear demonstration of confidence. He took a paper from his pocket and gave it to the servant. "This is all the information you'll need."

Nicolas took the paper and put it away. It was not appropriate to read it at the moment.

"Your help has been invaluable," the man in black praised him. "What was the code for Ursino?"

"CS," he said.

"We have an RO for the Spaniard, HT for the Turk, IS for the German, and KS for Ursino. What will Ratzinger's be?"

Nicolas was like a timid child who thought he knew the answer, but was uncertain and afraid to reply.

"Say it, man," the other ordered, not missing anything.

"If you will permit me to suggest, sir, I think that Ratzinger and Wojtyla have no code. It seems to me the code should be KHRISTOS."

The other reflected on this a few moments and then raised his hand to his forehead. "Of course. We're blind to the obvious, Nicolas."

"And now, sir?"

"Now follow the instructions I gave you. Our enemy

is now no longer Ben Isaac. We were deceived, but there is time to correct the error," he proclaimed vehemently. "The dice have been rolled."

"Certainly, sir," Nicolas replied, getting up. There was work to do.

"Wait. Kneel down with me. We're going to pray the Our Father together. He'll give us strength to finish this business."

Nicolas kneeled down promptly, hands joined, head bowed, eyes closed, and repeated the Lord's Prayer.

60

No matter how many turns the earth makes around the sun, it always ends up in the same place, as if it were a faithful servant of an unknown order, and although the orbit is always the same, day after day, night after night, year after year, the blue firmament is always different.

Life imitates this rotation, turning on itself and around others, passing the same places but in constant evolution, mobile, changing.

Sarah saw him and blushed immediately as soon as he entered the plane cabin behind Gavache. She had seen him a little more than six months before in this same city, and despite not being the same person herself, it was as if she had just seen him yesterday.

She hated blushing, but fortunately Gavache made sure all the attention was on him.

"Commander, get us on our way. First stop Paris, and then wherever you want. It doesn't matter to me," he said while he took off his overcoat and sat down heavily in a seat.

"We're going to Paris?" Jacopo protested. "What great service."

"How many times do we save lives every day, Jean-Paul?" Gavache asked as he looked out the window.

"Once, Inspector," Jean-Paul promptly answered, seated next to Sarah.

Gavache looked back at Jacopo and frowned. "My work is done for the day."

Rafael and Sarah exchanged looks quickly, then the priest sat down next to Gavache.

An attendant came out of the cockpit and entered the passenger cabin with a cell phone in her hand. "Captain Frank Terry has ordered electronic devices turned off. We'll be taking off in twenty minutes. We'll make a brief stop in Paris and continue on to Rome, our final destination. Estimated time of flight is four hours. I wish you a pleasant flight, and I look forward to serving you." She immediately went to Sarah with the phone. "You have a call, miss."

Sarah lifted the phone to her ear and blushed again on hearing, "Good afternoon, my dear." It was JC. "I hope this hasn't been a boring day." Always cynical. He never changed.

"On the contrary," she replied sarcastically. "The part when you suggested that Ben Isaac kill me was a brilliant touch."

"I couldn't resist, Sarah," JC confessed. "And it worked, as you see." He changed the subject. "I just left your beloved at the airport. Tonight he'll be back in the hotel where you're staying. You should be proud of him. He played his part perfectly."

"I heard." Sarah suddenly felt guilt for not thinking about Francesco. "How is he?"

"I gave him five-star treatment, Sarah."

I imagine so, she thought. But she also knew that Francesco wouldn't appreciate it for a moment. She would have a lot to explain.

"Do you want to give me a message for Cardinal William?" she asked.

"No, thanks. I'll get in touch with him personally. But give my thanks to Inspector Gavache. I'll arrange for his daughter to get into the Sorbonne, but don't tell him that. I'm only bragging. I have to ask you another favor, Sarah. Nothing too difficult."

Sarah closed her eyes. She remembered William in the Palazzo Madama, saying the same thing. *JC told us that Sarah was the right person for the job and no one else. He kidnapped the son of a famous Jewish banker. We're going to put you in contact with him to get back the parchments I spoke about.*

"How will I do that?" Sarah had asked incredulously in the middle of the gallery displaying the faces of Christ.

Just follow the instructions he'll send you during the operation. He gave her a cell phone. *You can't imagine how grateful the church will be for all you are doing.*

Everything had gone well. He'd sent her a message to say that he'd asked Ben Isaac to get rid of her, which made her apprehensive, but then he told her that Gavache and Garvis were on the way. Everything happened according to JC's plan.

Now he was asking her for something else. This man never stopped.

"Tell me," she forced herself to ask. She couldn't avoid it.

"Under the seat you'll find a package. Just follow the instructions. My regards to our favorite priest, also. He must not be very happy to have been left on the sidelines all this time. Until the next time, Sarah," he concluded with a chuckle before hanging up.

Sarah put the phone down on the arm of the seat and reached under. There it was. A white plastic bag. Marks & Spencer. She took out the contents, and her initial suspicion gave way to a suppressed laugh. On a Post-it stuck to the package was written, *Follow the instructions on the back*. JC was priceless. Always a step ahead. She read the text and remembered they were taking off in twenty minutes. There was time. She stuck the pregnancy test kit back in the sack, got up, and went to the lavatory.

In the front seats Jacopo sat next to a window with no one at his side, and on the other side, Gavache by the window, with Rafael next to him. Passing them, Sarah bent down to the inspector. "JC is extremely grateful." She stepped back to look at the priest. "He sends his greetings."

"What does JC have to do with this?" Rafael asked heatedly.

"So you can talk after all!" Sarah exclaimed sarcastically, leaving the men and going to the toilet.

"Are you relaxed enough to tell me what the hell's going on?" Rafael asked irritably.

"The deceived husband is always the last to know," Jacopo spoke from his seat with a smile.

"I'll take care of you later," Rafael warned him.

"Well, well, well," Barry's voice was heard. He'd come up from a compartment in the back of the plane to talk to Rafael, who was surprised but didn't want to show it. "Look who's here." He approached Rafael.

"You're here?" Rafael welcomed him. He had no idea what was going on but didn't want the American to know. "I thought we were going to have dinner tonight. Couldn't you wait? You missed me so much?"

Barry gave him a victory smile. "That trick with the taxi was very good." He shook his hand in greeting.

"It was one of my best moments," Rafael returned. "I see you're in JC's service also."

"Always in the service of the American people," Barry corrected him. "JC left us out of this, but he offered us this small participation as a reward for being so diligent in pursuing the truth."

"He has a special knack for getting people to do things for him without having to ask."

"I thought to myself, why not give him a little hand? What could it be that the church wants back so badly that they have to ask a living legend like JC to do it?"

"I understand you," Rafael said ironically. "They have

to be pretty desperate to ask the pope's assassin to do something like this."

"The alleged assassin," Barry corrected.

"The assassin of who?" Aris asked curiously, joining the group.

"I'd like to introduce my operative, Aris," Barry said. "This is the famous Jack Payne." He looked at Gavache. "And you are?"

"The no-less-famous Inspector Gavache of the French police."

"Pleased to meet you." Barry offered his hand.

Aris greeted the two men also, looking at Rafael more closely than good manners might dictate. "The assassin of who?" he asked again.

"Rafael was talking about JC, the alleged assassin of Pope John Paul the First."

"This is getting more interesting by the moment," Aris said.

"So you decided to give us a ride," Rafael concluded.

"Exactly. For old times' sake."

For a moment there was a feeling of tension in the air. When Rafael was a double agent under the name Jack Payne, he collaborated with the CIA as part of P2, a Masonic lodge controlled by JC. In truth it was a triple situation, since Rafael didn't loyally serve the CIA or JC, but the Holy Church. He was still not looked at kindly by the Agency, but he had earned the respect of the old man. Very few managed to deceive JC and survive.

"I imagine he's somewhere in Jerusalem," Rafael suggested to break the ice.

"You know how he is. Here today, there tomorrow. I didn't want such important documents on a commercial flight. The Holy See is grateful."

I imagine so, Rafael thought to himself. He knew that nothing Barry said was entirely true. Barry wanted to be in JC's good graces, a powerful ally it was convenient to cultivate. Then the Holy See would owe him a favor, whether they liked it or not. But above all, Barry wanted what all secret agencies want—information. Whoever has it comes out on top.

The flight attendant interrupted this pleasant conversation. "Excuse me. We're taking off now, and I have to ask you to take a seat."

"Certainly," Barry obeyed. "Later, Payne."

Rafael looked at Gavache with an unfriendly expression.

"I understand your irritation, Father," Gavache offered. "You've got to understand that sometimes to get the ship to a good port, you need to navigate in the fog."

"I don't understand why I had to come to this plane to meet that bastard," he said, pointing at Jacopo, "and Sarah . . ." Then he stopped, as if he couldn't say more. Of course. It could only be so. He began to shake his head. He couldn't believe it. He was a naive fool. He'd let himself be used like a puppet. He was losing his touch.

"Don't blame yourself, Father," Gavache said, grabbing some crackers the flight attendant was offering on a tray. "You couldn't have known. When we don't want someone to focus on something specifically, we simply—"

"I know how you work," Rafael interrupted. This made him even more annoyed. "You never needed me for anything, right? Jacopo was the bait, and I fell for it like a beginner on his first mission."

"What do you think, Jean-Paul? I never needed the reverend father?" He asked toward the backseat.

"Father Rafael was the one who discovered the Jesuit involvement, Inspector," Jean-Paul replied behind.

Gavache looked at the priest with an expression as if to say, *You see how important you were?*

"But you were working with JC," Rafael argued.

"The only thing I did for JC was guarantee that Sarah would leave Ben Isaac's house with the documents."

"Why did you call me to Paris to stage that scene with me over why I was there or not," Rafael pressured him.

"Why did I call the reverend father to Paris, Jean-Paul?"

"Technically, it was also JC who asked, Inspector."

"Okay, so I did two favors for JC," he responded, without a trace of shame. "That means he holds you in high regard." He took a deep breath. "The truth is, I have two related crimes on my hands, and your contribution to solving them was decisive. I know you'd like a more elaborate explanation, but I'm not the one to give it to you, Father," Gavache concluded.

Rafael blamed himself. How could he have been such an idiot? JC again pulling all the strings in the plot, but this time it was different. JC was involved with the Vatican. He looked at Jacopo angrily. He wanted to strangle him.

"Don't stare at me," Jacopo said uncomfortably. "I didn't know any more than the inspector," he said in his defense.

The engines of the plane started and emitted a rising roar. They were moving to the runway and finally taking off.

Rafael continued to reflect. He was going to have to do something very difficult: talk to Sarah. He looked at her seat, but she still hadn't returned. He began to hear an irritating noise at his side. Gavache was leaning against the window, making more noise than the engines.

While Rafael endured Gavache's snoring, Sarah waited in the bathroom for the result of the test. The instructions said ten minutes for the blue strip to change to red in case of a positive result. No change had taken place yet. She placed the test on the washbasin and avoided looking at it. Each minute seemed like five, a torture. She closed her eyes. Then she turned her gaze away, in case the test gave her a result ahead of time. She found herself hoping the strip would stay blue. Maybe she was selfish, but she didn't want to be a mother, not at this unpredictable stage of her life, when she didn't know where she'd be the following day or where she'd sleep that night. Perhaps in Francesco's cozy arms in their suite at the Grand Hotel Palatino . . . but was that what she wanted? Damn, Rafael made her doubt everything. He had so much influence over her without even lifting a finger, simply by being out there in one of the seats. She was tired, fed up, hungry, unhappy. She needed a hug. She thought about her mother and father and the estate in Beja, Portugal. She'd give anything to be there right now. She needed her father's embrace. The plane shook as if it were rolling down a street full of potholes. Soon they would leave the runway, and the engines accelerated to their maximum power to lift off.

Ten minutes had passed, and she didn't dare look at the verdict. She couldn't do it. She didn't want to face the hard reality. She feared the red strip, the positive result, the divine blessing of procreation. She didn't want to be ungrateful, but . . . two light knocks on the door.

"Miss Sarah, we're in line to take off. We're fifth." It was the attendant's voice. "In five minutes we'll take off."

"I'm coming. Thanks."

Reality was pressuring her. She got up and opened the door. "Excuse me," she called.

The attendant came to the door. "Can I help you?"

She gestured for her to come in. The attendant was surprised but did what she asked. On these flights one didn't question the passengers. For the fortune they paid, wishes were orders.

"Can you see that on the washbasin?" Sarah asked, her voice choking.

"Yes."

"Tell me what you see, please."

"What?"

"Tell me what you see."

The attendant went over to the sink and saw what she

was referring to. She checked it and gave Sarah an uncomfortable half smile. Tears were running down the journalist's face.

"Congratulations," the attendant said in a questioning way.

61

Tarcisio rode in the backseat of a luxurious Mercedes, and felt an unbearable absence, as if he'd lost a familiar part of himself. Trevor had been a dedicated assistant, and Tarcisio didn't return a third of the attention the young Scotsman devoted to him. A man as pious as the secretary of state should not feel remorse. His feelings were supposed to follow a sense of right, of purity, full of love and compassion. Still, he couldn't help but feel overwhelming guilt for having taken Trevor for granted, with never a friendly word of recognition. Although the Scotsman had never indicated he felt the lack of appreciation, Tarcisio now felt he should show a paternal concern for a life whose only detail he knew was his nationality. Tarcisio had been embroiled in his own problems, the church's problems. Never had he called Trevor at the end of the day to ask him about his hopes for the future, how his family was . . . if he needed anything. Trevor never missed work for an illness, never showed a lack of respect toward anyone. The church and the secretary of state were the first priority in his short life. He had died under terrifying circumstances without a friendly hand to help him. Remorse. That's what Tarcisio felt, though his position did not permit it.

His eyes couldn't camouflage his grief and guilt. If it weren't for the presence of Cardinal William and Father Schmidt in the car, Tarcisio would have cried openly.

The secretary didn't have the courage to look at poor Trevor's body splayed out in the corridor of the Domus Sanctae Marthae. It was a sight he didn't want to remember. William spared him that suffering and offered to go in his place. Trevor was not his assistant. He saw him often and always considered him a good person, but felt nothing more than the normal shock of seeing a life cut short in that way.

"This doesn't seem prudent to me," William protested vehemently in the backseat. "It goes against all security standards."

"You've already said that," Tarcisio answered impatiently, his voice breaking a little.

Daniel, the commander of the Swiss Guard, had also disapproved when he'd heard Tarcisio's intention in his office.

"There are security protocols that have to be complied with," he'd asserted. "With all due respect, the secretary of state can't leave the Vatican like a normal citizen or even like a normal cardinal. Your Eminence knows you are not a cardinal like the others, excuse my familiarity." This last remark was for William, who agreed with him and was not offended.

"It wouldn't be the first time," the secretary argued.

"It would be the first time under these circumstances. Two murders in one day. We're under attack, Your Eminence agrees, I know. The secretary of state is the most important prince of the church."

"You don't have to teach me my position, Daniel," Tarcisio grumbled.

"Your Eminence, pardon me, but I can't let you leave without security."

"Be reasonable, Tarcisio," William said.

Tarcisio persisted. "I'm the cardinal secretary of state of the Holy See," he cried, flushed with anger. "His Holiness is the face of the church, but I'm the one who has to expose my chest to the bullets. What happened here today and in the last few days must not happen again. The Society of Jesus wants to negotiate, and with these latest developments they're in a position to do so." His voice broke. "I don't want to belong to a church that won't defend its own."

Daniel took a deep breath after listening to the secretary's arguments. What a situation. "Very well, Your Eminence, I'll prepare a car. You'll take one of my men as the driver, and I'll go in back."

"I'd like to go with Your Eminence to help as much as possible," Father Schmidt volunteered.

Tarcisio laid a grateful hand on Schmidt's shoulder.

"I appreciate it, my friend, but you've been through a lot today, and I want you to get some rest. I'll take care of this."

"I won't be able to rest until you return. Let me go with you, please."

Tarcisio said nothing. He went to the window and looked at the sun setting behind the buildings.

"All right," he finally decided.

"I'll come also," William said.

Daniel held a Beretta up in front of Schmidt's face. "Do you know how to use one of these?"

Schmidt blushed and smiled nervously. "Of course not."

"I'll explain it quickly."

The Mercedes left twenty minutes later with a driver and two Swiss Guards, young but well trained, and two Volvos behind the Mercedes.

"Was it Adolph who called?" William asked.

"No, Aloysius."

"What do you expect from this?"

"I have no idea, Will. Not the slightest."

"But . . ."

"He threatened to kill more people, Will," Tarcisio suddenly confessed. "He said they would kill . . ." He hesitated. "His Holiness, to be specific. After what happened to Trevor, I don't believe I'm in a position to bargain," he added in defeat.

"The bastards," the prefect swore.

"We can't foresee their game, Will. We can only look out for ourselves."

"There's nothing that can be done?" Schmidt asked.

The two cardinals gestured negatively.

"The person who helped us with this tragic operation complied with what was specified. Our interest was only the parchments. They're in our possession," Tarcisio explained.

William didn't approve of the secretary revealing these details to someone unknown. They might be friends, but that didn't give him the right.

"Who did you trust with this job, if I might ask?" William insisted, with no embarrassment or hesitation to interfere.

Tarcisio looked out at the Roman street they were passing before responding, "The pope's assassin."

62

Everyone follows predetermined patterns. His weak father had chosen to be an alcoholic who abused his wife and three children. Being a bricklayer was no excuse for staggering home every night, reeking of alcohol and shouting insults at his children and the bewitching woman to whom he was married. He was cursed for life with the responsibility of being the head of a family . . . or at least that's what he blabbered during those long sessions with a belt in one hand and a beer in the other.

His mother never intervened. She always ended up asleep at the table, deaf to their wails and their father's roars. When he tired of beating them, he knocked her awake and dragged her to the bedroom, slamming the door. A few minutes later the creaking of the bed could be heard.

For years he hated his mother for her weakness, her lack of concern for them, for falling asleep during almost every supper, for having to take her plate away so that her stringy blond hair didn't get in the food, and for leaving them at the mercy of his father's belt. Sometimes he saw her swollen face or eyes, a look of suffering, or a more pronounced limp in a woman who must have been very beautiful once.

He spent the best hours of the day in school, when his father didn't make him come to work with him. He learned to read, though poorly, joining the syllables together with difficulty and stammering over the words like someone with a speech impediment.

One day when he was twelve, he found a book on a shelf in his parents' bedroom, the only book in the house, and started reading it every night. He heard it mentioned in the Mass they attended every Sunday morning. His father would shave, his mother dressed them in their best clothes—his only pair of shoes and the only shirt that wasn't torn—and they went with other parents and children to hear a man talk about Jesus and God. It was probably the only thing his father feared—not that he wouldn't quickly forget everything that very same night, when he would return to his drunken ways.

At first he read with great difficulty, but then he made progress. It was the best story he'd ever heard. He had no idea what the title, *The Holy Bible,* meant, nor did he understand everything he read, but the impression of the stories as a whole was overwhelming. He started reading it every day, over and over, imagining the worlds described, the stories of Abraham, Isaac, Rebecca, Moses and the freeing of the people from slavery in Egypt, the crossing of the Red Sea, the fall of Jericho, Samson, David and Goliath, David and Jonathan, Absalom's rebellion, the wisdom of Solomon, the birth of Jesus, His baptism, temptation in the wilderness, turning water into wine, calming the storm, finding refuge in Jesus's parables, in the special child whose parents loved him, sometimes at the end of one more violent night. The Bible was his fantasy world, Joseph and Mary the parents he wished he had, the Apostles his only friends.

One night he discovered something. His father poured a colorless, odorless fluid into his mother's drink and kept it in the bathroom in a cupboard full of dozens of medicines, many past their expiration dates. His mother slept at the table during supper; his father beat them with the belt. He thought of the Bible, the stories and Jesus, while he endured the belt. His father loosened his trousers to do the rest, but he recalled the Bible and shouted, "God will punish you. God will punish you." Then he shut his tearful eyes. He trembled and prayed, *Help me, Jesus, help me, Joseph and Mary*. His earthly father stopped hitting him with the belt.

"What did you say?" his father demanded, holding the belt up to hit him again, but the boy didn't say anything.

His father put down the belt and said nothing more. He staggered from the table, grabbed his mother, carried her to the bedroom, slammed the door, and moments later the bed began to squeak.

His father never touched him again, even if nights at home didn't change much. His mother appeared with her arm in a sling and her lip swollen, but for him it was as if he had achieved a new status as an untouchable, silent witness, until he couldn't take it anymore and retired to his room to take refuge in his book. But his brothers' cries and frightened gasps pierced his ears without his being able to do anything about them. "Make him stop, Jesus. Make him stop," he begged. He opened the Bible at random and read the first verse. The crying had quieted, and the bed in his parents' bedroom had begun to creak.

The next day he went over to his father, who was sleeping at the table and would not wake again. He struck his head so hard with a heavy plate that it broke. His mother thought it was strange when she felt her son's hand on top of hers. "He's not going to hurt us anymore, Mother."

She got up, upset, and tried to wake her husband without success. "What have you done, Nicolas?" she asked in panic. "What have you done? What's going to become of us?" She couldn't even look at her son.

One afternoon a few days after the funeral, two men in white coats came to get him from his room, just when he was about to read a passage from the Book of the Apocalypse. He struggled but couldn't free himself, and was dragged to a white van, clinging to his book.

Young Nicolas never saw his brothers again.

He was placed in a school, required to follow a rigid schedule of classes and study a lot of subjects, most of which he'd never heard of before. He learned Latin, Spanish, English, French, and Hebrew, but his favorite class was biblical studies, about his favorite book. Of course he read other books, getting to know other stories—*The Odyssey, Oedipus Rex, The Satyricon, The Decameron*—but none of them moved him with passion like the Bible. Perhaps because it had been his lifesaver until the death of . . . the man who said he was his father, but acted like a lunatic. His real father was Father Aloysius, who mentored him to adulthood and gave him his first mission with instructions. "This is God's will," Aloysius told him. "Fulfill it." Nicolas executed that mission perfectly and continued to do so until the present moment at this corner of Via Merulana and Via Labicana.

Night closed over Rome, but the activity remained frenetic, with sounds of cars, motorcycles, buses, vans, pedestrians, horns, and shouts. The impatient Rome of late afternoon. He looked at his watch, which read six thirty. It was time.

He took out his cell phone and waited for the call, which was not long in coming, just six minutes. When he saw the Mercedes, he crossed the street, taking out his gun.

63

Two Volvos followed the Mercedes closely. Daniel, the commander of the guard, was in the passenger seat in the first car, giving orders to a team of eight Pontifical Guards, distributed among the vehicles, including the two that were following the secretary's Mercedes.

The destination was the Basilica di Santa Maria Maggiore, and the GPS detector installed in the Mercedes showed them the way, following the predetermined route.

"This is a mistake," Daniel muttered to himself. "A big mistake."

They weren't using the customary motorcycle escort to clear the street ahead, since this wasn't an official visit. They had no other option than to get jammed up in the terrible traffic at the end of the afternoon, with night already fallen, in this wild autumn season that settled over the peninsula at the beginning of November like an army of rain, wind, and cold that offered no truce.

"Stand by, Adrian," Daniel addressed the driver of the Mercedes called over the radio. "Turn right on Merulana," he ordered.

"Understood. Right on Merulana," the radio answered.

A few feet later, at the Piazza di San Giovanni in the Lateran, the Mercedes cut to the right, following Daniel's orders. The Mercedes was traveling just under the legal speed limit, about two hundred feet in front of Daniel's Volvo. Between them was a number 714 bus and two SUVs. Daniel's attention was fixed on the device recording the position of the car, with only a ten-foot margin of error, which on a street as big as this was negligible.

The bus stopped to pick up passengers about thirty feet from the end of the street and caused a backup in the traffic. The GPS device indicated that the Mercedes was continuing ahead, according to the screen Daniel was concentrating on.

"Attention, Adrian. Pull over and wait for us. We're stuck behind the bus," Daniel ordered.

The GPS indicated that the Mercedes had stopped not far from where they were, close to the intersection with Labicana. Daniel couldn't see them, and this caused him some anxiety, despite his knowing that the secretary was well protected. He let out a deep breath in frustration. The cardinal should have listened to him.

"Nothing's moving in front," the commander protested.

He ordered the driver to pull around the SUVs and the bus, but as soon as the Volvo pulled out, the SUV in front did the same and came to a stop beside the other SUV, completely blocking the road.

"Shit," Daniel said, more to himself than to the others in the car.

The driver leaned on the horn, but there was no reaction. Daniel gestured to the men in the back to go see what was going on. They got out immediately, but were unable to speak to anyone. The drivers of the SUVs jumped out and abandoned the vehicles, slammed the doors, and ran in opposite directions.

The GPS in the Mercedes indicated it was starting forward again.

"What the hell?" This was not normal. "Take the sidewalk," Daniel yelled. "Take the sidewalk now."

The driver swung to the left onto the sidewalk. The pedestrians were forced to scatter, and one of them was even grazed by the taillight and ended up falling to the pavement.

"Keep going. *Keep going,*" Daniel shouted urgently.

The GPS indicated the Mercedes was still moving forward. It turned left on Labicana, moving very fast.

"Attention," Daniel called over the radio. "No order was given to proceed, Adrian," he alerted the agent in the Mercedes. "Attention, Adrian. Report your position."

There was no reply.

The agents who'd left the first Volvo got into the second one, since Daniel didn't want to lose time.

Staring at the screen, he noticed that the Mercedes was traveling in the direction of the Colosseum.

"Get this piece of shit moving," he shouted when they entered Labicana with tires squealing.

There were no traffic rules at the moment. The cardinal secretary of state was in danger.

"Attention," he repeated on the radio. "Report your position immediately, Adrian."

There was still no reply.

"Fuck it," he swore. "Faster, *faster*!" he shouted as he drummed his fingers on the dashboard.

The street was long, and the Volvo was already going too fast. Some vehicles had to pull over as far as possible or even go onto the sidewalk to avoid being hit. The agent drove skillfully. He'd been trained in evasive driving— defensive, and in pursuit—and was more than prepared for a situation like this . . . in theory.

The GPS indicated that the Mercedes had turned to the right to go up Via Nicola Salvi. Daniel had to make a decision. He needed to cut them off.

"Flavian," he called over the radio to the driver of the second Volvo. "Straight ahead. Go up Nicola Salvi."

"Understood," the radio responded.

"Turn around," he said to his own driver.

"What?"

"Turn around, now." As Daniel said this, he grabbed the wheel and turned it toward the left, to the clamor of horns and squealing brakes.

The Volvo accelerated again to the intersection with

Merulana and turned left toward the Piazza di Santa
Maria Maggiore. It was a suicidal high-speed drive at over
sixty miles an hour with traffic and blowing horns.

"Straight to Cavour," Daniel ordered, and grabbed the
radio. "Straight to Cavour, Flavian."

"Understood," came over the radio.

They finally came out on Cavour and careened left
with no concern for the bus coming from Termini, which
had to slam on its brakes to let them pass.

"Idiot," the bus driver shouted, among other insults.

The GPS indicated that the Mercedes had stopped a
few hundred feet from them near the juncture with Via
Giovanni Lanza, and they could see it, badly parked, with
a wheel on the sidewalk and all the doors open.

Daniel feared the worst. His chest tightened with anxiety, and sweat broke out on his face. The tires squealed
when the Volvos stopped abruptly near the Mercedes, one
on each side. Before leaving the car, Daniel could see that
no one was inside the Mercedes. Shit! He should never
have permitted this. Shit!

There was no sign of the secretary, Cardinal William,
Father Schmidt, or the other two agents. As the commander, Daniel could not show weakness or desperation,
but that's what he felt, complete disorientation and,
despite feeling cold as ice, an immensely destructive vol-
cano within.

"What the hell happened?"

64

Tarcisio couldn't believe what his eyes had seen. He would have preferred a knife to the heart, bleeding away the life God gave him. No one should have to suffer such an enormous betrayal.

A man had appeared in the middle of the street, pointing a gun at them. The driver's first action was to accelerate; since he was shielded, a pointed gun didn't pose any threat, but then something seemingly impossible happened. Schmidt and the guard next to the driver stuck guns into the driver's head.

"Stop the car immediately," Schmidt ordered.

"Wha . . . what are you doing, Hans?" Tarcisio asked uneasily.

"Shut up," Schmidt said coldly. His look was glacial, cavernous. Tarcisio had never seen it before, and he shivered.

William was likewise stupefied.

"Drop the gun, Hugo," Tarcisio ordered the agent who was pointing his gun at his colleague.

Schmidt slapped him in the face. "I told you not to talk unless spoken to."

They could hear Daniel's voice on the radio. *Attention, Adrian. Pull over and wait for us. We're stuck behind the bus.*

Schmidt pressed the gun tighter into the back of the driver's neck. "Got it? Even your boss is ordering you to stop. You don't want the secretary to see your brains splattered all over the windshield, do you?"

The driver didn't give in. He was trained to die for the pope or in his name. That was God's will.

"Stop the car, my son," Tarcisio ordered. "It's not worth risking your life for me."

Adrian obeyed the cardinal's order and put on the brakes. He was shocked to see his colleague pointing a gun at him, but said nothing. No one truly knows anyone.

"Good boy," Schmidt said scornfully.

The man outside the car came up beside the driver, opened the door, and plunged a syringe into his neck. It took the driver about five seconds to lose consciousness, and then he was thrown in the trunk of the Mercedes, and the stranger took over the driving.

"It's good to see you, Nicolas," Schmidt greeted him.

"Good evening, Professor Aloysius," Nicolas welcomed him and hit the accelerator.

Aloysius? He calls himself Aloysius? Was it he who had misled him to negotiate with Adolph? Tarcisio asked himself. He was, in fact, a complete unknown, this Schmidt who turned a gun on the two prelates with a forced smile.

"They're everywhere," Tarcisio whispered hesitantly to William, who continued watching all this without a word or a reaction.

Schmidt had a cynical smile on his face. "Did you think you could deceive the society?"

"How can you do something like this?" Tarcisio asked in consternation. He remembered Ursino and . . . Trevor. God, he'd been so blind. "Were you the one who killed Ursino and Trevor?" His cracking voice indicated defeat.

"I'm responsible for Trevor. Ursino liked younger men, like Nicolas." Schmidt was enjoying himself. "Isn't that so, Jonas?" he joked with the driver.

"How could you? After all you defend . . ." Tarcisio interrupted.

"Explanations, explanations. Let's not talk about the past. It's useless. It can't be changed. You know I'm a man of the present, and presently you have the parchments that we want."

"And you think that kidnapping the secretary of state and the prefect of the Congregation for the Doctrine of the Faith is going to get them for you?" William interrupted, recovering his self-control.

"We do."

At that moment, Daniel's voice was heard over the radio again. *Attention. No order was given to proceed, Adrian. Attention, Adrian. Report your position.*

"Turn off that shit," Schmidt, also known as Aloysius, ordered.

"Even if you kidnap His Holiness, you won't get them," William argued, enervated.

"I doubt that."

The Mercedes squealed to a stop so hard that William and Tarcisio were almost thrown into the front.

"We're here," Nicolas said.

Tarcisio tried to see where "here" was, but the street seemed the same as so many others.

They opened the car doors and pushed the elderly prelates inside a closed van that had stopped next to them.

"Get in," Schmidt ordered. "Get inside."

They continued on their way without rush. A few hundred feet further they saw one of the Volvos from the Holy See burst into the Piazza dell'Esquilino, almost colliding with a bus coming from Termini, and head for the Mercedes at full speed.

Nicolas and Schmidt smiled. "They're stupid," Schmidt gloated.

"Where are we going? Where are you taking us?" Tarcisio asked uncomfortably, seated on the floor in the back of the van.

Schmidt showed the same cynical smile with which he had mocked them at the beginning of the trip. "We're going to take a walk, boys. Behave yourselves." He turned to look at Nicolas and assumed a strict expression. "It's time to ask for the ransom."

65

The plane began its descent into Fiumicino Airport while flying over Livorno. They'd experienced some turbulence, especially over the peninsula. The stopover at Orly had been quick. Gavache said good-bye to them in his typical way with an "*Au revoir,* but I hope not" to the men, and a smile for Sarah. He insisted on lightly touching her hair, as if caressing a daughter. He made her promise a future visit to the City of Lights and then left with the faithful Jean-Paul at his back.

Twenty minutes later they took off for Fiumicino. Sarah and Rafael, who had been accompanied on the flight to Paris by Gavache and Jean-Paul, were now alone, each absorbed in their own lives and thoughts. Rafael thought about speaking to her. It would be a good opportunity to find out everything that had happened, but ever since that one-sided conversation in Walker's Wine and Ale Bar, their relationship had cooled to the point where it could no longer be called a relationship. A relationship was what she had with Francesco, the Italian journalist. Yes, he knew about the Italian journalist. He tried to keep himself informed about her life through surveillance. He enjoyed thinking that she knew, although she couldn't have. After Francesco came into her life, Rafael felt he shouldn't interfere. He did, however, investigate Francesco's criminal record. He wouldn't have forgiven himself if he hadn't. After finding a clean record, except for a few traffic tickets, he decided that she was in good company. Until Jacopo had burst into his classroom at the Gregorian to inform him about Zafer's death . . .

He should go to her. Should he? He should. Should he? Nervous, he sighed deeply. No woman should leave him feeling like this. He had a relationship with God . . . not only with God, but with the church, and he owed them fidelity and loyalty. But he had to talk to Sarah. Did he? Yes, he had to. At least to ask her forgiveness for his silence . . .

"May I?" he heard her ask. She had sat down before he could say yes.

"Of course," he stammered. Sarah already had her seat belt fastened.

She looked out the window and sighed. It was dark and there was nothing to see.

For a few minutes they just listened to the noise of the engine moving the plane over Lazio Province. Then they got used to the noise and didn't hear it anymore.

Rafael noticed her swollen, red eyes. She'd been crying. "Are you all right, Sarah?"

"Yes. Fine," she replied immediately, more an automatic response than a sincere one. "And how are you?"

"As you see," he said with a half smile, "I still don't understand what happened."

"That's not normal for you," she observed. "You're always ahead of things, not behind."

Rafael said nothing. It was true, and he felt uncomfortable with the situation. How could he protect her if she knew more than he?

"Unless you have a trick up your sleeve?" she teased.

Rafael rolled up his sleeves to show he wasn't hiding anything.

"JC again, huh?" he asked.

"Always JC," she replied evasively. *Bringing us together and separating us,* she thought without saying it, even though she wanted to.

"Was it the Holy See that asked you to recover the parchments?" Rafael was embarrassed to have to ask.

"Yes. I feel strange telling you these things."

And I feel strange asking, the priest thought.

He'd never felt so defenseless in front of her, so normal, so like a man.

"Cardinal William came for me at the hotel last night," she continued. Last night? It felt so much longer, like weeks. Fatigue was taking over. It was almost nice, after so many hours on edge, of being constantly alert, suspicious, upset. "He explained JC's plan while it was in action. Kidnapping Ben Isaac's son to make him release the parchments."

The death of the "Gentlemen" didn't matter to the pope's assassin, or to the church; only the parchments mattered.

"Have they discovered yet who was behind the murders?" Sarah asked.

Rafael nodded. At least one thing Sarah didn't know. "The Society of Jesus."

Sarah was surprised. "The Jesuits? Aren't they supposed to take a vow of chastity and poverty? How can they go around killing people indiscriminately?"

"It's complicated," Rafael confided.

"Everything's been very complicated. We are carrying around parchments written by Jesus Christ more than ten years after the Crucifixion," Sarah declared, implying that nothing could be more complicated than that.

"Allegedly," Rafael cautioned.

"Everything is alleged when dealing with the Holy See and Jesus. Even with JC. When I call him a murderer, he says the same thing." She paused, hoping Rafael would go on.

"Everything indicates that the society, contrary to what is thought, is a fanatical religious organization that hasn't hesitated to use any and all means to eliminate threats to the church for four hundred years."

"My God!"

"They are the faithful guardians of some important secrets of the Catholic Church with unimaginable power," Rafael added.

"Like P2?"

"Worse than P2. P2 was motivated by money. The society is motivated by religion, and they are practically everywhere. There's no comparison. Getting JC involved seems like a good decision," Rafael concluded.

Sarah looked shocked. She couldn't consider herself an expert on the affairs of the Society of Jesus, but she admired their work in helping the unfortunate and in teaching. The Pontifical Gregorian University was the heir to the Collegio Romano, a prestigious organization founded in 1551 by the Jesuits and supported in 1584 by Gregory XIII, to whom they paid homage by adopting his name. And there were countless colleges and universities they founded and ran. It was hard to believe the Jesuits could be fanatics, much less terrorists.

"Aren't the society and the church on the same side?" Sarah really wanted to understand this.

"They were," Rafael replied. "For three centuries. But things changed in the twentieth century," he declared.

From the beginning, the society acted like a marketing team for the Vatican. They had an easy way of explaining things that laypeople could understand, and they started various rituals that the church ended up adopting. One of these was confession, which, until then, didn't exist.

"Seriously?" Sarah found it curious. There were so many things people just assumed always existed without taking the trouble to realize that everything was the work of men.

Rafael nodded. Even today, with rare exceptions, a

Jesuit priest heard confession from the pope every seven days.

"Impressive," Sarah exclaimed. History only reveals one side, the winner's.

"Where does Gavache come into all this?" Rafael inquired, returning to a subject he disliked, but couldn't avoid.

"I presume that JC must have joined the useful with the pleasant. The crimes were related. He's one of the best inspectors in the French police, and probably a connection the old man has in France." She closed her eyes with a touch of regret. She shouldn't have referred to JC like that in front of Rafael.

He smiled. Silence settled in between them again, but not as awkwardly. Good conversations have their moments of propitious silence, and these should be respected.

The engines slowed, and the plane began its descent. An attendant came to inform them of this. Only Sarah and Rafael were awake.

They were silent, feeling inhibited by each other. The technical details were exhausted; only the personal questions remained.

"I'd like to apologize for my reaction in London that time," Sarah said.

He said nothing.

"I didn't have the right to ask you those questions," she continued. The white light in the cabin hid the blush on her face.

He remained silent. He should say something. He

couldn't stay so timid, as he had in Walker's Wine and Ale Bar.

Talk! Say something, he urged himself.

The plane banked right for a final pass over the runway.

"I'd like to congratulate you. . . ." he started to say.

Sarah was suddenly alert. Did he know about her condition?

"Thank you," she hurried to reply.

"He's Italian, as far as I know," the priest added.

"Yes. A journalist from Ascoli," she said with some relief.

"It will all be for the better, certainly," Rafael affirmed, somewhat embarrassed.

She couldn't help but feel angry with Rafael, Francesco, and her pregnancy. She tried to control herself. She didn't want to insult him, grab him forcefully, and yell, *I'm here, and I can give you things that your God never gave you.* Absurd. Better to end it all now.

"It will be. I'm pregnant," she heard herself say as the plane touched down on the runway. She closed her eyes. Saying it out loud made everything real, it meant accepting.

Nothing more was said.

The plane rolled up to its gate in the middle of Fiumicino Airport, officially named Leonardo da Vinci.

David Barry approached Rafael.

"We've arrived in your city."

"What now? Do you want to certify that the delivery is made?" the priest asked, getting up.

"No. I've got some things to take care of with Cardinal William and then I'll fly back to London."

Rafael knew that Barry just wanted to make sure William wouldn't forget him. That's how the world of secrecy worked. A favor always had to be repaid.

A van with four passengers was waiting for them at the parking area. Rafael was the first to disembark, then Jacopo, clutching the leather case.

The noise of engines and vehicles everywhere was deafening.

Rafael let Sarah enter the van first, then followed her.

"Good evening, Daniel," he said as soon as he sat down by Sarah in the backseat.

The commander's gloomy face didn't fool anyone.

"What happened?" Rafael suddenly asked. It wasn't worth beating around the bush.

Daniel seemed shocked and disoriented.

"Out with it, man!" Rafael urged him.

Barry, Aris, and Jacopo also got in and could see a defeated man.

"They've kidnapped the secretary and the prefect of the Congregation for the Doctrine of the Faith," Daniel stammered, his head down.

Everyone must have thought *What?* But no one said it out loud. No one had expected that, even Daniel.

"How did that happen?" Barry asked, intrigued.

"That doesn't matter now," Rafael interrupted. "They want the parchments, right?"

Daniel nodded.

"How much time do we have?"

Daniel seemed hypnotized, reliving every step since

leaving the Vatican, looking for a way around his incompetence and failure.

"How much time?" Rafael pressed.

"By ten tonight we're supposed to leave the parchments in the Curia Generalizia on Via dei Penitenzieri."

"Or what? Are they going to kill the secretary of state and the prefect?" Jacopo protested. "Do you think they have the balls to do that?"

"They'll kill all three," Daniel replied in a weak voice.

"Three? Who's the third?"

"The pope," Daniel said. "At the moment His Holiness is protected, but one of our agents was an infiltrator. I don't know who's clean and who's not now."

"We'll clean house later," Rafael said decisively. He looked at his watch. It was five minutes after eight. They had less than two hours. "One thing at a time."

"Shall we head for Via dei Penitenzieri?" Daniel asked.

"All this work to hand them over on a tray?" Jacopo complained.

"No. We're not going to give them anything," Rafael said. He turned to look at Barry. "Can I count on the station in Rome?"

"Those bastards kidnapped someone I need to talk to," Barry replied. "Let me make some phone calls."

"What's our destination, then?" Daniel asked. Rafael's certainty was contagious.

The priest took out his Beretta and checked the chamber. "We're going to find the secretary and prefect. I have an idea where they took them."

66

———◆———

Rafael didn't reveal their final destination. In the present state of distrust it was better to rely on himself. He gave the driver directions as necessary: *Turn left, right, straight ahead, enter here*.

They entered Via della Gatta, and Rafael told him to park in the Piazza del Collegio Romano. Rafael, Daniel, and two of his men got out, along with Barry and Aris. Only Jacopo, Sarah, and the driver stayed back. Rafael instructed him to drive around the city, far from there, until he received further orders.

"Can we trust him?" Rafael asked Daniel about the driver.

The commander sighed. "He's never failed me," he replied with frustration. "But Hugo never did, either."

Rafael looked the driver in the eye. You can't tell a person from his face. Every evaluation was subjective.

"Get out of the van," he ordered.

"What?" the agent asked, puzzled.

"Get out of the van," Rafael said, and looked at Jacopo. "Take Sarah for a ride."

"Are you kidding?" Jacopo asked. He was clutching the leather case that held the most important documents in Christianity, and he was clearly upset.

"Show her your skill as a driver." Rafael smiled.

Barry, who was on the telephone, clapped the priest on the shoulder. "Fifteen minutes."

"Okay," Rafael agreed. "Let's hope they aren't late."

He checked his watch. It was nine fifteen.

"Get out of here, Jacopo. Start driving," Rafael ordered, slammed the door, and gave it a slap with his hand. He gave Sarah a final look. He didn't want her stuck in the middle of that craziness.

Jacopo left, complaining about priests who ordered everyone around. He was tired and hungry.

"Give the orders," Barry said, impatient to get into action.

"Follow me."

They walked along the side of the enormous building that was once the Collegio Romano, administered by the Jesuits. It kept its educational mission, but belonged to the Italian government now. At the end of a narrow street they turned left and entered a small plaza, the Piazza di Sant'Ignazio.

Rafael thought about the information Gunter had given him before dying. At first he hadn't considered it important. But after the conversation with Robin, he remembered it. Five narrow streets ended in this small plaza in the heart of Rome, and it was surrounded by small buildings on all sides, except one. On this one a monumental baroque church rose up toward the sky, the Church of Saint Ignatius of Loyola at Campus Martius.

It was an impressive structure, and one couldn't take in the monumental facade all at once.

The church was built in 1650 and functioned as the rectory of the nearby Collegio Romano, located in an enormous building that had been built in 1584, when it became the Pontifical Gregorian University. Later the rectory was moved, but the church remained, dedicated to Saint Ignatius, and despite the former building of the Collegio Romano being turned into a school that no longer belonged to the society, the church remained one of the most important places for decisions the society made.

"Is it here?" Daniel asked.

Rafael looked a few feet above on the tympanum to see the cursed symbol that dominated the center of the facade, IHS. It was here.

The doors were closed. A panel at the side of the main door announced a concert for that night. They were going to play Franz Liszt. Red letters had been written over the announcement: CANCELED.

Two men in black were standing by the panel with

benevolent smiles, explaining to some tourists that the concert had been canceled due to the conductor's illness and that the church was closed.

Rafael told Daniel to order his men to go into the restaurant across the street, while they and the Americans sat in the esplanade, heated by powerful gas heaters. People were eating at most of the tables. A group of six young Spaniards were laughing and talking loudly.

"Are you going in all the chapels?" Barry asked Rafael, enjoying himself.

"How are we going to get in there?" Aris asked.

"By force?" Daniel suggested, before giving his men their orders. He wanted very much to rescue the two most important men in the church, after the pope. He immediately joined the priest and the Americans in the esplanade.

The church was like a fortress that couldn't be taken by force—solid, firm, installed on an entire city block of Jesuit buildings.

Barry picked up the menu to order a drink. "Sentries?" he asked Rafael.

"Look inside the cassock of the one on the right side," he replied.

Barry and Aris observed without being seen. The cassock wasn't buttoned. They could see the shape of a holster.

The waitress came up to get their order. Beers all around. Very friendly and gracious, she gave Rafael a special smile and went off to attend to other thirsty tourists, ignoring the chorus of flirtatious whistles from a group of noisy youngsters.

"What's your plan?" Barry asked.

"We're going to improvise," the priest replied.

Barry nodded his head in agreement and compressed his lips.

"What if the cardinals aren't inside?" Aris asked. There was always that possibility.

"Why have armed men in front of the church?" Barry countered. "It's a church for the love of God."

The young waitress arrived with the beers and set them around the table. She gave Rafael another sweet smile.

"Do you think you could find me a map of the city?" Rafael asked, deploying a little charm that seemed to win her over.

"Certainly."

"Are you going to celebrate Mass tomorrow morning, Father?" Barry asked with a big smile.

The young woman blushed and winked at Rafael, who swallowed a sip of beer. She hurried off to find a map.

"These women," Barry commented, shaking his head.

"The forbidden fruit," Rafael said, uninterested in the conversation. "I think you'd make a good Jesuit," he joked.

"Now that you mention it, I do, too."

The young woman brought the map, folded in two, and gave it to the priest. She took advantage of the opportunity to rub her hand against his. The Spaniards called her over for something.

"I'll bet you she wrote down her number," Barry joked provocatively.

It was very probable, but Rafael didn't look for it as he opened the page with the city center.

"Are you ready?" the priest asked.

"I was born ready. What about these people?" He was talking about the tourists sitting in the esplanade.

"Count on Daniel to create a distraction," Rafael said.

"I'll wait for your signal," Daniel said, ready to act.

"Don't forget, we're dealing with fanatics," the priest reminded them. "Barry, Aris, and I are going in. If I need you, I'll call you."

"I understand," Daniel said.

Rafael pushed back the chair to get up. Barry and Aris followed him. He left twenty euros to pay for the drinks, and walked toward the church door with Barry by his side and Aris behind them. Daniel called one of his men on the radio.

"We're lost tourists?" Barry asked.

Rafael nodded with the map open in his hand, as if trying to find some random place.

"Scusami," he said to one of the lookouts, coming up next to him with the map. *"Fontana di Trevi, dove?"* he asked, pointing at the map.

The helpful sentinel looked at the map with a friendly manner and found the fountain they were looking for. An elbow to the chest, followed by a punch in the nose, while Rafael bent his arm up his back made the lookout lose his balance, requiring him to be supported by the priest. Meanwhile, Barry and Aris overpowered the other with a kick in the knee and a blow to the head.

At the same time on the esplanade, Daniel, now on his feet, kicked the guard who had come to meet him, so hard that it sent him sprawling across the noisy Spaniards' table. Daniel threw himself on top of the table to continue attacking his subordinate, while the tourists and waiters watched apprehensively. One of the customers tried to separate them, but a young man in the same uniform as the fighters saw what was happening and stopped him with a hand on his chest. "Keep out of this."

Rafael and the Americans opened the church door and dragged the two unconscious lookouts inside. The first part was over.

On the esplanade the young man in the Swiss Guard uniform put his fingers in his mouth and whistled. Daniel, still struggling with his subordinate, stopped as soon as he heard the whistle. He got up and helped up the other as well. He composed himself as well as he could and shook the other's hand. "I'll buy you a drink later," Daniel said gratefully.

No one understood what was going on. The Spaniards watched silently, speechless. One thing was certain. It wasn't a good idea to get into a fight with those two guys.

Inside the church the three men were in the vestibule, protected by the inner doors.

"What now?" Aris asked, whispering so that his voice wouldn't echo.

"I'm going to enter on the right and follow along the

side nave. You do the same on the left," Rafael explained. "It's too dangerous to go down the center aisle."

"Okay," Barry agreed. "We'll see each other in front."

Rafael nodded and stuck his hand on the door on the right. "Boys," he whispered with a wink, "try not to get shot."

67

———

Jacopo's nervousness finally left him as they drove around the city. The traffic was lighter, and the stop lights were now the only obstacles to moving ahead.

Sarah turned out to be an agreeable companion, given the circumstances. All hopes for a positive outcome rested with Rafael. Jacopo didn't doubt his capabilities, proven over and over, but this enemy was very different from what they had encountered before.

They drove along Via di San Marco without a specific destination.

"This JC is truly intriguing," Jacopo remarked, taking his eyes off the street. He was not used to driving. "Have you known him long?"

"About four years," she replied, holding tight to the case with the parchments.

"He's not someone I'd want as an enemy."

Sarah knew that well. When she met him, he was just that, an enemy. Even today she didn't know how things had taken such a turn. She tried not to think about it.

"For the church he's an extremely important partner," Jacopo declared. "And after this," he said, pointing at the parchments, "he's an ally."

Sarah knew that their secret underworld was always changing. Nothing was certain: all alliances were tenuous, relationships did not last, words meant nothing. Only money and power mattered.

"Have you known Father Rafael for a long time, Jacopo?" This question had been on Sarah's mind since they had begun driving around.

"Oh, so long I can't remember," he replied nostalgically.

"Was he your student?" Sarah asked, trying to get an answer in another way.

"He was."

Interesting, Sarah thought. She couldn't imagine Rafael as a student. "Did you know his parents?"

"No. His life is a complete mystery, and the Holy See tries to keep it that way. No one knows where he comes from, his family . . . He came out of nowhere."

The mystery thickened. Who *was* Rafael? Maybe she could collect a favor from JC and ask him. *Oh, shut up,* she reproached herself. She was in a relationship, pregnant, and had nothing to do with Rafael's private life or his origins.

She clutched the case and took advantage of the opportunity to change the subject. Rafael upset her too much.

"Do you think this parchment was actually written by Jesus?"

Jacopo didn't reply right away. He obviously felt conflicted. "Everything is possible."

"I'd like it a lot if the things the church has been teaching us since childhood weren't lies," Sarah said with a fanciful expression. "But it seems more and more impossible to believe anything that comes out of there." She pointed at the cupola of Saint Peter's Basilica, which could be seen from where they were.

"You said it," Jacopo lamented. "What's born crooked can't be made straight."

"Still, it's lasted for two thousand years," Sarah observed.

Jacopo smiled. "As you said yourself, it's hard to believe everything that comes from there. One needs to question everything, including the heritage they claim."

Sarah understood what Jacopo wanted to say, or at least she thought she did. "Are you saying that Pope Ratzinger is not the heir to Peter or, consequently, to Jesus?"

"I'm saying it's possible he's not," the historian corrected her. "We have the right to question everything, Sarah. Think about it. You're carrying a gospel that puts the church in a difficult position. If in fact Jesus was the person who wrote it, how could that be justified? To say nothing of the historical impossibility of connecting Peter to Linus, the second pope, and consequently the popes that followed him."

"Seriously?" There were things that left even Sarah

puzzled. "That connection is the raison d'être of the church."

"It is, Sarah. But it was fabricated. Conclaves are very recent. The term *pope* itself came into use only in the third century, though back then it meant all Catholic bishops. In the sixth century it was used to designate only the bishop of Rome, and only in the ninth century did it become the official title it is now."

"What does *pope* mean?"

"It's thought it has to do with the first syllables of the words *pater* and *pastor,* but that's only a theory."

"How was it that a history that began so long ago in Israel could culminate here in Rome and turn Rome into the center of the Christian world?"

"Think about it. Rome was the capital of the empire that ruled Israel. Two plus two . . . for the creation of a new religion to subjugate the population, Rome had to play a predominant role."

"My God."

"The truth is, Sarah, that we've attributed what we can't explain to God from the beginning, and we continue to do so. Men in power understand this and use that knowledge for their own interests."

"But you work for a church that misrepresents things."

"We all have our price, Sarah," Jacopo confessed. "That said, what better job than to discover what's true and what's a lie?"

"Have you been able to discover that?"

"I've only achieved more doubts and questions," he replied with a frustrated smile.

"Have you seen what's inside here?" She pointed to the case.

Jacopo shook his head no. "I still don't have the courage."

At that moment Sarah's cell phone vibrated, announcing a new text message. She felt a moment of anxiety in her heart. Maybe it was Francesco saying he'd arrived. She read the text, but didn't understand it immediately, despite its being short and clear.

"News?" Jacopo asked.

"The driving around is over. We have to go to this location." She showed the screen to the historian.

He read the message and swallowed dryly. "Why didn't I stay at home?" he complained.

The Church of Saint Ignatius of Loyola, 15 minutes was written on the screen.

68

Rafael opened the inside door on the right, careful to make no noise, and entered silently. He closed the door and walked agilely through the side nave. He looked around the immense central nave, but neither saw nor heard anyone. The light was dim, favoring both sides.

He went past Saint Christopher's Chapel toward Saint Joseph's, using the columns and niches to shield himself. He looked over at the side nave on the left and saw Aris and Barry advancing cautiously in front of the chapel of the Sacred Heart of Jesus.

As he continued, he began to hear voices, imperceptible at first, disconnected, a murmur, and then words, entire phrases, a laugh he didn't recognize, Tarcisio's voice pleading for the craziness to stop, William's warning that they'd regret all this. The laugh again.

"God is going to punish us, Prefect?" The same male voice that laughed asked. "Even though you gentlemen hired a criminal to murder a Supreme Pontiff? I really don't know who deserves more punishment."

Rafael moved a little closer. He hid behind a column and peered around the edge. Tarcisio and William were seated on chairs turned toward the altar on the right side of the transept, dedicated to Saint Aloysius Gonzaga, a Jesuit who died in the prime of life from the bubonic plague. There were four kidnappers: a man in a cassock, much younger than the cardinals, and three younger men in suits. You can't trust a man in a suit or a cassock.

Beyond Saint Aloysius's altar, next to the high altar, he could see the funerary monument of Gregory XV and of Cardinal Ludovico Ludovisi.

"What can the pope's assassin do to us?" the priest continued.

Tarcisio and William were sweating profusely.

"You're not going to get away with it, Hans. The pope will concede nothing," the secretary argued.

"The pope has no choice," Rafael heard a voice say from the altar.

Rafael couldn't see where the voice came from, but he recognized the voice of Adolph, the superior general, who was walking toward the group with firm, decisive steps, a leader of men and the faithful.

"The pope is the Supreme Pontiff, the pastor of pastors. You can't do anything to him," William shouted.

"In theory you're right. But that's going to change

tonight," the superior general declared with a scornful smile.

The four kidnappers were silent and lowered their heads in respect. Tarcisio shivered.

"You're a heretic," William insulted Adolph, outraged.

"Infidel," Adolph answered with the same tone. "I want the pope to sign an agreement with us. Since that's something you're used to doing."

"I can't negotiate in his name, and given how you're treating high dignitaries of the church, I don't—"

"There's one thing I've learned in life, Tarcisio," Adolph interrupted. "Everything can be forgotten to preserve a higher good."

Tarcisio spread his arms dramatically. "*This* can't be forgotten."

Adolph smiled sardonically. "This never happened, you know very well. It'll never appear in the history books."

"What do you want?" Tarcisio asked, irritated.

"That Ratzinger sign an agreement to name a Jesuit to succeed him when God calls him to His side. Obviously."

"Are you crazy?" William reprehended him. "His Holiness will never agree to that."

"That's too bad," Adolph replied. "We guard your greatest secrets loyally," he added pointedly.

"Spare me, Adolph," Tarcisio protested. "You are the loyal guardians of a fraud. The bones of Christ, parchments that were probably written in the sixteenth century."

"How dare you repudiate our work that Saint Ignatius—"

"Don't make me laugh, Adolph," Tarcisio provoked. "Whatever he brought from Jerusalem weren't the bones of Christ but some John Doe nobody knows about."

Tarcisio sounded as if he possessed a higher truth.

"You have a very high opinion of yourselves," the secretary insisted. "Do you think if they were really the bones of Christ, the Holy See would have left them in your hands? You were used to carry them wherever the pope decreed. Nothing more."

Adolph's face twisted in rage. He looked at his watch. "Ten o'clock. Time's up."

A cell phone rang loudly at just that moment. Adolph took it out and listened without saying a word. He disconnected and smiled. "It appears His Holiness has conceded. His secretary and prefect are worth something to him, after all."

Tarcisio and William looked at him, puzzled. Rafael thought it all very strange.

"It's not what we agreed, but the parchments will be delivered here," the superior general informed them.

"How do they know we're here?" Schmidt asked, surprised.

"What does it matter, Aloysius?" Adolph interrupted. "What matters is the parchments will be in our power. If Ratzinger gives in on this, he'll give in on the rest." He smiled with good reason. "Tell the men to let whoever the Vatican sends come in, Nicolas."

Nicolas raised the radio to his lips. "Attention, Giovanni."

Rafael got up noiselessly. There would be trouble when Giovanni didn't answer.

"Giovanni, come in," Nicolas ordered.

No one answered.

"Go see what's going on," Schmidt ordered.

Nicolas took out a gun and left for the door. "Keep your eyes open," he said to Schmidt as he left.

Rafael would not have a better opportunity to act. It had to be now, though the telephone call Adolph had received confused him a little. It had to be quick. First the agents, then the priest, if necessary. He waited until Nicolas had walked through the central nave to the entrance.

One shot. Two. Right to the head to make sure. Schmidt couldn't react, only staring at the fallen bodies of the agents, incredulously.

Tarcisio blessed himself. William fell out of his chair. Rafael pointed the gun at Schmidt and approached him. "Quiet. Get on the floor." He looked at Adolph. "You, too. Get on the floor."

Adolph refused and looked at him sternly. "Do you know who I am?"

"I don't know, and I don't care," Barry grumbled, approaching them. "Do what he told you, old man, before God calls you to wash His feet."

Adolph got down, scowling with fury.

"Check to see if they're armed," Barry ordered Aris, who shook down Adolph and Schmidt, taking a gun and radio from the latter.

The adrenaline began to kick in.

"What was all that about the pope giving in?" Barry asked.

"I have no idea," Rafael answered, turning to the cardinals, who didn't know what was going on, either. "Let's wait and see."

"Call your man," Barry ordered Adolph.

The superior general, his head resting on the floor, gestured toward Schmidt. Aris returned the radio to the priest.

"Nicolas, where are you?"

The reply was immediate. "I'm up here at the entrance. I'm bringing you some company. There are Swiss Guards outside. Tell them not to come in, if they don't want to get covered with her brains," he threatened. "I'm not kidding."

Rafael felt as if he had been shot by them. Nicolas had said *her*. His heart was in his mouth, and he was upset, though not showing it. Was he talking about Sarah? If so, what the hell was she doing there?

"I'm coming back," Nicolas's voice came over the radio. "I'm not afraid of killing or being killed," he stressed so they'd know he wasn't joking.

Rafael watched the entrance and felt desolate when he saw them enter through a side door. Sarah and Jacopo with Nicolas behind them, a gun in each hand pointed at their heads. They were walking so slowly it would take them an eternity to join them.

Rafael wanted to know how this could have happened.

"What are they doing here?" Barry asked.

"I have no idea," Rafael replied.

"What now?"

Rafael sighed. "Let's be very careful."

"It'd be a shame to waste such a pretty woman," Barry said.

"I don't want any hasty moves," Rafael warned. *Nothing bad can happen to Sarah.* He'd never forgive himself.

Finally the three got to Saint Aloysius Gonzaga's chapel.

"Let the superior general and Father Aloysius get up," Nicolas ordered.

Rafael let them up. There were too many Aloysiuses in the story. Aris and Barry placed themselves behind them strategically, with guns pointed. They had to keep the game counterbalanced.

As Adolph regained his posture, his arrogance doubled. "Did you bring the parchments?" he asked.

Jacopo hung on to the leather case that Nicolas was trying to grab from him.

"This should be it," Nicolas said.

"You're not going to get away with this," Rafael warned. "There are agents everywhere outside."

"Shut up," Nicolas said. "This isn't over until we say it's over."

"Sons of bitches fanatics," Barry swore.

"Bring me the case," Adolph said.

Nicolas obeyed promptly.

"What now? Are we going to stay here staring at each other?" Rafael asked.

Sarah's frightened expression broke his heart. This wasn't in his plans. He wanted to avoid it at all costs.

"Let's stay calm," Tarcisio asked. "No one else has to suffer."

"I have what I want," Adolph said, holding the case tightly.

He opened it and cautiously took out the contents, handling them like the most valuable of prizes. He checked them and his solemn face turned angry.

"Is this some kind of joke?" He grunted, waving the pages in the air with no attempt to protect them. "Are you joking with me? Did you think you could fool me?"

No one understood, but the papers certainly didn't seem ancient rarities.

"That's what they gave me," Sarah argued.

"Do you think I was born yesterday?" Adolph shouted. "All that's in here are the agreements the Holy See made with Ben Isaac. "Don't fuck with me." He was completely beside himself.

"Let's stay calm," Rafael requested.

Things couldn't get out of control, precarious as they already were.

Sarah was mystified. Jean-Paul had gone to the vault. She'd seen him go there. He had given her the case, and no one had opened it until now. How could . . . ?

The superior general's cell phone rang. He listened. Someone said something, and he immediately disconnected and put it back in his pocket.

"How are we going to resolve this?" Rafael asked.

It could turn into a bloodbath.

Another phone started to ring. After a few bars the ringtone became clear: "The Star-Spangled Banner." Barry's phone.

"Barry," he said, answering it.

He listened a few seconds, then took the phone from his ear and punched a key. "Okay, you're on speakerphone."

"Good evening, gentlemen," they heard a voice say.

Sarah managed a half smile as she recognized JC's voice.

"Who is it?" Adolph asked angrily.

"You're very rude, Adolph. Hanging up without hearing what I have to say," the voice reproached him.

Adolph was not worried. "Who are you?"

"The last person who hung up on me is no longer with us. I have a very quick temper when it comes to bad manners."

"Cut the shit," Schmidt said arrogantly.

"Oh, oh, oh! What impatience, Reverend Father Hans Matthaus Schmidt, or do you prefer your Jesuit name, Aloysius?"

The voice made Adolph and Schmidt uncomfortable.

"My own name doesn't matter. You can call me JC."

"Pope Luciani's assassin," Schmidt whispered to Adolph.

"Men are the most predictable creatures in existence," JC continued over Barry's speakerphone. They don't understand each other, they don't share, they don't like to lose. I'm including myself. I'm the same."

"Is there some point to this conversation?" Adolph asked.

"I've decided neither one of you will get the parchments. I shall be their faithful guardian."

"That's not what we agreed," William put in, visibly discouraged.

"We agreed to recover the parchments. I never said I'd give them to you."

"That was implicit," William argued.

"I can be slow to understand," JC said ironically.

Adolph looked at Tarcisio furiously. "Do you see what happens when you get involved with criminals? The pope's assassin, for the love of God. What were you thinking?"

"I must add *allegedly* to your name-calling," JC corrected him. "In any case, I want you to lower your guns and go your separate ways."

Nicolas laughed; so did Schmidt.

"And we should just because you say so?" Schmidt asked.

"I'll excuse the reverend father because he's never heard of me. But I won't repeat my order to lower your guns," JC declared.

The impasse and tension remained: Nicolas with two guns pointed at Sarah and Jacopo, Aris covering Schmidt and Adolph, Rafael and Barry pointing their guns away.

"Kill them," Adolph ordered Nicolas.

"Stay calm." Rafael tried to aim in Sarah's direction to see if he could hit Nicolas, but Nicolas was shielded by the two of them. It would be a difficult shot.

Sarah closed her eyes in panic.

"Oh, my God!" Jacopo stammered, terrified.

"Kill them," Adolph said again, without a trace of emotion.

Two shots echoed through the immense structure of the church. Nicolas was thrown forward, arms wide, pushing Jacopo and Sarah aside with the impact of the bullets between his shoulders.

Adolph looked around, but saw no one. The CIA men and Rafael did the same. Nothing, no one.

A chuckle echoed over Barry's cell phone.

"If you disobey me again, Adolph, it'll be your head next time," JC warned.

The superior general was livid. Schmidt was sweating profusely. Rafael smiled to himself. Sarah was white as chalk, crouched on the cold floor. Jacopo was fleeing through the nave toward the exit.

The doors suddenly opened to admit a dozen agents under Daniel's orders. Jacopo passed them without stopping. No one cared about the cripple who went running after Jacopo.

"Both of your sides are defending a lie," JC offered. "You're all very far from the truth. If you knew . . . if you knew. You can kill yourselves some other day, not today, with my people involved. Remember one thing. I see and hear everything." He disconnected the call.

Adolph suddenly left in the direction of the sacristy, muttering imperceptible curses, frustrated profanities, with Schmidt at his heels. Nicolas dragged himself along painfully, bleeding from both shoulders.

Rafael went to Sarah and hugged her. "Are you all right?"

"I think so," she murmured.

Daniel came up to them. "How are you?"

"It's over for now," Rafael said. "We need to clean this up," he said, pointing at the bodies on the floor.

"I'll have it taken care of," he assured him, approaching Tarcisio and William to provide security for them. Then he prostrated himself before the secretary and cried, "Pardon my failure, Your Eminence."

Tarcisio placed his hand on Daniel's head. "You're not guilty at all. You couldn't have done anything, Daniel. The Lord's plans are unknowable. Get up, my son."

Barry extended his hand to Rafael. "The old man is tough."

They shook hands. "Thanks, Barry."

Barry looked at his watch. "Perhaps there's still time to dine at Memmo."

"Okay," Rafael accepted. "Just let me see if . . ." He looked in Sarah's direction, but she wasn't where he'd left her.

He caught a glimpse of her in the middle of the nave, looking at a trompe l'oeil fresco that created the illusion of a nonexistent cupola, an ingenious masterpiece by Andrea Pozzo. He ran over to her.

"You made things real easy," she was shouting upward, red in the face. "Real easy."

Rafael had never seen her like this; she was beside herself.

"I could have died, JC. You played with my life," she continued to shout furiously at no one.

A coughing attack made her double over. She raised a closed hand to her mouth to stop the coughing. Rafael ran to help her.

"Are you all right, Sarah?" He was worried.

She coughed a little more and then calmed down.

"Do you feel better?" he wanted to know.

"It's over, thanks. Something caught in my throat."

Rafael shook his head and looked at her hand.

Sarah followed his glance and understood. Her hand was full of blood.

69

It was like a rebirth.

When Myriam saw her son coming down the steps from the plane at Heathrow, a little after midnight, thin, rumpled, with a knapsack on his back, it was as if she'd given birth to him a second time. Her tears flowed uncontrollably as little Ben embraced her, crying and smiling, too, like a newborn. His father also hugged him tightly, feeling as if he'd recovered a part of himself he thought he'd lost forever. The entire nightmare had vanished with his son's smile and the opportunity to touch, embrace, and caress. Everything was good.

"You can never go out again without my permission, son," Myriam said, with a voice still heavy with emotion.

"I need a vacation, Dad," Ben said with a smile.

"Of course, Ben. I'll take care of everything."

They got into the backseat of the car. Myriam gave both of them an unhappy look. "You're going to delegate authority, Ben. All three of us are going on vacation, as a family."

"Please, not another cruise," Ben Isaac objected.

"We will not be taking another cruise. I promise."

"Take us home, Joseph," Ben Isaac told the driver.

Having his son safe and sound was worth any price, all the money he had . . . any parchment.

They looked at the London streets as if seeing them for the first time. The long lines of traffic didn't matter, nor did taking more than an hour to get home. The lights in the dark streets were comforting. The most important thing was that they were all together. They were a family again, or for the first time.

Myriam wanted everything to last forever. Her husband, her son, together, united, the Isaacs.

"I'm going to call Dr. Forster to see if you're all right," Myriam advised when they arrived at the house.

"That's not necessary, Mother. I'm fine."

"Your mother's right. We want to make sure," Ben Isaac admonished him. "Do you want me to call a psychologist?"

The experience could have been traumatizing.

"Not for now," the young man declined. "Let's see how things go and decide later, okay?"

He couldn't lie to himself. It hadn't been a walk in the park. He'd been tortured, and had seen an innocent person killed in front of him. That couldn't be erased, wiped from his memory like a computer hard drive.

"That seems sensible to me," his father agreed. "What about you, Myr?"

His mother held his face in her hands and looked at him directly. "Don't hold things in. That does no one any good. If you need help, we're here."

Little Ben didn't say yes or no. The car parked at the door of the large house inside the Isaac property.

"I'm going to take a long shower and go to bed," the young man declared as soon as he got out of the car. Coming home was a wonderful feeling.

"That sounds like an excellent idea," his father said jovially.

"Ah!" Little Ben remembered something, opening his pack and taking out a package for his father.

"What's this?" The older man asked curiously.

"Your friend sent you this. He said you should guard it in the vault, and it couldn't be in better hands."

Ben Isaac had no idea what his son was talking about.

"You've never mentioned him," little Ben observed.

"Who?" his father asked.

"JC."

"Let's go, darling," Myriam called, hugging her son. "Go take your shower and rest."

She walked her son to the door and stopped to look at Ben Isaac.

"Are you coming?"

"In a minute," he replied.

He walked to the vault with the package in his hand. It should contain a large bound book inside.

He descended the twenty steps and walked to the solid door. He was nervous. Who was this JC, whom both his son and Sarah mentioned?

He entered the code to open the door: KHRISTOS.

He placed his eyes in front of the screen and a blue light read his retina. Entry authorized.

He entered a cold chamber as soon as the heavy door opened. He didn't have the courage to look at the showcases. He felt sad about not being able to look at the written words of the parchments again.

He turned in front of the door to unwrap the package his son had given him. Inside was a book protected by a plastic bag with a hermetic seal. There was a Post-it attached. He read the message.

Nothing has changed, except only you and I know, and I've already forgotten.

He opened the seal and took the book out very carefully. He was completely perplexed. Nothing has changed?

The cover revealed nothing, but the first page said it all.

The History of Jesus, the Nazarite.

The entire text was written in Hebrew.

Tears ran down his face. The experience sent waves of anxiety through him.

He turned some of the pages, yellowed with time, of the ancient transcription. The story of Jesus according to Mathew, John, Simon Kepha, Judas Tome, Phillip, Bar Talmay, Myriam. It was all there, a testimony from those days.

He would guard it in one of the showcases, since there was room now. He went over and looked at the displays, astonished. There, immune to the passage of time, were the Gospel of Jesus and the inscription placing Jesus in Rome in A.D. 45. How could that be? Only one of the showcases was empty, the one containing the Status Quo agreements of 1960 and 1985.

He read the Post-it over again and smiled incredulously. *Nothing has changed, except only you and I know, and I've already forgotten.*

Who was this new unknown friend, known by two letters that could mean nothing? He glanced at the inscription and the Gospel of Jesus again and locked the new item very carefully in the empty showcase.

He returned to the heavy door and looked at the three showcases. He took a deep breath and turned his back. The world always sets things right.

70

God had expressed Himself, but for the first time he hadn't understood Him. He first found Him in the Holy Scriptures that had turned him into His most faithful servant. He had sent him Aloysius, who had guided him through the meanderings of the Word and the Mystery, teaching him the true meaning of all the passages of the Bible.

Tonight God had sent him a message he couldn't decipher. The pain in his shoulders made him almost lose consciousness. He was laid out on the backseat of the car Aloysius was driving.

"I should take you to the hospital, Nicolas," his worried tutor advised.

"No, Professor. I'll deal with this at home," he said, in pain.

"I hope you know what you're doing."

Aloysius, or Schmidt, or the Austrian iceman, was devastated by what had happened. Everything overthrown by a stranger, a legend.

He had no doubt he had started a war with the church, and if things were bad now, they would only get worse.

She was already in bed when they arrived. She was awakened by loud knocking on the door. She hurried to open it, and saw an unknown man walk in behind Nicolas, who was wounded.

"My God!" she stammered, frightened.

Nicolas lay down on the floor, full of pain. "You don't need to stay, Aloysius. She'll take care of me. Get some rest."

Aloysius looked hesitant, then said to him, "If you need anything, call me. Do you hear?"

"Of course," Nicolas agreed.

"Did you hear me?" Aloysius asked her arrogantly.

"Yes, sir," she replied.

Nicolas twisted on the floor, sweating, moaning, and shivering. "Get me the first-aid kit," he ordered his wife.

She hurried to obey. She heated some water, brought clean towels and a knife to use as a scalpel if necessary.

She took scissors and cut his shirt away from the wounds to begin the operation. None of the bullets had exited.

"You're going to have to get them out," he told her. "Go and get the case out of my dresser drawer."

She obeyed and came back in a few moments with a small black case. She knelt down by him and opened it. It was full of containers, needles, and a syringe. She recognized the syringe and could almost feel the fluid injected into her veins, more times than she could remember.

"Attach the needle to the syringe, insert it into the flask, and extract the fluid," he explained, almost fainting.

She did it with some difficulty, then repeated the gesture she'd seen him perform so often, squeezing the syringe until a few drops left the needle.

She started to insert it into his arm, but he grabbed her hand hard. He gasped with pain.

"Wait. Get the book from the pocket of my shirt."

She put the syringe on the floor and found the book easily. It was the paperback Bible.

"Open it at random," he ordered.

She did.

"Choose a verse and read it to me."

Her voice was nervous, but then gained strength at the end. *"Behold the eyes of the Lord are on those who fear Him, on those who hope for his mercy."*

He thought about the words she read him for a few moments and made a decision. "I'm ready."

She looked at the needle and injected the contents of the syringe. It would take 120 seconds to take effect.

He raised his head suddenly and frightened her. He seemed delirious.

"Will everything be all right, Mother?" he asked. "Tell me everything will be all right, Mama."

She stroked his hair.

"*Shhh.* Rest. Everything's fine, my son. It'll go away."

Two minutes passed and Nicolas fell into a deep sleep. There was no more pain, doubt, or disillusion. Everything was perfect.

She opened the small pocket Bible again at random and read the first verse her eyes hit upon. *I will place my hopes in the Lord; I will hope for the God of my salvation; my God will hear me.*

She took a deep breath and picked up the knife she'd found in the kitchen. She looked at Nicolas's serene face, breathing peacefully, imprisoned in a drug-induced sleep. Her first stab was right in his heart, the second, an inch or so to the side. She continued stabbing his chest eighteen times, her fury increasing with each motion. When she stopped, she looked again at his peaceful face. He wasn't breathing.

She took her time washing Nicolas's blood off her skin. A hot, restoring bath, whose steam billowed into a cloud on the ceiling of the bathroom. She put on a blue dress with a jacket and packed a small suitcase into which she put Nicolas's Bible. He didn't need it anymore. She carried the suitcase to the hall and went to his room, to his first dresser drawer, where there was another case, larger than the one that held the syringe. Inside were stacks of fifty-euro bills. She emptied the box and went to the hall for her suitcase. She looked at Nicolas's corpse one last time. He appeared to be sleeping.

"We'll see each other in hell, Nicolas," she said bitterly before going out into the cold, dark night.

71

The next day dawned sunny, as it often does after a storm.

Rafael had spent the whole night in a chair at Sarah's side in the Policlinico Gemelli, courtesy of His Holiness Pope Benedict XVI, who intervened personally to make sure the journalist was treated with every comfort.

Tarcisio had called Rafael early in the morning to meet him at the Basilica of Saint Paul Outside the Walls on the Via Ostiense, where Tarcisio was presiding over a ceremony celebrating the founder, Don Bosco. It appealed very much to the secretary's heart, since it was a Salesian ritual, and he himself was a Salesian brother.

Rafael showed up at the designated hour, ten in the morning, in the basilica where the bones of the apostle Saint Paul are exhibited. A line of Salesian priests and brothers filed past the secretary, who was seated next to the altar. The ceremony lasted about fifteen minutes, with a choir singing the praises of God, and then there were many petitions, since it was not every day they had the privilege of speaking personally with such an important figure. Rafael stood next to the tomb of the apostle, who never knew Jesus but contributed decisively to His immortality. Rafael watched. The wide nave with eighty columns was full of tourists taking photos of the portraits of the popes displayed throughout the edifices, from Peter to Benedict—the sixteenth to use that blessed name.

The stampede of brothers eased up gradually as they went to enjoy a simple meal being served in the cloister. Tarcisio delayed a little to exchange words with the rector of the Salesian congregation—instructions and recommendations from someone in an influential position important to the order.

The secretary returned to the sacristy. An assistant who had taken Trevor's place came over to Rafael next to the canopy.

"His Eminence can see you now," he said.

Rafael followed him to the sacristy, where Tarcisio was waiting.

"Good morning, Rafael. I'm sorry to have kept you waiting. Sit down, please," he said, gesturing toward a chair next to a large oak table. "Did you get any rest?" Tarcisio asked.

"I dozed a little in the hospital."

"Is Sarah all right?"

"We'll have to see," Rafael replied.

"I'll mention her in my prayers," Tarcisio offered.

Rafael knew he would.

"Your Eminence never questions things?" Rafael asked, a little intimidated by the question he couldn't hold back.

"What do you mean?"

"Do you ever doubt your faith?"

Tarcisio sighed. "Someone who wants to believe must first doubt. Faith comes after doubts, not before."

Rafael took a deep breath. It was a profound response.

"Whoever never doubts never really knows what it is to believe," the secretary added.

Rafael was a man with doubts, but he was in the presence of one of the most powerful men in the world. He didn't know how to express his doubts without showing a lack of respect.

"Yesterday I realized things that . . . that . . ."

"That put your faith in doubt," Tarcisio concluded for him.

Rafael neither confirmed nor denied it.

"My dear Rafael, I understand your confusion, your doubts, but let me say that they're unfounded."

"I'm afraid everything is just a misunderstood exaggeration of history by Paul, whose bones may not even lie in that tomb out there."

"They're in there, for sure, Rafael," Tarcisio reassured him.

"Then what is the society guarding?"

"A great lie. A Jesus who never existed. Don't forget

something, Rafael. We're His heirs. This is not based on anything that can be denied."

Rafael wanted very much to believe this, but he felt a storm of doubts at the moment. He didn't have the clarity of thought to distinguish between true and false or a plausible invention.

"Excuse my presumption, Your Eminence, but why are you a Catholic?"

Tarcisio smiled condescendingly. "For two simple reasons. Because I want to be and I can be."

It was an affirmation of freedom, in fact, that put faith on the level of a simple choice. Either one accepted freely with a spontaneous will or rejected it, purely and simply.

"I called you here because His Holiness asked me to give you this." Tarcisio handed him a rare book with extremely worn pages.

Rafael opened it carefully. It was written in Latin with the title *Jesus the Nazarite*. The priest turned his eyes to Tarcisio, astonished.

"His Holiness doesn't want any of his flock to have doubts or confusion. The answers to your questions are there," he explained. "It's a loan. His Holiness would like it back when you're finished."

"Of course," Rafael said with a smile. This gesture made him feel better.

A piece of paper fell out of the book. It was a photocopy of a carbon-dating test showing that the material analyzed belonged to a male from the fifteenth century.

"What's this?"

"It concerns the bones the Jesuits have been guarding."

The fifteenth century, not the first. This is why Tarcisio always spoke of a fraud. He knew.

"What's going to happen now between us and the society?"

"Don't tell me you don't know?" Tarcisio exclaimed, assuming a sardonic tone.

Rafael shook his head. What was there to know?

"Something very strange happened," Tarcisio revealed. "Adolph has suffered a severe attack of food poisoning and is being treated at this moment in the hospital. But it seems his last hour has not come," he said ironically. "Next time it could be worse. Food can kill you, Rafael. You just never know. Schmidt or Aloysius, however you prefer to call him, had worse luck," he continued. "He fell off the metro platform at Lepanto when the train was coming in. A tragedy." There was a trace of sorrow in his voice, even if Tarcisio sounded sarcastic.

Rafael thought about these latest developments. Proof of the power of the church that could destroy the society next time. Whoever had been the strategist—Tarcisio, William, or the Supreme Pontiff—was brilliant.

"Your contribution was very important, Rafael. We won't forget."

"But I still feel lost. You could have told me about JC's involvement," he argued.

"It was William's strategy, and I didn't want to interfere."

"Where is it that they guard the supposed bones of Christ?" Rafael asked jokingly.

"The supposed bones of some Christ from the fifteenth century, is that what you mean?" the secretary corrected Rafael. "Where else would they be but in the Church of the Gesù?"

"How ironic."

"We have another problem, Rafael, not related to this."

There's always something, the priest thought to himself.

"It's about Anna and Mandy, her daughter," Tarcisio revealed.

Rafael focused on the names he knew well. "What's going on? That affair was resolved."

"It was, true, but Anna's receiving visits from reporters, and she could never keep a secret, as you know."

Rafael knew this well. Anna and Mandy were a daughter and granddaughter of a pope. Anna knew this, but Mandy had no idea. She didn't even know that Anna was her mother.

"We have to resolve this problem," Tarcisio said.

It was good to see how rapidly the church recovered itself. Everything was returning to normal . . . or almost everything.

"I'm not going to be able to help you with this right away, Your Eminence. Please ask Jacopo and Roberta to argue the case during my absence. As soon as possible I'll go see Anna and see what I can do," Rafael informed him.

Tarcisio got up and put his hands behind his back. He walked off through the sacristy with a proud expression. He was the secretary of state in all his splendor again.

"I think we can hold off for a while," he suggested with a smile, and extended his hand to say good-bye.

Rafael went off again toward the interior of the enormous basilica to look at the altar. He passed the baldachin on his way through the immense nave and looked at Paul's tomb. He went down some marble steps to the crypt, knelt down, joined his hands, and prayed.

"I've never asked anything. I've always served You without question." He opened his eyes and looked at the chest that held the apostle's bones. "The time has come to ask You humbly to protect her because only You can do so. Give me light and support my steps. I've got to do it, but I can't do it alone."

72

There's a first for everything, and certainly Sarah never expected to find herself stretched out in a hospital bed with a tube pushing oxygen through her nose and a catheter stuck into the back of her hand, receiving fluids with unpronounceable names. At least she'd been able to sleep last night, probably with the help of some drug that soothed her eyes, convincing them to close, and quieted her mind, obliging her to rest. When she woke in the morning her vision was clouded, but she made out a figure seated in a chair against the wall. He seemed to be dozing as much as his uncomfortable position allowed.

"Were you here all night, Rafael?" she asked with a voice that came out a squeak.

"Who's Rafael?" the figure asked, straightening up in the chair and then getting up to come to the bed.

It was Francesco. She could make out his features now that he was closer. She touched his face.

"How are you?" she asked.

"Don't worry about me. Are you okay? What happened?" He was worried.

"I still don't know. They gave me a battery of tests last night, and then I passed out."

Francesco took her hand and breathed deeply, a sigh that resembled a lament. "Sarah, I don't know if I can deal with this."

His eyes were moist, a tear was about to fall from them, but he wiped it away.

"I never thought your life was like this. I never imagined this existed," he tried to explain. "I don't have the strength. I don't have the strength."

"We're going to have a baby, Francesco," she announced without thinking about it. "He's going to need a father."

Francesco looked at her, amazed. "The nurse told me you weren't pregnant, Sarah."

No? But the test came out positive. The attendant had congratulated her, and she couldn't avoid looking at the red strip on the pregnancy test that showed positive.

"No?" she said, doubtful. "But . . ."

Francesco pressed her hand again. "Give me time, Sarah. Please, give me time."

Now it was her eyes that filled with tears. Francesco was a good man, but she hoped with all her might that the nurse was right. She was selfish and he didn't deserve a woman who couldn't love him completely.

Francesco kissed her on the forehead. "I'll call you later, okay?"

She agreed, wiping the tears, and watched him leave helplessly, without a *Wait! Don't go! Don't leave me!* Nothing. She simply let him leave. She remembered crying like a baby, the nurse asking her what was wrong, and answering nothing. She wasn't crying over seeing him leave but over her own disappointment in herself, and she couldn't say that to the nurse.

She slept and woke up, slept again and awoke, not knowing how many hours had passed and not caring. Finally she awakened to a feeling of well-being. Someone was holding her hand and caressing her hair. Was it her mother or father? She opened her eyes, and it was him.

"Rafael?" she stammered. "What are you doing here?" She pulled herself together and tried to draw her hand away, but he wouldn't let her.

"You're not pregnant, Sarah," he told her. "You have a choriocarcinoma."

She felt as if he'd punched her in the stomach.

"A what?"

"A trophoblastic cancer in the ovaries. That's why the pregnancy test was positive, and why you had nausea and coughed up blood. Perhaps you also felt short of breath.

Those are some of the symptoms. But there's a high rate of success for treatment. I've already talked with the doctor. He'll explain everything to you shortly." It was best to say it all at once.

He didn't mention that the doctor had told him she was in the third stage of metastasis. Having cancer was bad enough news.

She didn't know what to think. She hadn't expected this particular misfortune. She had cancer. Everything had changed in seconds. One moment she was pregnant, and the next she was at the gates of death. Nice irony, God! Maybe it was a punishment for rejecting a child, but a God who punished wasn't God. At least the God she'd grown up with loved all beings unconditionally. Good, bad, criminal, saintly. A father and a mother always loved their children above everything else.

"You're going to overcome this, Sarah," Rafael assured her.

She smiled sadly. "This time you can't protect me."

The priest looked at her seriously and pressed her hand again. He gave her a timid smile, pleasant, or at least she thought so.

"I know there's a part of me somewhere inside you. Only you know where it is and what it could be. Use it to protect yourself. I've never let you down, have I?"

Tears ran down Sarah's face. She shook her head. No, he'd never let her down.

"That Rafael you have within you will never let you down," he repeated.

She closed her eyes. She felt pain. "I don't know if I can make it alone," she confessed through her tears.

He made her look at him. "I'm not going anywhere, Sarah," he assured her. "I'm not going anywhere."

73

Five years had passed since that first night, but it seemed like fifteen. His hair had turned white, his back bent with the weight of humanity, of believers, non-believers, heretics, infidels, all of whom weighed upon him every day.

Night was worse than day, when he gave himself over to his thoughts, caught in the meshes of loneliness in the middle of a colosseum filled with lions and gladiators.

Ratzinger was alone in his office, the light dim, conducive to thought and meditation. A whiskey appealed to him. Perhaps he'd have one.

The last several days had been terrifying. Filled with conflict, murders, disrespect for God. As pope he was accustomed to this. The majority disrespected Him, or, at best, accepted Him only in times of trouble. No one ever needed Him or even lost time thinking about Him when things were going well. Why? God was only necessary to satisfy the most important requests, the most tormented, while the others were insignificant. Success was always attributed to the individual, failure to others, society, destiny, or chance, and then, yes, God's presence was missing.

No one seemed to care that God was always present in good and bad times, whether He was celebrated, called upon, or ignored. It was the one immutable certainty.

Someone knocked on the door and partly put his head into the room.

"Your Holiness."

"Ah, Ambrosiano. Are seven days over?" he asked in a firm voice.

"Yes, Your Holiness," the other replied. "How do you feel today?"

"Perfect, Ambrosiano. And you?"

"This weather makes my joints ache," the other complained.

"God always knows where to grab us," the pope agreed.

"Are you ready to make confession?"

"Not today," Ratzinger decided, pushing an envelope toward the front of his desk. "I'd like you to give this to the superior general."

"Certainly," the other replied, taking the envelope and putting it away carefully, showing some discomfort. "When do you want me to come back, Your Holiness?"

"We'll see later," the pope answered shrewdly. "It's my

will that the provision made by my predecessors Clement the Seventh and Pius the Ninth be canceled."

"What did Your Holiness say?" He couldn't have heard right.

"The ritual of the first night will not be repeated. My successor will not put his eyes on the content of that letter which you faithfully guard. I order it to be destroyed immediately."

"And the secret, Your Holiness?" Ambrosiano asked, visibly uncomfortable and suspicious.

"What secret? There you have a copy of a letter sent by Loyola to Francisco Xavier. Nothing which you guard is real. It was all a hoax."

The other was ashamed.

"Jesus, the Nazarite, was crucified and rose from the dead on the third day," Ratzinger proclaimed. "His body was never found, nor will it ever be, because He ascended into the heavens to join His Father, where He sits on the right hand. That's what Scripture says. That's what actually happened."

The priest retreated in defeat, without turning his back on the Supreme Pontiff until he reached the door.

Ratzinger sighed and got up with difficulty. He looked out at Saint Peter's Square through a slit in the curtains. A few camera flashes from the Roman side recorded the facade of Saint Peter's Basilica for posterity.

The whiskey could wait. He gave a sad sigh and retired to his bedroom. "That's what actually happened."

Acknowledgments

Every book is much more than its writer.

I want to show my deep appreciation to Monsignor Sansoni, who brought me the magnificent world of Jesus the Nazarite, and to Dr. David, who explained the Jewish tradition and the inconsistencies in the story of Jesus, and to Ben Isaac, who found history as history should be found and for having shown me what I never expected to see (despite not understanding most of what I saw).

Special thanks to my marvelous agents, Laura Dail, Maru de Montserrat, and Eva Schubert, who have been much more than just agents.

My thanks to Robin McAllister, my translator, who, starting with *The Holy Bullet*, has helped make these writings legible to readers of English. We've made a great team, Robin; many thanks.

To the super team at Putnam—Ivan Held, Chris Nelson, Stephanie Sorensen, Kate Stark—my respect and admiration. Thanks to my publicist, Summer Smith, who's done a magnificent job; I appreciate the innumerable hours of dedication in promoting me. And, last but not least, to my editor, Rachel Kahan, to whom I bow in deep admiration and gratitude for all that she has done for me.

In Italy I owe a debt of gratitude to Roberta Hidalgo and Raffaella Rosa, for their invaluable assistance with my book. To my marvelous friend Vincenzo di Martino, director of the Grand Hotel Palatino, the Sun King of hotel directors, my sincere thanks. I feel privileged to enjoy your friendship.

In Portugal I cannot forget to thank Carlos Almeida and João Paulo Sacadura, for all their help and encouragement; and Luisa Lourenço, for putting up with my whims as a writer in the full process of creation at any hour of the day or night. Your friendship is precious to me.

To JC, wherever you are.

Finally, to my readers all over the world. I am grateful for the privilege of telling you the story of Sarah and Rafael, whatever their names in real life.

From the bestselling author of *The Last Pope*
LUIS M. ROCHA

THE
HOLY BULLET

The attempted assassination of Pope John Paul II in 1981 has long been considered a conspiracy of international proportions.

An international journalist, a war-weary Portuguese veteran, a Muslim with visions of the Virgin Mary, a rogue priest, and members of the world's most powerful—and secretive—organizations come together after the suspicious death of Pope John Paul I. A few operatives bold enough to penetrate the Vatican's shadowy inner circle will investigate what actually happened—and try to prevent the popular new pope from meeting the same fate.

penguin.com